SHIVA

SHIVA

CAROLYN McCRAY

THOMAS & MERCER

The characters and events portrayed in this book are fictitious. Any similarity to real persons, living or dead, is coincidental and not intended by the author.

Printed in the United States of America.

Published by Thomas & Mercer
P.O. Box 400818
Las Vegas, NV 89140

ISBN-13: 9781611097177
ISBN-10: 1611097177

To Ben.
He knows why.

PROLOGUE

MONTSERRAT, SPAIN

694 AD

Vasco Borgoña soul would be damned until the End of Days and beyond if he did not finish his glorious task. Vasco squinted at his carving as the candlelight flickered, the wick nearly drowned in melted wax. How long had he been gone from his bed?

His joints ached from the cold, but still, he could not force himself away from the eyes that stared back at him. Dark. Haunting. Instead, Vasco drew the rough-spun blanket tighter around his shoulders.

Sleep could wait. A roaring fire could wait. The wooden sculpture could not. Vasco hadn't traveled from village to village, never staying longer than a fortnight before leaving his humble abode to melt into the wilderness, carrying only the statue and the tools necessary to create it, to wait upon sleep. Those who sought to destroy his work had the coin and determination to follow him to hell and back.

In truth, it was not just his enemies who kept Vasco from a sound slumber. Those who had commissioned the sculpture were as fierce, and possibly even more deadly, than those sworn to destroy him and his work. A chill, not of the northerly wind that whistled through the thatched roof, coursed down Vasco's back.

Still, he could not turn away from the carving. Each time he looked into the woman's eyes, he found himself warmed. It had taken him nearly a year to achieve the exact curve of her cheek. He placed his hand against the wood. Was it his imagination, or did his palm tingle each time he touched her beauty?

It was said the model for his sculpture had been Tzipora, Moses's wife. Vasco did not know the veracity of such things. He had only received a sketch on an ancient piece of parchment, along with a deerskin full of coin. He had been a simple artist, his belly aching from hunger, so happy for the gold he did not question as to why his benefactors had wanted such a carving or how endangered his life would become if he dared lay chisel to wood.

Vasco let his hand drop away from the sculpture. How many times had he cursed his luck? How many times had he wished to go back and spit upon that deerskin?

Yet, knowing all that he did, Vasco would still have taken the commission. How could he not? How could he have gone on living without bringing this creation to life from the wood of five different trees?

Now all that was to be done was the final painting of her dress. Then she would be ready to be introduced to the world.

Vasco dabbed his paintbrush in the pool of gold flakes mixed with his own spittle. Long after his name died upon people's tongues, a part of him would still be with the wooden woman he had come to love better than any lady made of flesh and blood.

He did not get the opportunity to lay down a single stroke, as the thin slat door burst open, bringing with it a slap of mountain air. Vasco turned, raising an arm to shield his eyes from the burning torches. His sword lay not a few feet away, yet Vasco did not bother to lunge for it. Not with the hatred in the intruder's eyes. Not with the silver cross that glistened on the man's chest. Despite the symbol of eternal life, Vasco would find no mercy here.

The man's blade slid into Vasco's flesh so easily he almost could not believe it to be a mortal blow. But as the sword came out of his belly with a wet slosh, Vasco knew his end was near. Others rushed in behind the attacker, knocking cups from the shelf, setting his straw bed alight.

Clutching his belly, Vasco slumped to his knees, splashing blood onto his nightshirt as the attacker stood before him, unmoved, unmoving. Flames crackled all around. His small abode consumed in fire. The attacker turned from Vasco and raised his sword over the carving.

Vasco tried to reach out to protect the statue, but all he succeeded in doing was falling onto his side. Helpless to stop the man, the blade came down upon the wood, splitting the babe in the lady's arms from her embrace. Not satisfied to part a child from his mother, the man swung the sword again, cleaving the woman's head from her body. The wooden head bounced off the table, landing near Vasco.

Such hatred in a man supposedly walking the righteous path of God.

Then with the same swiftness they had entered his world, shattering it, they left. Only the roar of the fire and the burning in his belly marked their passing. Vasco could hear shouts and cries from the street. Not for him or his creation, but for the flames. A fire such as this could spread throughout the homes, ravaging the entire village.

As flames licked his feet, Vasco kept his eyes forward, looking into the lady's face that he had so very carefully carved. From the corner of her perfect eyes, bright red streamed down her face, making it look as if she cried blood. The burgundy a stark contrast to her ebony skin. So like the color of Moses's Ethiopian wife.

Vasco should have known they would never allow his dark Mother to survive.

His sole comfort was in the fact that this was not his first Black Madonna. Nay. This was a second statue. The first long in the hands of his benefactors.

Despite the raging fire, cold took hold of Vasco, numbing his body, stilling his heart.

His last sight, that of this dark Virgin.

Mankind's last hope at salvation.

CHAPTER 1

CATHEDRAL PARISH, SOUTH CAROLINA

AUGUST 26, 2:38 P.M. (EST)

Dr. Rebecca Monroe tried to ignore the bustling around her. Instead, she stared at the reflection in the mirror. It was so strange to see her blonde hair swept away from her face. And not in a loose, messy ponytail, either. The hairdresser had used enough hair spray and bobby pins to keep her notoriously difficult-to-manage curls under control. Her eyes seemed to float in the reflection, with enough black eyeliner to make an ancient Egyptian queen happy.

Was this really her? Was this really happening? Then she looked down at her long white wedding dress. Okay, not exactly pure white. She was in her thirties, and Brandt had just received an annulment from a woman who claimed to be carrying his baby. So pure white seemed a stretch. Bone white seemed a far more appropriate color. For many, many reasons.

"Don't you dare start crying," Bunny said, nudging Rebecca away from the mirror. "You've just got to make it twenty-one more minutes."

Dear God, she was getting married in less than a half hour? Tears threatened. She struggled against them, but it was futile. After everything Brandt and she had been through? Chased across continents. Hunted by religious zealots. Hounded by ruthless mercenaries.

In the mirror's reflection, Bunny smiled, helping to tuck one loose blonde strand back into its proper place. The younger woman's bright-red hair also had that sheen only a can of hair spray could produce. Despite trying to keep an upbeat attitude about the day, Rebecca couldn't help but notice Bunny's lean frame and young "I don't need a support garment" bustline.

Despite the fact her maid of honor was clothed in a rather uncomplimentary peach-colored bridesmaid dress, Bunny radiated beauty. And if anything, the other two bridesmaids, Brandt's younger sisters, were even prettier. Not beauty pageant pretty. But "I swept all the categories in the pageant" kind of pretty.

Both were slim with rich, dark hair. Rebecca wasn't the prettiest one in the room. Hell, she wasn't even in the top five.

What did Brandt see in her? He had grown up around Southern sophistication. He was used to women who were actual *ladies*. Rebecca's skin chaffed at the lace edging her dress, and seriously, who wore panty hose in Charleston in *August*? With a full-length skirt and four-foot train, who the hell was going to see her legs?

But Brandt's mother had been quite insistent. Actually, she had been quite insistent on everything. From the peach bridesmaids gowns, to the nylons, to the flowers in Rebecca's bouquet.

Nothing about this wedding had been decided by Rebecca, and you know what? Rebecca was more than happy about it. She would have just eloped, but Brandt had family, and by God, his family wanted a Southern wedding.

"Oops," Bunny said, pointing out a red scrape along Rebecca's temple. A wound courtesy of a little "outing" Bunny and she had taken earlier in the week. It had begun as a simple research trip to Iceland. The theory had been to do some research into a strange Viking connection with the Disciples of Moshe, the religious fanatics who had plagued them across Europe. Of course, nothing had gone routinely about the trip.

But maybe that was what Brandt saw in her. An ability to take a head blow and not faint—or at least not for long.

Bunny turned to one of Brandt's stunning sisters. Rebecca was still trying to figure out which was which. "Hand me a little cover up, would you?"

As Bunny applied the extra makeup, an itch sprang up in Rebecca's foot and traveled up her calf, settling in her knee. She knew the rules about breathing, let alone moving in her elaborate wedding dress, but she couldn't help it. Rebecca reached her hand down, but before a single finger could touch the fabric, a whip-slender woman rushed across the room.

"No, no, no, dear," Mrs. Brandt chided with a Southern drawl. How come if people said things with that drawl you couldn't take offense to it? "You must pick up the dress at the sides so that you don't crease the chiffon."

Little did her mother-in-law-to-be know that Rebecca had almost dared to *scratch* the fabric. Rebecca decided to keep that little gem of a plan to herself. Because Mrs. Brandt turned out to terrify Rebecca more than any of the aforementioned threats combined.

"Sorry, ma'am," Rebecca mumbled.

"Do not *ma'am* me, young lady," Mrs. Brandt corrected in that silky-smooth tone, scolding as only a Southerner could. "Call me Mama."

Yeah, that was never going to happen.

"Oh no," one of the sisters exclaimed. "There's a piece of lint!"

Apparently, in wedding day mode, that constituted a five-alarm emergency. Brandt's other sister—Kaydria, Rebecca thought—dove for the lint brush as Mrs. Brandt took a magnifying glass, an actual *magnifying* glass, to the wedding dress.

Okay, this was shaping up to be the longest twenty-one minutes of her life. It seemed the entire family was trying to wipe away the memory of Brandt's first awkward overseas marriage by putting on the largest, most glamorous wedding Charleston had ever seen.

Which wasn't easy to do, given it was Charleston, and this was the Cathedral of St. John the Baptist, the largest church on the southern seaboard. This dressing room alone had enough gilded crosses to give the Vatican a run for its money, and Rebecca would know.

"Don't worry," Bunny whispered. "None of it dates before the eighteenth century." The younger woman gave a wink. "I checked."

And Bunny would know as well. The redhead was nearly as well versed in proto-Christianity as Rebecca. Which had come in handy several times in the past few months.

Still, Rebecca felt compelled to study the religious icons to assess if there wasn't some deeper, hidden code buried in them rather than preparing to get married.

Get married.

Okay, those two words were really starting to freak her out.

Bunny must have sensed Rebecca's rising anxiety, as she tried to herd the Brandt women to the door. "I think the bride might need a little air."

It looked like Rebecca might get a reprieve from all of the clucking when Holly, Brandt's youngest sister, burst into the room. "They're still not here!"

The other women dropped Rebecca's dress and rushed over to the teen.

"What do you mean?" Mrs. Brandt demanded. "Vincent said they were stuck in traffic and going to be a tad late"—she looked to her silver watch—"but the groomsmen should be in position by now."

"Yes," Bunny encouraged, "why don't you go see about that?"

In a rustle of satin, the mother of the groom and three of Rebecca's bridesmaids rushed from the room as Bunny closed the door behind them.

"They'll be here on time," Bunny reassured her.

Of that, Rebecca wasn't so sure. This was Brandt, after all. If any man on the planet could find a way to get in some kind of international trouble on his wedding day, it was her fiancé.

The only thing Rebecca was certain of was that the men weren't stuck in a traffic jam.

With Lopez driving, that was an absolute impossibility.

Sergeant Vincent Brandt clutched the machine gun to his chest as his other hand grabbed hold of the train car's panel to keep himself from being hurled out the window. Yes, he was clutching a machine gun on his wedding day. That didn't stop the train from nearly derailing as it took a sixty-degree turn at sixty miles an hour. Physics was not their friend today.

"Slow it down!" Brandt yelled to Lopez but knew that it was futile. Especially as the corporal lashed out a hand to catch the video camera before it slid off the console.

"Gotcha!" Lopez announced, not to Brandt, but to the camera as he set it up again.

Another one of Operation's bright ideas. Filming their missions. Even though the brand-spanking-new Ricoh military spec camera was solid, state-eyes-only encrypted, with a self-destruct module, Brandt thought it was possibly the worst idea to come along since, well, since ever. And it didn't help that Lopez was already a little too Evel Knievel for Brandt's tastes, but now? Now that he was being filmed for posterity? Forget about it.

But the upper brass's new thing was accountability. They wanted proof of a mission's objectives. Brandt thought if they wanted that kind of deal, they might want to come out in the field with his team for a week. Strangely, no one took him up on his offer.

The crack of a shot came from the right as Davidson cursed under his breath. Clearly, the private hadn't hit the driver of the train car in front of them. How could he? The kid was good—*damned* good. However, the train they chased was just a speck on the horizon. And strong winds coming in from the east were making any long-distance shot reliant on prayer.

Davidson pulled himself back into the car and stretched out his scarred fingers, shaking off the pain. How the kid could shoot at all after all those burns was amazing. The fact he could outshoot most snipers with ten years his training? That was about as near a miracle as you could get. Brandt's lips turned down as he studied the melted ruin of Davidson's left cheek.

Had that fire truly transformed the sniper? There were times Brandt felt the old trust building, then Davidson would take a single step out of place, and it would be shattered. Brandt wished he could wipe the memory of Davidson pointing a gun at Rebecca away, burn it to ashes, but it refused to be uprooted. Was the sniper reformed or just a scorpion biding his time?

"Throw on more wood!" Lopez yelled over the clacking of the train, snapping Brandt back to the present.

Picking a steam-powered antique train as their chase vehicle hadn't been the most efficient choice, but it was what they had, so they had to make it work. Ahead of them, a stolen train car filled with live munitions was booking it.

"Levont!" Brandt ordered. "You heard the man!"

The team's new point man bent over, grabbed a large log, and tossed it into the old-fashioned furnace. The burly guy made it look easy. The train picked up speed, hurling down the tracks of an abandoned railway on the north side of the Charleston Naval Weapons Station.

"Nineteen minutes!" Talli shouted.

Damn it. The naval base had over three *thousand* active-duty personnel, yet here Brandt and his team were, chasing down the bad guys. The upper brass was worried that this string of ammunitions thefts were inside jobs, hence why they had no military back up. And now, with less than twenty minutes to go before his wedding? *Typical.*

There was absolutely nothing Brandt could do to speed up the chase as the Charleston countryside rolled past. Thick grass blanketed the meadows hemmed in only by the weeping willows. It smelled green. Not that muted, dusty green of the rest of the world, but that bright, shiny green he'd only found in South Carolina. It smelled like home.

"Watch it!" Davidson snapped at Talli. "If you can't get a shot through the window, don't take it."

The team's "official" sniper bristled at the rebuke. However, Brandt backed their "unofficial" yet infinitely more talented sniper. Ever since Davidson had rejoined the team, Talli had been trying too hard. Which was not helping the man's accuracy one damned bit.

Honestly, Brandt doubted Talli had been targeting the train car itself. In truth, Brandt was pretty sure Talli had *meant* to hit the window. The man kept trying to take shots outside his range to keep up with Davidson. Which just wasn't going to happen.

Normally, Brandt would let it slide. He would let Talli find his footing. The problem was, right now, Talli's quest to prove himself could get them all blown up.

"Look, we've got no idea where they've stored the stolen ordnance," Brandt said, trying to use his sensitivity training. The upper brass was now also all for caring about feelings. Brandt was supposed to be careful not to deflate Talli's ego. He failed miserably. "It's the engineering window or *nothing*."

Talli's jaw clenched as he lowered his eye back to his scope. Brandt noticed, though, that Talli didn't fire. Good man.

Davidson took several more shots, all equally unsuccessful. Brandt squinted. Were they catching up? Had the other train car slowed? Or had they sped up?

Then Davidson's rifle snapped up. "Crap."

"What?"

"They're stopping," the private reported.

"Great!" Lopez whooped.

"No," Davidson said, shaking his head. "They're stopping because the tracks end up ahead."

Not even Lopez could find the silver lining in that. Not with their brakes shot. Gone. Done. Nonexistent.

Brandt turned to Levont. "Any luck?"

The tall black man shoved another log into the furnace as he indicated with his head to the antique control panel. "Maybe if we had Henry Ford to help…"

The lack of brakes had seemed like a nonissue when the chase began. How often did Lopez use them, anyway? Now, however? Now brakes kind of seemed important.

Lopez's smile returned. "You know what I say?" Brandt really didn't want to know. However, he had a wedding to get to in nineteen minutes, so he let Lopez continue. "I say throw on *all* the wood."

A retort was on Brandt's lips, but it stalled as he saw the long-term strategy of Lopez's plan. It wasn't just that Lopez wanted to set the world speed record for a steam engine *and* catch it all on film. It wasn't even to get to the enemy before they unloaded all of the ammunition they'd stolen. It *was* to ram this train into the other at the highest speed possible, *detonating* all of those live munitions.

It was a "if you can't beat them, join them" kind of plan. Better to have those dangerous explosives go up here where they could do minimal damage than where the terrorists planned to use them.

Brandt turned to Levont. Even though the man had only been with them a few months, he didn't need the order, as he grabbed a log in each hand, chucking them into the furnace.

As the train surged forward, Brandt had only one little problem to work out.

How the hell to get off the train before it exploded in all its fiery glory?

Minor detail.

Rebecca held her tongue as the Brandt women once again fussed all around her. Apparently, wedding preparation involved constantly readjusting every inch of her dress.

"Maybe," Brandt's youngest sister blurted, "maybe Vincent's had second thoughts."

Mrs. Brandt took a supposedly playful swing at her daughter, although when it connected, Holly grimaced. "Hush, child. Vincent is having no such thing." The older woman then turned her attention to Rebecca. "Don't you worry. Vincent *will* be here."

Rebecca was pretty darned sure that the woman said it more for her own sake than any bride's. The teenager couldn't help herself, though.

"But Vincent is never late for—"

"Holly!" Mrs. Brandt snapped, tugging her youngest away from Rebecca.

"Mom!" Holly complained as she was dragged off. "You ruffled my dress!"

As the two smoothed out the peach chiffon, Rebecca looked to Bunny, who pushed a tumble of red curls out of the way, arching an eyebrow.

"Never late?" the younger woman whispered. "How about, don't bother to make plans because he is probably on another continent?"

Brandt had clearly done a great job of protecting his family from his true occupation. They all thought he was regular army, stationed over in Germany. That worried them enough. If they knew what he really did? If they knew the danger he put himself in on a daily—no, *hourly*—basis?

They would not be nearly as worried about chiffon—that was for certain.

"I'm sure Vin's got a good reason," Kaydria said as she squeezed Rebecca's arm.

That was exactly what had Rebecca concerned. Not that Brandt had ditched her. That thought had never crossed her mind. He would take a bullet for her. Actually, he'd taken several for her, so worrying about his level of devotion was kind of a moot point.

No, she was worried he and his team had gotten themselves into the kind of trouble they couldn't get themselves out of.

The hot South Carolina air blasted Brandt in the face as he climbed up onto the roof of the train. Although, the blazing summer heat was nothing compared to the inferno inside of the engine car. Levont had stoked the fire so high that flames shot out of the furnace. That was their cue to leave.

The only "safe" location was on top of the train, which gave you an indication of exactly how insane their plan was. Lopez swore he had a backup contingency, but sometimes the corporal confused contingency with prayer. And there was no time to discuss the difference.

Levont looked over the side of the train to the ground speeding past. "If we throw ourselves off..."

Yeah, a broken back would probably be the best-case scenario. Right now, the only other option was to crash into the munitions car and die in a ball of flame. So there was that.

"Sarge!" Talli yelled, pointing to what appeared to be a fly on the horizon. The faster it zipped toward them, the larger it became. That was no fly. It was a helicopter.

"When the general said *no* base support," Brandt growled at Lopez, "he meant *none*." The whole reason Brandt's team had been pulled in was the concern that this heist was an inside job.

Lopez smiled, though. "I took it he meant *this* base, Sarge, not the other three in the area."

The corporal had a rebellious streak a mile wide, but damn, he was inventive in how he expressed it. The helicopter's nose was down, pushing the envelope on air speed.

Brandt glanced to the stopped train car ahead of them. Would the helicopter get to them in time? Could they clear the blast zone in time? Was Rebecca freaking out at the altar?

Unfortunately, the only question he could answer was the one about the helicopter.

"The helo's not going to make it." Talli sighed next to him as Davidson lay belly flat on the train's roof, taking shots at the fleeing terrorists. Apparently, the would-be thieves had realized their incredibly well-planned-out mission was a bust and ran for the hills. Literally.

At the least, the terrorists had abandoned the vans that contained all of the stolen ordnances. Enough live ammunition to blow a city block. Instead of trying to drive the van out of here, the terrorists fled on dirt bikes. The perfect vehicles for the countryside. Clearly, they hoped to melt into the thick forests surrounding the base.

That just wouldn't do.

Time to get even crazier than Lopez.

"Get up!" Brandt shouted to the men as the train hurled toward the explosive-laden train. He tugged Davidson up by the bulletproof vest but spoke to Lopez. "Tell the helo to drop the lines."

Lopez's brows furrowed, then arched up. "On it!"

Brandt counted off in his head as the helicopter streaked toward them, black rope pouring out the sides like dark spiderwebs. Maybe the helo couldn't get to them in time, but that didn't mean they couldn't get to it.

"On my mark!" Brandt yelled. He glanced over his shoulder as the details of the munitions car came into sharp relief. He could read the car number 429. Even Talli could hit the damn thing by now.

Davidson must have just gotten wind of Brandt's plan. "Okay, then. I guess we are doing this." The sniper slung his rifle over his shoulder, securing it.

Levont smiled. "They said your team was off the hook."

Good to know.

"Three," Brandt shouted.

Christ All Mighty, that car was coming up fast.

"Two."

Each of the men kneeled down, preparing for the burst of speed and *height* they were going to need.

"One!"

Brandt and the rest sprinted across the train's roof. His barely healed obliques screeched their protest to the plan, but he kept running. As Brandt hit the edge of the roof, he pushed off, launching himself into the air. For a brief moment, he worried Rebecca would get the call all families of the military feared they would get. He could even see her tear-stained cheeks. A wedding suddenly turned wake.

Then a rope smacked him in the face. He grabbed it, wrapping his wrist around it, letting it take his weight.

Not everyone else was so lucky. Davidson had the speed and the height—there just wasn't a rope in sight. Lashing out, Brandt snagged the edge of Davidson's vest. The force changed his trajectory enough to allow the sniper to grab the tail end of Brandt's rope. Unfortunately, the added weight knocked the helicopter off balance.

Davidson, though, flung himself like a monkey in a tree, casting himself off Brandt's rope and grabbing a free line.

The chopper righted itself, zipping away as the engine car hit the munitions train. A fireball Michael Bay would have been proud of exploded high into the sky, the heat blast hurling them all forward. The three vans were engulfed in flame yet they didn't blow. Weird. They should have been filled with explosives.

Lopez whooped, waving the camera. "Got it! In HD color, baby!"

Before he could figure out what that meant, Levont swung closer. "They were right. *Off. The. Hook.*"

Brandt frowned. "You think we're *done*?"

"Hell, no!" Lopez shouted as Brandt gave the helicopter the signal to give chase to the dirt bikes.

Davidson felt his lips—well, at least his good lip—pull up into a fierce smile. His bad arm hurt like hell, and his fingers were cramped around the rope, but he'd never felt so alive as the hot air pushed him back as the helicopter accelerated.

Who wouldn't want to hang out of a helicopter chasing after terrorists? God truly was gracious giving him such a second chance. His first military tour had been shrouded in lies. Lies he'd convinced himself were necessary. In the end, though, he couldn't serve the cult that raised him and his country at the same time.

And his country had suffered for it. Worse, Rebecca had suffered for it. Brandt had suffered the most.

Not this time. The man clinging to a rope going a hundred miles an hour was the *real* Davidson. Free of the Knot, he could truly be committed to his cause. To make up for every death he'd caused while under cover. And there had been many. Too many.

He pushed aside the sight of that jet in France. While he hadn't pulled the trigger, those deaths were on his shoulders as surely as the terrorist who launched the RPG. God would decide his punishment for wandering from His way.

In this life, Davidson could do only one thing to make amends. And that was to take out the bad guys.

Luckily, it looked like there were six of them right ahead, trying to outrace a helicopter. Given that he was the lowest on the ropes, Davidson's feet skimmed the tall, bright grass, so he had the opportunity to be at bike level. The guy on the motorcycle genuinely looked surprised when Davidson flung himself from the rope and knocked into him. An elbow to the jaw and the guy was off the bike.

It took both hands on the handlebars to stabilize the motorcycle before it pitched over. However, Davidison didn't take the bike much farther. He'd just preferred to stop the bike on his own rather than plowing into the ground.

Instead, Davidson braked hard as he slung his rifle off his shoulder. The other bikes were so close, it was almost too easy. Like target practice. After the day they'd had? Davidson would take it. His first shot took out the back tire of the nearest motorcycle. It tilted over into the high grass. The next shot hit the third biker in the back. Not checking to see what happened to that bike, Davidson aimed at the fourth and hit the gas tank. His next shot set it on fire. Before he set up the shot, the fifth terrorist stopped his bike, his hands high up in the air.

Davidson looked up to Brandt, still on his rope. His question for the sergeant clear. Take the shot or not?

Brandt shook his head. The guy had surrendered. He was a sleazy terrorist, but he'd given himself up. Sirens sounded from across the field as naval MPs finally caught up with the action.

Given that Davidson had single-handedly taken down the terrorist cell, Brandt gave the private a nod toward the rope.

Normally, Brandt would have felt slightly cheated that someone else had had all the action, but with his wedding sixteen minutes away? Today he could have laid a lip-lock on Davidson.

Feeling confident that the slew of MPs heading their way could take care of the cleanup, Brandt gave the signal for the chopper to pull them up.

As their lines zipped upward toward the helicopter, Brandt glanced to the inferno that used to be a train car. All those explosives had been meant for elementary school children visiting the Smithsonian Museum on a field trip. It felt pretty damned good to see that hailstorm of pain and anguish burning benignly in a meadow.

However, today wouldn't be a complete win, not if he missed his own nuptials.

Shrugging off the help of one of the airmen in the helo, Brandt climbed onto the deck of the chopper. Of course, Lopez went forward to the pilot's seat. And of course, the air force pilot refused to give him the stick. Normally, Brandt would have sided with the guy who brought the helicopter to the party. However, today wasn't normal.

"Lopez will be flying," Brandt added.

"Sir, this is an air force vehicle," the pilot shot back. "And no one but a—"

Davidson pulled out a piece of paper from his flak jacket and handed it to the copilot. The man quickly scanned it. When he looked up, he seemed confused. "It is a letter of suspension of *posse comitatus* for the team."

The pilot's eyes narrowed. They all knew what that meant.

"That's right," Lopez said, waving his hand at the pilot. "And it is signed by the president of the United States, so get out of the chair already."

The document in Davidson's possession overrode the federal law prohibiting military personnel from operating on civilian soil. Which allowed Lopez to fly them wherever the hell they wanted. In fairness, it had been issued in case the chase after the live munitions had carried them past the base's borders, *not* to get Brandt to his wedding on time, but hey, Brandt would deal with his commander once he slipped that ring onto Rebecca's finger.

With a displeased grunt, the pilot rose from his chair, handing the stick over to Lopez. The helicopter lurched and bucked at the transfer and Lopez demanding maximum speed ASAP.

"Sorry, folks," Lopez yelled over the whine of the engine. "A little learning curve."

"More like performance anxiety," the pilot grumbled, although even he threw a hand out and grabbed a hold as the helicopter nearly jumped forward responding to Lopez's urging.

"How long?" Lopez asked to no one in particular.

"Thirteen minutes," Talli answered.

"Pshhh," Lopez snorted. "I thought this was going to be some kind of challenge."

With the cathedral's tall steeple nothing but a blip in the distance, Brandt was pretty damned sure getting them there on time was in fact going to be a challenge, but he didn't bother voicing it. Lopez would just snort again and take offense.

Levont turned to Brandt, beaming. "Like I said. Off—"

"You really think we're done?" Brandt asked, shoving a package into the point man's hands.

The rest of the men answered for him. "Hell. *No*."

CHAPTER 2

THE CATHEDRAL OF ST. JOHN THE BAPTIST

2:58 P.M. (EST)

Rebecca looked to Bunny as the younger woman placed a hand on hers. Rebecca hadn't even realized she had been chewing on a very well-manicured finger until Bunny glanced to the digit.

"Sorry," Rebecca murmured, pulling her hand down from her mouth.

"Hey, it's your wedding pictures," Bunny teased. "If you don't mind a few chipped nails, then I don't."

Activity buzzed in the crowded hallway. It was like a hurricane of chiffon had been bottled in the passage. Rebecca couldn't help but sneak a peak around the corner. The huge white altar was still unmanned except for the priest, who, for the thousandth time, glanced to his watch. Like the guy had anything better to do right now.

"What are we going to do?" Holly asked, the teenager treble replacing her usual "I am older than I look" tone.

"I don't…" Mrs. Brandt, for once, seemed at a loss for words.

If Brandt did miss their wedding, Rebecca felt way sadder for his mother than she did even for herself. The poor woman had been through a sham marriage, embarrassing annulment, and now a no-show groom. Mrs. Brandt's social standing might never recover in this bastion of Southern traditions.

Then something sounded overhead. Rebecca craned to look up the tall bell tower. She could have sworn she heard something on the roof. There it was again. Rebecca would recognize a man repelling onto a roof any day.

She looked over to Bunny, who smiled back. They were here. Their men.

"Let's get this wedding started," Rebecca announced.

"Deary, what do you mean?" Mrs. Brandt asked, clearly flustered.

"Tell them to strike up the organ music," Bunny ordered an usher. When he balked, she gave the young man a shove. "Now."

Her voice had enough authority to override Mrs. Brandt's shrill protests, and the guy was on his way. Guess surviving multiple RPG attacks could give a redhead some confidence.

"There's no time to explain," Rebecca said to Mrs. Brandt as she adjusted her bouquet. "Brandt's here, so get those bridesmaids down the aisle."

"But there's no groomsmen to lead them," Mrs. Brandt protested.

Rebecca squeezed her soon-to-be mother-in-law's arm. "This is a new century. Girl power and all. I'm sure they can make it to the altar on their own."

"Oh dear." Mrs. Brandt sighed, clearly on the edge of tears. "This is not how things are supposed to go."

"Just imagine if Vincent pulls this off," Rebecca encouraged. "It will make the morning paper."

A flicker of a smile crossed Mrs. Brandt's lips as the bridal march began, resonating throughout the church. The woman turned to her daughters. "Girls, what are you waiting for? You know the drill."

Brandt's sisters, clearly accustomed to taking orders from their matriarch, lined up expertly, ready to go. Holly was the first. All those teenage nerves disappeared as she stepped onto the red carpet that lined the aisle between the pews. The others followed, with Bunny bringing up the rear.

Next it was Brandt's young cousins as the flower girl and ring bearer. Unfortunately, there still weren't any men.

"They're still not here," Mrs. Brandt hissed.

"Just take your seat," Rebecca encouraged, needing the woman to head down the side hallway and slip quietly into her seat up front.

"Deary," Mrs. Brandt said, overriding Rebecca, "you have to move your engagement ring to your other hand."

"I hadn't—" Rebecca said as the woman pulled the ring from her left hand.

"He's got to have somewhere to put the wedding ring, doesn't he?"

"I wouldn't have thought of that," Rebecca admitted as Mrs. Brandt put the ring onto her right finger.

"That's what family is for," Mrs. Brandt said with tears in her eyes, although Rebecca felt they were tears of joy this time. At least she hoped they were.

"Thank you," Rebecca said, giving the woman a hug. There hadn't been much said of Rebecca's lack of relatives. She'd lost her parents in college, and they had been a small family to start with.

Finally, with Mrs. Brandt on her way, Rebecca looked to Mr. Brandt. The reedlike man in a dark-gray suit. How he got next to her, Rebecca had no idea. The man always seemed at the periphery of his wife's entourage, yet was there if you needed him. And Rebecca needed him now. The only other man that might have qualified to give her away, Dr. Archibald Lochum, had succumbed over a year ago. So Brandt's father had agreed to do the honors, or at least Mrs. Brandt had offered his services.

"Ready?" Rebecca asked.

He simply nodded.

If Rebecca thought his son was a man of few words, she clearly hadn't met Brandt's father. As a matter of fact, the guy could be mute for all she knew. But none of that mattered. Not as the wedding march played. She took Mr. Brandt's arm and followed him from the shelter of the hallway and stepped out into the church proper.

Most brides would be greeted by the sight of their groom standing, waiting for their arrival. Instead, Rebecca had a church full of freaked-out guests. Anxiety, worry, and even a tinge of recrimination painted their faces. Rebecca's belly started fluttering. Could she be wrong? Could this crowd be right? Would Brandt stand her up?

Then she remembered the look in his eye, his bloody eye, as Brandt proposed—for the second time. His fervent promise to her.

In that moment, Rebecca felt sorry for the doubting crowd. Clearly, they didn't know the determination of her man.

"*Fuck. Fuck. Fuck*," Brandt cursed under his breath as he hung onto the church's ledge with his fingernails. This was the fifth goddamned window they had tried to open, to no avail.

"Sarge," Lopez suggested, "we're going to have to smash one."

Great. Now not only was he late for his own wedding, but he would have to destroy divine property.

"Wait!" Davidson yelled. "I've got it!"

As soon as the window popped open, the men poured through in various states of dress. Thinking ahead, Davidson had packed their tuxedoes. What they hadn't counted on was having to get dressed on an extremely bumpy helicopter ride streaking over Charleston.

"Boss," Lopez said, "that tie won't do."

Despite being the last one to be able to don his tux, Lopez was by far the most put together. Guess it wasn't a surprise, though. It was Lopez.

The corporal trotted backward, fixing Brandt's tie as they hurried down the hall.

"Enough," Brandt announced as they reached the steps down to the altar. "She's seen me far worse."

Talli chuckled. "At least you don't have a bullet in your belly."

"Exactly," Brandt agreed as he went to make his way down the steps, but Levont stopped him.

"No, Sarge, we go in reverse order," the point man said.

"What in the hell difference does it—"

"For the video, man," Levont insisted, nodding toward Lopez. Then the point man straightened his tux and headed down the steps. Talli followed close behind.

Lopez lingered at the landing. The first time Rebecca and Brandt had been engaged, it had been a no-brainer that Lopez would be the best man. After that stunt where the corporal didn't bother to inform Brandt that he, too, had slept with his supposed baby momma? Lopez had kind of lost the whole best man gig.

Davidson shifted from foot to foot. "Sarge, I don't mind, let Lopez—"

"No offense, Ricky, but you let me *marry* another woman," Brandt said to his corporal.

"No offense taken," Lopez stated, heading down the steps after the other groomsmen.

Which left Brandt and Davidson. At one time, he'd thought the younger man to be a brother. Not just in arms, but in his heart. Then, shortly thereafter, Brandt wanted to kill the son of a bitch. Yet here they were now. Despite all of that, they were standing here, ready to say his vows before his family, and God, he was glad for Davidson to be by his side.

"Thank you," Brandt said, putting his hand out.

Davidson gulped, putting his scarred hand in Brandt's. "No, sir. *Thank you.*"

Brandt turned away before they both got all emotional. Davidson led the way, hurrying down the steps. Brandt was certain he wasn't the proper number of steps behind his best man, but seriously, he didn't give a crap anymore. He just wanted to get to the damned altar before Rebecca walked. Nobody would blame her.

The music was still playing, so that had to be good. He couldn't tell how far along the procession she was, as all the guests were standing, blocking his view of the aisle. A smattering of clapping went up as Davidson took his place. Brandt made his way past the men and stepped onto what he thought his spot at the altar should be, when a cheer erupted from the entire crowd.

Guess they didn't have much faith the groom was going to make it.

Then he looked down the aisle to the angel floating toward him.

Rebecca. She'd had faith. She'd trusted he'd be there.

Breath caught in his throat as if he'd been punched in the solar plexus. She was a vision. An absolute vision. And she was *his*.

Rebecca felt tears spring to her eyes. Bunny would be so upset.

The sight of Brandt in a rumpled tux, though a bleeding cut on his forehead and knuckles raw, was everything she had ever dreamed of. Who knew where the injuries came from? All she cared about was that he was here. Ready to marry her.

The rest of the walk up to the altar was a blur. Literally a blur as tears spilled down her cheeks. Mr. Brandt made certain her hand was firmly in his son's before the older man backed away.

Brandt helped her up the small step to the altar. She clutched him as tightly as she had in their mad race down the Alpine avalanche, needing his strength to stay upright. The improbability and perfection of the moment took her breath away.

No matter she didn't like her dress or the fact that the bridesmaids looked like baby peaches or that she didn't have any family to witness the event. The world shrunk down to just her and Brandt.

The priest began speaking as Brandt urged her to face the clergyman. Since they'd had to cancel the rehearsal last night because neither she nor Brandt was in the country, the protocol was all a mystery to Rebecca. Her future mother-in-law had tried to explain it to her, but anything that happened before Brandt burst onto the altar was gone. Just gone.

How could she think when the dreams she'd had since she was a child were suddenly coming true. Okay, fine, they had to go through a gauntlet of bombs, bullets, and ballistic missiles to get here, but here they were now.

Nothing could spoil this day.

Nothing except the sound of feet landing on the steeple of the church. Someone was repelling onto the cathedral's roof.

Rebecca's head swung around to her fiancé. "Did you invite anyone else?"

In answer, Brandt's hand flew to his hip, only there wasn't a gun there.

Then the vaulted ceiling above their heads exploded.

Brandt threw himself on top of Rebecca, shielding her from the debris. Why the fuck wasn't he armed? And why the hell hadn't he posted snipers outside? He had two right here, standing next to him. A lot of good that did.

Well, it did do a little good since the rest of his men did come armed. Davidson was firing up into the Charleston sky as he yelled for the civilians to evacuate, but who knew who heard him above the terrified screams?

No one needed much prodding, though, as the guests fled the kill zone. Tucking Rebecca's head down tighter under him, Brandt looked to his sisters, who scattered from the altar and joined his parents in the front row.

"Go!" he yelled to his father. "Get them out!"

His father seemed hesitant, though. After serving two tours in the Gulf, you could see him wanting to help. But given who had blown that roof, there would be no help.

"Now!" Brandt bellowed, jolting his father out of his indecision. In a flurry of peach and gray, his family rushed off.

Gunfire erupted all around him as his men laid down heavy cover fire. Was it the bullets that kept the enemy from repelling through the breach? And was it just Brandt, or was the enemy not firing back? Had the Disciples not expected them to be armed? Whatever the reason, Brandt meant to take full advantage of it.

Brandt whispered in Rebecca's ear. "On the count of three."

She only nodded. He didn't need to tell her what they were going to do. Rebecca reached a hand out and grasped Bunny's. On three, they were getting the hell out of here. Backing themselves toward the other men and their cover fire. From there, they would find a place to make a stand.

But first they had to get to three.

"One," he whispered when a sharp piece of debris hit him in the back. *That fucking hurt.*

"Two," Brandt slurred as his body slumped against Rebecca's. Hand flailing, he found the source of the problem. A dart. A tranquilizing dart.

What the fuck?

As the world spun and compressed down around him, he never did make it to three.

"Sarge!" Davidson yelled, but Brandt didn't answer as Rebecca crawled out from under her groom. She checked his pulse and gave a thumbs-up. So Brandt was still alive, but why the hell had he collapsed?

They were only five seconds into the firefight, and already, things were going sideways.

"Cover me!" Davidson shouted. Before he could even make it a step closer, a harness dropped down from the breach in the roof.

A blow horn announced from above, “He has sixty seconds to live. Get him in that harness or he dies.”

Davidson glanced over his shoulder to Lopez, who technically was in charge. However, even the corporal looked to Rebecca. She clung to Brandt. Her beautiful white dress now streaked in soot.

Davidson rushed to her side, but all Rebecca could do was shake her head. He felt Brandt’s pulse. It seemed to be weakening. The church had fallen eerily quiet as the parishioners fled into the street, taking their screams with them. Far away, the distant sound of police sirens wailed. But they would never get here in time.

None of them could do anything for Brandt in time. Except for the enemy.

“They want him alive,” Davidson said to her, not knowing what else to say. They simply didn’t have time for anything else. “We’ve got to trust in that.”

Rebecca raised her face as black mascara tear tracks etched her features. “Give me the harness.”

Quickly, they hooked Brandt into the apparatus. Once done, Davidson tugged on the rope. Immediately, Brandt’s unconscious body was pulled off the ground. Rebecca hurled herself forward, catching Brandt. Davidson feared he was going to have to pull her off of him, but she kissed the sergeant hard on the lips.

“We are *right* behind you,” she whispered, then let Brandt go.

The unconscious sergeant sped upward as the Disciples wasted no time claiming their prize. The helicopter hovering over the church banked away the second Brandt was loaded into the chopper.

Davidson spun to the other men to find out their next orders, only to find Lopez gone.

“Where’d he go?”

Talli shrugged. “Where do you think?”

With a tight smile, Davidson turned back to Rebecca just in time to catch her as she slumped to her knees.

"Are you injured?" he asked.

Shaking her head, Rebecca wiped her cheek with the back of her hand. "Why Brandt?"

"I don't know."

"Why not *me*?" she asked, choking back a sob.

Davidson pulled her into his arms, having absolutely no idea of how to comfort her. "I don't know, Rebecca…I don't know."

Brandt jerked his eyes open, then wished he hadn't. The world swam in a sea of reds and oranges. Whatever the fuck they had given him as an antidote, he swore he could see the blood vessels in the back of his eyes. That couldn't be good.

Despite the terror that spiked in his veins, Brandt couldn't move. Not his arms or his legs. Nothing. Even his eyelids were beginning to drift down. It took every effort to keep them open.

A man with a shaved head lowered himself to the floor of the helicopter. His face pierced with steel and his skin riddled with tattoos. One especially prominent. The Star of David with a rod through the center. The sign of the Disciples of Moshe.

Fuckers.

"Where is *she*?" he asked almost reverently.

What *she*?

Last Brandt had seen, Rebecca and Bunny were still in the church. Did these ass-bites screw up? Leaving the woman they wanted and taking him instead? But the Disciples were anything but stupid. The capture had been expertly done.

Then what *she*?

"Do not worry," the man said. "You will tell us."

Brandt wanted to punch or kick at the guy—hell, he'd settle for biting him—but his muscles wouldn't cooperate. It was like his whole body had been injected with Botox. Not a great feeling. Worse, it was keeping him from doing the one task he really needed to get done.

He tried to get his tongue to work, but there was no way he could even form a curse, let alone pop the false crown off his tooth. Nope. He was going to have to get the Disciples to do it for him.

Brandt was going to have to count on their cruelty.

Summoning up every ounce of energy he had left, Brandt spit in the man's face.

For a moment, rage contorted the inked markings, but then his captor's face smoothed back into the mask.

"You cannot bait me. I walk the righteous path."

Really? Brandt got the one Disciple slow to anger?

The man rose and sat back down, his eyes closing in what looked like prayer. Seriously, a guy couldn't get kicked in the face around a Disciple?

Then one of the mercenaries hauled back a leg and kicked Brandt square in the jaw.

Finally.

His molars slammed together so hard that the crown cracked in two. Brandt could feel his gum bleed, but that was of little consequence. His tracker was now primed. The only problem? He needed to activate the damned thing.

The guys in R&D really needed to take field conditions into consideration. Brandt wasn't complaining—fine, maybe he was—but they needed to seriously factor in curare poisoning into the equation.

Gathering the blood into his mouth, Brandt spit again, this time at the mercenaries' feet.

The merc reared back, kicking Brandt right in the solar plexus. His mind careened from the pain and lack of oxygen, but damn if his jaw didn't clamp down.

Vision blackening, Brandt could only hope that it was enough.

As Davidson released her, Rebecca imagined what Brandt would be doing right now if it were she who had been the one kidnapped. Well, besides saying, "Christ, stop crying," because that was not going to happen any time soon. Her groom had just been kidnapped. She deserved a few tears.

His next admonishment would be to stop feeling sorry for herself—again, not going to happen—so instead, she did the next best thing and took stock of her assets.

Right now, standing in front of a demolished altar, she couldn't think of any. Her groom was in the hands of the Disciples, the extreme religious organization who had nearly succeeded in killing them all earlier in the year.

Except, unlike most disappointed brides, she did have a crack Special Forces team on her side. She sniffled, pulling back in the tears. They also had a getaway driver equal to none other. These brave men hunted where others feared to tread. They had the skills. They just needed something to give them the speed.

And if the kidnappers were in fact the Disciples, they were going to have to move quickly. Because Brandt *had* to be alive. The religious fanatics had staged this kidnapping down to the smallest detail. They wanted Brandt for something. Even as the tears streamed down her cheeks, she couldn't think of why.

It had been she and Bunny who had decoded the tablets that held the Ten Commandments and so much more. Why hadn't the bastards taken either of them? Sure, the Disciples would want

Brandt dead for the major blow he'd delivered them, but alive? His abduction made absolutely no sense.

Those thoughts could wait as the skies darkened above her.

A helicopter. Not the one with Brandt, but a helicopter nonetheless.

Davidson raised his gun, but Rebecca shoved the barrel down. "It's Lopez."

The corporal must have tracked down the helicopter that had dropped the men off at the church in the first place. Or he stole one. Or a little elf delivered it to him. With Lopez, you were just never certain.

Ropes being flung out the sides confirmed her suspicion, though.

Lopez had gotten them the speed. Now they just needed to take advantage of it.

As sirens sped toward them, Rebecca gathered her skirt. Davidson put a hand up.

"I'm going," Rebecca stated, daring him with her look to argue. Nothing could stop her from getting on that helicopter.

"Duh," Davidson answered. "I'm helping you attach to the line."

"Oh," Rebecca demurred and accepted his help.

After he got the bride situated, he turned to Bunny, but she backed away.

"I'm so sorry," she said, her red curls loosening from the pins that tried to keep them contained. "I can't. I just can't."

The other men secured their lines and zipped up toward the chopper. Davidson took Bunny's hand.

"It's all good," Davidson said, cupping her face in his scarred palm. "I'm glad you are staying."

Bunny cocked her head. "Don't lie."

She was right. His protective instincts should be taking over, wanting to keep her safe, but he couldn't help himself. He was going to miss her.

"No one is going to blame you for staying behind."

Snuffling back a tear, Bunny put her hand over his. "Like I said, don't *lie*."

Again, Bunny was correct. There was going to be some judgment about her bailing, but if Bunny's heart wasn't in it, there was no getting around that fact.

As police officers burst into the back of the church, Davidson kissed her gently on the lips. It was amazing how well the body could heal if given the right incentive. A few months ago, Davidson couldn't feel the entire right side of his face.

Now? He enjoyed every moment of their PDA.

He didn't want to break off the kiss, but they did have an audience. "They are going to want some answers."

Bunny gave him a peck on the cheek. "Which I *can't* give them. Don't worry," she said, shooing him away. "Go."

Davidson grabbed ahold of the rope, wrapping it around his good wrist as the zip line jerked him upward. He watched his peach-colored girl as long as he could. She rushed forward, informing the cops that the men fleeing were not terrorists. Just as Lopez angled the helicopter away, Bunny looked up.

A sad smile on her face.

He would have smiled back if he hadn't nearly been impaled on the huge cross that topped the church. The other men helped haul him up into the chopper as Lopez really lay on the throttle.

"Took you long enough," Lopez grumbled.

Davidson ignored him and prepped his rifle. "Any luck?"

Lopez nodded. "Got a ping hauling ass north by northwest."

"Wait," Rebecca said over the roar of the rotors, "you mean we've got a location on Brandt?"

"*Had*," Lopez corrected. "The ping was a few minutes ago."

Rebecca looked from Lopez to Davidson. "What does that mean?"

Davidson encouraged Rebecca to sit down and strap in. "After our last mission, we all got fitted with intradental tracking devices."

"That's good," Rebecca said, pushing her veil to the side. "That's great, right? We can find him."

He glanced to Lopez, though. It would be great if the signal were *continuous*.

"Only, we haven't gotten anything since that original ping," Lopez stated.

Rebecca tugged on Davidson's tuxedo cuffs. "Tell me what the hell is going on."

"The tracker requires kinetic movement for energy..."

The woman had three PhDs. She could easily piece together the scenario.

"So if the tracker isn't transmitting, it means that Brandt isn't moving," Rebecca said in a rush as the helicopter veered to miss a high rise. "He must be unconscious again."

"Or..." Davidson couldn't bring himself to say it.

"Or," Rebecca finished his train of thought, "Brandt is dead."

CHAPTER 3

UNDISCLOSED LOCATION

5:57 P.M. (EST)

Frellan leisurely studied the soldier curled up on the floor of the helicopter. The Master had made this man out to be nearly a god. The man who had stolen Moses's tablets and destroyed God's twin cities. Bringing their most vaulted warrior, Aunush, his sister, to her knees.

Though, he did not think it took a god to bring Aunush down. Though they had bathed in the same womb, they could not be more divergent. Aunush, since her first squall, had wished the world to know of her might. She had flaunted her elevated position and taken pride in her accomplishments, indulging in her passions.

Including the man who sat across from Frellan. Her sniper, Mikhal.

She had toyed with the sniper. Baiting him, thinking her sexual conquest would keep her safe. In the end, Mikhal had turned her in to the Master. But how long had the sniper played both sides against one another? Had he truly brought Aunush to the Disciples out of duty or out of expedience? Had the sniper hedged his bets?

Whether or not Frellan trusted the sniper mattered not. Mikhal was a weapon. A very useful one if the reports from Aunush's last operation were any indication. The only one to survive the encounter with Brandt and his team.

Frellan's eyes scanned farther down the row of mercenaries, who sat stoically through the long flight, until he paused on Monnie's face. Beautiful auburn eyes shone from a blemish-free mocha complexion. So young and tender to be a watcher.

However, after Nannan's untimely death in Jordan, the young woman was the most studied of the watchers. Monnie was seeped in the Messiah's prophecies. Not just the ones detailed in the Bible, but she was also well versed in the oral history from Moshe and Yoshua, carried down the line through the Disciples' history.

Frellan had been reluctant to bring the young woman along, but the Master had overridden him. The Master was concerned that if this girl in the Congo truly was the Messiah, she might be naive to her station, her power. Their savior might think herself just a scared little girl. It might be best to have someone on the team who wasn't a mercenary forged by God's will. A *feminine* touch.

Monnie must have felt his gaze upon her, as she looked up from the scroll she had been reading. He saw the flinch of fear in her eyes as she surveyed the many tattoos and body piercings that riddled his face. Frellan did not balk despite the disdain he found in her features.

While his sister's life had been led in the light, Frellan's had been spent in shadow. The only marks of his passing were those etched upon his skin. For every quest, every victory, every defeat was recorded in ink or steel.

Few had seen his face and lived to tell the tale.

Her eyes flickered back to her precious scroll. *That is right, child*, Frellan thought. His piercings had another purpose. Intimidation. If he would do such to himself, what might he do to an enemy? Or an ally who had disappointed him?

Frellan looked back down the row of the mercenaries. They, too, had deep ritual scars, but even they gave him a wide berth. He found Ugudo, his second-in-command. The man sported a new spiked rod through his cheek, after they failed to obtain the information they needed in the Congo.

The piercing was a work of art, really.

It was not that Aunush and he did not share the same desires. That they did not both revel in creating, nurturing, and exploring pain. He'd just found a way to elevate his to beauty. Something God would smile down upon.

He wondered what he might do to this supposed god at his feet, Brandt. The man had been trained to withstand torture, but torture was not what Frellan employed. He made sure even if his subject survived his ministrations, they bore his mark for life. Would his woman want him then? Knowing what Frellan had done to him?

When his spleen poked out through his flank? Or a hooked bar pierced his member?

The thought of all that he could do to the paralyzed soldier aroused Frellan. He took a deep breath. His was to experience pleasure but to serve God. Especially with the Messiah's appearance to be so close at hand.

This man-god's gnats were in the air, searching for their lost leader.

Little did they know that the tablets were but one of many secrets the Disciples held. In many ways, the tablets, while holding the fascination of the Master and Aunush, were of little consequence. They held only the announcement of the female Messiah. They did not hold where or how she would come into the world.

The tablets might be lost again, but the Disciples' purpose was redoubled.

Since the moment Aunush had sent word that the tablets were in play, Frellan had listened for the whispers in the night of the Messiah. Was she already born, or had she yet to be conceived? The Disciples must be the first to find her, bring her into their fold, so that she might be raised amongst the true Word.

Even in this modern age of computers and the Internet, combing through a world filled with nearly seven billion people was a laborious task. Then a scout assigned to shadow Brandt and his men had stumbled out of the Congo jungle, telling of a girl who could heal even the most mortal blow. A girl who Brandt had saved. A girl who he had personally seen to it had been secreted off, deep into the forest.

Did the soldier know whom he had come upon? Or was he as blind as he was impotent?

Many within the fold were shocked that this soldier might have been in contact with the possible Messiah. To Frellan, there was a perfect symmetry to their meeting. God, in His great wisdom, did not unfold his plan for all to see.

He lived in the shadows as did Frellan. But now, in this glorious age, it was time for both of them to taste the sun on their skin.

"You must have heard wrong," Rebecca said, shaking her head so hard her neck muscles complained.

Still, Lopez lay off the throttle, banking them toward the north. "Nope," the corporal said. "We have been ordered to stand down."

"They want another team to take over the search?" Davidson asked, clearly as befuddled by the orders as Rebecca.

"Yep," Lopez replied as they flew toward the Charleston Airport. They had stayed in the general vicinity of the abduction, awaiting another signal from Brandt. They needed to know in which direction to head, but nothing. Over an hour and nothing.

Rebecca really didn't think that she had any more tears to shed, but moisture sprang to the ready. In disbelief, she watched as Lopez angled them toward the helipad of the airport, prepping them to land.

She looked to Davidson, but he just shrugged. "That's brass for you."

This couldn't be happening. Brandt couldn't be kidnapped. They couldn't be losing control of the search. And what the hell was wrong with the men? Why weren't they throwing a huge fit? Her own fists shook in quiet rage as her mind raced to find a way to convince the men to stay on the trail.

The only *huge* problem? That would require her to convince the men to disobey a direct order, not from Brandt, but from the Pentagon. At the least, that would be a court-martial offense. At worst, it could be construed as treason punishable by death.

Words caught in her throat as Lopez lowered them to the large red-and-white helipad. Could she really ask that of them?

Um, as she stepped on her wedding dress and tore it, again, *hell yes* she could.

Lopez brushed past her as he exited the chopper. Rebecca was right on his tail. He was in charge. She had to convince him.

Rebecca placed an arm on his. "Ricky."

The corporal seemed vaguely annoyed. Like her asking to save the man she loved was a bother. "What?"

"We can't just give up."

Lopez cocked his head. "No kidding." He turned to Davidson. "I'm guessing you are in."

The younger man shrugged. "How much more trouble could I really get into?"

"Talli?" the corporal asked. After the sniper nodded, Lopez turned to the new point man, Levont. "You've only been with us a few months. No one will think you're a bent helmet for waving this one off."

"Are you kidding me?" Levont said with a broad smile. "I see this going down one of two ways." The point man swung his assault rifle onto his shoulder. "One, you guys save the world, *again*. Or two, you go down in a flaming blaze of glory. Either way, I am *so* going to be there."

Lopez put his hand over Rebecca's. "So, little missy, if you aren't too busy questioning our dedication, would you like to help me steal a plane?"

These men might not wear Brandt's ring on their finger like she did, but they were equally bound to him. Having no other way to apologize, Rebecca just threw her sweaty, grimy, torn wedding-dressed self into Ricky's arms.

He laughed, picking her up, swinging her around, so she was pointed in the direction of the private plane hangar. "That's more like it."

Brandt felt his body slosh over. Actually, not slosh. There was no water, yet that's what it felt like. Had someone replaced his muscles with lumpy oatmeal? Or Jell-O, maybe Jell-O. Whatever the hell it was, it wasn't responding to his mind's repeated, urgent request to get up. *Now.*

The best Brandt could manage was to crack open his eyelids. He was on some kind of air cargo plane. Not US military. It felt Italian in manufacture. Although his brain was about a hundred times more functional than his muscles, he wasn't about to ask it to come up with the exact make and model. Besides, it didn't matter. The Disciples probably stole it from a maintenance yard or plane graveyard, making the transport nearly impossible to trace.

His limited, ground-level vision swept the area in front of him. Pairs upon pairs of combat boots were lined up. A tactical team. No great surprise there, either. The Disciples were transporting him from South Carolina to somewhere *not* in South Carolina.

Even if he had full, or even minimal, use of his limbs, he probably couldn't figure that out. Not without one hell of a fight ending in a huge body count. One of those probably being his.

No, instead, he needed to concentrate on his tooth.

Closing his eyes and marshaling every reserve he had left, which wasn't much, Brandt tried to clench his jaw. The best he got was his incisors barely grazing each other. That was not going to do.

Brandt clearly remembered the briefing by the scientists. They were so giddy. "All you have to do is chew," they said, nearly giggling.

It sounded so fucking simple. Chew or, more appropriate in Brandt's case, grind your teeth, and the motion fueled the transmitter. So simple.

So not happening.

"Just ten good chews and the activated transmitter will send out a burst with your coordinates."

Ten good chews. Who couldn't chew ten times? Apparently Brandt. Plus, come to think of it, what about if you had a ball gag in your mouth? How could you chew then?

Yeah, those were two scenarios the squints hadn't thought of.

Knowing that his life depended on his ability to masticate, Brandt bit down harder. He nicked the side of his tongue, but who cared? Pain shot up from the broken shards of porcelain cap. Concentrating, Brandt bit down again and again and again. At least ten times, but nothing.

The first time he'd activated the tracker, the damn thing had given him a little jolt in the gum. Now nothing.

Ten chews his ass.

Clearly, that had been an optimistic number.

Taking in a slow, deep breath, Brandt prepared for another round of overriding a massive paralytic.

He could only hope someone was watching on the other end.

Davidson allowed the whine of the plane's engines to soothe his jangled joints. The last few hours had not been kind to any of them. This was the fourth plane they had lifted, and Lopez was having a harder and harder time staying clear of any civilian or military's radar.

But they needed to stay close to Charleston. To strike out in any one direction could cost them hours later if Brandt had been taken in the opposite direction. So they had stayed as close to the church as they could. However, word had clearly gone out that their team was AWOL. The Pentagon was probably spending as much time tracking down them as they were Brandt.

No one was taking the waiting harder than Rebecca. She sat across the aisle from Davidson on the twin-engine prop plane, her stained and tattered wedding dress a visible accounting of the hell they had all been through.

Her veil, the anchor of it so firmly tangled in her hair that the best they could do was cut off the shiny fabric, no longer flew in front of her face. However, it looked like some sort of mutant white tulle creature growing from her head.

She had been such a beautiful bride, for all of about two minutes.

And this waiting wasn't aging well on her. She bit at her manicure, ripping the polish off until she could chew at the nail itself. If she didn't stop soon, she'd have nothing but bloody fingertips to show for it.

Finally, it appeared that she couldn't wait any longer. She unlatched her safety belt and pushed herself between Lopez and his copilot, Talli.

"We've got to do something," she implored.

Equally frustrated, Lopez answered. "Tell me what to do, Rebecca," the corporal said, turning to her, "and I'll do it. *Anything*."

Rebecca threw herself back into her seat, knowing that Lopez was right. There was absolutely nothing else to do but wait. She must have known that flying around in circles simply wasn't Lopez's style, either.

"Wait," Levont said, pushing the tracking monitor toward them, "I think it's pinging."

"What do you mean *think*?" Lopez asked.

Davidson looked at the monitor. Rapidly, the screen was realigning itself, squeezing the search grid down and down again. "Something definitely is happening...But it's not showing Brandt's location."

Rebecca leaned over, her stubby veil brushing Talli's back. "Why is the screen doing that?"

"Doing what?" Lopez asked, clearly agitated that, at such a critical juncture, he still had to fly the plane.

Davidson watched as the map pulled in tighter and tighter, expanding the area covered to far beyond their search area. Then the screen took an abrupt leap to the right.

"Oh my God," Rebecca breathed out.

"*What*?" Lopez demanded.

"He's gotta be..." Levont started, then stalled.

The little light flashed brightly against the blank blue background.

"Which way do I turn?" Lopez begged, glancing over his shoulder.

But given that the blip was coming from somewhere over the middle of the Atlantic Ocean, there would be no turning anywhere.

Davidson took the map from Levont, readjusted it so that Lopez could see the coordinates, then put the screen in front of the corporal.

His mouth opened, then closed as Rebecca sobbed quietly in her seat.

"Well," Lopez announced, starting his descent, "guess we are just going to have to steal a bigger airplane."

Bunny sighed and crossed her arms, forcing the pout of all pouts onto her lips. But the guy across from her seemed to care less. Weird. That usually worked on most guys. Perhaps Lt. Daniel Prenner didn't bat for her side. After the repeal of "Don't ask, don't tell," it was kind of hard to know.

"Brenda," the man coaxed.

"It is *Bunny*," she replied. "And I am telling you that you don't have the clearance to hear my side of the story."

"Corporal Lopez and the rest have gone AWOL after being ordered to stand down," Prenner said, as if that was going to surprise her. "You've got to know how much trouble they are in."

Really? After Moscow, Slovenia, and Jordan, she should be worried about Rebecca and the rest? *Please*. Running around the American countryside avoiding MPs was like eating breakfast—in bed. Which is kind of why she didn't grab that repelling line from the helicopter.

She'd grown to love Rebecca like a sister and Brandt like a brother-in-law, but chasing *after* the Disciples? That was sheer crazy talk. Whenever the Disciples were involved, you needed to run away—as quickly as you could.

Prenner hit a key on his laptop that started cell phone footage of her and Davidson's kiss. "Clearly, you care for this man."

Bunny shrugged. "He's grown on me."

Which wasn't exactly true. There was something there, but between his aborted court-martial, reinstatement, then five missions back-to-back, it had been a little hard for them to explore exactly the extent of that "something."

She closed the laptop. "Just get me my CIA handler."

Which was kind of weird to say. Her life had certainly taken a left turn since last year. During her graduate studies, the closest that she had come to interacting with the Central Intelligence Agency had been watching reruns of *Covert Affairs*.

Now she had her very own CIA handler.

"As I said," Prenner stated very slowly, "Emily Jannus doesn't exist."

"Of course she doesn't. Ugh." This was going to be a very long night.

Then the door opened as a woman dressed in a long black gown, her hair tucked into a sleek bun, strode in.

"This is a closed interrogation," Prenner growled, but the woman put her hand out.

"Nice to meet you. I'm Emily Jannus." The woman smiled, looking like she had just stepped into an elegant cocktail party. "And Bunny. So nice to see you again."

Bunny scooted her chair over to make room for Emily, suddenly feeling underdressed for the occasion. Why did Mrs. Brandt have to go with peach?

"My understanding is that you have a few questions for Ms. Hollingford?" Emily pleasantly asked the lieutenant.

"My commander is *not* going to stand for this," Prenner warned.

Emily chuckled. "Who do you think held the door open for me?"

An older man in full dress uniform stepped into the room, his chest bristling with medals. "I am afraid my hands are tied. We are to cooperate fully with Ms. Jannus, or whatever her name truly is."

Bunny's CIA handler just bent her head at a cute angle, demurring to the fact Emily wasn't her real name but not giving any further details. Turning her attention from the men, Emily smiled at Bunny.

"Now, why don't you catch me up?"

"Well"—Bunny looked to the officers, not sure how much she could say in front of them—"the wackos kidnapped Brandt."

Emily pulled out a small tablet device and queued up the keyboard. "That much I know."

"Then it got weird," Bunny said, nodding to the army men. "Apparently, the military tried to pull Rebecca and Brandt's team from the pursuit."

"That I hadn't heard," Emily stated as she typed rapidly.

"Of course, they disobeyed those orders."

Emily's eyebrows went up. "Of course." She turned to the general. "Why would you pull a highly decorated Special Ops team from the search for one of their own?"

"The order came from above." Bunny noted that the general would not meet Emily's eyes. "Directly from the DOD."

"See?" Bunny asked. "Weird. It makes no sense unless…the wackos have someone pretty high up."

"What are you insinuating?" Prenner asked.

It was Emily who answered, though. Her breezy manner evaporating. Replacing it with a cool confidence. "I'm sorry, but you don't have high enough clearance for me to even approach that question."

Prenner bristled as Bunny gave him a well-deserved "I told you so" look. The lieutenant looked ready to lash out, but the general intervened, indicating that Prenner should leave. "Regs are regs."

"Oh, I'm sorry," Emily continued. "I meant *both* of you."

The general's brow creased, but he seemed too much of a professional to sputter in front of the CIA agent. Before they could turn from the room, Prenner's cell phone buzzed. He read the text, then flashed the message to the general.

For a moment, they didn't look like they were going to share.

"Gentlemen?" Emily asked. "Do I need to call my director?"

With a soul-deep sigh, the general's shoulders sagged. "Brandt has been located."

Bunny sat up straight in her chair. This was the best news since…well, ever.

"And?" Emily prompted.

"It looks like he is heading to the Congo."

Emily turned to Bunny, but she shook her head. "I have no idea why the wackos would take him there."

Prenner cleared his throat. "I think I might know." All eyes turned to the lieutenant. "That was the location of Brandt's last mission."

Still, it made no sense. Bunny vaguely knew Brandt and Davidson had been on the African continent, but it had sounded like a routine mission. Nothing that ran afoul of the Disciples.

"I think I've heard enough," Emily said, rising from her chair. "I'll be taking care of Ms. Hollingford."

The men didn't argue, but neither did they part to let them leave.

"Prenner goes with you," the general stated. Emily went to open her mouth, but he continued. "Otherwise, I *will* call your director. Then he will have to call a meeting at the White House with the Joint Chiefs. I take it you don't want to wait that long?"

A frown crossed over Emily's lips, then curved up into a smile. "Prenner it is."

With that, the men parted, and Emily whisked Bunny out into the hallway, with the lieutenant close behind. Their heels clicking on the tile floor, Bunny asked, "Where are we going?"

Emily grinned. "The Pentagon, of course."

Right. It involved Brandt and Rebecca, so of course it involved the Pentagon.

Duh.

CHAPTER 4

OUTSIDE OF MBANDAKA, DEMOCRATIC REPUBLIC OF THE CONGO

MAY 27, 5:05 P.M. (CAT, CENTRAL AFRICAN TIME)

Brandt's head banged against the Jeep's window. Just add that to his collection of bruises. His body wanted to sink back into a drugged haze, but his mind had other plans. The next time the Jeep dipped into a huge hole in the dirt road and bounced out of it, Brandt braced, demanding that his muscles obey.

And they did. Well, at least a little bit. The paralytic must have been wearing off. Obviously, the Disciples were prepared for this fact since they had zip-tied Brandt's hands and feet.

Squinting his eyes open, Brandt took in his surroundings. Actually, he took in the enemy number first and foremost. Besides the driver and the ever-so-pleasant Disciple, there were three other men in the Jeep. All black. Not just black, but with ritualistic face scars. These weren't just any mercenaries. These men had been carrying a weapon since childhood. They had been boy soldiers who had grown up to be highly trained mercenaries.

He'd dealt with this brand of men before. Just last week, as a matter of fact. Taking in the passing scenery, Brandt realized he'd seen that too. Just last week as well. Lush jungle lay ahead as they drove through the misty, low-rolling hills of the Congo.

Why the hell would the Disciples bring him back here? Brandt's last mission didn't have anything to do with the Ten Commandments or even religion. A World Bank envoy had been kidnapped and needed extraction.

Sure, the mission had gotten bloody. Any mission in this impoverished part of the world invariably did. But what did the Disciples care about that?

Apparently a lot.

There were at least three Jeeps in front of them, and as they made a curve around a large hill, it seemed at least three Jeeps behind them. The last carrying the young woman from the plane. The Disciples had come in force.

Again, for what, though?

A zap from his molar brought Brandt back to more practical matters. All of this backcountry driving, chattering his teeth, must have fueled his transmitter. He was pinging his location, for who knew how long.

The Jeep's engine groaned as they began the steep climb up into the dense rain forest, heading toward, Brandt could only guess, the war-torn village where his last mission had culminated.

What the Disciples would do to him there was anyone's guess.

With a drug-besotted mind, Brandt tried to calculate when he'd activated his transmitter and how long it would take for his team to catch up. With a sigh, he slumped back into his seat. Even if his team had left the States the moment he had pinged them, the Disciples were at least six to eight hours ahead. Add in the time it would take to arrange transportation into the mountains, and his team would be ten hours behind.

Ten hours that the Disciples could spend torturing him.

Not even Lopez and his need for speed could make up that difference.

"We are totally going to beat them there," Lopez announced.

Rebecca raised an eyebrow. However, the other men seemed to believe the corporal.

"Don't believe me, *chica*, but we will," Lopez insisted.

Of course, that made no mathematical sense whatsoever. Even without her laptop, Rebecca knew they were nearly half a day behind Brandt. Granted, Lopez had made up a ton of time over the Atlantic, and it had turned out to be way faster to simply land and steal another plane in Lisbon rather than wait for a refuel, but still, that left a minimum of a four-hour gap, which Rebecca couldn't see how they were going to make up.

Then she noticed the men getting parachutes out.

"No," Rebecca hissed, suddenly understanding how Lopez planned to make up the difference.

"*Yes*," Lopez teased, his eyes wide with anticipation. "We are coming in from the other side of the mountain and dropping directly into the village."

The corporal raised his hand for a high five, which Rebecca did *not* return. Talli fulfilled the action for her. The sniper actually had a smile on his face. "All's that stands between us and setting up an ambush is a little low-altitude jump. My fave."

"I...I've never...skydived," Rebecca admitted. Normally a paleo-archaeologist whose specialty was genetic migration wouldn't feel ashamed about such a thing, but most PhDs weren't hanging out with Special Forces.

"Never?" Davidson asked behind her as he strapped himself into his parachute.

She shook her head.

"Dude," Lopez snorted. "What the hell were you and Brandt doing all this time?"

Rebecca's face reddened. Oh, they were doing lots of stuff, just not anything that could be mentioned in mixed company. Besides, having way too much action in their work lives, they liked their downtime to be...*down.*

Not up, jumping from planes.

No matter her hesitation, Davidson handed her a parachute. She studied the myriad of straps.

"No worries," he coaxed. "I'll get you hooked up. Then we'll tandem jump."

"Yeah, right," Lopez retorted as he rose from the pilot seat. Talli followed.

"Um," Rebecca stammered. "Who is going to fly the plane?"

The corporal waved his hand at the controls. "The autopilot is set to fly past the mountain and crash in Uganda."

Rebecca didn't even have time to digest that news when Lopez grabbed for her parachute. "No, Ricky. I think I'd rather have Davidson."

While just as insane as the rest, Davidson did have some concern for her personal safety. Lopez, on the other hand? His motto? Personal safety was for the dead. Which didn't even make sense, but he certainly said it frequently enough.

Besides, she and the corporal had being staying at arm's length since that unfortunate incident of mistaken identity in Russia.

Lopez was having none of it, though. "Please. Chica. Look at those hips of yours."

She glanced down to her tattered gown. Rebecca liked to think of her figure as hourglass.

The corporal nodded to the lean Davidson.

"Do you really think that skinny-ass frame could handle your curves?"

"Hey," both Rebecca and Davidson protested at the same time.

"I am team leader," Lopez said, surprisingly serious. "Chica and I are doing the tandem tango."

Davidson backed down with a shrug. However, Rebecca didn't have the same deference to military chain of command. As Lopez started strapping her in, she complained, "Ricky, I really think—"

"Look at his hands," Lopez whispered in Rebecca's ear. At first, she had no idea what the corporal was taking about. Then she noticed Davidson shake out his arm. When they came to rest again, the sniper's fingers, especially those on his severely scarred left hand, began to twitch.

It was no wonder. They were all trashed. After twenty hours on the road, who wouldn't be? And Davidson was under the most strain of all. Usually, after a mission, he would have to have several hot paraffin treatments to soothe the pain from his tortured hands. Davidson tried to shield it from the rest, but Rebecca had been there through the multiple surgeries to cut out the scar tissue. She knew the pain even routine movement brought on, let alone the strain of an operation. And he'd gone right from the conflict in South Carolina to this cross-continental plane hop. All of that strain showing in those twitching fingers.

"If anything happened during the jump…I'm not sure if he could hold you," Lopez continued. "We need his hands for shooting."

She looked to the corporal with a bit more appreciation for his leadership skills. Far better to tease her about her hips and Davidson about his slight frame than embarrass the sniper with his much more pronounced weakness.

"Besides," the corporal followed up, "it's been a while since I've held you."

Typical Lopez. Profoundly insightful one moment, then *Lopez* the next.

"Let's just make sure that weapon of yours is holstered," she challenged back.

With a broad smile, Lopez settled the weight of the parachute on Rebecca's back. "We shall see."

Readjusting the straps onto her shoulders, Rebecca realized this was like wearing the world's most uncomfortable bra. The straps already dug grooves into her skin. Nothing about this experience was going to be pleasant.

As the plane's yoke inclined on its own, dropping altitude, Rebecca frowned. It just seemed wrong they trusted the computer to drop them off at the right place.

"Ricky, are you sure about this?"

Lopez finished adjusting his parachute before answering. "Oh, please. In these calm skies? The autopilot will be fine…"

"Unless?"

A boom sounded off to the left. The plane veered as fire filled the sky. Lopez grabbed hold of her, breaking her fall as the tip of the wing shuddered, then broke off.

"Unless we're attacked," Lopez answered, jumping up, springing for the pilot's seat.

Davidson searched out the plane's window. Scattered clouds blocked the view of the ground. Then bright-red flared.

"Incoming from the left!" he shouted.

Lopez banked to the right. Just in time. Still, the explosion rocked the plane, sending them careening.

"Another!" Levont yelled.

They avoided another direct hit, but that wasn't going to last long.

"I'm opening the hatch!" Davidson announced, making sure Rebecca had tight hold of a seat. Bracing himself so he wasn't sucked out, Davidson opened the door. Wind whipped around them. "Somebody get ready to hold my feet!" Davidson announced as he dropped to the floor.

As Levont grabbed his dress shoes, Davidson swung his rifle to bear. Ignoring the fact he was only a few inches from falling from the plane, he yelled, "Turn into it!"

Lopez obliged, tilting the plane toward the left. Through the scope, Davidson scanned. *Where are you?*

The attackers weren't the Disciples. They were far too north for that. No, this attack was simply the cost of doing business in Africa. Some tribal lord thought that a nice, expensive Learjet would bring in some good money. And the chief wouldn't be wrong. Selling the jet scrap metal could probably feed the village for a year.

The only problem was that Davidson and the rest still needed the plane. Intact.

There it was. That flash as the RPG was fired.

"Into it!" Davidson shouted. Lopez, as always, was right on it, cutting under the RPG as it sailed over them. Davidson fired before the cloud cover obscured the launch site. They were impossible shots. He didn't expect to hit anything or anyone. He just wanted to give the men on the ground something to ponder. Passenger planes usually didn't shoot back.

Unfortunately, the attackers didn't seem to care.

"Here!" Tallie said as he shoved an RPG launcher at Davidson. The metal object slid across the floor. Davidson snatched it before it went over the side.

Now this, this might give them something to seriously ponder.

Before he could get the launcher up onto his shoulder, Rebecca screamed, "Incoming!"

She was right. And this one was coming straight at them. Lopez tried to maneuver, but there was no way they could get out of range. The trajectory was all wrong, and Davidson was all about the trajectory.

There was only one thing to do.

Rebecca watched as the RPG seemed to swim out of the clouds and streak toward them. Despite Lopez's best efforts, the RPG was still going to hit them. Maybe in the tail of the plane now, instead of the nose, but they were going to get hit.

Then Davidson fired his RPG. The rocket shot out of the aircraft, scorching the chairs next to Davidson. She expected the RPG to sail downward, but instead, its path was nearly parallel to the plane. Right at the incoming missile.

In a fiery explosion, Davidson's RPG slammed into the enemy's. Close. Too close. The shock wave cracked metal, sheering off an entire wing. The plane tumbled onto its side as the seam that held the front and the back of the plane split open.

"Go!" Lopez yelled from the cockpit. "Jump!"

Davidson scrambled to his feet, letting Talli and Levont follow orders and leap from the plane as he tried to make his way to Rebecca. Then the unthinkable happened. The plane cracked in two. Davidson lunged forward, trying to grasp her wrist, but their fingers barely brushed. She was on her own.

Without any thrust of its own, the back of the plane tilted nearly vertical and fell, with her *inside.*

Tears ripped from her eyes, Rebecca latched onto the edge of a seat, her feet dangling, useless. Then she passed Talli and Levont, their parachutes already open. She could see the men point at her, but what could they do?

Pull it together, Rebecca thought. You're just falling at terminal velocity. Okay, that didn't help. No, she needed to get out of the plane. She needed to climb to the top and jump, getting clear of the wreckage. Or pre-wreckage.

She tried to grab hold of the armrest in front of her, only to have her grip slip. Dangling by one hand, Rebecca tried to push the panic down. What would Brandt say?

"You're still alive, so stop whining."

God, she loved him, but his voice really wasn't all that helpful in a crisis.

"Rebecca!"

She looked up to find Davidson curled into a ball, cutting his wind resistance, hurling toward her. He pantomimed for her to grab a cord on her parachute and pull.

Not even thinking about it and all the things that could go so horribly wrong, Rebecca jerked the cord. Or at least the cord she thought she should pull. But nothing happened. Rebecca looked up to find Davidson nearly on her.

"The orange one!" he yelled.

Fishing around, she found the orange one and pulled it.

Davidson waited until the parachute flung open. It hit the side of the plane, but the wind caught in its canopy and jerked Rebecca up and out of the tail. As he pulled his own cord, Rebecca shot up past him.

That was okay. He'd rather have her up above him than hurling to her death. His own parachute popped open, sucking in air, snapping his risers, just as the tail of the plane crashed into the mountainside. Guess the tribal lord was going to get his cash, after all. Then Davidson was whisked upward as the skirt caught air. He sailed up and slightly past Rebecca. Guess Lopez was right. He must be a little lighter than her. Not that he would ever tell Rebecca.

Sheer terror masked her normally pretty features. He guided the braking lines, slowing his ascent to match hers, pulling them almost even. His intent was to grab hold of her rigging and help control her descent, but Rebecca's eyes stared over his head.

He looked over his shoulder to find the plane's front half plummeting out of the sky—with Lopez standing on the nose of the plane.

"Quick!" he yelled. "Somebody get this for Ricky Junior!"

Davidson ignored the corporal. At some point, Lopez was going to have to pull the cord. Picture or not. Davidson's priority was getting Rebecca down safely. Carefully positioning his canopy over hers, he inched into position. They were close enough he could see Rebecca's terror returning to her eyes.

"See?" he tried to coax. "It's not so bad."

Rebecca scowled, but at least she didn't look ready to hurl.

Maneuvering around her lines, Davidson brought them nearly nose to nose.

"I'm just going to tether us, then cut your shoot. Okay?"

Gulping, Rebecca nodded, seeming more than willing to hand over the landing to him.

"On the count of—"

A shot split the difference between them. More bullets came as men ran through the forest, tracking them. Guess the tribal lord wasn't just satisfied with the plane wreckage.

"Why are they shooting?"

The better question was why hadn't they hit them yet. They were sitting ducks up here. Then Davidson realized their strategy. They weren't trying to hit them. They were trying to hit their parachutes. They were forcing them down onto the tribal lands.

"They want us for ransom," Davidson said quietly, trying to keep to the task at hand. Getting Rebecca and him tethered.

"Ransom?" she repeated, clearly trying to wrap her head around the idea.

He didn't have time to explain that a major part of rural African economy was ransom. And people falling out of an expensive Learjet? Even better. Given the fact that Rebecca was in a wedding dress and all the men were in tuxes. The best.

Little did the tribesmen know they'd downed a Special Forces team. Davidson would let them figure it out once they were on the ground and could marshal some defenses.

His fingers fumbled as he tried to latch on the carabiner. Then another shot, one that sliced through Rebecca's canopy, ripped her out of his grip. He tried to hold on to her as Rebecca's fingers dug into the flesh of his palm, but his scars spasmed, and she was gone.

The tear in the skirt spread like wildfire as she flailed to get control of the damaged parachute. She didn't have the experience to do it, though, evidenced by her rapid, haphazard descent.

There was only one thing left to do.

Rebecca's body was jerked to the left as the wind caught the intact portion of her parachute. She picked up speed as the gust carried her past a peak. Davidson, however, was drifting down like a good skydiver would. Then he pulled out his gun.

Too late, she realized what he was planning on doing.

"No!" she screamed.

Davidson pulled the trigger anyway, shooting at his own parachute. Dear God, she loved military men, but they were freaking crazy. The newly damaged parachute bucked and fought him. However, Davidson had far more control than she did. As a matter of fact, he rapidly gained speed and accuracy, coming right for her.

Unfortunately, the tear in his chute angled to the left, ripping a huge hole in the fabric, dragging the chute away from her. Davidson had to follow. With a desperate cry of "Rebecca," the private disappeared behind the peak.

She would cry too, except that green jungle was coming up fast. Unable to guide the chute, Rebecca let go of the handles and covered her face. Her body slammed sideways into the thick vegetation. Through her arms, she could see leaves flapping and branches snapping. Her leg hit a tree trunk and bounced off of it.

The parachute got caught in the foliage, threatening to nearly tear her in half. Then she was falling again as the fabric tore away. Birds burst all around her, startled by her falling form. Monkeys hooted in the distance, and still, she fell. Something snagged her cheek. Her dress ripped. A bone-white shoe dropped off, and still, she fell.

Then her harness caught on a branch, jerking her to a sudden stop. The slightly stretchy material sprang her up, then down, bouncing her like a baby in a swing.

The sole problem? She was a good twenty meters from the forest floor.

But you know what? She'd take it.

Davidson ran through the dense underbrush, heading toward the sound of the shots. It was about ten degrees off the path he'd calculated for Rebecca, but if he could gather a few more men, all the better.

Raising his weapon, he jumped a moss-covered log and burst into a small clearing. Four guns turned toward him. Luckily, they were his team. Half a dozen bodies littered the ground. Guess the tribesmen had gotten in a little over their heads.

"Where's Rebecca?" Lopez asked.

Gulping air, shame burnt Davidson's face. "Her chute…she got…I lost her."

"They were shooting at all of us," Levont said.

Davidson glared at the new point man. Having someone defend him made his failure sting all the worse.

"Whatever," Lopez said, gathering ammunition and weapons from the dead men. "We'll catch up with her."

"Are you sure?" Talli asked.

Both Davidson and Lopez glared at the supposed sniper.

"Whoa," he said, holding up his hands. "I'm not saying someone shouldn't go after her, but we have a narrow window of opportunity to get in ahead of Brandt. I'm just saying we put the majority of our manpower to laying the ambush."

The man was correct, which bugged the crap out of Davidson. His shame had prevented him from seeing the whole picture.

"Talli's right," Davidson admitted. "I'll head out and catch up with you at the rally point."

Levont stepped in front of him, though. "You are kidding, right?"

Davidson looked to Lopez.

The corporal nodded. "Davidson did just fine last week."

"That was with an entire team. With vehicles, sticking to the roads," Levont pressed. "But out here? In the jungle? How much forest tracking experience do you have?"

Still bristling from the prickle of shame, Davidson was not in the mood to be questioned. "Enough."

"Do you speak Lingala?" Levont asked bluntly. "Dude, you are a white guy in a tux who doesn't even speak the official language of the country. How far exactly do you think you are getting?"

"He's got a point," Lopez stated.

"No." Davidson had lost her. He had to get Rebecca back.

Lopez dug his shoe into the dirt. "We've got GPS coordinates to guide us back to the village. Finding Rebecca out here in this"—the corporal indicated to the dripping leaves that formed a green sky above their heads—"is going to take some mad skills."

They shouldn't even have been having this discussion. If Brandt were here, they wouldn't be. Brandt would already have struck out after Rebecca.

"We've got to give Rebecca *and* Brandt the best chance at survival," Lopez concluded.

"I'll find her," Levont added. "Or die trying, I swear."

"We're not soldiers," Talli chimed in. "We are a team. We've got to work as one."

Great. Talli being more logical than him. It didn't get much worse than that.

Lopez must have read Davidson's capitulation before Davidson even knew that he capitulated.

"Levont," Lopez said, handing him several extra weapons, "go."

"My last spotting marked her about eleven degrees north by northwest."

With a nod, the tall black man took the guns and ammo, tucking them into his tux's pocket as he turned and headed into the forest. Davidson watched Levont's back until it disappeared amongst the foliage.

Talli struck out in the opposite direction. Still, Davidson stood rooted in place. Not sure which direction to head.

Lopez patted him on the back. "I am going to leave it up to you," the corporal said, then turned, walking backward. He looked over his shoulder, apparently making sure Talli was out of earshot before whispering harshly. "But *damn*, I could use a *real* sniper on this rescue mission."

Davidson sighed. Brandt's chances did go down sharply if he didn't join them. Whereas Rebecca's chances were best with Levont.

"Flattery will get you everywhere," Davidson said as he followed Lopez.

"That and taking the plane elevator," Lopez frowned. "I need to get a better name for it, but you get what I mean."

Unfortunately, Davidson did.

Brandt braced himself as the open-aired Jeep slid in the thick mud. If the driver didn't correct, they were about to go off the side of a very steep cliff. Thankfully, the driver was probably born and raised amongst these treacherous, slick mountain "roads," as he turned into the spin, hitting the gas, bumping them up and over the mudslide.

However, the Jeep in front of them did not fare so well. It couldn't fight the force of gravity as the rear wheels went over the edge. The men tried to scramble from the vehicle as it hung from its front tires, but again, those laws of physics didn't seem to give a rat's ass. Which apparently, neither did the men's team. No one so much as reached a hand out as the Jeep slipped from its perch and plummeted down the side of the cliff, the men's screams filling the misty mountain air.

Then quiet returned to the jungle.

"See what the problem is," the lead mercanary barked at the driver.

Using his legs, Brandt lifted himself off the seat and looked ahead, finding the problem that had brought this little convoy to a screeching halt. Ahead of the lead Jeep was a huge gouge in the road. More than likely the Congolese government's countermeasure to rebel activities. It was a common ploy. Cutting gouges in the road stopped motorized vehicles from disappearing back into the jungle, which made it much harder for the rebels to make blinding strikes in the lowlands. It could take hours to build any kind of stopgap measure to get across.

Brandt had never been so glad for a ruthless, oppressive government in his life.

Until now, the Disciples had been well organized and executed a Special Forces–style snatch. Too bad their luck seemed to have run out. As everyone's did eventually. Had the Disciples prepared for this contingency? They were now six men down. Which meant that Brandt was still facing twelve-to-one odds. Odds that were now doable.

"Frellan, we will have to go by foot," the merc leader stated as he grabbed his pack from the Jeep. The Disciple didn't seem any too happy by the fact. Guess the guy didn't do as much research on the African side of this mission as he should have.

Brandt and his team had met with a similar problem last week, approaching from the eastern slope. However, they had brought sturdy planking along. Lopez had gotten them underway within ten minutes. Clearly, Frellan didn't have anyone of Lopez's caliber, which meant if they wanted to get the Jeeps across, they would have to stop, cut down trees, craft planks out of them, and hope they held the Jeeps' weight.

And every hour they delayed here trying to build their bridge on a sliding slope of mud was an hour the army could spot them and send in troops.

Guess the Disciples were learning the hard way that Africa was a fickle mistress.

Worse, the group had only made it halfway up the mountain, and even the Jeeps' engines had strained at the grade. There was no way Brandt was going to make it in his current condition. And Frellan knew it.

The tattooed man drew in a deep breath. "Administer the antidote."

Brandt kept his face placid, neutral, accepting.

But on the inside? Oh. On the inside, he was grinning ear to ear.

CHAPTER 5

PENTAGON, WASHINGTON, DC

10:59 A.M. (EST)

Bunny sat in a room not all that unlike the one back in South Carolina. Painted gray, with no windows and a stark metal table. Guess the Pentagon wasn't big on spending their budget on interior decor. She shifted in her chair, trying to get comfortable. Even in a borrowed pair of slacks and a blouse from Emily, Bunny still felt woefully underdressed. The few people they had met coming in through the south parking entrance were in full dress uniform.

She sipped on her can of Fresca. Emily remembered her well, even the exceedingly rare flavor of grapefruit mint. Setting the can down carefully, so as not to spill anything on the dozens of files scattered on the table, Bunny reached for the report on Brandt's last mission.

These after-action reports read about as easily as a freshman's term paper. For all of Brandt's virtues, engaging prose was not one of them.

The door swung open as Emily and Prenner rushed in. Neither could hide the look on their faces. Bunny popped up from her chair.

"What happened? Is it Brandt?"

Bunny knew that he had activated his tracker and the Disciples had taken him back to Africa, but had his usefulness run its course?

Emily gulped, nodding to the chair. Bunny didn't sit down. The woman sighed. "No. Brandt is still en route to the African village. No…" Emily gulped again. "The plane we believe was carrying Corporal Lopez's team and Dr. Monroe was shot down deep within the Congo basin."

Bunny sat down. Hard. "Are you sure it was them?"

"Just before it was downed, it looked like someone was trying to break the sound barrier with a Learjet," Prenner answered.

Okay, the lieutenant was right. That had to be Lopez, then. But if Lopez was at the helm, how the hell did they get shot down?

"The Disciples?" she asked.

Her CIA handler shook her head. "The last satellite images we had showed a tribe on the move. I think this was simply a matter of opportunity for them."

"Okay, then," Bunny stated, shifting her mind out of freak-out mode and into figure-it-the-hell-out mode. "You guys have obviously scrambled up some kind of rescue effort."

By the shared pained expression on Emily and Prenner's face, that was a big fat *no*.

She shouldn't have been surprised, though. The men's mission last week had been uber secret. A last ditch effort, as a matter of fact. The African country was on the brink of civil war at all times. Trying to negotiate even the most basic humanitarian aid was fraught with danger. Add in a major American military move? That spelled disaster.

"So they are on their own?" Bunny asked despite already knowing the answer.

"Which is why we need to figure out the Disciples' angle. I have assets in the region, but I can't engage them until we know the end game," Emily said as she sat down across from Bunny. The CIA operative pushed the after-action reports toward Bunny. "There has got to be something in here that gives us a clue."

Bunny shoved the papers back. "I've been over them a thousand times. There is *nothing* in there."

"What about what *isn't* in there?" Prenner suggested.

Bunny's eyes narrowed. "What do you mean?"

"All military units are known for let's say 'fudging' their after-action reports. Special Forces, though? Theirs are nicknamed 'time-savers' since they save the redactors all that precious ink blacking out parts that will never see the light of day."

"Can you give me an example?" she asked, still not quite understanding how any of this was going to help save Rebeca and the rest.

Prenner pulled out a specific file. The one that covered their time chasing after the Ten Commandments tablets. "Did Brandt describe everything that happened in this?"

Bunny snorted. *Hell, no.* The indoor helicopter incident? Where Lopez stole a Russian military helicopter? Not very likely. The lack of Talli's sniper skills? Completely missing. The report was more a general gist kind of document rather than giving the actual blow-by-blow.

"It looks like you are getting where I'm headed," the lieutenant stated.

She didn't bother answering him. Instead, she dug through the pages, trying to find the ones that had bugged her. The ones that seemed incomplete.

Rebecca watched the snake's forked tongue flicker.

An African rock python.

Genus: *Python*. Species: *sebae*, if she weren't mistaken. And mistaken she wished she could be. The rock python was the largest of all African snakes, and that damned tongue of its was forked to increase the surface area so that it could more easily detect tropotaxins. Chemical cues that prey was around.

Basically, if exhaustion had a smell, Rebecca was doused in it. The snake probably tasted an easy meal on the horizon. She had nearly been squeezed to death by a cousin of its in Ecuador and really did not want to relive the experience. However, as the metal clasps of the parachute's harness refused to budge, Rebecca feared a repeat performance. Especially since she had been watching the damn snake for about five minutes and had yet to see its tail. It was really annoying that she knew the snake could be as long as twenty feet and could easily consume her, tattered wedding dress and all.

Even if she somehow got out of the tangled harness, there was still that nasty twenty-foot drop. Although, right about now, she would take a broken leg over suffocation via python.

Not a great Plan B, however.

As a branch snapped as the snake coiled itself around the parachute, working out its crushing muscles, Rebecca worked frantically on the latch. She understood that they didn't want you falling out of the parachute at a thousand feet up, but seriously, did they have to jungle-proof it?

The buzz of insects, so many insects, rang in her ears as if they were cheering the python on. Not that it needed much incentive. Side to side, it winded its way down the parachute, that tongue testing the air. Making sure she was still an easy mark.

One of the latches finally gave way, taking an acrylic nail with it. She slipped through one of the loops, dropping a good foot. The snake must have sensed its meal getting away, as it sprang open its jaws, striking toward her. Rebecca ducked as its head flew past her. Undeterred, the snake swung back, pulling itself back for another strike. It hadn't spent the last half hour climbing this damned tree to let her go so easily.

Frantic, Rebecca worked at the other carabiner, spinning the lock until it, too, released. Just as the python reared back for another, Rebecca threw herself forward. The scales of the snake's head slid past her arm, leaving a trail of python saliva on her skin.

Caught by her leg, Rebecca dangled upside down, pointed toward the jungle floor. Tangled in the rigging, Rebecca really wished she'd done all that "core body" conditioning Bunny bragged so much about. But seriously, who would have thought she would need that kind of muscle strength to escape a python? Bunny probably could have folded herself over and pulled her body weight up to extract herself from the harness.

The best Rebecca could do, however, was keep from puking as she swayed above the lush underbrush. Mr. Python wasn't taking this development lying down, either. His body squeezed the rigging above her so tightly that even if she had Bunny's abs, Rebecca probably couldn't get her leg out now.

Then the insects silenced. Like all at once. The only sounds left were her pounding pulse and the crinkle of the parachute as it was crushed within the python's coils. Maybe the insects didn't have the stomach for what came next, after all.

Blood rushing to her head, Rebecca thought her vision was blurring when she saw movement to the right. But there it was again. Could the men have found her?

"Davidson!" she cried. *Dear God, could the cavalry really be here?*

Then a stick hit her in the head. *What the hell?*

The source of the projectile charged out of the dense brush directly beneath her. A chimpanzee. Not one, but a whole troupe of chimpanzees. And apparently really pissed-off chimpanzees.

Face heating up and her leg throbbing, Rebecca was really annoyed that she knew there were two species of chimps. One that warred and one that lived in communal harmony. Of course, man evolved from the war ones. And apparently these chimps were pretty ticked off at their descendant. They hooted and shook the underbrush.

But usually, even these chimps weren't so aggressive. Rebecca guessed it was that earthquake last week. Between it and the after-shocks, the animals were on edge. Territorial. Deadly.

The snake's head slid across her foot, its tongue flickering across her skin, apparently making sure that she tasted as good as she smelled.

Snake above. Mad apes below.

This day really couldn't get much better. Rebecca could only hope the men were faring better than she.

"We're so screwed," Lopez whispered.

Davidson couldn't argue. Not as he watched through his sniper scope the trail of men tracking through the jungle. This was not how this was supposed to go down. The Disciples were supposed to be in open-air vehicles. They were supposed to pull up, en masse, to the center of the village. The kill zone that Davidson and Talli had set up. Then on Lopez's order, the shooting was supposed to begin.

Under the cover of that fire, Lopez was going to speed in with the beat-up Pajeros he'd "borrowed" and whisk Brandt out of there. They would then all meet at the rally point five clicks north.

That plan clearly had to be scraped. Unfortunately, there wasn't any easy alternative. The Disciples' mercenaries were spread out far and wide, many hidden deep within the thick foliage. Davidson had counted eight already, and who knew how many others were out there? He hadn't even spotted Brandt yet.

And traveling on foot, the enemy was going to be far more vigilant than they would have been in a vehicle. Tracking through the jungle, they had to be.

Water dripped from the ridge of Davidson's nose, onto his rifle, and down the long barrel. The cloud burst had been short but had dropped nearly half an inch of water. Puddles pocked the road through the village as mist clung to the mountainside. The Disciples must have lost their vehicle, then taken to the jungle to avoid the downpour.

Each event making their job of extracting Brandt all the harder.

A splash announced Talli's arrival. "What are we going to do?"

Davidson looked to Lopez. The corporal's lips turned down. Which was not their usual direction. As a matter of fact, it was weird to see Lopez with a frown on his face.

"We really need some thermal imaging," Talli stated, nodding to the forest where the only way you knew men were out there was by the sway of the branches.

Lopez snorted. "Yeah, let's call Command and say, 'Hey, I know we went AWOL and all, but what the heck, since we are in Africa, how about you give us some tactical support?'"

Talli looked down and away, but Davidson saw the edge of Lopez's lip turn upward.

"Why don't we?" Davidson suggested.

"What do you mean?" Talli asked

Lopez, though, pulled his radio out of his pack. "He means we've gone AWOL. Why the hell don't we ask for tactical help? The worst they could do is say no."

"Or use the transcript against us at our court-martial," Talli added.

"Or that," Lopez said as he shrugged, dialing the phone.

There was one thing that had bugged Bunny while reviewing the files. Two things, actually, but she had to find the first. Bunny couldn't articulate the vague sense of unease she felt. But now that they were trying to prove a negative, Bunny knew she'd found something. Finally, she found the page. It detailed Brandt's extraction from the Congo.

"Why didn't they hit their first extraction window?" Bunny asked. She had noticed that fact before but really hadn't cared about it. Why should she? Now, though? It was of paramount importance because the after-action report was completely silent about the cause.

Prenner shrugged as he searched through the files. "Looks like they just said they couldn't make the window and requested a secondary pickup."

"And nobody found that weird?" Bunny chuckled. "That delay cost them nearly thirty-six hours. Brandt missed his rehearsal dinner because of it."

She didn't even wait for Prenner's response. Instead, she dug through the report to find the third page. Another fact had nagged at her. Bunny found the paragraph.

"*A girl, along with her caregiver, provided intel on the location of the rebellion's base.*" When Bunny looked up, Emily and Prenner both frowned. They didn't get it. At least not yet. She shuffled the pages until she came to the end of the report. "*Fortunately, there was only one civilian death. Unfortunately, it was that of the girl's caregiver.*"

Again, the other two frowned. "You clearly do not know Brandt and Davidson."

"Apparently not," Prenner stated, although not with nearly the attitude he might have had a few hours ago.

"In that part of the world? What would happen to an orphaned girl?" Bunny asked, not expecting an answer. They all knew that human slavery, rape, and worse awaited an orphan in the jungle. "There is no way Brandt would have left that girl unprotected."

Prenner squinted, reading the report over again. "You are saying that he took that thirty-six hours and found the girl a safe home?"

"Yes," Bunny said, nodding vigorously. "I'm certain that is the aspect of the mission the Disciples are honing in on."

"Certain?" Emily said as her eyebrow rose. "Why?"

Bunny immediately regretted her choice of words. She was certain. Only, she couldn't tell them why she was certain. Another of those things that not only got left out of the after-action report, but hadn't even been reported to Brandt. Rebecca and she had kept the information to themselves.

The knowledge that the tablets of the Ten Commandments spoke of the *daughter* of God. Not *son*. Not *child*, but *daughter* of God prophesized to rise to be the Messiah.

And now, suddenly, the Disciples were taking such interest in a girl deep in the African jungle. There had to be a connection. Not that she could tell Emily that.

"You are just going to have to trust me," Bunny answered.

"My, my," Prenner commented, nodding toward Emily, "I guess someone else doesn't have the clearance they need."

Bunny felt bad for holding back on Emily, but this was more than a pinky promise she'd made with Rebecca. This was a sacred vow.

The secret of the female Messiah was safe with her.

Turning to Emily, Bunny tried to get them refocused. "Now all we have to do is figure out where Brandt took the girl."

"Oh, is that all?" Emily shot back.

Prenner's phone buzzed. He read the text aloud. "*Contact made with Corporal Lopez. Eyes on Brandt approaching the village. Requesting thermal imaging of area.*"

Bunny caught herself on the edge of the table. Davidson was safe. They made it out of the crash and sounded like they were moments from rescuing him. They might really be able to pull it off.

However, even in the euphoria of the moment, Bunny still wondered, *Where is the girl?*

Rebecca squelched a scream as the python's coils tightened around her legs. Knees knocking together, she tried not to panic. However, she was finding it more and more difficult to keep perspective. Hanging upside down was certainly not helping.

Hooting and hollering, the chimps were throwing what she could only hope was mud at her as the snake made its slow, painful advance. Rebecca had tried to remain still, allowing the python to think her subdued. She didn't need those long fangs sunk into her. When the moment came to make her move, she needed to be able to...well, move.

She blocked out the chimps' war cries. In her right hand, she held the metal comb from her veil. The removal of which had been made at great cost to her scalp. Even now, she held a chunk of hair in her palm. Her only hope was to let the snake get close enough, then use the sharp comb as a weapon. Although, the closer the python got, the more her desperate plan seemed even more desperate and unrealistic.

What else did she have?

Just as she gripped the comb, readying the blow, a figure burst from the forest. Tall, lean, and shirtless, the older man's dark skin melted with the shadows. Then he opened his eyes. One obsidian black, the other a milky white. Waving a thick cane over his head, he yelled fiercely.

Rebecca wasn't sure if it even contained any words or if it was just a visceral utterance, but the chimps took note. Many fled, while others became even more agitated, jumping into the trees, rattling the branches.

Mr. Python stopped his slow descent, lifting his head, flickering his tongue at the newest arrival. Rebecca could feel the snake tense. Apparently, he did not want to share his meal. Opening his jaw wide, the snake made ready to strike.

Hand shaking, Rebecca clutched her comb. However, no matter how sharp, it seemed a meager defense against those teeth.

Then the largest chimp launched itself from a neighboring tree. Its body slammed into Rebecca. *Not the face, please not the face* was all Rebecca could think. Its fingernails dug into her dress. Then the python struck, nailing the chimp in the shoulder. The ape howled its pain, then bore its own rather impressive set of fangs and dug them into the snake.

The python, apparently forgetting all about its human prey, released Rebecca. Instead, the snake reared, trying to slither back up to the high shelter of the canopy. The chimp climbed over Rebecca like she was a jungle gym, racing after the snake. Hissing, the python flung itself from the parachute to another tree.

The motion ripped the fabric.

Dropping, Rebecca closed her eyes. This was not going to be pretty.

But the harness caught, jerking her to a stop. More panicked than with purpose, Rebecca thrashed her legs. Finally, the strap gave, freeing her foot.

Nothing but the ground stopped her this time.

Stars, literal white stars, danced in her vision as her head struck a log. Blurry images filtered into her mind. The strangest being a little girl dressed in a bright-orange traditional kaftan with matching *gelee* headscarf.

"Hello," the girl stated with a thick Congolese accent.

Not sure if the child was real or simply a consequence of her concussion, Rebecca passed out.

CHAPTER 6

OUTSIDE OF BOMONGO, DEMOCRATIC REPUBLIC OF THE CONGO

8:12 P.M. (CAT)

Brandt pretended to stumble on a thick vine. Frellan had the men cut the zip ties on Brandt's legs but had insisted his hands stay bound. Which was fine by Brandt. It allowed the other men to relax around him. Especially after Brandt had been such a good boy the whole trek up the mountain.

Was his presumed compliance enough to give him a window of opportunity? Things had gone his way as they ventured into the jungle. The men had been forced to spread out, leaving only four men in his immediate vicinity. Others were in the nearby forest, but with only four nearby, Brandt might just be able to dispatch them before the others could assist.

Wiping his brow with his arm, Brandt prepared to go from zero to sixty. This might be his last chance for escape. As the men chattered, Brandt picked up enough from their excitement to know that they were nearing the village. If he allowed them to secure him in the village, he was screwed. They would probably dope him again or begin the torture brigade. Either way, getting away would be next to impossible.

Taking a moment to center himself, Brandt breathed in. This could go badly. Like seriously badly. He was only one man against a dozen. Not just any dozen, but a dozen of highly trained mercenaries who knew this mountainside like he knew each and every one of Rebecca's curves.

Rebecca.

Stuff it down, Brandt. Don't get all maudlin. You are *going to see her again.*

Well, if luck swung his way.

A leaf fluttered next to him. Funny, a hole was blown through it. He glanced behind him, to see the rear guard slump to the ground.

What the fuck?

His head snapped forward. Beyond the forward guards, there was just more forest. Absolutely no window for someone to get a shot through. Unless your name was Davidson. Brandt's heart soared, like literally beat a hundred times stronger. His men were here. He stumbled again, this time not faking it. His limbs simply couldn't believe how fortunate they were.

What had been an insane gamble was now a fucking doable plan.

Brandt stared at the back of the closest guard's head.

Game on.

"What are we looking at?" Bunny asked, sitting down in an extremely comfortable computer chair.

Prenner had led them out of the dismally gray room, down several corridors and several security levels until they arrived in this distinctly colorful room. The room itself was nearly a cavern divided off into smaller sections by glass walls.

"We've got the thermal imaging Lopez requested," Emily answered, then off a frown from Prenner, bowed her head, sat down, and made the motion of zipping her lips closed and throwing away the key.

"At least for right now," Prenner stated. "The satellite had already been retasked for Nigeria, but we are catching a slice of the Congo for the next six minutes."

"What would you need to see in Nigeria?" Bunny asked.

By the set of Prenner's lips, she was not going to find out.

"Remember, Bunny," Emily reminded her, "everything you see is classified."

No kidding. Just a glance through the glass separators and Bunny could make out at least ten other military missions being monitored. Exactly how many missions did the Pentagon run a day?

"There is Brandt," Prenner announced, pointing to a throbbing blue glob overlaying a red glob on the screen. That certainly didn't even look human, let alone Brandt shaped. "That blue signal is his intradental transmitter."

"So they are transporting him through the jungle, then?" Emily asked.

Prenner gave a sharp nod.

Brandt was flanked by three men. Bunny could only assume those were his Disciple guards. There were many other orange globs scattered throughout the forest. Many, many other globs. That was a lot of men.

"What are those?" Bunny asked, pointing to several light-yellow figures that stayed stationary.

"Dead bodies," Prenner answered.

Bunny's hand flew to her mouth. Was one of them Davidson?

Emily patted her arm. "Watch there."

Not knowing why her handler was pointing to a speck so far away from Brandt, Bunny watched what appeared to be a villager. Then a bright-red flash. She followed Emily's finger to another orange glob that slumped over, rapidly turning yellow.

"Davidson is using our scans to pinpoint the enemy's location," Emily explained.

Prenner nodded. "He is thinning the herd."

"So the Disciples are just going to let themselves get picked off and let Brandt walk out of there?"

Emily looked to Prenner, clearly wanting the lieutenant to give Bunny the bad news.

"Not exactly. You can only cull so much until someone notices."

"And then what?" Bunny asked, almost afraid to voice the question.

"Then the hell storm begins."

Brandt felt his respiratory rate increase despite his explicit instructions to his lungs to keep anticipation on the down low. It wouldn't be good to have his escape discovered before it had even begun.

With every passing moment and no further activity, or at least none that he could see, it was becoming harder and harder to wait it out. Had something happened? Was it back to him to make the move? They couldn't be more than a few hundred yards from the tree line. Once exposed, his luck would be up.

Then one of the men ahead of Brandt tripped and nearly fell. The others laughed cruelly at the man's awkward flailing to stay upright. He pointed down to his leg. It was caught in a game snare. Or at least it had been made to look like a game snare. Brandt noticed that the wire seemed a bit shiny for an old snare. He worried the guards would notice, but they were too busy berating the man for his oafishness.

Brandt kept his head down, plodding along, hopefully playing the part of the disheartened prisoner to perfection.

Despite the man's protests, the other two moved forward, waving him off. Even though Brandt didn't understand the native tongue, he knew body language. The other guards' bodies said, *Take care of it yourself*, very, very loudly. They traipsed off ahead, moving more quickly to the village.

Even hardened mercenaries missed their beds and home-cooked meals. If Brandt weren't mistaken, the scent of roasted goat drifted on the air. Both men seemed eager for dinner. Even Brandt's stomach rumbled, and he was not all that fond of goat.

As Brandt approached the snared man's position, he tensed. Was this a sign? Was he to incapacitate the man, take his weapon, and shoot his way out? They really needed to get better backup plans for a wedding-abduction scenario.

Just as Brandt brought his hands back, getting ready to thrust at the man's windpipe, the guy jerked upright, bright-red blood squirting from a slice across his neck. He gurgled once, then slumped into his attacker's arms.

Talli.

He put his finger to his lips as he propped the dead guard against a tree. Talli spread out two fingers, indicating to the remaining guards. Then he tapped a finger to his wrist and brought up one finger. Sweeping that finger out, he pointed in the direction of the village.

Brandt gave a curt nod. *Got it.* Talli melted back into the forest.

Then Brandt continued onward before his guards suspected anything.

In one minute, Davidson was going to take out the two remaining guards.

In sixty seconds, the shit was going to hit the fan.

Davidson checked his watch. Forty-eight more seconds to go.

He watched Brandt's slow forest march through his glasses's translucent lenses. The glasses were picking up the feed from the Pentagon's satellite imagery. It was as if he could see their body heat. Pretty dang cool.

However, it wasn't perfect. There was the subtlest of time delays, which made hitting men trekking through the jungle, going under and over obstacles, a tad difficult. Unfortunately, accuracy was kind of the name of the game for snipers. They were grossly outnumbered, and Brandt was in the thick of it. If they didn't execute a clean extraction, the Disciples might easily decide to kill Brandt on the spot rather than let him get away with any information they believed he had.

This had to be quick, or it was going to get ugly.

He took the few moments he had left to scan the jungle around Brandt. Talli had retreated north, deeper into the jungle, securing Brandt's exit. Other men were scattered amongst the huge old forest trees, creating a fan pattern.

It looked like they still had surprise on their side.

Not too bad for a plan put together while running up a mountain.

Davidson brought his attention back to Brandt. The thermal feed was flattening out, distorting distances. It couldn't be helped, though, as the satellite was passing out of range soon, and the farther along the horizon it sank, the more distorted the image. Not ideal, but better than nothing. They only had about four minutes left of coverage, but they should only need a fraction of that.

Otherwise, they were in big trouble.

Well, bigger trouble than Brandt being kidnapped and Rebecca lost in the forest.

He had to trust Levont, though, just as Brandt was trusting him.

Settling back into his shooting form, Davidson adjusted his chin, relaxed his jaw, and steadied his breathing. He didn't need to look at his watch any longer. He knew the countdown as well as if he had a metronome inside his skull.

Targeting the guard who lagged a few feet behind the front man, Davidson prepared his shot. Five more seconds.

They each ticked off in his head.

The man suddenly jerked Brandt forward, nearly level with him. Only inches separated the two.

Steady, Davidson admonished himself, *you can see which is which.*

Then his glasses went blank.

Nothing but static.

Davidson did the only thing he could.

Shoot and pray he hit his target.

The bullet zinged past Brandt, hitting the guard in the ear. The man howled, grabbing at the wound, not understanding what had just happened.

Davidson had missed.

Christ All Mighty, Davidson had missed.

A cry went up behind them. One of the bodies must have been discovered. The guard brought up his weapon. Brandt had nothing but his own body as a weapon. Make that his forehead.

Brandt slammed his head into the guards, dazing them both. It was enough of a window for Brandt to throw his foot out, landing it squarely on the guard's knee. The guy dropped to the ground. That wasn't enough. Brandt grabbed the chain, wrapped it around the man's neck, and jerked him up just in time for the guy to take several bullets meant for Brandt.

Bullets ripped through the foliage, although none hit their mark. What the fuck was wrong with Davidson?

And now the others were honing in on his position. Still constrained by the zip ties on his wrists, Brandt grabbed hold of the now dead guard's gun. He didn't have time to aim. He only had time to squeeze the trigger, sending a spray of lead from the automatic weapon. Lady Luck must have forgiven Brandt, because one of those bullets hit the guy square in the belly.

Then Talli was there, charging forward, laying down cover fire.

Brandt pulled the chain off the guard's neck, taking his leash back.

Sprinting, Talli and he dove into the thick of the forest. Bullets chased them, digging into the mossy ground on all sides.

"What's wrong with Davidson?" Brandt growled as a shot tore through his tuxedo pant leg.

"We lost satellite feed," Talli answered, puffing as he ran. "He's shooting blind."

Well, that would explain it. Brandt could also assume that losing the feed had not been a part of the plan. Which might mean they were screwed. Especially as Talli and he hit a part of the mountainside that was nearly vertical. The mercenaries would catch up in no time.

Then an SUV burst from the trees, sailing over several lichen-encrusted logs, landing hard on the soft forest floor.

Doors flew open as Lopez yelled, "Elephant!"

Not understanding the code word, Brandt hauled ass to the car, throwing himself into the backseat as the corporal hit the gas, spinning the rear wheels in the mud. He ground the gears, getting them into four-wheel drive, but still, they spun, useless.

They were as much sitting ducks as if they were climbing that steep incline.

"I don't mean to complain…" Brandt said as Talli cut the zip ties from his wrists.

"I got one word for you," Lopez said between clenched teeth. "Elephant."

"What the—" Brandt didn't finish the question, as an elephant, an actual elephant, burst from the trees, straight for the SUV.

"Hang on!"

The long, straight tusks lowered as the elephant charged, an angry trumpet warning them of what was to come. Before Brandt could bring his weapon up, the beast slammed into the SUV. Using those tusks, it lifted the rear of the car. Then, with a heave, sent it flying end over end.

In the tumble, Brandt's shoulder hit the roof of the car just before he was slammed against a seat. Rinse and repeat. Finally, they came to a stop, wheels down. Lopez gunned the engine, skidding them out since the elephant did not seem quite done with them.

Granted, the car was moving. However, they were going backward down the steep slope. Lopez steered like crazy, avoiding the huge trees and equally dangerous saplings. And now it seemed the rest of the elephant herd was joining in. You know, just for fun.

"Why are there elephants?" Lopez yelled.

"Yes," Brandt responded, prepping his weapon for a shot, "why are there elephants chasing us?"

Lopez shrugged that shrug of his as he narrowly avoided them ramming into a huge stump. "I might have challenged them to a race. Maybe getting a little too close to the herd."

That's what Brandt thought. He did not know much about elephants, but buzzing their family was probably not a good idea. Brandt raised his gun to shoot, but Talli forced the barrel up.

"The forest elephant is endangered," Talli said, then hurried on as Brandt glared. "Besides, we don't have anything large enough caliber to penetrate its skull. You'd just piss it off with that."

As the elephant trumpeted again, gaining ground, Brandt found it hard to believe it could really get much angrier.

"Is somebody taking video of this?" Lopez asked, his head craned over his shoulder as he tried to steer. Even so, he must have felt Brandt's ire. "What? For Ricky Junior!"

Davidson ran across the thin tin roof, hurling himself across the open space between buildings. He'd run out of village, though. Davidson hated losing the high ground, but sometimes the high ground was simply lost. He jumped the eight feet from the shanty-town roof to the ground.

He landed with a gun in his face. The gunman's dark face split by the flash of a white smile. There was no way Davidson could get his gun up in time to shoot.

That didn't mean it was useless, though. Pretending to surrender his weapon, Davidson bowed over. In a single motion, he swung the gun hard, nailing the guy in the crotch with it.

A shot went wide overhead as the gunman stumbled. With his good hand, Davidson pulled his knife from its sheath. Wielding it backhanded, Davidson slammed the blade into the man's belly. He removed it and stabbed again and again. The gunman slumped against Davidson.

You could see the surprise in the man's eyes. He had thought he was capturing a sniper. Well, just because he was a perimeter specialist didn't mean Davidson wasn't highly trained in hand-to-hand combat. Not Brandt level, of course, but he could get the job done.

Still, Davidson took no pleasure from the man's death. He could only be glad to have come out still breathing. Although, that was not guaranteed to last, as shouts rose all around the village.

Gunfire spat at his feet as he released the deceased and sprinted for the tree line.

Lopez and the others should have been here by now. The plan had been to drive by Davidson's roof so that he could provide cover fire until the last second. Then he was supposed to jump onto the roof of the SUV and be gone.

Given the shouts and strange trumpeting from the jungle, that was not going to happen.

Time to improvise.

Without thermal imaging, Davidson just had go by his gut.

And his gut told him to take to the trees.

"I thought elephants were sprinters?" Lopez demanded as the elephant lowered his head and butted the SUV.

"Watch out!" Talli yelled, but it was too late. Lopez hit the gunman head-on. The wheels thumping over his body.

Bullets pinged off the SUV as other gunmen burst from the jungle. But equally quickly, they threw themselves back into the bush as the elephant swung its huge tusks side to side, knocking one man off his feet and ten feet into the air.

"Hey, maybe there's an upside to this!" Lopez, ever the silver lining kind of guy, shouted.

Then, of course, the elephant lowered its head again, but this time, instead of butting the SUV, aimed its tusks and shoved through the grating. And given the steam spraying, the bull elephant had also punctured their radiator.

Lopez gunned it, hurling them down the slope, disengaging them from the tusks.

The elephant shook its massive head, seeming rattled by the exchange. Good. Maybe he'd given up.

"Stop!" Talli screamed.

"Stop?" Lopez retorted. "But I'm—"

"Stop!" Brandt ordered, now seeing what Talli had. He could see clear sky past the trees. Unfortunately, that was a hundred-foot drop on the other side.

Lopez slammed on the brakes. The SUV skid side to side, tires laying down rubber, trying to find traction on the slick jungle floor. Luck, if you could call it that, put a tree right in their path. Lopez turned into the trunk, slamming the SUV to a stop.

Jarred by the impact and more than a little shaky from his near-daylong drugging, Brandt tried to pull it together. However, he doubted that even if he was at the top of his game, he could come up with a better plan as the elephant stood, ears out, flapping them in agitation. Tail swishing across its haunches. The bull seemed to be very aware he had them cornered.

"I'll provide cover while you two jump out." There was no saving all of them. They had to split up to increase their odds that *any* of them would survive. "Head in opposite directions and—"

"No way," Lopez said as he whipped out his gun. "I can—"

Then a shot rang out, accompanied by a high-pitch shriek. Far to the back of the herd, a baby elephant explored a long wound along its flank with its trunk. Another shot forced the baby to step away from its mother. The entire herd vocalized their distress.

Davidson.

Maybe they couldn't hurt the bull elephant, but clearly the little one was not nearly as invulnerable to gunfire. For now, the sniper had only grazed the little guy. Brandt was loathe to do anything more, but that really was up to the elephants. Brandt was sorry for trespassing, but work was work.

The bull searched the trees, finding Davidson perched in the basket made up of the canopy's intertwining branches. Was the animal intelligent enough to know its choices? Could it see past its rage to the danger of its offspring?

Apparently not, as it turned back toward the SUV, its enormous ribs heaving, drawing in breath for a final attack.

"Don't worry," Lopez said. "I am totally getting this on film."

Brandt shoved the corporal toward his door. "On my mark."

Before he could give the order, several gunmen burst from the brush. In a panic at the site of an entire herd of elephants, they sprayed the animals with bullets. Talli had been correct. The gunfire barely scratched the adults. But now they had a new focus to vent their anger upon.

The herd charged in unison, stampeding toward the gunmen. The bull took one last look at the SUV, then turned as quickly as a two-ton elephant could and charged after the herd.

"Classic, man!" Lopez yelled, turning his digital camera back to himself. "Can't wait until you're old enough to get chased by elephants, RJ."

Brandt wasn't so sure Maria was going to be quite as up for "take your son to work" day.

Lopez lowered the camera and revved the engine, getting them the hell away from the cliff as Davidson scrambled down from the tree. He waved the SUV over, then leaped onto the roof and squeezed his lean frame through the damaged window frame.

Once settled, Davidson turned to the rest. "Does it seem like that was way too easy?"

Brandt couldn't agree more. That wasn't an escape. That was a release back to nature. It should have been impossible, but the Disciples must have had the frequency for his intradental tracker.

"All right," Brandt said with a grunt. This was not going to be pleasant. "Who is up for removing my tooth?"

When no one replied, Lopez's hand shot up. "Not me, but I'll film it!"

Great.

"What's wrong?" Bunny demanded.

Emily held up a hand as she listened on the phone. Prenner stood over the technician at the keyboard, his stiff body language asking the same thing.

Still, static filled the screen. It had been like that for nearly ten minutes. Davidson had been ready to take out Brandt's two remaining escorts and then poof. The feed was gone.

"The feed was overwritten," the technician finally announced.

"We've been hacked?" Prenner demanded.

That couldn't be, could it? They were in the Pentagon. They should be hack-proof, right?

"No," the tech reassured them. "Someone within this building overrode my commands and turned the feed off from the satellite itself."

"Who would do that?" Bunny asked.

Emily hung up the phone. "That is something my boss would like to know."

"It is something everyone wants to know," Prenner shot back.

"Yes," Bunny agreed. "However, that isn't going to help Brandt and the rest in real time. What are we doing to help them right now?"

Prenner shrugged. He actually shrugged. "Like I said earlier, they are on their own."

"On their own?" Bunny couldn't keep the exasperation from her voice.

"The men went AWOL."

"To save a decorated hero!"

Prenner pulled up to his full height. "Black ops men know the risk."

Bunny was about to launch into the tirade to end all tirades when Emily stepped between them.

"Now, now," she cooed. "I've asked the Brits for a spot of help."

Bunny's mood brightened. "Vanderwalt?" she asked. He had been super helpful during the whole Jordan debacle. And his crooked smile was kind of sexy.

Emily nodded. "We should have a feed on the area within the hour, and they have some 'aid' workers even closer than I do."

Bunny sank into her chair, not realizing tears were at the edge of her eyelids. She wasn't built for this. She always read the last page of a book so that she didn't have to stress about the characters the whole time. And if the heroes didn't win in the end? She just didn't read the book.

Her CIA handler squeezed her shoulder. "It is going to be over forty-five minutes before we can even get a glimpse of the area. Why don't you go lay down?"

Wiping the tears away, Bunny shook her head. "No. I want to be here. I *have* to be here."

"Very well," Emily stated. "Then I think it is best we all get some food—some *real* food—in our bellies." She turned to Prenner. "Is the Moulin Rogues still in the Pentagon Row?"

The technician shook his head. "Nope. Closed down last summer, but Panda Express is just around the corner and has a drive-through."

"Well then, Panda Express it is." Emily turned to Prenner. "I'll write our order down."

"What the hell?" Prenner countered. "I'm not your dinner bitch."

Emily cocked her head in that really cute way. "Really? Because I am pretty sure that the department that has a big, fat mole that ruined a black ops mission, putting all of our assets in the region in danger, gets to go get the food." She looked to Bunny. "Right?"

Bunny might just have a new hero. "Right."

"It's a rule." Emily turned back to Prenner. "Maybe not written, but a rule nonetheless."

To Bunny's surprise, Prenner sighed. "Give me the list," he said, "and I'll get a private to do it."

Bunny could taste the egg rolls now. Although, even the best soy sauce wasn't going to make the next forty-five minutes go by any faster. She could only pray the men were safe until then.

Safe. Not dead. *Safe.*

Maybe if she repeated that frequently enough, she could make it come true.

CHAPTER 7

UNDISCLOSED LOCATION

9:47 P.M. (CAT)

Rebecca awoke facedown on a cool earthen floor. She felt like she'd fallen out of a plane, through a rain forest, and then been squeezed by a python.

Oh, wait, she had.

A little worried about where she had ended up, Rebecca was loath to open her eyes. The Disciples were in the area and had already snatched Brandt. Had they found her, too? Would she be staring at a room filled with torture instruments?

Squeezing her eyes shut against the horror wouldn't make it go away. At the least she needed to get her bearings.

Cracking her eyelids open, Rebecca found a typical African hut. The curved walls were made of braided vines. Although, these had some adornment. Scattered throughout the walls were brightly colored strands. The contrast created a random yet beautiful pattern.

Tied to these walls were a line of gourds, primitive storage vessels. The roof above was made of wide green fronds. Unlike the round huts of the African plains, tribes in the moist Congo region could not use dried thatch. Otherwise, they'd have mildewed walls within days.

No, the rain forest tribes had adopted nature's own waterproofing, using the waxy plants of the forest to construct their homes. Which would have all been great fodder for a scientific paper on aboriginal African hut building. Unfortunately, she was not on an academic assignment.

Rising up on one elbow, her eyes explored more of the hut.

There was a small central fire pit that spit sparks at a chunk of meat being grilled on a skewer. Her fingers felt the soft ground beneath her until she realized it wasn't ground at all. It was a loosely woven rug of moss.

Again, ingenious use of natural resources, but not exactly information she could use to formulate her escape.

Soft footsteps carried from outside the hut. Rebecca lay back down, closing her eyes.

"*Jambo*," a sweet voice called out.

So Rebecca hadn't been hallucinating. She opened her eyes to find the same little girl sitting on her haunches next to her. The girl opened her small hand to reveal half a dozen burgundy berries. Strangely, they smelled of rose petals.

"Kola," the girl urged.

Tentatively, Rebecca took one from her palm. The girl urged her to bring it to her mouth. However, when Rebecca bit down, she found it wasn't a berry. Instead, it was brightly colored nut. A nut with a rather tough exterior.

The little girl giggled, shaking her head as she sat down cross-legged. Tucking her skirt over her knees, she used the orange fabric as a bowl. Picking out a seed, the girl used her fingernail to crack open the burgundy exterior to reveal a smooth white shell. This, too, she opened. Inside the shell were four small seeds.

Rebecca accepted one from the girl, sniffing at it. This seed certainly didn't smell like roses. Actually, it smelled like her face wash. But the girl pantomimed that Rebecca should put the seed in her mouth.

With that bright smile, how could Rebecca refuse?

Popping the seed into her mouth, she realized that not only did the seed smell like her face wash, it tasted like her face wash, with a bit of astringent mixed in for good measure. But the girl, even though wincing herself at the bitter taste, kept chewing, giving Rebecca the universal thumbs-up. So Rebecca kept chewing. And the bitter became sweet.

It was weird. The more she chewed, the sweeter it got. Plus, the pounding in her head receded, and she felt stronger. Rebecca looked down at the seeds with more appreciation.

The kola nut. The basis for the original cola soft drinks. That was caffeine racing through her veins. Usually, she tried to avoid stimulants of any kind, but after the day she'd had? Rebecca grabbed the other two seeds and started chewing.

A grunt came from the other side of the hut. Rebecca cringed as the tall man with skin the color of night stood to his full height. That one milky eye staring straight ahead.

Instead of moving toward her, though, he moved to the spit, rotating the meat above the fire. Again, Rebecca normally tried to stay away from charbroiled game meat, but she couldn't help it as her mouth started to water.

The little girl pointed to a coiled carcass.

The python.

Rebecca's stomach turned as she realized the meat on the spit was the snake that had tried to eat her. In the jungle, the *real* jungle, it truly was eat or be eaten.

And damn if Rebecca wasn't really, really hungry.

Brandt's jaw throbbed as the SUV's engine smoked. Lopez cut the engine.

"I think we've ridden this pony as far as she is going to go," the corporal admitted.

He couldn't disagree with Lopez. It was just that Brandt had been hoping for a few more minutes of sitting. Not hiking. Not climbing up a huge-ass mountain. As always, fate didn't seem to give a crap what he wanted.

As Talli opened the passenger door, Brandt asked, "What is our extraction point?"

When no one answered him, let alone looked at him, he knew something was wrong. Really wrong.

"We do have an extraction plan?"

Lopez snorted as he climbed out of the vehicle. "Well, yeah, duh, we had a plan."

"Had?" Brandt asked, touching his swollen cheek, then regretting it. Davidson might be a phenomenal sniper. A dentist, not so much.

Lopez glanced to Talli, who looked to Davidson. Okay, this must be bad if they wanted Davidson to deliver the news.

"Yeah, um…" the younger man said, digging his toe into the moist rain forest soil. "We kind of have to make a detour."

Brandt's eyelids narrowed. "Detour?"

"And..." Davidson said, then licked his damaged lips. "We're not quite sure where."

This was going to take an extremely long time if Brandt incredulously repeated the last asinine statement the men made.

"Out with it."

"Well, you've probably noticed that we don't have Rebecca," Davidson said.

"Rebecca?" Brandt spat out. As much as he swore he wouldn't just repeat things, he couldn't help himself. "What the fuck would Rebecca be doing here?"

"Sarge," Lopez interjected, stepping between Brandt and Davidson, "she was like Bridezilla on steroids. There was no keeping her off the plane."

Brandt's fury rose, threatening to blind him. He wanted to lash out, but all that came to the tip of his tongue were swear words. Lots and lots of swear words. A litany of them. Yet they stalled there, unable to pass his lips.

He could still hear her words as he was lifted into the Disciples' helicopter. "We are right behind you." Not "The men are right behind you." Or "They are right behind you," but "*We* are right behind you." He should have known Rebecca would find a way to tag along. Not even his Death Star gaze could have stopped her. And on her wedding day?

Maybe he did need to cut his men some slack. Just a little.

"Fine," Brandt snapped. "Where is she, then?"

Again, Davidson became obsessed with a patch of moss on the ground.

"Davidson..."

"Look," Lopez said, "there was a plane crash, and then some crazy tribesmen—"

"Where?"

"We don't know," Davidson finally admitted. "I couldn't hold on…And she went down somewhere in the forest."

Brandt wanted to strangle the sniper, but something about the way his voice hitched with shame kept Brandt from fulfilling his desire. As a matter of fact, all the men seemed equally upset that Rebecca was missing.

Which didn't fucking change the fact she was missing.

"But hey, we sent our best tracker, Levont, out for her before we hoofed it here," Lopez explained.

"And?"

Lopez frowned. "Um, we haven't heard from him."

Brandt didn't bother repeating that. No point.

"And what exactly is Command doing to locate both of them?"

The moss kicking again. Talli actually turned to look deeper into the forest as if keeping sentry. Yeah, right.

"What the fuck are they doing?" Brandt demanded.

Davidson sighed. "They tried to reassign us, so we kind of went AWOL."

Brandt tried to keep his temper in check. Unfortunately, that usually meant grinding his teeth, and well, one of them was fucking missing at the moment.

"Please specify what 'kind of' AWOL means?"

"Hey," Lopez jumped in, "they weren't sending anyone after you. We had to come."

"Which would simply make you AWOL," Brandt added.

"Right, and they cut us off," Davidson said. "But once we were here, they hooked us up with thermal imaging of the village."

"Which would then make you on active duty."

"Yeah." Lopez sighed. "Then they cut us off. Not sure why."

Brandt glared at each of his men in turn. Including the back of Talli's head.

"Let me get this straight," Brandt said as calmly and cautiously as he could. "You brought my bride to Africa, lost her in the jungle, and now have no way to find her?"

"True, all," Lopez said, nodding. "But I've got great video." The corporal must have felt the wave of rage coming his way as he raised his hands in surrender. "Sorry, sorry." When Brandt backed off a step, Lopez continued. "Too soon?"

A glare shut him up.

"Silver lining here," Davidson added. "Levont was supposed to gather Rebecca and take her to the spot we dropped the little girl. So we do have a secondary staging point."

Brandt just picked up a pack—he didn't even know whose it was—and set off north. Lopez trotted to catch up with him.

"Come on, Sarge, I know you are worried, but this is Dr. Monroe we are talking about. Rebecca and the jungle are BFFs. Remember Ecuador?"

That was the problem. The first time Brandt had laid eyes on his bride-to-be was seared into his brain. At the time, she had gotten herself tied to a stake with an anaconda about to squeeze the life from her.

So he would consider their relationship a little more on the frenemies side. Vicious, cold-blooded frenemies.

He hoped the jungle knew what it was doing when it messed with Rebecca.

Frellan breathed in through his nose and whistled the air through his teeth as he stared down at the blip on the screen, which was supposed to give him the exact location of Brandt. It was the only reason they had allowed the man to escape. The Master had thought that Frellan would take too long in his ministrations. She had put them on this path.

Of course, the Master had not counted on the rest of his team arriving so rudely unannounced. Why have someone placed so highly in the US government if they were not forewarned of such things?

Across the clearing, Mikhal glared that glare of his. The sniper was still angered that he had been taken out of the equation. But how exactly were they to allow Brandt to think he'd run off on his own, if they had revealed they had the sniper with them?

Had the sniper taken a single shot, Brandt would have known he survived only by the Master's good graces. And another, more closely held reason burned in Frellan's chest. He would not allow the sniper to share in the glory of finding their Savior. That alone was reserved for Frellan. He alone must atone for his family's sins.

But now, now here he stood, staring down at a tooth. The white enamel glistened brightly against the deep-green ground. The words *Fuck You* dug into the loam.

Ugudo kicked the thing deeper into the forest.

They were not without their resources, though. He turned as one of their trackers trotted up to him.

"There is a clear trail for the SUV heading due east."

Even someone with half of Frellan's experience would know that there was a clear trail east. It was *not* Brandt's ultimate path. Frellan looked through the trees to the position of the moon. They would not have the British satellite feed for another half an hour. Brandt was in no shape to make a speedy escape from the region. This escape attempt reeked of desperation.

There was no reason to linger here. He gave the signal to return to the village.

Frellan let his body shift side to side as it navigated the treacherous road back to the village. Closing his eyes, he let the rhythm bring him closer to God. He did not resist the rough course that He had put him upon. As they made the last hairpin turn into the village, Frellan opened his eyes to find Monnie standing on the wooden stoop of a dilapidated hut. She bent her head in supplication as he exited the Jeep.

He ignored her. His only want was to find a quiet hut and a subject to express his desires upon. As he went to pass, she whispered, "Master Frellan."

There was something beguiling in that soft tone. Beguiling enough for him to turn to her. "Yes, Monnie?"

"I believe I have found someone you should speak to."

Frellan had not even noticed the older woman huddled at Monnie's feet. You could smell the fear on the woman. Her dark eyes tried so hard not to stare at his piercings, yet they failed. He knelt beside the old woman, cupping her face. Ah, so many wrinkles to work with. Her sagging features a worthy canvas for him to work upon.

"She says she has information if we agree to not harm anyone in the village."

"And you agreed to such terms?"

Monnie would not meet his eye. "Yes, I thought it better to—"

He held up his hand. Her arrogance would be dealt with later. Perhaps she was used to such latitude, given her new position as a watcher of the Word. In the sanctuary, the title held great power. In the African forest? She would learn. What message would it send the Master if he marred that smooth skin of Monnie's?

He let none of that show on his face, however. He simply nodded. The woman prattled on in a smattering of French and Lingala. Frellan, however, caught the salient points. The girl had been entrusted to a local witch doctor.

"There," she said in English, pointing up the mountain.

Frellan turned to Ugudo. "The helicopter." He turned to the next man. "Leave no witnesses."

"No!" Monnie cried out. "You promised!" she said as she went to slap his face.

Frellan caught her hand in midair. "No, Monnie. You promised that which you could not honor." Her hand shook as shots, then screams rang out across the village. His only regret that it would all be over so quickly. Frellan usually liked to take his time. Put true effort into the taking of someone's life. They deserved as much.

"So you will never speak for me again?"

Auburn eyes swimming in tears looked up at him. She had never been more beautiful as she sobbed. "No."

Rebecca chewed on the last of her portion, trying to suppress her gag reflex. How she wished that python tasted like chicken. It did not. Not at all. It tasted like…well, charbroiled snake. She would not recommend it.

But with some food, no matter how gross, in her belly, some fresh water, and a few more kola seeds, Rebecca was feeling almost as good as new. And from the girl next to her's beaming face, she was feeling pretty darn good as well.

"Do you speak English?" Rebecca asked.

"*Un peu*," the girl responded.

Which of course was French for "a little bit."

And Lord knew Rebecca's French was a bit atrocious. She looked over to the older man, who had taken to butchering the rest of the python. All twenty feet of him. While she was grateful for all that the man had done for her, Rebecca had to look away.

Besides, he didn't even seem eager to speak the native language, let alone English.

"Is that your grandfather? *Grand-père*?"

The girl shook her head. "Just *lehrer.*"

Teacher. Rebecca knew that term in German. Hell, she knew it in just about every language.

"I am Rebecca," she said, extending her hand. The girl took her hand, then cupped her own elbow. A sign of respect across Africa.

Even though the gesture was usually used to show reverence to elders, Rebecca mimicked the action, nodding in synch with the little girl, whose smile radiated nearly as brightly as the fire.

"Vakasa," she answered.

"Thank you, Vakasa," Rebecca said, but when the girl looked confused, she added, "*Merci beaucoup.*"

Vakasa shook her head, though. "*Salamat.*"

"Thank you" in Filipino. "For what?"

The girl spoke quickly in like five languages. The words whizzed past so quickly that Rebecca wasn't sure if she'd translated properly. *For what is to come.*

Rebecca had started to ask the girl what she meant when she heard the distinct sound of helicopter rotors. Since they were not squealing in complaint, Rebecca could only assume it was *not* Lopez.

That wasn't good.

As the old man grabbed his spear, he seemed to agree. Their eyes met over the fire. Then his gaze slid from Rebecca to the girl. The message obvious. I will hold them off. You get the girl out of here.

Or at least that's what she meant, because that was Rebecca's plan.

Bunny watched as the screen bloomed to life. The green of the African jungle punctuated with orange blobs. A lot of them.

"What's going on?"

Prenner leaned against his fists on the desk. His eyes scanned the data. For a remote forest, there were a lot of blips. Some much smaller than a human. Some much, much bigger. The jungle seemed abuzz with activity. Given the aftershock of a few hours ago, it wasn't surprising. Then there were the human-sized blips. But which of those were Brandt's team, which were the Disciples, and which were just villagers going about their business?

In addition to the bright oranges, there were stark-yellow markers that slowly turned a light blue. The dead. So many of them, too.

"There," he said, pointing northeast. "Those four blips. They are on the move. It's got to be Brandt and his men."

"You didn't order any air support, did you?" Emily asked the lieutenant.

"No," he said, shaking his head. "Everything we have is tied up in Somalia."

Bunny was about to inquire why Emily had asked. Then she noticed two fairly large blobs moving at a very fast speed toward the peak of the mountains.

"No," she groaned. They were helicopters. The damn Disciples were well outfitted. Too well outfitted. And here Brandt and the rest were traveling on foot.

"Looks like they are converging on these three figures," the tech stated as he drew a bright-red circle around a small hut in the middle of the jungle. That had to be Rebecca and Levont. But who was the third small blip? Bunny watched as the helicopters quickly made up the distance. "And it looks like those choppers are going to win the race."

Bunny gulped and turned to Emily. "And what are you going to do about it?"

Emily grabbed Bunny's hand and gave it a squeeze. "Pray."

Davidson set up his shot with patience. He would not get another like this. Not only to take out the lead helicopter, but with any luck at all, make sure the second chopper hit the debris.

He ignored the squeaks of the forest's insects. He ignored the large frond that had draped over his leg. He ignored his own impatience.

Nothing mattered but the bull's-eye on the Disciples' helicopter's rear rotor. He needed their crash to be messy.

Davidson had squared his shoulder, ready for the impact of the recoil, when a bullet flew past his ear. He jerked his rifle to the left and fired in the same motion. He put a hole in the side of the second chopper, but it was cosmetic damage at best.

Through his scope, he could see the Disciples' sniper haul himself back into his chopper. A broad smile on his face. Davidson almost cursed. Almost. He had been too shortsighted. Apparently, the sniper hadn't died back in Jordan. Just because the man hadn't let off a shot didn't mean he wasn't attached to the mission.

Snapping his gun up, Davidson made his way down the tree as the other men shot at the fleeing helicopters. It did no good. The choppers were too far away for the range of their guns. It had been Davidson's duty to neutralize the helicopters.

His.

Another failure atop of losing Rebecca.

He landed hard on the ground, right next to Brandt. The pain in the man's eyes seared Davidson. Those choppers were headed only one place. Straight to Rebecca's staging site. The Disciples might be after the girl—clearly, they had found out about her—but now they were on the trail of Rebecca as well.

"I am—"

"Save it," Brandt grunted, rolling his neck from one side to the other.

"But the Disciples are—"

Brandt's eyes narrowed. "I know what the Disciples are doing."

Everyone stood silent as Brandt stretched out one arm, then the next.

"Um, Sarge?" Lopez asked. "What are we going to do?"

"Run."

With that, the sergeant charged up the forest slope, heedless of the steep grade or the thick underbrush.

Lopez grinned. "Last one up writes the after-action report!"

Davidson strapped his rifle onto his back. This was one race he was not losing.

CHAPTER 8

NORTHEAST CONGO JUNGLE

10:42 P.M. (CAT)

Since Rebecca's rescue from the python, the jungle had descended into darkness. The constant chatter of African gray parrots had transformed into the unnerving creaks and squeaks of unseen wildlife. The forest pressed down upon her as she held the girl close. They followed the old man wordlessly through the rain forest.

To the south, the helicopter had landed, and the men had already trashed the hut. Search parties had quickly been sent out. It would only be a matter of time before they were caught.

And when they were caught—there was no doubt they were going to be caught—the only weapon they had was the old man's long, hollow stick.

The old man stopped, sniffed the air, then urged her deeper into the jungle. It seemed this was where he planned to make his stand. How this spot was different than the other hundred they had passed in their silent trek, Rebecca had no idea.

As she moved past him, Rebecca reached out and touched his ritually scarred arm. "Thank you."

His response was an annoyed grunt and head jerk toward the path he had set them on.

Taking no offense—she was used to Brandt, after all—Rebecca went to oblige, but the girl wouldn't budge. Taking her small hand from Rebecca's, Vakasa hugged the old man. At first, the elder did not seem to know quite what to do. Then he put a hand on the girl's back and gave it a pat.

The girl murmured something in Romanian, ancient Greek, and Swahili.

As much as Rebecca could cobble together, it meant, "I'll see you again." Or Vakasa wanted a mocha latte.

The old man shook his head sharply, but the girl only hugged harder. "*Promesse.*"

Promise. Or at least that's what Rebecca thought. Her French wasn't exactly Grade A.

With one final, awkward pat, the man forced Vakasa away from him and put her hand in Rebecca's.

"Go," he whispered in heavily accented English.

Squeezing the girl's hand, Rebecca headed out into the forest, still dripping from the latest downpour. Moonlight streaked through in thin slices, edging its way through the thick canopy.

Vakasa's hand was warm in her palm. So little. So trusting. Rebecca was the one used to being protected. She wasn't built to be the protector. Was she?

Shots sounded behind them. A war cry that resounded in Rebecca's bones was the answer. The battle headed north. The warrior was drawing the men away from her and the girl. Not wanting to waste his efforts, Rebecca broke into a run. The sound of their flight masked by the fight to the north.

She had absolutely no idea where they were running. Rebecca only knew that she had to get as far away from the hut as possible, as quickly as possible. Then Vakasa stopped cold, nearly jerking Rebecca's shoulder out. She tried to coax the girl forward, but the child's lip trembled as she pointed ahead.

Three men stalked from the trees.

Rebecca's heart sank so hard that she was sure she heard it hit the ground. The Disciples had set up a perimeter. Bastards.

She pushed Vakasa behind her. The men wanted Rebecca. Perhaps if she gave up, they would let the girl melt into the forest.

"I'll go quietly," Rebecca said as she stepped toward them.

The nearest man backhanded her. The force snapped her head to the side as she fell to the ground. *What the…?*

He then lunged and grabbed the girl, jerking her toward him. He laughed harshly, speaking in broken English. "So much dollars for something so small."

The men wanted Vakasa?

Seriously, Rebecca couldn't get kidnapped to save her life today.

"They've got the girl," Bunny whispered to no one in particular.

"You were right," Emily stated.

Prenner just frowned, staring at the small dot surrounded by three much larger dots. A fifth dot lay off to the side. Rebecca? The dot held a steady orange, so she must be alive, but for how long?

Not far, but too far away, Brandt and the men surged ahead. Bright-red flashes marked their gunfire. The splashes of color made the forest look afire. This was another reason why Bunny didn't get on that helicopter with Davidson. Yet her heart lurching at each burst and the smell of gunpowder in her nose, she might as well be there.

"At least they are able to hone in on the enemy," Prenner said, indicating the live feed to the men's devices.

Bunny glanced to the blobs that appeared to be Rebecca and the girl. How had the Disciples honed in on *them* so well? They were out in the middle of the jungle. Bunny presumed they had stayed quiet. Then how?

"Turn it off!" Bunny shouted, realizing that the Disciples were honing in on Rebecca the same exact way Brandt was honing in on the enemy. By the satellite feed.

"What are you—" Prenner tried to demand, but Bunny elbowed him out of the way and got up alongside the technician.

"Cut it!"

"Are you kidding me? Do you know how hard it is just to keep the damn thing aligned and transmitting?"

Bunny slipped off her stiletto and smashed the heel into the keyboard. "I take it that might make it harder?" The screen warped and fuzzed, losing detail, but not enough. Bunny turned to take on the CPU, but Prenner caught her wrist.

"Oh, no, you don't."

Well, Bunny had two shoes, didn't she? Kicking backward, she plunged a heel into the CPU, which sparked and hissed. The screen went an icy blue.

"You just took away the slim advantage they had!" Prenner growled.

"Yes, I did," Bunny responded, then glanced to Emily. "The *Disciples*' advantage. We've got to shut down the British feed in case they are getting their intel from there."

"On it," Emily said, flipping open her phone.

Prenner looked from the CIA operative to Bunny. "You can't really think they are *live* hacking us."

"That's exactly what I think," Bunny said as she jerked her wrist out of his grip. She turned to the tech. "We've got to find the source of the hack."

The guy indicated to his fried keyboard and CPU. "Kind of need a work station to accomplish that."

Bunny nodded to the glass walls revealing dozens upon dozens of options. "I think we can find a replacement."

The tech looked to Prenner, who gave a sharp nod.

"Sure." The tech rolled his chair back from the desk, then stopped. "I just gotta say…"

"Yes?" Bunny urged.

"That was kind of hot."

Bunny shoved the guy toward the door. What was he, nineteen? Still, it was nice to know she still had it.

Now to just figure out a way to give the advantage back to Rebecca and Brandt.

Fuck.

The damned feed was still down.

There was no fucking waiting around for Command to get their asses together. They knew Rebecca's last known location. That was going to have to be enough.

"Now!" Brandt yelled, laying down cover fire.

From the corner of his eye, he saw Davidson sprinting east. They had to get ahead of the bulk of the forces. And damn it if Davidson wasn't the fastest amongst them. Brandt wanted to be the one running to Rebecca right now, but this was a shit storm, and seldom did one get what they wanted in the middle of a fucking shit storm. Lopez, ducking, running low, headed north. That left Brandt and Talli to not only keep these fuckers busy, but advance their position.

No biggie.

"Let's do this," Brandt ordered Talli, who dropped to one knee.

He fired broadly as Brandt scrambled forward, pushing aside underbrush. A thorny branch snapped back, slicing his cheek. Even the forest was against him. Brandt fought a few more feet, then dropped to his knee and began firing.

"Go!"

Talli made his way by, passing Brandt and establishing a forward position about ten feet in front. The corporal dropped to his knee. "Go!"

As leaves shredded all around him, Brandt took a bullet to the upper bicep. *Great.* Another stain on his tuxedo. They were so not getting their security deposit back. However, he made it a good twelve feet forward. Of course, they were nearly a quarter of a mile from Rebecca.

Did she know to hold on? He had to believe that she did.

That they were coming for her.

Rebecca tried to push the foot planted on her chest off, but the mercenary just chuckled, putting enough pressure so that she could barely breathe. Vakasa was faring no better as the other two men tossed her back and forth between them, taunting her. Rebecca couldn't follow the native language, but she could imagine what they threatened.

"Frellan wants her unmolested," the man holding Rebecca down barked when one of the other mercenaries went to kiss the young girl.

"Who cares what the *farang* wants?" the other man spat.

She might not speak Lingala. However, she knew a racial slur when she heard one. Frellan must be white. And more than likely a Disciple. The master to these mercenaries.

The man holding Rebecca down brought his gun to bear against his own men. "The *mzungu* pays us, and I won't lose my bonus." Rebecca was momentarily relieved when the men released Vakasa, until it became clear why the mercenary was using English. "However, he said nothing about the *nyeupe shetani*."

White devil.

All eyes turned on Rebecca. She was a member of Amnesty International. She knew what these men were capable of. The war crimes they had already committed a hundred times over. She swore she could feel her spleen squeeze in terror. Even though the thought of their hands on her body nauseated her to the core, Rebecca couldn't let them hurt the girl.

She had to place her trust in her men. They would get here. Brandt would get here before…before she became another statistic.

"Yes," Rebecca blurted before she lost the courage. "Take me," she added, trying to keep the tremble out of her voice. She failed.

The man removed his foot and jerked her to her feet. He pressed his body against hers. "Not a virgin, I see, but you will do."

Rebecca couldn't watch as he put his nostrils against her skin and inhaled up her neck. Instead, she found Vakasa's eyes. "Look away," she whispered desperately. But the girl did the oddest thing.

She winked.

Then she bit the hand of the man holding her. He howled in outrage, shaking the wounded appendage. The other man laughed at him. Even so, the mercenary holding Rebecca let his grip loosen just a bit. Using every bit of close-quarter training Brandt had ever showed her, Rebecca used her shoe and scraped it down his shin. Then as he bent over in pain, she brought her elbow straight up into his solar plexus.

In a pained rush of air, he teetered, then slumped to the ground. The other men's guns snapped up, aiming at her. Rebecca guessed she had about a second before they pulled the trigger.

As Vakasa rushed over to her, one of the men's necks split open, gushing blood. Yet he strangely turned and shot his partner.

"Get down!" a vaguely familiar voice yelled.

Not worrying about who it was that had come to their rescue, Rebecca dragged Vakasa down to the ground with her. Even as they hit the dirt, she watched the last mercenary stagger up. One hand on his sternum. The other on his gun. There was no way their rescuer was going to get him in time.

Then the man's head snapped to the side. The mercenary lurched, trying to get his bearings, when that long, hollow stick hit him in the back of the knees. Legs knocked out from under him, the mercenary tumbled to the ground, his shots going wild. The stick came down flat onto his nose, crushing it.

Rebecca looked away, tucking Vakasa's head away from the violence.

It wasn't until a few seconds after the last moist thud that Rebecca glanced back up. Levont. Was that his name? Brandt's new point man offered her his mud-covered hand.

"We've got to get moving."

Once up, Rebecca looked around for the old man. He had melted into the night again.

"Thank you," she said shakily to Brandt's man.

"Appreciate it, ma'am, but my boss would be awfully disgruntled if I rescued you, only to have us captured again."

Rebecca snorted despite herself. Levont was right. Brandt would be pissed.

"Where is he?"

Levont's answer was a nod toward the literal storm of gunfire across the jungle. However, the man moved north instead of toward Brandt.

"Where are we going?"

"To get the hell out of here."

Yeah, Rebecca couldn't agree more.

"Can you do it?" Bunny demanded.

The technician's fingers flew over the keyboard. "In a week, maybe."

Bunny looked over at Emily. "I'll get someone at Langley on it."

The ploy worked, as one of the tech's hands flew up. "Hang on."

The screen in front of them—a new screen since shrapnel from Bunny's CPU attack had damaged the last one—bloomed to life. Orange and yellow and red flared.

"You are sure you aren't broadcasting to Brandt's team?" Bunny asked.

The tech rolled his eyes. "Like I said, we are broadcasting to nowhere."

"But it is live inside the system?"

"Jeez, yes. Now, which way do you want me to have them going?" the tech asked.

"South," Bunny answered.

"Why south?" Prenner asked.

Bunny didn't answer. Probably because south was just a hunch. But after everything that had happened over the last year, she'd learned to trust her gut. Bunny smacked the tech on the shoulder.

"South it is," the tech said, moving one of the medium-sized orange globs, along with the smallest blip, down the screen. "And the others?"

"Have them converge on the last location of the main enemy's force."

It was a good thing the kid's background was in video game development before the DOD recruited him.

"Not so fast," Prenner suggested. "Brandt would never move that cautiously. Lopez, the blip to the west might, but not Brandt."

Bunny nodded. "Good point. Davidson would also set up in a tree somewhere, so keep him stable."

"Seriously, people," the tech complained, "I am doing like five people's jobs right now, so let's keep the personalized monograms to a minimum."

She gave the tech a squeeze on the shoulder as a little motivator. Davidson wouldn't mind, not if the gesture helped save his life.

"Fine," the tech said, typing rapidly. The figures on the screen moved in a corresponding fashion.

Bunny pointed to the blip next to Brandt. "Talli isn't that good a shot. Don't have him be that Rambo."

With a minimal of fussing, the tech did as asked.

The chess pieces were on the board. In hopefully the exact opposite direction of the actual soldiers.

Now to see if the Disciples would take the bait.

Brandt dropped to his knee and pulled the trigger. Only, nothing came out. He didn't bother cursing. He simply pulled his sidearm out of his waistband and fired. This time squeezing off the rounds one by one.

Talli pulled up beside him rather than leapfrogging.

"I'm almost out as well."

What the hell were Lopez and Davidson doing?

Brandt and Talli were in place. Actually, they had pushed past "the place," just to keep up the charade of trying to reach Rebecca. Now, though, with limited ammunition? Something had to happen. Something *big* or they would be pinned down within minutes.

"Spare your rounds," Brandt said, letting Talli provide the cover fire while he thought through the mess they were in.

What could have gone wrong with the plan? Besides about sixteen thousand things?

Brandt cocked his head. Talli wasn't firing. "Run out?" he asked as he fired into the jungle.

"No," Talli said, pushing Brandt's gun arm down. He was about to complain, quite stringently, when Talli put his finger to his lips. "Listen," he whispered.

And Brandt did. And people were still firing at them. Or were they? Sure, shots were being fired, but they seemed to be going east. At a clipped rate. What the hell was going on? It was like the enemy was chasing ghosts.

They stayed silent in the brush for a few more moments, letting the enemy charge in the wrong direction. Could he trust this bizarre golden opportunity? Could he trust that somehow an escape path had opened up?

Given how light his gun felt in his hand, Brandt figured he could.

"Ready?" he asked Talli.

After a deep breath, the corporal nodded.

This was it.

Brandt took a step to the west. Then another and another, gaining speed as he went.

After all of that, their plan might still work.

CHAPTER 9

CONGO JUNGLE

11:18 P.M. (CAT)

Ahead of them, Levont skid to stop, putting his hand into a fist. Rebecca pulled Vakasa close as they hunkered down in the brush. There had been several other times men had run past their location. Strangely shooting in the wrong direction. It had forced them to take a far more circumventous route than Levont had proposed.

Through the heavy leaves, Rebecca spotted their final destination. Awash in moonlight, two helicopters sat on an outcropping of rock.

Rebecca inched her way to the point man. "What is the plan?"

"Not sure," he answered, sweeping night-vision goggles over the area.

"Um..." Levont was new to the team. Maybe he wasn't used to sharing intel with her. "Can you give me any specifics? Brandt is totally candid with me."

"Oh, it's not that I'm withholding," he said with a grin. "It's because I don't know."

Rebecca rocked back onto her heels. That was not the answer she was looking for. "Then why did you have us haul our butts over here?"

Levont nodded to the helicopters. "Those are the only vehicles for twenty miles. You think Lopez could keep his hands off of them?"

Well, Levont may be new to the team, but he certainly had Lopez pegged.

"So what do we do?" Rebecca asked as Vakasa crawled onto her lap. The young girl leaned her head against Rebecca's shoulder. Somehow the terror faded. At least a little.

"Wait."

"For what?"

One of the helicopter's blades slowly started spinning.

"For that..." Levont said with a broad grin. Guards, attracted by the sound, rushed the helicopter. Levont took aim, knocking each one either down or back. "I may not be Davidson, but I've got my uses."

Apparently, the point man did.

"You know how cover fire works?" Levont asked.

"Yes, *unfortunately*," she answered.

"All right, then," he said, getting his shot lined up. "On my mark, you are going to get the girl to the helicopter. You are not going to worry about me. You are not going to look back. You are not going to wait for me to catch up. Got it?"

"Got it."

Levont turned to look her straight in the eye. "I mean it."

"So do I," Rebecca answered. "You are on your own."

The point man grinned. Then his face got grim. "Three… two…"

Ugh. Rebecca knew the rest as she gripped Vakasa's hand.

"Stop!" Frellan yelled, yet his men charged forward. Had he heard something?

"*Simama*!" Ugudo yelled in Swahili. The group of mercenaries was so diverse that it was the only common language amongst them. The dark-skinned commander waved the men back. "Your orders?"

Frellan cocked his head, listening. Nothing. In the deep jungle, was his mind playing tricks on him? He looked to the video feed of the heat signatures, then to the jungle. Beyond where his men had just come, there was no movement. Not a single branch out of place. Brandt and his team were good, but not that good. No one was that good.

Then gunfire erupted. *Behind* them.

"The helicopters," Ugudo confirmed.

No. It could not be. Brandt and the rest were in *front* of them.

However, as more and more shots sounded, Frellan had to accept this new reality.

He studied his handheld receiver. The signal had been a decoy. A *decoy*. Someone dared bait him? Bait the *Disciples*?

Was this how Aunush failed? He had read her reports. He had shaken his head at her constant blaming of faulty intelligence. Yet here he stood, in the middle of the Congo, with a device that had betrayed him.

God truly was testing him.

Once he caught Brandt, Monroe, and the child, though? Ah, then he would have the time he craved. All the time in the world to etch betrayal into their very souls.

Rebecca turned the handle of the helicopter's door and jerked it open as the rotors wound up.

Lopez winked at her. "Long time no see."

"Just fly, Ricky," Rebecca urged, even though she couldn't help but grin as she helped Vakasa into the helicopter.

"Why, how lucky can a guy get?" Lopez commented. "His two favorite girls loading into his helicopter?"

Vakasa had no trouble flashing a huge smile at the corporal, until a bullet bounced off one of the blades.

"Levont should be right behind us," Rebecca said as she got Vakasa hooked into her seat, latching the restraints in place. What did it say about her life that she could do so without even looking?

"Doesn't look like it," Lopez commented as he lifted them a few feet off the ground. Rebecca looked to the tree line, to see Levont retreat back into the brush as bullets flew. "He's going to need some cover," Lopez added. "And I'm, well, a little busy."

He eyed the gun sitting on the seat next to him. Rebecca shied away. Despite their rather desperate need, she was loath to pick up the gun. She hated guns. She hated everything they represented. She hated that her life and that of everyone else's relied on them.

Then Vakasa was there. Her little fingers picked up the heavy weapon.

"No!" Rebecca shouted, pulling the gun from the girl's hand. "No."

The girl looked puzzled. Clearly, she'd grown up in the war-torn region. Vakasa probably had more shooting experience than Rebecca. Yet she could not allow the girl to be the one to shoot. She couldn't let the girl be the one to carry the burden.

Opening the helicopter door, Rebecca braced herself and pulled the trigger. The recoil shot pain up her wrists to her elbow and all the way to her shoulder. She fired again in the general direction of the guards. Still, Levont couldn't poke his head out of the leaves without bullets pushing him back.

"Fine. Lopez to the rescue," the corporal stated, lifting the chopper up and tilting it toward the tree line. "Keep that door open!"

They skimmed the damp grass, speeding toward Levont's position. The others must have realized what Lopez was attempting, as they moved to cut the chopper off. Rebecca raised the weapon and squeezed off another two joint-jarring shots. This time the men paid attention to her errant bullets, firing back.

Ducking, Rebecca kept the door open even as the jungle tried to push it closed. Levont scrambled out from the brush as the helicopter bucked and fought Lopez. They lurched up four feet. Levont tossed his weapon over his shoulder and leapt for it. His body hit the opening.

Rebecca grabbed his hand, trying to help haul him up. One of Levont's feet caught some purchase on the helicopter's struts. He was about to push himself into the chopper when one of the mercenaries charged. Rebecca didn't even think. She just shot.

Blood splattered across the man's shoulder. Howling, he dropped his gun. Shaking, Rebecca dropped her gun as well. She'd shot someone. She could see the pain in his features. She could see the blood she'd freed from his body.

"A little help," Levont groaned, hanging on with one hand to the doorframe. The other arm was tucked up against his abdomen. Whether his arm was hit or his belly, Rebecca couldn't tell.

She reached over him, grabbed him by the belt, and pulled. He was nearly inside the chopper when he became twice as heavy. The mercenary had jumped up and grabbed Levont by the leg.

Seriously, give it up.

But the guy seemed intent on taking Levont down.

"Close the door!" Lopez yelled.

"He's not in yet," Rebecca responded, still tugging up with all her might.

"Do it!" Lopez shouted.

She had no idea what he had in mind, but it was probably incredibly stupid. And dangerous. So with one hand still on Levont's belt, she used the other one to bring the door as closed as she could under the bizarre circumstances.

Lopez tilted the helicopter precariously thirty degrees to the right. The blades chewed up branches, sending wooden shrapnel everywhere, but especially at the mercenary. Levont grit his teeth as his own leg took some of the damage.

Still, the guy would not let go. As a matter of fact, he was climbing up Levont, trying to make it into the chopper. Rebecca gripped the chopper door, then threw her weight into it. The metal hit the guy in the head, knocking him back. He lost his traction on Levont's tuxedo pant leg and slid down to his shoe.

With one good kick, Levont freed himself of the mercenary.

Now half as light, the point man easily made it into the helicopter. Once inside, Rebecca slammed the door shut.

Despite a bleeding arm and half a dozen scratches, Levont beamed. "Off. The. Hook."

Then bullets flew as Lopez banked them away from the forest. The bulk of mercenaries had clearly returned.

"Thor!" Vakasa cried, pointing to two men approaching.

Thor?

Hell no, that was Brandt—and Talli—running across the clearing!

Only Lopez had to climb higher and higher and push the chopper faster and faster to avoid the storm of shots coming from the forest.

Fuck. Fuck. Fuck.

They were too late. The helicopter had been forced to take off as the rest of the mercenaries arrived.

"Retreat," Brandt ordered.

Talli obeyed, backing into the jungle, laying down what cover fire he could while clearly still trying to conserve ammo. The only lucky break they had gotten was that the Disciples were way too busy worrying about the helicopter getting away to chase them down.

Lopez's chopper, with a hail of bullets chasing it, sailed overhead. Pressed against the glass was Rebecca's face. She was *alive*.

He wouldn't be much longer if he stood there all doe-eyed. Heading back into the jungle, Brandt tried to think like Lopez. Which kind of made his head hurt. They didn't have a third staging area. What were they thinking? From now on, they needed about five of them.

Retreating outside the range of the mercenaries' guns, Brandt studied the enemy. There were still eight of them, not including their leader. So storming the second helicopter wasn't an option. Besides, he wasn't much of a chopper pilot, and he wasn't about to risk it to Talli.

Most of the mercenaries loaded quickly into the chopper, leaving only a few on the ground to provide protection for their launch.

Which, it turned out, was going to be a while. The pilot had tried to start the helicopter when smoke plumed out the engine. Brandt took a moment to feel just a little satisfied. Lopez didn't have any C4, so he did the next best thing to prevent the other chopper from taking off.

Good old-fashioned sabotage.

The only problem? Now that the enemy didn't have a quick pursuit to care about, they all turned their attention to the jungle.

Time to hightail it.

But where?

"Any thoughts on where Lopez is heading?" Brandt asked as he crept deeper into the jungle.

"You are asking me?" Talli asked.

True. The two men couldn't be more diametrically opposed.

Great. Time to play "Where in the World is Lopez?"

Not his favorite game.

"We've got to circle back," Rebecca demanded.

"Can't, darlin'," Lopez answered, swerving the chopper under the canopy, avoiding the tree trunks. Which was about as difficult as it sounded. Chunks of bark flew all around them. It was like flying through a wood chipper.

Rebecca hissed out a breath, trying to regain her composure. It was just a little hard to do after flying over your husband-to-be, abandoning him to the Disciples. But she knew, after everything Lopez had done, that he couldn't possibly be leaving Brandt and Talli behind.

She took another breath before asking, "So you have a plan?"

"Duh," Lopez said, ducking his head as they mowed through a palm tree, its leaves smacking the windshield.

She counted to ten before speaking. "Do you care to share?"

"Isn't it obvious?"

"*No*!" Rebecca just couldn't help it.

Lopez only smiled, though. "If you've only got two staging areas and one is compromised, what do you do?"

"Go to the other," Levont answered from behind her.

Vakasa kneeled next to the large man as he prepped ropes and riggings. It seemed like he was getting ready to pull the men into the chopper from the ground. But what if the men weren't there to pull?

"That's great and all, but does Brandt know this?" she asked.

Lopez made a face. "Um, he better, or we are so screwed."

Brandt glanced over his shoulder to Talli, who was having a hard time keeping up. He'd twisted his ankle or something. For a guy with not the best aim in the world, you would think he would keep the klutziness to a minimum. Clearly, Talli was a contrarian.

At full speed, were they even going in the right direction? Brandt was operating on gut instinct alone, returning to their last rally point. Would Lopez think to double back? The man did have a fairly linear—make that acceleration-oriented—mind.

Still, it was their best shot.

He broke through a particularly stalwart pair of branches and stumbled into the clearing around the hut. Although, it wasn't exactly clear any longer. And the hut wasn't exactly a hut, either. The Disciples had torn it down to nearly its last thatch. Leaves, pots, and snake parts littered the ground.

"Incoming!" Talli yelled, limping over to the right.

Sure enough, a speeding helicopter swooped and dodged trees, making its way to them. A most welcome sight. Only, one slight problem. They weren't slowing down. Or landing.

"We better take this at a run," Brandt suggested as the helicopter's door opened. Talli tried, he really did, but he was never going to make it on his own. So as the chopper sped toward them, Brandt fell back, throwing Talli's arm over his shoulder, urging him along.

The helicopter flew overhead, pausing only briefly to hover over them.

Levont reached out a bloody arm to help Talli up.

"Why can't you land?" Brandt yelled over the rotor wash.

"Giraffe!" Levont shouted back.

Giraffe? What the hell did—

Then Brandt saw them. Giraffes. Tall, lanky, and apparently pissed, coming right at them.

Giving Talli's ass one good shove, Brandt got his sniper in the chopper, then running, keeping up with the now traveling helicopter, Brandt got a foot onto the strut. Hauling himself up, he dove into the chopper just as the door was slammed closed by a tree.

Then giraffes were all around them. Their long necks rocking back and forth as they ran. One took a swipe at the struts, nearly knocking the helicopter ten feet off course.

"I swear I didn't challenge them to anything," Lopez yelled from the front of the chopper.

Brandt was about to answer when Rebecca was suddenly in his arms. He hugged her fiercely, then pulled her away, enough to look into her eyes.

"Don't you ever follow me again," Brandt said, but joy danced in her eyes. Brandt would have kissed her, except for, you know, the giraffes.

Rebecca grabbed hold of a seat as the helicopter rocked when it was hit by another giraffe.

"Why are there so many freaking animals?" Lopez demanded.

Nursing his ankle, Talli answered, "We are smack dab in the middle of a wildlife reserve."

"Still..." Lopez exhaled. "And is somebody filming this?"

Rebecca plunked her forehead against Brandt's extremely stained white shirt. For a moment, amongst all the chaos, she just let his chest lift her forehead, then lower it as he breathed in and out. His heartbeat pounded against his breastbone, creating a beautiful symphony. He put a hand on the back of her head, stroking her hair. She felt his lips brush the top of her head.

Brandt was not just alive, but safe, too. Well, as safe as any of them as Lopez struggled to keep them somewhat aloft. Rebecca barely noticed. Instead, she took in the moment. Then the little girl threw herself at Brandt, wrapping her little arms around his leg.

"Thor!"

Yes, Vakasa's dark-haired, green-eyed Thor was Brandt. There must be a story there, but they certainly didn't have time to tell it, as Lopez yelled, "Hold on!"

When Lopez told you to secure yourself, you *secured* yourself.

Brandt grabbed Rebecca and Vakasa, lowering them to the floor as he grabbed hold of the base of a seat. Lopez hit the thrust, taking them up. Up through the thick jungle canopy. Huge fronds whacked the chopper, tousling its path. The rotors ground, screaming their complaint, but still, they ascended.

Until, finally, they popped out of the forest, streaking upward. It was like they'd escaped the earth's atmosphere and hurled into space as stars twinkled in the sky. Then Lopez stabilized their speed and ascent.

They hovered over the forest. The huge hole they'd cut in the canopy was already closing as branches unfolded, spreading a leaf bandage over the jungle.

"There!" Talli shouted, pointing to the other helicopter whose rotors began turning.

She laid her cheek against Brandt's chest.

His words rumbled against her ear. "I thought you sabotaged it?"

"Wait for it," Lopez said, skimming them over the canopy, heading north.

Brandt waited, with Rebecca safely stowed in his embrace, as the mercenaries loaded into the chopper even as it lifted off. The chopper that was supposed to be inoperable. Like, not able to lift off.

"Lopez..."

As their own helicopter gained altitude, Lopez scoffed. "Kind of the point of 'wait for it' is to *wait*."

Even after the other chopper had lifted off completely and swung around to give chase, Lopez still kept smiling. There was waiting, and then there was being stupid. Suddenly, the Disciples' rotors lurched, spinning erratically. The chopper dipped and spun as the pilot tried to get the vehicle under control.

"I knew they would comb the helo looking for other sabotage points, so I taped some rocks deep within the gear box."

"I don't get it," Rebecca said, tilting her chin up to look at Brandt. Her tear-streaked, mud-caked features should have been on the cover of *Vogue*.

Levont answered as Talli tended to his arm wound. "The heat and vibration of the liftoff loosened the tape, releasing the rocks into the gear box."

"I figured, why just incapacitate the chopper when I might be able to take out the whole crew?" Lopez boasted, not inaccurately, as the Disciples' helicopter limped its way over the forest. Clearly trying to find a place to land.

If Brandt weren't holding Rebecca so close, he might have hugged the corporal. Vakasa loosened her grip from his leg to look around.

She asked in a mishmash of Russian, Hebrew, and possibly Incan. Brandt took her to mean, "Where is Scarecrow?" Davidson.

Good question.

"Lopez?"

Again, the corporal scoffed. "Why do think we're not halfway to Rwanda?"

As the Disciples' helicopter zigged and zagged its way west, losing altitude, then shooting up the next second, Lopez maneuvered his way back to the clearing. A hand waved from the trees. For once, they had a sniper in the perch and didn't have to use him.

Brandt moved Rebecca and the girl over to make room to open the chopper's door.

One team member left to rescue and they were the *hell* out of Africa.

Davidson emerged from the canopy as Lopez brought them alongside the tree line. Winds buffeted them a bit, but the sniper would only have a few feet to jump and be home free.

Brandt reached out his hand. “Nice to see you, Private.”

A smile flashed as Davidson secured his rifle. He took in a few breaths, then launched himself. Everything was going great—the helicopter’s stability, Davidson’s trajectory, everything.

Until it wasn’t.

Pain lanced Davidson’s neck as warm blood gushed from a bullet wound. The force knocked him back and down. His fingers desperately sought the helicopter’s struts, but his hand instinctively pulled back to clutch the bleeding wound. And his weak hand couldn’t support his weight.

Brandt clutched at his sleeve, but he could never pull him up in time and, all the while he tried, gave the Disciples’ sniper all the time in the world to deliver a fatal blow to the chopper.

“Take two,” Davidson said before he let go.

The sergeant refused to release his sleeve until bullets pinged off the chopper.

“Fuck,” Brandt blurted, then let gravity do the rest.

Davidson crashed into the canopy, the leaves and thick stems breaking his fall. He only fell through three layers of trees before he caught a branch under one arm. One hand staunching the bleeding, Davidson’s other hand helped him climb up onto the branch.

When would he learn that the Disciples’ sniper had the patience of, literally, a saint? And worse, he was smart. Why show your hand until you could go for the checkmate shot? The other sniper knew he couldn’t take out the team until he took out Davidson. So he had laid in wait. Tempering his urgency with his desire to eliminate his competition. Patiently staying his hand until the kill shot.

And another half inch and it would have been a fatal injury.

Davidson pulled his palm away from his neck and gently probed the wound. The bullet had taken a small chunk out of his flesh but missed the jugular. Which didn't mean it wasn't bleeding like a *mother*.

Ripping the hem from his jacket, he packed the wound and tied a band as tight as he could without cutting off blood flow to his brain.

Now to figure out a way to get back on that helicopter without getting them all shot.

Frellan leaned in as the helicopter veered left, as if blown by a fierce wind. Instead, they were undone by child's play. Pebbles in the gear box had brought them low. Not just low. It had nearly crashed them.

He looked to the empty seat across from him. Mikhal's seat. The sniper had refused to board. He had refused to chase after the heat signatures. He had gone up a tree and refused to come down.

What report would he write to the Master? How Frellan not only lost the Messiah, but killed his entire team in the attempt? Mikhal prized stillness. Who knew sitting out the fight could actually make you the victor. Well, Frellan had combed the world for near on a decade for the Messiah.

And now, after seeing her? Frellan wasn't about to yield his duty or his honor.

"We must jump," he ordered Ugudo as the helicopter bucked again, nearly falling into the trees.

The man shook his head sharply, his words rattled by the unstable rotors. "Can't chance landing in the river."

Frellan looked out past the tree line to the Congo River. It snaked past, slow and sluggish. "The water will break our fall."

All the men around Frellan snorted. "We will take our chances here," one said.

"*Mamba*," Ugudo said. "Bad *mamba* here."

Frellan studied the smooth waters as best he could as the helicopter jumped and bounced in the air. He knew of the crocodile danger. Anyone who dared travel in Africa knew of the *mamba*. It was one thing to snatch a kayaker from his boat. Quite another to take on an entire armed team.

He went to argue with Ugudo, but the man leaned his head against the hull. "You jump? You jump *alone*." Even with that barbed bar in his cheek, the man still defied Frellan. He did not take that lightly.

Frellan nodded his concession. Seldom did he allow subordinates to dictate terms, but if Ugudo was willing to risk another session with Frellan, he must have his convictions.

"Then we land," Frellan instructed.

"The pilot is trying to get us back to the—"

"*Now*," Frellan ordered. "If he must crash us, he crashes us."

The African's eyes dilated. It was one of the mercenaries who spoke. "That is quite the risk."

Frellen raised a pierced eyebrow to Ugudo. "You wished to take your chances, did you not?"

"That's right, sucker!" Lopez yelled through the windshield. That was until a shot bounced off a rotor. The corporal backed them away several hundred yards. "How about now, huh?"

"Lopez," Brandt admonished, "let's stop antagonizing the guy with the sniper rifle…" Then Brandt remembered the elephants and the giraffes. “On second thought, let’s not antagonize anyone or *thing*.”

“I gotta tell ya,” Lopez said, “I don’t have a whole lot of fuel left…”

For so many reasons, they were running out of options. But they couldn’t leave Davidson in the jungle, either. However, to go in close enough to the forest’s edge to retrieve the private would be nearly suicide for both Davidson and everyone on the chopper.

“What are we going to do?” Rebecca asked, slipping her hand in his.

Jesus, he wished he had an answer for her.

“Get us close enough, and I can try to take a shot,” Talli suggested.

Brandt shook his head. “Your gun doesn’t have enough range. Nothing we have does.” *Plus, it is you on the trigger*, he thought but did not say aloud.

“I say we take the fight to the sniper,” Levont announced from the back of the helicopter.

“Great plan, only how do you plan to avoid a massacre?” Brandt said as he turned to his point man.

Levont didn’t have to answer as he hefted an RPG launcher from a metal bin.

“I couldn’t agree more,” Brandt said as he squeezed Rebecca’s hand. “Let’s get everyone strapped in.”

God, he had never loved Rebecca more than when she simply nodded and went to get Vakasa secured. No argument. No questioning the logic. No fussing.

If they survived the next few minutes, she was definitely a keeper.

CHAPTER 10

SKIES ABOVE THE CONGO

11:29 P.M. (CAT)

Rebecca urged Vakasa to cover her ears, but the little girl just stared wide-eyed at Levont as he prepped the rocket launcher.

"Lopez, move us in," Brandt said, then turned to everyone else. "Remember, we are going to have to take some fire until we are in position."

Of course, they would have to take some fire. When didn't they? At least this was for a good cause. Getting Davidson back. She'd take some fire for that. Apparently Vakasa would as well, as she gave a thumbs-up. Such a remarkable little girl. It seemed she spoke over half a dozen languages and knew her way around American idioms.

"Ready?" Lopez asked, then didn't bother to wait for an answer.

Instead, he tilted the chopper forward, running straight at the sniper's position. Bullets cracked the windshield, but still, they streaked forward.

"Now!" Brandt shouted, and on a dime, Lopez turned the helicopter ninety degrees so the door was facing the sniper.

Rebecca covered her ears, wincing as the rocket ignited, flying from the launcher toward the western jungle. Just as quickly, Lopez spun the helicopter away and hauled ass across the clearing. She looked over her shoulder to watch the rocket hit the trees and burst into flame. They had no chance of actually killing the sniper. They just needed him running for his life from the explosion.

And sure enough, not a single shot sounded in the night as they raced to Davidson's position. Somehow, even though injured, he had climbed back to the top of the canopy, deeper in the forest so they couldn't pick him up at the tree line, but Levont had the ropes and harness ready.

They were prepared.

Except, of course, for the helicopter to start sputtering.

Davidson watched the helicopter's speed cut in half. Fuel streaming out of a bullet hole explained a lot.

Crap.

There would be no second chances this time. Ignoring the stabbing pain from his neck and just about every other body part, Davidson knew he had to make up the distance. No time to make sure the branches could carry his weight.

He just had to have faith. With a prayer on his lips, Davidson ran across the canopy. Never landing long enough to sink into the jungle. His momentum would not last long, though.

The helicopter veered toward him, then dropped a good twenty feet down the riverside cliff. Davidson was almost there. Minor details, but now that the helicopter was lower than him, the spinning rotors were in the way.

It was clear, however, that as the helicopter staggered and sputtered, it was never going to make up the altitude.

Davidson could only pray that Lopez knew what he was about to do.

Gritting his teeth, Davidson launched himself out of the jungle and toward those spinning rotors.

Just in time, the helicopter tilted left, angling the rotors away.

Davidson hit the fuselage hard. His finger scrambled to find a hold on the fuel-slickened metal. His feet flailed, trying to find purchase on…well, anything.

Then there was a hand on his collar.

"I've got you," Brandt said. Standing on the struts, braced against the door, the sergeant was a sight for sore eyes. "Let's get you inside."

Davidson certainly didn't argue there. He let himself slip the rest of the way down the body of the helicopter as he was guided to the safety of the struts. As the helicopter righted itself, Davidson was pulled into the cabin.

"Thanks."

Brandt frowned, though. "I wouldn't thank me yet."

The sergeant nodded toward the Congo River. The surface of which was fast approaching as Brandt secured the door.

"What are you talking about?" Lopez scoffed. "We are totally going to make it."

The far shore seemed, well, pretty far off, given how quickly the helicopter was losing thrust.

"Okay. I lied," Lopez admitted. "We aren't going to make it."

No kidding.

Rebecca watched as, for one glorious moment, it looked like Lopez would prove himself wrong. The bank wasn't forty feet away. You could see the individual trees on the other side. You could make out the ripples in the mud.

Then the helicopter's engine gave one last sputter. The rotors ground to a halt, and the chopper just fell out of the air. Straight down into the Congo River. They hit the water hard, but not all that hard because, well, they just weren't that high in the sky.

"Evac," Brandt barked, flinging off his restraints.

Water lapped at the front windshield as they sank into the river. Rebecca unbuckled herself, then Vakasa. The girl climbed into her arms, clutching her neck. Rebecca didn't blame the girl. If she could have sought shelter in Brandt's arms, she would have done it. Unfortunately, Brandt was busy gathering as much gear as they could salvage. He trusted her to buck up. To be brave. Or at least fake it.

Talli went to grab the chopper's door, but Brandt shook his head. "Grab anything you can."

"But the higher the water gets, the harder it will be to—"

Lopez nodded to the bullet hole-ridden windshield. "Dude, we are not going to create a vacuum in here."

Rebecca nearly lost her balance as the helicopter slid down the muddy riverbed, deeper into the Congo. The water level was over halfway up the windows.

"Got mine," Davidson announced as he threw a fifth bag over his shoulders.

Surprisingly, Brandt didn't have anything on his. Instead, he handed out the equipment to the other men. "All right. Levont you are going out first. Then I will escort Rebecca and Vakasa. Talli—"

"What the hell is—"

Out of nowhere, a mass of flesh with a glistening row of teeth surged in the water, hitting the windshield head-on. The glass cracked, sending a spiderweb of flaws through the windshield.

In the glow of headlights, the giant crocodile shook its head and several front teeth fell out. Clearly, the ancient predator was not used to the concept of glass. However, those dark eyes did not seem deterred in the least. A meal was to be had.

"Watch out!" Lopez yelled as another crocodile, a good four feet longer than the first, slammed into the window next to her. The sliding door rattled violently. Then another slammed into the other side of the helicopter.

Talk about shooting fish in a barrel. Only, they were the fish, and the crocodiles planned to latch onto them and drag them to the bottom and drown them.

Vakasa shook in Rebecca's arms. The girl hadn't flinched at the sight of guns, but crocs? Crocs she was clearly terrified of.

The sliding door buckled as a crocodile rammed it again.

"This bird's taken too much damage," Lopez said.

"And the water we're taking on," Talli added as the river filled the chopper. It was up to their knees now.

Brandt looked to her, grief detailing his features. They would have to make a run for it. And clearly not all would make it. And the chick in the wedding dress and a young girl? Vegas bookies would not be betting on them.

Then the door came off a hinge as the persistent reptile crashed into it again. Rebecca clutched Vakasa to her, throwing them both back as the croc used its wide snout to push open the door and its powerful tail to thrust itself halfway into the chopper.

Mouth wide open, it charged. The only thing that stopped it from grabbing them both was Davidson slamming the door closed on its neck. The croc thrashed against the restraint, hissing its fury.

For a moment, a memory of Rebecca's guide in the Amazon filled her vision. One second, he had been there. The next, a set of teeth had grabbed hold of his shoulder, and her guide was gone. She remembered watching helplessly as the alligator shook Yerato as he pulled him into the murky water.

This croc meant to do the same.

Brandt pulled his gun, but Levont pushed it down. "We can't have blood."

"What the fuck—"

"We only have three to deal with," Levont pleaded. "You get blood in the water, we'll have a hundred."

As if the crocodile were listening, it stopped its thrashing and simply floated at the water level, doing its best to convince them it was only a log. A nice big log that wanted to eat them.

"Stealthy mothers, aren't they?" Lopez observed.

Then the broken-toothed croc slammed into the windshield again. Creating cracks so deep that Rebecca doubted the glass would hold up to another ramming. As the croc repositioned itself for another strike, they were about to find out.

"Any fucking suggestions, then?" Brandt asked Levont.

"We just have to tie its mouth closed."

"Oh, *just* that."

Levont, though, grabbed some rope and quickly made a lasso out of it. "Talli, you are going to have to poke it."

"What?"

Brandt shoved Talli over, snatching a rifle. "Don't worry," Brandt assured Levont. "I'm not going to shoot it."

"Vincent..." Rebecca called out. It must have been bad if she was using his first name.

The other crocodile—you know, the one that was trying to break in through the windshield—slowly paddled just at the edge of the headlights. Keeping himself steady and ready to attack.

Since he couldn't do much about that one, he turned to the croc actually inside the damned helicopter.

"Ready?"

Levont just nodded.

Brandt held the rifle at its butt and shoved it hard right under the croc's eye. He was ready for a lot, but not the explosive power of the predator. The thing had his rifle, crunching it between its jaws, faster than Brandt could blink. The croc spit the mangled gun back at him.

Brandt stumbled back a step, his hands shaking from the assault.

Levont, though, was at the ready, flinging the noose around the croc's snout. The thing shook its head side to side violently, but the point man had a grip of steel. Too bad the rope wasn't as strong as he was.

They all saw the fraying. It must have got snagged by a tooth on the way in.

Hell no.

Brandt reached for his belt, unbuckling it and whipping it loose. As he rethreaded it, the irony that it was croc leather did not escape him. This time prepared for the ferocity, Brandt grabbed the rifle, poking the giant reptile. The croc swiveled impossibly quickly, knocking the gun away. But Brandt was there, slipping his belt around the nose.

Riding the damn thing like a bucking bronco, Brandt wrapped the leather twice around the snout, then secured it with the buckle.

"Davidson!" he shouted to the man on the door. "On my signal!"

The sniper nodded, still leaning his body weight against the metal to keep the croc pinned.

Brandt braced his hands against the croc's shoulder, avoiding the flailing head and surging river water.

"Now!"

Once the door was released, Brandt shoved hard against the nobby skin, pushing the beast back into the river. Davidson wasted no time shutting the door. The last thing Brandt saw of the beast was the croc spinning and thrashing, trying to slip its restraint.

"Vin!"

Brandt turned to find Rebecca pointing at not just a pair of red glowing eyes, but three, no, four sets made it five.

Guess they didn't even need blood in the water to attract the crocs' relatives.

Looks like they had gotten rid of one crocodile, only to invite in a whole group of them.

Fuck didn't even begin to cover it.

Even though Brandt tried to turn her away from the charging crocodile, Rebecca wouldn't let him. It was a sight to behold. Even in the murky water, she could make out the forty-eight teeth capable of delivering up to five thousand pounds per square inch. She could even see the pink of its tongue and upper palate. Many a tribesman and even a pharaoh or two had witnessed this as their last sight.

Brandt nearly crushed her with his embrace as the croc's tail surged side to side, powering the reptile right at the cracked glass.

Then a blur from the right knocked the crocodile from its trajectory. A brownish, blobbish streak had saved them.

"Hippo!" Lopez yelled, swinging his camera around.

"The dolphins of the Congo?" Talli asked, staring out the windshield. "Did it just save us?"

"No, no, no," Rebecca said, shoving Brandt toward the door.

Levont was right with her, sloshing through the now thigh-high water. "Hippos are extremely territorial. They will—"

The helicopter shuddered as it was hit on the side. On the second attack, the chopper didn't just shake, it physically rolled over. Rebecca put her hands out to brace her, slamming into the roof of the chopper. Her fingers fished around for Vakasa, but could barely keep her head from smashing up against the metal.

And the hippopotamus didn't stop. Using his wide head as a battering ram, he rolled the chopper down the steep riverbank until the entire vehicle was underwater. Rotors and all. Metal squealed and glass groaned until the windshield couldn't take any more stress.

Shattering inward, the Congo came to claim them.

Rebecca was thrown backward by the rush of water, stripped from Brandt's hold. Then the door's frame bent, leaving just enough room for Rebecca to get sucked out into the river.

"Rebecca!" Brandt cried, but the water had him plastered against the back hull.

She fought the current to get back inside the chopper, but the hippo hit it again, tumbling it farther down the bank.

Something knocked against her leg.

Log, crocodile, or another hippo were only a few of the possibilities.

The best thing she could do for Brandt was to save herself, giving Brandt the leeway to save himself.

She kicked hard in the direction she prayed was the surface.

Davidson got churned under the rolling helicopter. A twisted rotor knocked him upside the head. Dazed, he drifted to the right just as the chopper flipped again. Its headlights creating a kaleidoscope of light and dark.

He wasn't sure where he was. Heading toward the shore or deeper into the river? Was his head pointing to the surface, or was he just striking for the riverbed? His lungs begged him to gasp. From the pain and for the oxygen. But there was nothing but murky water all around him.

Stay calm, he tried to remind himself. *Let your natural buoyancy guide you.* He'd had plenty of water-survival training. However, none of the courses covered a hippo attack. The water was cut by so many currents even it didn't seem to know which way was up.

Darkness crept into the edge of his vision. The lack of air and blow to the head conspiring to black him out.

Then there was orange. Bright, playful orange.

A small hand reached out to him.

Davidson took it.

The girl struck upward and to the left. Davidson didn't hesitate to follow her course. He was running out of oxygen, though. Like, aneurysm out. Then they broke the surface. Davidson gulped the precious moist air as his limbs tried to right his course.

"*Kusimama*," the girl urged.

Levont had been right. Davidson's African dialects could use some work.

"*Kusimama*," Vakasa repeated, jerking on his arm.

Her actions were bringing him nearly vertical. And then he felt it. The riverbed. Feeling incredibly stupid, Davidson planted his feet and stood up. He was only knee high in the water.

Yep, he'd nearly drowned in kiddie pool-deep water. Still, they were way too deep to feel safe from the crocs or the hippo.

Grabbing the girl's hand, he splashed his way to the bank. Talli, Lopez, and Levont repeated the process up and down the bank. Once on dry land, Davidson spun around, trying to find the others.

Rebecca's head popped up, water spraying from her mouth. She was alive.

However, she was not alone. And that figure next to her in the water *wasn't* Brandt.

Above the ringing in her ears, Rebecca couldn't make out what Davidson was screaming. Then, out of the corner of her eye, she spotted the large "log" floating not ten feet from her. Funny, though, logs usually didn't blink.

She stopped struggling in the water. She let the river buoy her. The log didn't seem fooled, however. Not as it drifted *against* the current. Rebecca's eyes slid toward the shore. There was no way she could outrun the croc. No way. And how they were situated in the river, the men had no shot. Besides, if Levont was right about crocodilian anatomy, it wouldn't matter, anyway.

Maybe if she didn't move, the log wouldn't move.

Yeah. Right.

She noted a glint of silver caught in one of the log's teeth. The remains of Brandt's belt buckle. If the croc had gotten out of that, he certainly wasn't going to let an easy meal escape his grasp twice.

There was only a ripple in the water to warn her he was coming. Rebecca threw herself back, knowing it was useless, but her body insisted.

Teeth surged from beneath the surface, shining brightly in the moonlight.

Then Brandt was there, leaping from the side. He landed atop the croc's jaws, wrestling them closed.

"I've got him!" Brandt yelled. But Rebecca wasn't so sure about that as the crocodile rolled, taking Brandt with him. Once they popped back up, Brandt shouted, "Go!"

God, she didn't want to, but given the other ripples in the water, if she didn't get herself to shore, Brandt would have two of them to worry about. And if anything, Brandt seemed to be winning.

Until the crocodile surged up on its back feet, which were once used to walk upright eons ago. Brandt dangled from the croc's jaw, holding on for dear life. It wouldn't be enough, though, as the reptile, so adapt at surviving, tipped backward, crashing them into much deeper water.

"Come on!" Davidson yelled from the shore.

Never taking her eyes off the spot where Brandt had disappeared, she made her way up the bank. The churning water quieted to smooth as glass. As if Brandt had never existed.

This was a fucking losing battle. The croc had the upper hand. Brandt was no reptile expert, but he did know the fucker could hold its breath for like two hours. And the death roll? Even on the outside of it, Brandt was getting knocked the fuck around. He simply couldn't gut it out. The croc would win.

And that was simply unacceptable.

Even with Levont's warning ringing in his ears, Brandt pulled a knife from its sheath on his calf. Now, where the hell did the point man say to hit?

The ear. Straight in the croc's ear to hit the golf ball-sized brain.

Except, um, where the fuck was the crocodile's ear?

Still gripping the beast's jaw shut with one arm, Brandt arced the blade up and stabbed where an ear ought to be. Lukewarm blood squirted out of the wound. But the fucker kept rolling. Brandt brought the knife up again, and this time sunk it into the hilt. The croc's body spasmed, convulsing.

Not taking any fucking chances, Brandt ground the blade, twisting it on its axis. Take that, golf ball.

The croc's head arced back. Its eyes rolling like a china doll's. Not until its body went slack, totally slack, did Brandt tentatively let go. No opened jaws. No attack. The fucker was dead.

But blood spread all around him. There would be more. Like, quickly.

Pushing off the croc's body, Brandt struck for the sky, knife still in hand. He surged out of the water, shaking his head, trying to get his bearings. The shore wasn't that far off. It was doable. He could make it there before the rest of the croc brigade showed up.

Then why exactly were the men waving their arms, screaming?

"Hippo!"

Of course there was a fucking hippo behind him.

Brandt let his adrenaline do the work. Running to meet him, the men fired at the three-ton hippopotamus, but the thing had a hard-on for Brandt. Slipping in the mud, Brandt scrambled up the bank. He grabbed a vine and hauled himself up the slope, swearing that he could hear the jiggle of the hippo's fat.

The loud sound of splashing told Brandt he was running out of time. Grasping another branch, he lurched upward, every muscle fiber complaining of the abuse. He chanced a glance back. The fucker was fast. How the fuck could something so fat move so fucking fast?

And now that it was on land, it was smoking.

"Stop!" Levont yelled. "Stop running."

That was the stupidest damned advice Brandt had ever been given.

Then Rebecca chimed in. "They are only territorial in the water!"

Did he trust Encyclopedia and Brittanica over there or his own gut?

Given the fact that his legs were giving out, he came to a stop. The hippo's charge stalled, but its jaw was still wide open. Brandt could smell its retched breath. He could make out the grooves in those ivory teeth that could crush his spine.

The thing took a few more steps forward, then closed its mouth, its wide nose sniffing the wind. Then, as if it had nothing better to do, started grazing on the grass.

What the hell?

"Just slowly back away," Rebecca advised. "As long as you aren't making fast movements, it doesn't care about you on land."

Easy to say when you were forty feet away.

He was a little limited on options, though, so he did as instructed.

The first step felt like a leap of faith. The second felt more like a prayer. The third was actually almost normal.

But it wasn't far enough. Not when another crocodile flew out of the water, aiming right for Brandt.

A spear came out of nowhere, skewering the crocodile in the vulnerable underbelly. Just as quickly, the dark-skinned medicine man shoved the crocodile back into the river. Its body, grabbed by its breathren, pulled underwater.

The hippo gave a glance over its shoulder, blinked twice, then went back to grazing. Just another day in Africa.

Brandt stepped back carefully, making for the tree line as quickly as he could without angering the hippo. He wanted to make it into the jungle, but his adrenaline high gave out like a balloon let free. Stumbling a few steps, his butt hit the ground.

Rebecca rushed to his side as the men fanned out, keeping a close eye on the grazing hippo.

"Are you okay?"

"Honestly," Brandt asked as he lay back onto the cool ground, "hell if I know."

Rebecca ripped open Brandt's bloody shirt. So far, the red stains had been from other creatures' blood. Not Brandt's. He had a lump on the side of his head the size of a goose egg. A literal Canadian goose-sized egg. He had bruises up and down his side, but she could see the color coming back into his lips as he breathed in and out.

The hippo, apparently not liking this much company for its foraging, slipped back into the water. Once submerged, the Congo looked as peaceful as a church. Forget the fourteen ways you could die in an instant. And they had weapons. And training. Rebecca tucked Vakasa tight under her arm. This jungle was no place for a little girl.

"Thor," Vakasa said, patting her forehead, then bowing deeply.

Brandt smiled weakly. "Hey, kid." He glanced around. "Where's the medicine man?"

"He disappeared back into the forest," Rebecca answered, glad that Brandt seemed well oriented.

He smiled again. "He has a habit of doing that."

She smoothed his sopping-wet hair down and kissed his forehead. "Yes, he does."

“Everyone else okay?” Brandt asked, although his eyelids had slid back down.

“Yeah, babe,” Rebecca answered. “We’re knocked around, but good.”

Brandt smiled faintly.

“I mean, I don’t mean to be the downer here,” Talli said as the consummate downer, “but some of the Disciples must have survived on the other side. They aren’t going to wait around forever.”

Levont grunted his approval. “Do we have an evac plan?”

No one answered as the crickets sang their little hearts out.

“But hey, on the bright side,” Lopez said, raising his camera, “I got it all on film!”

CHAPTER 11

PENTAGON

7:22 P.M. (EST)

"The hack is on the inside," the tech announced. Finally. "I mean, I hate to admit it, but Bunny is right."

Bunny knew she was right. It was the only thing that made sense. "Thanks... Tech."

"Stark," the kid corrected. "And not Tony."

She snorted. "Of course not. I can only assume you take after the *Farscape* character. Season one. Episode nineteen."

The kid's eyes dilated. Oh, he definitely batted for her team, and after that sci-fi geekery? Batted for *her*.

Emily didn't seem nearly as impressed, as she asked, "Which means the Disciples probably know that *we* know the hack is within the Pentagon's servers?"

The tech just nodded, pulling his fingers back from his keyboard as if the keys had suddenly become distasteful.

"So even if we were able to get another satellite in position, we would be letting the Disciples know exactly where Brandt and the rest were?" Prenner asked.

"*Exactly* where they were, yes," Stark answered.

"Okay, then," Bunny said. "Plan B."

"Huh?" the tech said as only a teenager could. "Maybe you don't get it. We are effectively neutered. Anything I do, the Disciples know."

Bunny grabbed her purse. "Exactly. Which is why we need to get out of here."

She turned on her heel-less shoe and walked out of the *supposedly* most secure place in the world. For all their shiny toys and high-tech gear, they could be breached just as easily as Troy had been by a wooden horse. No wonder Brandt went off the book so frequently.

"Wait," Prenner called out, trotting to catch up with her, "where do you think we are going?"

"To go on a little shopping spree."

Prenner stepped in front of her, blocking her exit. "Not without a little more explanation."

Bunny studied the lieutenant's features. He was handsome if you liked that chiseled-jaw "I was a star quarterback" kind of look. Which Bunny didn't. His arrogant bluster had mellowed, though, into a more subtle "I hate losing power" kind of vibe.

"How many years have you spent under the radar?" she asked him. "One? Two years?"

Prenner's lips formed a hard line.

"I spent two and a half with Coti and another six months in Russia. I know a thing or two about laying low but getting the job done."

Emily caught up with them. "That she does."

Stark, who had his arms full of equipment, ran up, panting.

Bunny shook her head. "You gotta let it go, dude."

"But—"

"Anything that has even seen this building has got to go."

Both Emily and Prenner nodded.

With tears at the edge of his eyelashes, Stark laid the components on a desk. "Good-bye, Lady Bug." He patted his customized mouse good-bye.

And people thought she loved her Prada a bit too much.

"Where are we going?" Emily asked, with her trusty phone at the ready.

"You'll see," Bunny said as she walked through the pressurized doors. The fewer people who knew what she was up to, the better.

Frellan favored his left ankle. A bit of shrapnel had dug its way next to the bone. Ugudo, perhaps relishing the chance, had been none too gentle in removing it. To think the girl had been just a short river crossing away. But he had seen the crocodile attacks. He had seen what happened to anyone foolhardy enough to enter the Congo River, especially at night.

And given that what remained of his team was bloodied to their core, getting in that water was not an option. The only exception to their injured list was, of course, Mikhal. Besides his blond hair being a bit singed at the tips, the man looked like he had just walked out of their beloved sanctuary.

There were rumors Mikhal was kissed by God's graces. Frellan was unfortunately starting to believe such gossip.

The burning village came into view as they reached the rutted, muddy road. Their transportation should be here within three hours. They could begin the hunt again. As they approached the huts, Frellan made out a lone figure standing vigil.

Monnie.

The watcher must have observed their descent toward the village, as she ran to meet them. Her eyes scanned the men, finding no Messiah with them.

"Where is She?" Monnie asked, her tone tinged with recrimination.

Frellan moved his hand, and she flinched. Clearly, she did not know him well enough. A slap would be juvenile. No, what he planned for her took far more maturity and especially patience.

Instead, he took her hand, stroking the smooth skin. Such smooth skin. "She is just a river's width away." Imagining how easy it would be to drill through the finger joint. Her hand trembled in his. Tears streaking down her face. Monnie must have heard the rumors about him then. Frellan followed a vein as it crossed over the bone. "We shall retrieve her in the morning."

Monnie snatched back her hand. "There is something you might want to see."

Wiping away her tears, Monnie turned and headed toward the heart of the village, which was nothing much more than a gathering of burned-out shacks.

She ducked into one of the few structures still partially intact. The rough mud walls sloped inward due to the heat of the fire. Monnie pointed to the far wall. At first, Frellan did not understand why. It looked just like the other walls. Pocked and flawed by the villagers' crude construction methods. Walls of mud.

"Look more closely," Monnie suggested, then took a quick step backward as he swung his frown toward her. She best learn not to order him about.

Taking another step forward, Frellan realized there were tiny writings etched into the mottled surface. Some were scrawled in Aramaic. Some in French. Other letters were of Congolese origin. The sliding mud had mixed it all together until it was jibberish. He reached out a finger and traced the garbled words.

These were the first documented writings of their Messiah.

He looked back at Monnie. She dared not give voice to it, but he could hear her thoughts as clearly in his head as if she had spoken them.

And you have destroyed them.

Frellan would pay a price for such an act. But not yet. Not before he delivered the Messiah to the Master.

"Block the camera, would you?" Bunny asked Prenner. The man obliged by sliding in front of the ATM, his back to the lens.

Bunny pulled out a bank card and pushed it into the slot. She rapidly cycled through the prompts to get cash.

"They can easily trace that, you know," Prenner said while scanning the street.

"Back to Tori Rinklehouse?" Bunny countered. "I say go for it."

She could feel Prenner study her face. That was fine by her. Let him figure out she wasn't some bubblegum-popping sorority girl. Well, at least not anymore. The last few years had changed her. And in moments like this, it felt like for the better.

Bunny accepted the five hundred dollars the ATM spit out. She got out another card and repeated the process. Then again.

Prenner frowned. "That's a lot of stashed cash."

"Let's just say I made a few 'specialty films' back in college."

The lieutenant's eyebrow went up. Wouldn't he like to know the exact nature of those. But alas, that was a story for another time.

Grabbing the last of the cash, Bunny turned toward the car. Well, not actually a car, but a beat-up Gremlin. While there was no way to electronically follow that old of a car, it did kind of stand out in a crowd. Kind of like how Stark wanted it to. Thumbing his nose at the man, the whole while desperately wanting the man to notice him.

An older model, neutral-colored Toyota pulled up to the curb. Emily. Now, this was a car that could blend in with traffic. And all without a backfire every quarter of a mile.

"Oh man," Stark pouted.

Avoiding the ATM's camera range, they climbed into the Toyota.

Emily turned to Bunny. "Where to?"

"Make a right, then two blocks later a left."

Within moments, they arrived at the rather sketchy-looking "used" electronics store. Every town had one. And DC? They were usually next to the bail bonds offices. The best part about them? While they had cameras and signs posted that they had video surveillance, they didn't record a single second. Their patronage was not hot on being caught on camera.

Which was fine by Bunny. Her foursome exited the car and entered the store.

"I can't use any of this," Stark said with a sneer, not touching any of the merchandise, it appeared, for fear of catching a virus.

Bunny ignored him and walked up to the unshaven clerk at the desk. "I am sure they have something a little more your speed."

The clerk picked something from his teeth. "No idea what you and the suits want, but you won't find it here."

"We don't want any trouble," Bunny said as she pulled a wad of one-hundred-dollar bills out. "We just need a few toys."

The clerk looked to Prenner, then Emily, then Bunny.

"Come on, any arrest would be entrapment at this point," Bunny encouraged.

Finally, the guy looked down at the cash. *Gotcha.*

He took out a huge ring of keys and unlocked a door behind him to reveal a room filled with gutted high-end electronics. "We've got just about everything, but you've got to rebuild it yourself."

Stark stared at the glut of electronica, his jaw slack. "There is a God." The tech was so easy to please.

She turned her attention back to the clerk. "I am going to need some disposable phones."

"How many?"

"Twenty should do."

"*Twenty*?"

Bunny nodded. "With international minutes, please."

As the clerk moved off, Prenner asked, "And what are you going to do with those?"

She looked to Emily. "Are the rumors true?"

Emily just gave that sly smile of hers.

Bunny turned back to Prenner. "It looks like I'm going to call a friend."

Brandt had stopped counting the injuries as he leaned heavily against a moss-laden tree. They were hiking north, striking for the border of the *other* Congo nation. More than likely, the

Disciples had paid off this republic's government generously. Another country all together? They could hope not.

The going was slow, though. Everyone was banged up, and adrenaline only got you so far.

A buzzing stopped the group in their tracks.

"What the hell was that?" Lopez asked, looking around to the group.

"What the hell is right," Brandt rumbled. All electronics should have had their batteries pulled. For Christ's sake, they were using a compass to guide them. Nobody better have a cell phone on them.

Davidson pulled his pack off his shoulder. "It is the sat phone."

Brandt counted to ten. Seriously, on a mission of this sensitivity, the kid didn't remember to pull the fucking battery out of their sat phone?

"I gutted it, I swear," Davidson said as he pulled the phone out. And sure enough, the battery backing was off and the battery was out. Still, somehow the phone was still vibrating in the sniper's hand.

"Look," Talli said. "There's a screw."

Davidson had the thing out within seconds. And there it was. A tiny crystal set into the body of the phone.

"Damn, is that what I think it is?" Lopez asked.

Levont nodded. "A photonic crystalline battery, yep." The point man turned to Brandt. "Command really does love you guys. Those things are supposedly just theoretical."

Yet there it was, powering the most basic of the phone's functions.

"Would have been nice for them to tell us," Brandt grumbled as he pushed off the tree.

"What should we do?" Davidson asked.

"I guess put the damned full battery back in and find out who is calling."

Davidson obliged and read the caller ID. "Looks like a burner phone."

"Might as well take it," Brandt ordered.

"Hello?" Davidson asked, then frowned as he pulled the phone from his ear to speak to the group. "It's Bunny."

"Bunny?" Rebecca repeated, sounding as surprised as the rest of the group. She then said, "Sorry, just really? Bunny on the secret sat phone?" Louder, she added, "No offense, Bunny."

Davidson held out the phone. Brandt reached to take it, but the sniper shook his head. "No, she wanted to talk to Rebecca."

"Me?" Rebecca repeated. Ugh, she hated it when she sounded like a parrot. But why in the world, with the seven of them stuck out in the jungle, would Bunny want to talk to her?

Still, she accepted the phone from Davidson. "Hi?"

"Is it *her*?" the tinny, statical voice asked.

"Her who?" Rebecca asked back. Was it just she was so damned tired, or was none of this making sense? It didn't help that all the men were staring at her.

There was a delay. Had they lost the connection?

Then Bunny's scratchy voice asked, "You know…the daughter. The one Moses was so worried about."

Rebecca's brain shifted focus, away from the rain forest and back to the caves under the Dead Sea. The tablets that contained the Ten Commandments held so much more than references to civil behavior. Including a reference to a female Messiah.

Now she understood why Bunny was being so cagey. She must have people on the other side listening in, just as Rebecca had her own audience. Bunny and she had resolved to never tell anyone of those passages.

Still, Rebecca was clueless. "I have no idea."

"Have you even asked her?" Bunny demanded.

"Asked who?" Rebecca answered, the exasperation of the last two days coming out in her tone.

"The girl with you," Bunny implored.

Wait. What? Rebecca nearly dropped the phone. She sought out Vakasa, who was snuggled up against Brandt's leg. Bunny couldn't possibly be suggesting…

No.

That couldn't be.

"Rebecca?" Bunny asked, sounding farther away than the seven thousand miles that separated them.

"Yeah," she answered absently. The majority of her brain was working on the fact that Vakasa could be…well, the Messiah foretold all those millennia ago.

"Think about it," Bunny rushed on. "Why else would the Disciples be hot on your heels?"

Vakasa being God's daughter certainly did resolve several questions. However, it brought up like a million. Rebecca couldn't even look Brandt in the eye as she talked.

"I will have to get back to you on that," Rebecca said.

"Can I?" Brandt asked, holding his hand out for the phone.

Bunny listened as Rebecca and Brandt exchanged words. She couldn't tell what they were, but it was pretty damned clear Brandt was none too happy. So Bunny wasn't surprised when the sergeant's voice came over the line.

"I don't know what is going on, which makes me just a little grumpy."

Just a little?

"We are trying to determine the Disciples' angle here."

"And?" Brandt demanded.

Bunny walked a few steps down the trash-strewn alley, away from Prenner and Emily. "Our theories are…evolving."

"Look, if I wanted that evasive crap, I would talk to the CIA." Brandt was definitely grumpy. "I want answers. *Now*."

Perhaps he couldn't boss his fiancée around, but that didn't mean he could shove Bunny any harder. She also knew the sergeant, though. He wouldn't let go of one bone unless you gave him another.

"How about I know where you need to go next?"

A pause told her Brandt's pit bull–like jaws were trying to decide if he liked this new bone well enough to let go of the other.

"And are you going to tell me, or do I have to figure out the Sphinx riddle."

Bunny chuckled. "Funny you should say that. It is looking like you need to head to Egypt."

Brandt exclaimed something. If Bunny was a betting woman, she could guess it was his favorite four-letter expletive.

"Yeah, well, we will be there in…I don't know…five and a half years at this rate."

Bunny noticed Emily snap her phone closed. Holding her hand over the mouthpiece, Bunny asked, "ETA?"

"If they head due north the choppers should be there in under two hours."

"Brandt?" Bunny said into the phone. "Continue on your current course. Turn your phone back on in two hours, and your evac should be there."

Silence greeted her. She would have worried the call dropped, except she could hear insects buzzing in the background.

"Bunny?" Davidson asked.

Her heart soared. She hadn't let herself doubt for a moment that the sniper had come through the ordeal alive.

"Yep," she said through tears.

"Sounds like we owe you a great big thank-you."

Wiping a single drop streaking down her cheek, Bunny answered, "You can deliver it when you get home."

Davidson's voice was about five times huskier than normal. "You know it."

The phone beeped, signaling her money was about to run out. Shocking how fast you could burn through a hundred bucks calling the Congo.

"Gotta go," she said. Bunny would never know what he said back, as that annoying "You have been disconnected" beep sounded in her ear. She closed the phone, stepped on it with her heel, then dropped the plastic carcass into the dumpster.

"Are you going to share why you are sending them to Egypt?" Prenner asked.

Putting a knuckle to the corner of her eye to draw away the tears before her makeup was totally ruined, Bunny shrugged. "I'd prefer not to."

By the look on both Prenner and Emily's faces, that wasn't going to fly.

"Fine," Bunny conceded. "But we are going to need some coffee first."

No one disagreed there as they made their way back to the Toyota.

Which was good, because what she had to share, no one was going to like.

CHAPTER 12

SKIES OVER AFRICA

8:29 P.M. (CAT)

Rebecca's head lolled to the side, rousing her. She cracked open her eyes, taking in the luxury jet. Their fourth plane since hopping the British aid helicopter back in the Congo.

Looking out the plane's window over the dark desert, it was hard to imagine the press of the jungle. Not that Rebecca was trying very hard, of course.

Oranges sparked along the horizon. The sun must be setting. Which meant she had slept far longer than the three hours she had allotted herself. Nestled in the crook of Brandt's arm, she would not be complaining any time soon. Under his other arm was Vakasa.

A little girl who held such big secrets. Or was she just a child like any other? The Disciples were on a hair trigger after the destruction of the tablets. Had they jumped to conclusions? Or was Rebecca looking at the Messiah? Even asking a question such as that sounded absurd. And to have to explain it to Brandt? That seemed downright impossible.

Vakasa rubbed her eyes, looking around.

"Where are we?" Rebecca asked for the girl.

Brandt moved, stretching his arm. Rebecca was loath to leave his embrace, but she lifted her head up to give him room to work out the kinks.

"Chad? Sudan? Libya?" Brandt answered. "I can't remember what Levont said."

Levont? Rebecca was surprised to find Lopez crashed in the overstuffed chair across from them. The corporal must have been truly exhausted if he let someone else fly the plane. Must have been all that filming.

Davidson stood up from the other side of the couch and leaned to the right, then left. "O for three," he said, indicating the eastern window. "Check it out."

Rebecca was confused, until she noticed a glistening ribbon of blue flanked by a greenbelt in the distance. The Nile. They were already in Egypt.

"Levont is giving Lopez a run for his money."

"I heard that," Lopez said, unfurrowing himself from the pretzel-like position.

"Yet it is strangely so much easier to sleep with Levont at the helm," Davidson teased the corporal. "Far less structural shaking."

Rebecca knew Lopez would never take that lying down. He hopped to his feet, yawning. "Easier to do when you aren't being shot at."

So true. To imagine they had made it an entire flight without an RPG strike? They truly had hit the jackpot. Rebecca noticed that no one said a thing, though. For how brave the men were, they were pretty damned superstitious. No one was about to jinx their luck.

As Davidson and Lopez stretched, Brandt leaned in close.

His presence was intoxicating. His words were not.

“Are we going to talk about it?”

Before she had to answer, Davidson turned around. Either he hadn’t heard Brandt’s question or was coming to her rescue. “Like the selection?”

Rebecca found a pair of jeans and a black T-shirt on the seat next to her. She picked up the items and brought them to her nose. Clothes. Real, actual clothes. No more torn and stained wedding dress.

“Not sure if they are the right size,” Davidson added. “Found them in a closet in the back…You gotta love private jets.”

Yes, Rebecca loved them, all right.

“They have even got a shower back there.”

“Do *not* be teasing me about that,” Rebecca stated.

Davidson laughed. “Dead serious. Hot water and everything.”

Rebecca felt herself almost melt at the thought.

Grabbing the clothes, Rebecca rose.

“Don’t take too long,” Davidson added. “We should be landing in forty minutes.”

Lopez scoffed as he headed to the cockpit. “Make it thirty-six minutes.”

Rebecca would take anything at this point. As she headed toward the back, Brandt caught her hand.

“I’ve been exceedingly patient.”

And that he had been.

“Then can I beg you for another thirty-six minutes?” she asked.

The corner of his lip twitched up. “How about thirty-one minutes and you give me five minutes to get cleaned up?”

"You got it."

He released her hand, sliding their palms against one another. If there wasn't a little girl in the room, she might have suggested they share that shower, but there was a little girl in the room. One who might be…

No. Rebecca wasn't going to think about that. She was going to enjoy possibly the most decadent shower in her life.

Then she would have to explain to Brandt…well, everything. And she'd thought the information she had learned in that Roman cave last year was bad.

The gold cross around Brandt's neck caught the light and glistened.

Could his faith survive the news she carried?

Sighing, Rebecca continued toward the shower. That was a question for thirty-six minutes from now.

Bunny rubbed her eyes. She could only look at the computer screen for so long. How Stark did his bug-eyed stare for hours upon hours was beyond her. The activity of the all-night Internet café had settled down, but not died. It was pretty amazing how many people wanted an anonymous Internet connection at midnight.

Emily walked up to their table. "My sources confirm Bunny's calculations."

She looked over to Prenner and gave the lieutenant her best "I told you so" look. Because, well, she had told him so.

"I still don't understand how you went from a few runes in Iceland to deducing the one man in all the world Brandt and the others need to talk to is living in Cairo," Prenner grumbled.

Probably because you don't think a civilian, a chick, might know something you don't. But Bunny took in a big breath. She had held off explaining the entire thing until they had confirmation from Emily that she was on the right track. And given that it had been super early in the morning over in Egypt, that confirmation was a while in coming.

Bunny brought up several pictures that Rebecca and she had taken in Iceland. *Crap, had it only been four days ago?* Bunny could have sworn that little adventure was four months ago.

Ah, sleep deprivation. How it skewed your perceptions.

She pointed to a row of symbols. "The Vikings were all about their runes. And documenting their conquests." Bunny flipped through the pictures. "This set recounts their arrival on Iceland and beginning a settlement there."

"Not exactly earth-shattering information," Prenner interjected.

"Perhaps," Bunny said, then scrolled down to the last picture. "Except, they happen to mention the Disciples and thank them for all their help."

"What?" Prenner said, now glaring at the symbols like he could read them.

"Bunny," Emily chided, "they don't exactly talk about the Disciples."

"They might as well," Bunny defended, then translated the runes from Old Norse to English. "*We hailed from the east. We conquered sea and beast to find our home. But we could not have done so without the help of those that do not wish to walk the halls of Vallahalla. Those of one God. Those of Moshe hold great secrets. Oden has blessed us with their companionship. To might. For might. Forever.*"

Bunny looked up. "Tell me that isn't about the Disciples."

"And the Egyptian connection?" Prenner asked, still looking a bit skeptical.

Bunny flipped through several pages on the laptop that Stark had jury-rigged for her. Wires poked out from the frame, and she had gotten more than one shock from using the trackpad, but hey, it was untraceable.

"Rebecca and I were not the only ones making the Viking connection," Bunny explained. "As a matter of fact, we followed this article—*The Found Tribe of Dann: Did the Scales of Justice Migrate as Far as Newfoundland?*"

From the blank look on both of their faces, Bunny was pretty sure neither Prenner nor Emily was well schooled in ancient Jewish studies.

"Dann is one of the 'lost tribes.' As a matter of fact, it was the northernmost tribe of Israel until they got booted out of the Holy Land by the Canaanites." Off of their blank expressions, Bunny asked, "Ring a bell?"

"Vaguely," Emily answered.

Great. They wanted quick answers, but it was going to take Bunny a semester to get them up to speed.

Prenner leaned back in his chair. "I think we get the whole lost tribe thing. Those Jewish tribes disappeared from the historical record after the Canaanites invaded. But why the focus on the Dann tribe? Isn't it as lost as the others?"

"All right, this is a bit more obscure but all the more important for it," Bunny said as she brought up the passage Rebecca had found. "The legions of Dann…" Bunny stopped to explain. "Dann was the second-largest tribe." She restarted. "The legions of Dann will leap from *Bashan* to become those prophesized."

Bunny looked up. "So you can see why we were so interested."

"No," Prenner said with a chuckle. Maybe the guy *was* human. "Not at all."

"Bashan is to the *east*," Bunny emphasized. Still, they didn't seem to get it. And people called *her* an airhead. She brought up a map of ancient Israel. "The Danns settled to the far north. That passage makes absolutely no sense. The Danns had never been granted or settled land to the east. And not a single scholar knows why the passage clearly says they would come from the east."

"Okay…" Emily said. "I am sure that just gets religious scholars' panties in a bunch. However, I am with Prenner in that I still don't *care*."

"Well, Nyura Massari would certainly disagree," Bunny said as she brought up the Viking article again. "He has brought together a huge amount of research on the Jewish tribes and where their genetic markers have spread across the globe. He has spent his whole life trying to track down the Dann tribe."

"I am sure Rebecca is fascinated by this stuff—"

Bunny cut off Emily. "It is more than academic minutia. You really don't see it?"

The woman cocked her head, squinting her eyes. The CIA operative clearly did not like being behind the curve. You could see her mind trying to unwind the mystery. Finally, Bunny put her out of her misery and pointed to the author of the article's name.

"Massari? It means 'Egyptian' in Arabic," Bunny explained. "It is the equivalent of saying you are Mr. Smith."

"So he is using a false last name?" Prenner clarified.

"Oh yeah," Bunny said as she brought up the letters and shuffled them. "But when you shake them just a bit, you get… Saramias."

Emily sucked in a breath and stepped back from the laptop.

"What?" Prenner said. "What am I missing?"

Bunny smiled, then looked to Emily. "Should I tell him, or will you?"

Emily just waved her off as she opened her phone and walked toward the corner of the café.

Bunny turned her attention to the lieutenant. "Saramias is Aunush's last name. I believe the author of that article is Aunush's father—apparently the only person to ever get away from the Disciples. Of course, until *us*."

Stark looked over his shoulder. "Why do you think he isn't *with* the Disciples?"

"You do not publish work on the genetics of ancient Jewish genes showing up in current populations if you are with the Disciples."

"Why not?" he asked.

Bunny sat down, pointing at the screen. "He is obviously trolling for their new Messiah. He is scientifically trying to find..." Bunny had to stop herself before she blurted out one of the most tightly held secrets in the world. "He is trying to find an individual of high value to them."

"But why publish if he is in hiding?"

Rebecca and she had asked the same question before heading to Iceland. "I don't think Saramias can travel freely, so he has been publishing to try and induce others to follow up on his research. We call it 'leapfrogging.' You take someone's conclusions and go out and prove or disprove them, moving the research forward."

"So you are sending Brandt to Egypt to interrogate this Mr. Saramias regarding the Disciples' interest in the African girl?" the lieutenant clarified.

"I gotta give it to you, Prenner," Bunny said, glad that he hadn't asked why the girl was such a priority for them, "you do catch on quickly.

Brandt tried to dry off. Except, that meant he had to apply pressure to his bruised and scraped skin. The deep purple of his most recent shoulder scar stood out against his skin. His finger followed an older, lighter scar that ran ragged along his side and down his groin. He looked like a patchwork doll, sewn by someone not all that skilled with a needle. Brandt knew he was lucky. Damned lucky.

The shower had proved a great wake-up, though. Now to get some thick, Egyptian coffee, basically a hit of straight-up caffeine, and he might actually be ready for the day.

As he dressed, the only sign that the plane had landed was the slightest rattle of the gilded faucet. These luxury jets certainly were worth every penny. Now, if he could only convince Command to put a couple hundred million into one for his team, he'd be a happy man.

Pulling on a bulletproof vest over his shirt, Brandt walked out into the plane's "great room." A crystal chandelier hung in the center of the "room." Gold-veined mirrors lined the "walls." A huge sectional couch wrapped around in a U, creating a conversation "circle."

Like he said. *Luxury*.

Last night, when they'd boarded, all Brandt had cared about was the fact that the plane was dry and had no wildlife. Now, though? The place was insane. Like they'd walked into an oil billionaire's mansion.

Rebecca turned, unconsciously smoothing back her hair. She hated those strands that framed her face when they got all wavy and unruly. She called them her "little seditious streaks." Brandt, though, liked the way they went their own way. Smiling, Rebecca walked toward him.

So you know what? Strike that whole two-hundred-million-dollar luxury plane. He was already a happy man.

Vakasa spotted him and jumped off the stool that was cozied up to the old-fashioned ice cream parlor counter, on a *plane*. That was the super rich. Gilded mirrors and strawberry malts. As a matter of fact, Vakasa's lips were rimmed in bright pink from her shake.

It had killed him to leave the little girl back in Africa. Even with a medicine man who swore to protect her. But Brandt hadn't even bothered to ask the brass to extract her from the Congo. He knew the policy regarding noncombatant civilians, even orphans. They just couldn't take home every kid. Besides, if he had asked, then Command had declined, someone might have asked what the hell they were doing that day and a half it took to stash her deep in the jungle.

Now, though? Now that the Disciples were interested in her? Now she got her own luxury jet, at least for the next little while.

Vakasa ran to him, arms up, so when she was close enough, despite all his injuries, Brandt swooped her up in his arms and spun her so fast that her feet flew out behind her. She giggled as only a child could. All the horror she must have witnessed erased, at least for a moment, by a good spin.

Unfortunately, his body could remember all too well the abuse he'd put it through. Not that he would admit it to anyone, but he'd gotten a tad dizzy. Easing into a stop, Brandt propped Vakasa up onto a hip. The girl's arms draped around his neck as she leaned her cheek against his chest.

"Thor…" she sighed.

Rebecca's eyebrow went up.

Brandt patted his sidearm. "Lopez told her my gun's name was Thor's Hammer."

"Ah," Rebecca said. She headed over. "So anyone wielding his hammer must be Thor."

"Apparently," Brandt responded, soaking in this moment of quiet. Soon, too soon, they would be out again, outwitting and most likely outrunning the Disciples.

"Want one, Boss?" Davidson asked, holding up a stainless steel cup, pouring a spoonful of malt powder into a vanilla shake.

"No, thanks," he answered. He was about to ask where the rest of the men were when they strolled from the forward compartment.

Lopez held up his hand. "My fault we are one minute and twelve seconds behind schedule, Sarge. We'll make it up, I promise."

Of that, Brandt had no question. "A low-profile car, Lopez. *Low. Profile.*"

The corporal was tasked with getting them a car. Unfortunately, his taste in automobiles ran nearly as rich as his taste in aircraft.

"This is Egypt. I get it," Lopez stated, waving him off as he headed toward the hatch.

Talli and Levont followed behind. They had their own shopping list.

"Sarge…" Davidson asked with a frown.

Normally, the private was their procurement guy, but his blond hair and blue eyes were not going to charm the Egyptian merchants. Especially with all those scars. His most recent round of surgeries had helped tremendously. However, in Egypt, his flawed Midwestern good looks were going to rouse suspicion. In this part of the world, Talli and Levont blended in perfectly. Even Lopez's darker complexion helped.

As the other men left and closed the hatch, Brandt looked to Davidson. "Sorry. You are going to have to sit this one out."

The private frowned but didn't complain. Rebecca, on the other hand, suddenly got very busy straightening the couch's elaborate cushions.

"Davidson, could you give us the room for a few minutes?" he asked.

At first, the sniper stiffened, probably thinking Brandt asked him to leave as a reprimand. Then the kid looked to Rebecca, who looked abundantly guilty. After seeing that look, Davidson couldn't get out of the room fast enough.

"Absolutely," he said, coming over and taking Vakasa out of Brandt's arms. "Let's get you cleaned up, kiddo."

Brandt locked eyes with Rebecca as Davidson left the room.

"Time's up," Brandt said. "I need the truth. *Now*."

Rebecca had been dreading this moment. She hated hurting Brandt's feelings. She could still remember the pain in his eyes when they thought they were hunting after Christ's bones. She still hadn't shared with him what she'd found in that Roman cave.

Here, though? She couldn't hide what she knew any longer.

"Sit down," she urged.

Brandt tilted his head to the side. The gesture he did when he wasn't quite sure where she was going with a conversation.

"Trust me," she said. "You are going to want to be sitting when you hear this."

With a sigh, Brandt crossed to the couch and sat down. Rebecca joined him.

"Now, take a deep breath."

"Rebecca..."

She put a hand on his knee. "Seriously, Vincent. Take a deep breath."

Brandt's eyes scanned her face. He should know she didn't ask for any of this lightly. Finally, he closed his eyes and took in a deep breath, only flinching in pain at the end. Then he opened his eyes. "Any other delay tactics you would like to try?"

Rebecca wished they were just delay tactics. She needed to be sure Brandt didn't blow a blood clot when he heard what she had to say.

"As you know, the tablets that contained the Ten Commandments—"

"*Supposedly* contained the Ten Commandments," Brandt interjected.

"Yes, well, let's just for the moment assume they were the real ones," Rebecca answered. "They contained a great deal more information than just the ten laws."

Brandt nodded for her to continue. She moved her hand from his knee to his palm and gave it a squeeze. He returned the affection even though his lips wore a frown.

"They stated, in pretty specific detail, the story of the Messiah."

"And?" he asked with that edge back in his voice. He really didn't like his Scripture messed with. Which only made this all the harder.

"And it also made it clear that the Savior would be the *daughter* of God."

Blinking twice before he spoke, Brandt's expression darkened. "*Daughter*? As in female? As in a woman as Messiah?"

Rebecca looked in the direction Davidson had taken Vakasa. "Or a girl." She squeezed his hand. This time he did not return the gesture.

"So you want me to believe that not only is God's son actually a *daughter*, but that it is the little girl we just scooped up from Africa?"

Wincing, waiting for the scathing rebuttal, Rebecca nodded.

Instead, Brandt gave her hand a gentle squeeze. "Well, if that's all." He patted her knee as he rose. "Want a malt?"

"What?" Rebecca blurted. Where was the argument? The wrestling to the ground to prove her wrong? "No. What?"

He offered his hand to her. Still stunned, she took it, and he pulled her up into an embrace. "I don't believe it," Brandt said softly. "Sorry. I know you are entertaining at least the idea," he said, smoothing her hair back. "And clearly the Disciples believe wholeheartedly, but I don't. I know my Savior. I'm good."

Brandt kissed her on the forehead, then went over to the shake machine. Rebecca followed slowly as he opened the small refrigerator. "Can you believe this?" he asked, peering into the cooler. "Look, they've even got sliced fruit. Want some fresh strawberries in your chocolate shake?"

"No, thank you," Rebecca answered automatically. "Are you really okay?" She also wanted to ask, *Or did you have ministroke?* but thought it more prudent *not* to ask.

Brandt kind of liked seeing Rebecca this way. A little unbalanced. Surprised. At a loss for words. It happened so seldom he decided to enjoy it.

"Yep," he said as he put a third scoop of ice cream into the cup. "I'm hungry but great."

He knew what she'd expected. She'd seen it before back in France, Budapest, and Rome. More recently in Russia, Slovenia, and Jordan. His shock, horror, and revulsion of what he considered a sacrilege. Then he'd had an epiphany.

"Faith is faith," he said with a shrug.

Rebecca's eyes narrowed. "Faith can be shaken."

"That it can be," Brandt answered. "That's why I'm going with the whole God works in mysterious ways thing."

His fiancée watched as he mixed in the fruit, then loaded the cup into the mixer. She stayed silent as the machine whirled the ice cream, chocolate syrup, malt powder, and strawberry slices together. How had he gotten along all this time without a shake machine at his fingertips?

"You don't even want me to go over the passages from the Ten Commandments tablets and how they relate to other religious works? How across history there is precedence for a female Messiah? Why we need to go to Egypt to try and prove if she is or isn't the Messiah?"

"Nope," Brandt said, taking a long draft of the shake. He licked his lips once he was done. *Damn that was good.* "I'm at peace with my God."

How could he not be? Here he stood, against all odds, drinking a shake with the love of his life, not forty-eight hours after being drugged and kidnapped. If that didn't prove God was pretty awesome, he didn't know what would.

After draining the cup of its contents, Brandt set it down on the counter and pulled Rebecca into a hug. "Come here."

She laid her hands on his chest. "You are freaking me out a little here."

"In a good or bad way?" he asked, pressing their hips together.

Her cheeks flushed. "Well, I'd thought the bad way, but now…"

"But now, what?" he asked as his palm caressed her cheek, his thumb stroking the soft skin.

Rebecca's one hand snaked up his neck, pulling him down toward her. Her other hand made its way down his belly, tugging his shirt up until she touched flesh. His skin rippled under her touch.

"Now?" she murmured. "I'm pretty sure there is a king-sized bed upstairs."

He loved how she thought.

Their lips met. Hers warm and inviting. Despite all the trauma it had been through, his body responded the way it always did. Roused, he pulled her even tighter to him. His hands coursed over her back, tugging up her shirt. Their tongues intertwined, foreshadowing what their bodies would be doing very, very soon.

If it weren't for the fact that Vakasa could stray out at any moment, Brandt would have taken Rebecca right there and then.

"Whoa!" Lopez shouted as he entered, throwing a hand over his eyes. "Put a sock on the door or something."

They broke off the kiss, but did not break their embrace.

"Having difficulty finding us a suitable getaway car?" Brandt asked, hoping that his tone backed off Lopez.

"Difficulty?" Lopez snorted, entering the room. "Finding a beater car in Egypt is about as hard as finding a corn on the cob at a state fair."

Of course the corporal had found a car in under five minutes. It was *Lopez.* Brandt knew he should get back to work, but damn if Rebecca didn't feel so right in his arms.

He couldn't exactly order the corporal out of the room so he could make out with his fiancée. He'd have to find a more creative way. "Perhaps you would like to—"

Then Lopez spied the parlor. "Shakes? Are you kidding me?"

Rebecca loosened her embrace as the corporal ran over to the counter.

"If they've got peanut butter, I can make it into ribbons for a Reese's-style shake!"

Sighing, Brandt let Rebecca back away from him. Maybe having a shake machine around all the time wasn't such a great idea.

CHAPTER 13

UNDISCLOSED LOCATION

1:18 P.M. (EST)

"We've got a problem," Stark said, stirring Bunny out of her semi-sleep.

"What?" Prenner asked, his tone as starched as his uniform. How the guy could go all night and not wrinkle his jacket went against all that was right.

Stark pointed to the screen. "Mr. Saramais has been receiving numerous payments—from numerous countries and agencies."

Bunny scanned the bank account list. Several names popped up. The Bahamas Commonwealth Bank. Probably one of the most famous CIA front companies out there. She turned to Emily.

The woman gritted her teeth, flipping open her phone. "On it."

Another account that stood out was the New Hong Kong Import Company. Bunny had seen the name before. Like how they had traced funds from that Chinese front company to the team that had attacked them in Russia.

Another line item was from the Iranian government—directly. No cover or front there. Just the Islamic Republic of Iran Treasury.

"What are all these payments for?" Bunny asked, a question that she felt was rhetorical, except Stark answered it.

"Research," he stated. "Or at least that's what the grants say."

"On what?" Bunny thought out loud. The Viking study probably cost a grand total of a couple hundred thousand dollars. The totals on this ledger added up into the millions, tens of millions.

Stark stretched out his fingers, cracking the knuckles. "That is going to take me a while. Saramias has got his own shell companies, plus a Swiss *and* Cayman Island account."

"I guess if you are trying to hide from the Disciples, you would need a ton of capital," Prenner suggested.

But what if Saramias wasn't hiding from the Disciples? What if Saramias was out there as bait? A lure that she had just advised Rebecca to take?

"We've got to warn them," Bunny stated.

Prenner shook his head. "We agreed to radio silence until they leave Egypt."

Bunny bit the edge of her fingernail. It turned out it was just as hard to be on this side of the radio as it was in the field. As she rubbed the scar that came around her rib and ended at her sternum, she realized maybe not quite as hard as out in the field, but pretty damned close.

Rebecca adjusted her *jilbab* so that it completely covered her clothes. The long, flowing black robe obscured any figure Rebecca might have liked to think she had.

Talli held out another garment. "This is your *niqab*."

"I thought it was a burka?" Davidson asked.

Rebecca shook her head, studying the hat-like garment that would cover her head and face. "No, a burka is a single garment. It isn't worn nearly as commonly in Egypt as it is in Saudi Arabia." Rebecca took the *niqab*. "This way, once inside, a women can easily take off the *niqab* yet still be modestly dressed from the neck down."

"Modest?" Lopez snorted, sucking down his third shake. "More like 'get thee to a nunnery.'"

"I think that is the point," Rebecca stated. She knew dressing in the local fashion was important. It was important to blend in. To mask her very Western features. Still, she hesitated to put on the *niqab*. Many woman around the world voluntarily covered their hair and face as a matter of their religion. Many others didn't do it voluntarily. In countries like Saudi Arabia and Iran, they could be beaten or whipped for showing their face to nonrelated males.

"You could stay with Lopez," Brandt suggested.

Rebecca shot him a look. Like she'd pass up the chance to ask Saramias what the hell was going on? Yeah, right. Besides, she had just nearly gotten squeezed to death by a python. A veil shouldn't be that big a deal. As Rebecca donned her *niqab*, the little girl next to her did as well. Even though the child was going to stay with Lopez in the getaway car, it was best to keep her identity under wraps.

"Don't worry," Rebecca murmured to Vakasa as she lowered the eye veil. The girl gave a thumbs-up as she adjusted the veil to fit properly. It appeared she'd worn one of these before.

Rebecca wasn't quite so comfortable veiling up the only part of her body that the *jilbab* and *niqab* didn't cover. But her blue eyes were a standout in this part of the world. They had to be concealed.

Dropping the veil over her eyes, Rebecca felt a wave of claustrophobia. And she wasn't even claustrophobic. She had read somewhere that wearing the eye veil was like wearing a dark pair of sunglasses. Um...They were wrong. A pair of sunglasses made you feel sexy. To her, the veil blanked out her identity.

Brandt put his arm around her and kissed the fabric. "You're still beautiful."

She shoved him away. "You say that to all the black-robed, indistinguishable women you meet."

"If it helps any, I'm wearing a hat, too," Brandt said as Talli finished with the head garment. The scarf was a bright red with a white-checkered pattern, carried down from the days of Mesopotamia.

"It's called a *keffiyeh*," Rebecca chided. "And it has a function, to keep the heat and sun from the top of your head."

Talli indicated to the flap on the side of the scarf. "Use this to guard your mouth and nose if we get into any sandy areas."

"With any luck, we should be going into a building, then right back out to the airport," Brandt said before turning to the men. "All right. In light of recent events, this is a country in unrest. We have got to lie low...Lopez?"

The corporal adjusted his *agal*, the rope that kept the fabric secured to the head. "Army crawl, Sarge. That's my goal."

Brandt seemed satisfied, nodding for them to move out. He took Rebecca's hand, helping her down the short staircase to the hangar floor. If she'd thought the *jilbab* was bad on the plane? Try wearing a black all-consuming garment in ninety-five-degree-plus weather. Rebecca was already sweating.

And was it just the eye veil, or did the car they were walking toward seem a bit…beat up?

"Lopez?" Brandt asked in that tone of his.

"What?" The corporal asked, pointing to the derelict car. "It's a Chana CM8. The single most popular car on the road in Egypt."

"How is it going to fit all of us?" Davidson asked.

Besides having more dents than Rebecca could count, the thing was narrow. Like, little, tiny Smart car narrow.

"It seats seven," Lopez insisted. "Now get in."

Brandt hesitated, though, which made everyone hesitate.

Finally, Lopez sighed. "Okay. Fine. It's going to be a tight fit. But if we put Brandt up front. Davidson, Rebecca, and the girl in the next row. That leaves Talli and Levont in the backward-facing seat." When everyone still hesitated, Lopez waved them on. "Now get."

Surprisingly, Lopez was right. Once loaded in, they were rubbing elbows, but the doors shut, and they were secure. Sort of. The engine rattled the entire car as it churned to life.

Brandt glared at his corporal, but Lopez just shrugged. "Army crawl, remember?"

Then the car pulled out onto the tarmac, passed through a gate to the road that led away from the Cairo airport. Lopez horned their way into the jam-packed traffic. It had been a while since Rebecca had been in Egypt. Lopez had been correct. Their beat-up, dusty, on-its-last-legs vehicle did fit right in. Cars in far worse shape flanked them.

"Told you," Lopez said, giving her a wink. Too bad he couldn't see the smile she flashed him, as it was hidden under the dark cloth of the *jilbab*.

"How long?" Brandt asked.

The corporal indicated to the wall-to-wall cars. "We're only twelve-point-four miles from Giza. However, in this traffic…"

Lopez brightened. "Unless you want me to hop off this freeway and take the side streets."

"That would be a definite *no*," Brandt answered. Bad things happened to foreigners on the back streets of Cairo. Even armed ones. Under the current political climate? Perhaps even worse to the armed ones.

How Brandt wished he could have left the girl back at the plane. But going into a black-box situation like this? He needed all his men on deck. Which meant Vakasa and Rebecca had to come along. Like he could have really kept Rebecca away. She'd skydived into the Congo, for God's sake. Trying to talk her out of going to a business suite was *not* going to happen.

As they eased their way out of the Cairo International Airport's wake, the traffic let up a bit. Enough so Lopez had to lay on the horn and force his way between cars. Normally, Brandt would admonish him for such behavior, but in Cairo? That *was* the norm. Cairo drivers used the car horn like teenagers used their cell phones to text. Only, a hell of a lot louder.

Finally, they made their way west, turning left onto Ring Road.

"This part never gets old," Rebecca said as they went over the long bridge. Brandt looked down to find they were crossing where the Nile forked. Yes, the water was pretty. A shimmering green with reeds lining the shores. Unfortunately, he knew that Nile crocodiles, notoriously even more aggressive than the Congo version, lurked just under the surface. Brandt was kind of done with rivers for a while. Even the Nile.

Lopez took the second exit after they crossed the Nile onto Salah Salem. The traffic became more cluttered as they entered the business district of Giza—Mohandesin.

"Look!" Vakasa said as she pointed out the window. In the far distance, you could make out the Great Pyramid. Or at least one of the pyramids. Brandt wasn't sure which one. And really didn't want Rebecca to go into a half hour lecture on them.

Instead, Brandt nodded politely as Vakasa babbled away in half a dozen languages.

"Visit?" she asked in English.

Brandt didn't need her to take off her eye veil to know she was using her super-cute expression. He had three younger sisters, so he knew the look well. To think Rebecca suspected this typical little girl was the Messiah? He'd spent several days with her last week. Even out in the Congo, she knew who Justin Bieber was and could hum his songs.

He had worried that Rebecca would drop a true bombshell of information back at the plane, but this? This he had down cold.

"Maybe later," Brandt half promised.

A few turns later, some of which Brandt wasn't sure were entirely on purpose, Lopez pulled them into the underground parking lot of the German Industry & Commerce Tower. The structure looked pretty new. It didn't have the same sand-etched surface as most of the other buildings they passed.

"Do we get to stop?" Rebecca asked from the backseat.

"Funny," he replied. Although, thinking about it, he usually was asking her to exit vehicles at high speed. This time, though, he thought they could actually make a stop. Or at least a Hollywood stop.

Lopez tapped the breaks, rolling them to the curb. "Mysterious ex-Disciple exit."

Brandt helped Rebecca out of the car as Talli and Levont unloaded the equipment. For their current urban surroundings, it looked like they'd brought out four large briefcases. Only, they weren't exactly filled with papers.

As Lopez pulled them away from the curb, Vakasa flipped her eye veil up and waved good-bye to them with such enthusiasm that she wasn't prepared when the corporal really hit the gas, sending her head over heels off the seat.

Brandt looked over to Rebecca. The question on his face pretty damned clear.

Her? The Messiah? Really?

Rebecca shrugged, or at least that was all he could tell with her covered head to foot in black.

"Davidson isn't joining us?" Talli asked as he picked up one heavy-ass briefcase.

"No," Brandt admitted. "He is setting up across the street to get our backs." It was a good thing Talli had dark skin. Otherwise, it would be way too easy to notice his cheeks flush. Brandt threw him a bone. "Don't worry. You are going up on the roof to guard our front."

And hopefully you'll be close enough you can actually hit something.

Talli crisply nodded, unaware of Brandt's true feelings. Perhaps, after they ended this mission, it was time to send him back to sniper school or something. It wasn't fair to him or the team to have one functional sniper and then Talli.

As their "sniper" headed to the freight elevator, Levont hit a button on a much more upscale keypad. Two other men joined them as they waited for the elevator. Both were dressed in Western-style business suites. Brandt was pretty sure they spoke Plattdeutsch, a lower-class version of German. Which made sense. The Germans had a vested interest in natural gas. Egypt was not blessed like some of its northern neighbors with huge oil reserves. No, Egypt's main export was natural gas.

And since the Russians started jacking up the price of natural gas to Europe? Suddenly, Egypt had a whole new bargaining position.

The bell dinged. Brandt stepped out of the way for Rebecca, but Levont blocked him, indicating for the businessmen to enter.

Crap. You are in Egypt, Brandt.

Women, especially such traditionally dressed women, walked *behind* their men. A fundamentalist man would never allow a woman to enter first. *Pull it together.*

He nodded to Levont, thanking him for the etiquette save. He also kept his hand firmly planted at his side. The instinct to put his palm on Rebecca's back really gnawed at him. His mother would be so disappointed he wasn't being a gentleman. Instead, he followed Levont into the elevator. Rebecca waited, then entered and put her back to the wall, bowing her head. She clearly had been to Egypt before. She seemed to know the customs better than he.

The other two men got off on the sixth floor. Levont punched the button for the penthouse, which, given they were in Giza, was only five more floors up. As they were lifted upward, Levont opened his briefcase and handed Brandt his gun. Quickly, he tucked it into his waistband, then straightened his clothes just before the elevator door opened.

To his surprise, they were greeted by an elderly gentleman dressed in Armani.

"Ah, Dr. Rebecca Monroe, to finally meet!" he exclaimed in a thick Middle Eastern accent.

Rebecca really, really hated it when people knew who she was. Since he knew her to be American, it made no real point to continue to wear the *niqab*. She pulled off the garmet, shaking out her ponytail as the man guided them into the affluent office.

The desk was made of solid mahogany and the floor covered in a thick Oriental carpet. The view through the office windows was a full 360 degrees of Giza. To the west, you could make out the Pyramids and Sphinx. To the east, Cairo sprawled out into the distant smoggy desert. The Nile lay between the two. To think this view had been enjoyed by businessmen and pharaohs. The ancient capital of Egypt was due south at Memphis. Civilization had called this region home for millennia.

Brandt stepped in front of Rebecca. "You know who I am. Who *we* are."

The man's neatly trimmed beard parted in a smile. "Of course, we have been expecting you."

Rebecca could feel Brandt's muscles tense. This wasn't at all how this was supposed to go.

"And you are Dr. Nyura Saramias?" Rebecca asked.

The man nodded vigorously, leading them over to a wet bar. "We do not frequently have guests that drink alcohol. However, I have brought in fine brandy and whiskey."

Clearly, the guy was not exactly clear on what Americans really drank or when.

Levont broke away from the group, checking out the rest of the room.

Nyura just smiled. "Ah, yes, please check. But be assured, after this long, we have our antibugging protocols down."

We?

Then Rebecca noticed a figure standing behind the desk. Her burka seemed to blend in with the mural of the Middle East that covered the back wall.

"My wife," Nyura stated as he urged them to sit.

None of them did.

"How did you know we were coming?" Brandt demanded, apparently deciding small talk was not needed.

The man ignored his question. Instead, he looked to Rebecca. "What do you think of her? Is she the one we have sought for so long?"

"I don't know," Rebecca stated. At least being able to tell the truth.

"Please, *sit*," Nyura insisted.

Awkwardly, Rebecca sat down and urged Brandt to do the same. Levont, however, seemed pretty intent on standing guard by the door.

"I know that you are worried," he said, "but my only concern is for the girl. And to make sure that she does not fall into the Disciples' hands. I will help in any way that I can."

Rebecca could feel Brandt's distrust wafting off of him. It beat against her skin. She could only imagine what Nyura felt. The sergeant was a lot of things. A delicate negotiator was not one of them.

"I assume that you would want something in return," Rebecca stated.

Again, the man's bright smile illuminated the room. "Of course, of course."

"And that would be?" Brandt rumbled.

"A strand of hair," he said. "That is all."

Before Rebecca could answer, Nyura's wife moved across the room, offering them tea in dainty porcelain cups.

"If you will not drink my whiskey, please, have some tea."

Rebecca took the cup but had no intention of drinking it. Brandt waved off the woman.

"I asked," Brandt pressed in that tone of his that threatened violence if he wasn't answered, "how did you know we would come *here*?"

"You really do not know?" the man asked, looking to each one in turn. "The girl, she sent word two weeks ago." Off their shocked looks, he chuckled. "I am only teasing. A little Messiah humor, sorry."

This Nyura was definitely not what Rebecca had expected. For one thing, they were in a room filled with light. That right off the bat was weird. These conversations usually took place in caves or run-down tenement buildings. And certainly not with someone as forthcoming as Nyura *appeared* to be.

"If the stand-up routine is over," Brandt stated, "would you like to answer my question?"

The man sombered, but not much. "The earthquakes were our first indication the Messiah may be ready to reveal herself."

The older man, his hair more salt than pepper, smiled that smile of his. Perhaps it charmed some. Rebecca seemed to be buying into it at a least a little, but then again, everyone knew her soft spot for older gentlemen.

This guy hadn't stayed alive this long without some serious ability to manipulate. The congenial yet affluent facade had probably served him well over the years. Not today, though. Brandt smelled a rat. Like, literally. There was something off about the office. The smell of fresh paint was one of them. Someone had gone to a lot of effort to make this space feel occupied, but Brandt doubted if it had been used for more than a week.

There was another smell. An odor that made him nauseous and hungry at the same time.

"Once Dr. Monroe found the Viking runes in Iceland," Nyura explained, "I knew that it would only be a matter of time that you would come knocking on my door." The man leaned back in his chair. "Then, of course, once the Disciples kidnapped you and sent men into the Congo after a little girl, well, we do understand our arithmetic. One plus one and all."

"And if we refuse to give you the girl's hair?" Brandt asked. With a man this skilled at spy craft, there was no reason to beat around the bush.

Nyura glanced to his wife, indicating he would like a refill on his tea. He took a nice long drink, then sighed. "*Americans.* Always the bottom line. Always testing the size of our relative reproductive organs. How big a stick am I wielding? That is what you wish to know?"

Okay, Brandt would have put it another way, but he could roll with it. "Yes."

"As I said, I only have the girl's welfare at heart."

"Bullshit," Brandt said, gaining the first frown for the day from Mr. Saramias. "I'm a decent, moral guy," Brandt went on. "And even I don't have *only* the girl's welfare at heart. I've got to balance the safety of my team, my superior's orders, and a whole crap load of regulations."

Nyura leaned forward, far more intense. "Ah, that is where we differ, Sergeant. I have no superiors. No regulations. And no team. I have me and my life's work, which is centered around this Messiah. *She* is my only concern."

Brandt glanced to Rebecca. What harm would giving him a single hair cause? Nyura could have taken the girl in the parking lot if he had really wanted to. Yet something tugged at Brandt's gut. If somebody wanted something this badly, it invariably was far bigger a deal than they let on.

So why hadn't he taken Vakasa when he could have? Did they stay their hand, as Nyura had stated, due to safety concerns, or was this impressive office just a front? Were they incapable of pulling off the grab?

"You supplied Bunny with this address," Rebecca stated breathlessly as if she had just had an epiphany. Brandt liked it when she had epiphanies. It meant his brain didn't have to work overtime understanding what in the hell was going on.

CHAPTER 14

GIZA, EGYPT

9:03 P.M. (CAT)

Rebecca watched as Nyura's expression went from affable to guarded. "Yes, yes, we did plant it for her to find."

She had read Bunny's e-mail. Rebecca had followed the logic tree that had gotten them here. But now that Rebecca was sitting in this luxurious office with a man offering to spill all of the Disciples' secrets for a bit of Vakasa's DNA, the trunk of that tree felt like it was branching off at odd intervals.

Obviously, Brandt was worried about the man's motives. That he would either take the DNA by force or not give them the knowledge he'd promised, even after they handed over the hair. Rebecca felt the deception went far deeper than that.

The dynamic between husband and wife, for one. If he truly was a Disciple, that meant he was Jewish—hardcore, super-traditional

Jewish. Which his wife was. For Arab visitors, Rebecca could see why they would keep up the Muslim traditions. But in front of Brandt and her? Why? Why not take off the burka?

It felt as though she were in the middle of the play *Hamlet*. That this scene was staged for some benefit, only Rebecca couldn't figure out for what purpose. In her mind, she traced back the lines of logic.

The Viking article by Nyura that she and Bunny followed. The anagram name switch. The German building.

Wait. Only the last name was switched. The first name seemed intact. Her Arabic was seriously rusty, but wasn't Nyura…?

"Nori," Rebecca blurted.

The woman couldn't help but turn in her direction. The woman tried to cover the recognition of her name by spilling some tea, but Rebecca had no doubt what she had uncovered.

"What just happened?" Brandt asked, jumping to his feet.

Rebecca noticed that Nyura's, or whatever his real name was, expression lost its joviality.

"Nyura is a unisex name," Rebecca stated. "Like an American 'Terry.'" She looked to Levont, who nodded his agreement. "Nori is the feminine nickname most women go by."

"So," Brandt said, his eyes flicking back and forth between the man and woman, "the real doctor is her?"

"I believe so," Rebecca stated.

In response, Nori lifted the burka up and over her head to reveal a crisp business suit. Unlike her husband, with his more Arabic features, Nori's nasal ridge was far more prominent, along with a higher forehead. A far more classic Jewish phenotype. Her dark-black straight hair was only lightly peppered with gray. Her eyes, though, showed her age. As a matter of fact, she looked perhaps a decade or two older than her husband. Lines etched the corner of her eyes. Wrinkles zigzagged her forehead.

Was this what Rebecca would look like if she continued to chase religious mysteries? A face filled with regret and purpose?

"What gave me away?" the older woman asked as she straightened her dark navy-blue jacket.

Rebecca nodded to her feet. "Ultimately, your shoes."

She had unconsciously noticed the click of heels when the woman walked around the room, offering the tea. Then Rebecca saw a blue leather top to a rather expensive set of shoes peak out from under the burka. Women in burkas just didn't wear upscale heels.

"We were in such a rush..." Nori said with more than a twinge of sadness.

"Does somebody want to explain what the hell is going on?" Brandt demanded.

The woman moved from behind her husband's chair to stand next to him. "The first thing I must tell you—"

Then the woman grabbed her stomach, nearly doubling over.

Brandt's gun flew up. He scanned the windows. Not a single bullet hole. And looking closer at her white dress shirt, there was no blood. Another ruse? Rebecca rushed over to help hold up the woman.

"Well, perhaps the first thing I must tell you," the woman said, "is that my dearest husband appears to still be loyal to the Disciples."

Retraining his aim, Brandt focused on the husband. "I have no idea what she means, but it isn't sounding very good for you."

"He has been poisoning me for weeks," the woman spat out. "And I believe he gave me the final, fatal dose this morning once we heard you would arrive."

Brandt might have thought she was faking, except for the fact her skin went gray as she struggled to breathe. You couldn't fake that level of shock. "Rebecca, get away from her."

"The good news, though?" the woman said, then coughed heavily. "I returned the favor."

The man's eyes dilated as his hand went to his stomach. "The tea?" he questioned, then spasmed. "You *bitch*."

He rushed his wife before Brandt could intervene. He needn't worry, though. The old woman buried a hidden knife up to the hilt into her husband's chest.

"For *Her*," she said as the knife slipped from her hand.

"Damn it," Brandt rumbled. "I could have interrogated him."

As the man slumped to the floor, his eyes already glazing over, Rebecca lowered the dying woman to the floor. Brandt signaled Levont to check the man.

"He wouldn't have told you anything," the woman said, then spit out blood. "Besides," she said, smiling to reveal red-streaked teeth, "I've wanted to do that for a very long time."

Damn it. This meeting was so far sideways it was doing doughnuts.

"We've got to get out of here," he said to Rebecca, urging her up.

"There's no computer or files that I can see," Levont informed him.

Of course there weren't.

Brandt had Rebecca halfway up when the woman grabbed her hand. "Please, they are coming, but a moment only."

Rebecca knew they needed to get the hell out of there, but she just couldn't deny the woman's dying request. Lowering herself back down to the floor, Rebecca cradled Nori's head.

"Is she as glorious as prophesized?" the woman asked.

Picturing the laughing, giggling little girl, Rebecca was not necessarily lying. "Yes, she is."

Nori squeezed her hand. "I have nothing else to share with you but my research."

The woman coughed, moist and wet. It was a disturbing sound. A sound Rebecca had heard back under the caves of Rome. A sound that only ended in death.

"You will find it hidden with the people of the Euskaldunak." Nori squeezed hard, although Rebecca wasn't so sure she was conscious of it. "You know the place. You must study the monks—"

Rebecca held the woman as another coughing fit claimed her. When it was over, the woman sagged in Rebecca's arms.

"Nori?" There was no response.

"Here they come," Levont reported from the door. Brandt helped the point man move a large bookcase in front of the door.

Rebecca wiped blood off the woman's cheek as her breathing turned shallow and rapid.

"Nori?" she whispered.

It was hard to imagine this woman, ashen and weak, was once a Disciple. Aunush's mother no less. Then again, she did just kill her husband.

"Nori," Rebecca repeated. "You fought them your whole life. You fought for *her*. You've got to give me more so I can protect Vakasa."

The woman roused enough to flutter open her eyelids. "Shechinah," she uttered before blood trickled, then gushed from her lips.

Brandt grabbed Rebecca by the elbow and propelled her up. She wouldn't voluntarily leave the dead woman.

"I don't understand," Rebecca said, holding out her hands, which were covered in the old woman's blood.

Brandt grabbed the woman's burka and wiped Rebacca's palms. "I don't either, babe, but we've got to book it."

Rebecca's eyes lost that far-off stare and focused on him. "Yeah, right. Okay."

"Levont," Brandt called out, "you want to start our daring escape?"

"Damn right," the point man said, walking to the western, centermost window. He picked up a chair and smashed it through the glass. A rope dangled down from the roof.

Brandt urged her over to the window. Rebecca looked to the rope, then back to Brandt. "You never thought Talli was going to have to shoot. He was our back up out of here, wasn't he?" She was smart.

"Yeah." Brandt chuckled. "Our meetings never go well."

Levont was out the window, climbing up the rope to the roof. The plan, once he got up there, was to throw down a harness so the men could haul Rebecca up there while Brandt held down the fort.

So they had a few seconds. Brandt pulled Rebecca close.

"I love you more than life itself," he stated.

Rebecca's eyes scanned his. "Ditto," she said, seeming confused. Declarations were not exactly his thing.

"But I want you to promise me before we get to that point," Brandt said, indicating to the dead couple, "we'll get a divorce."

A smile flickered on her lips. "I *so* promise."

Davidson watched Rebecca find her footing on the roof as Brandt slung his rifle over his shoulder and climbed up after her. They knew they would be attacked at the office. It was a no-brainer.

The Disciples were just that. Disciplined. Smart. Fast. And well connected. A visit to a supposed ex-patriot of theirs would not go unnoticed. Equally certain Rebecca needed to get more information on Vakasa. The only way to get ahead of the Disciples was to figure out their end game.

Why did they want the girl? Rebecca seemed to have some idea, but even she appeared unsure.

Even though the Disciples' men broke through into the penthouse office, Davidson held his fire. Talli and Levont shot at any head that dared peak out of the window. The Disciples would mount an offense to the roof, but Talli had secured that door pretty damned well.

Besides, Lopez should be here with their helicopter at any moment. Long before the enemy could pin Brandt and the rest down on the roof.

Davidson scanned the other buildings. Yes, they had made excellent time from Africa. Such good time that there was no way that Frellan and the sniper could be here. Except, Davidson was pretty darned sure that they *were* here.

He was not going to underestimate the Disciples ever again.

Glare caught his lens. The last rays of a sun about to give up for the night. The air was blustery red and orange as the desert flowed yellow. The Nile sparkled in the dying light as streetlamps flickered on. He would have to switch to night vision soon.

A flare of white caught his attention.

He swung his rifle sixty degrees, surveying the windows in that direction. He scanned across the entire row of offices, then across one, then up a row, tracking that floor. Nothing.

Was he being too hypervigilant? Was his mind interpreting minor input and creating a crisis out of it?

Then the flare shone from a window. Davidson honed in on the light source. His vision blurred for a moment as he adjusted his magnification. Then he wished he hadn't. Snapping his rifle up, Davidson frowned.

Just a man's watch reflecting the late-evening sun. A man who was having a rather inappropriate relationship with a coworker. It was situations like this that sniper school just didn't prepare you for.

Shrugging off the image of something the Quran definitely did not condone, Davidson went back to his systematic survey of the area. Then he heard it. A distant buzzing that got closer and closer.

That did not sound like a helicopter.

He slid his rifle around to face the oncoming aircraft.

It was definitely not a helicopter.

The only thing definite about it was that Brandt was going to be *pissed*.

"Is that what I think it is?" Levont asked.

Brandt jerked the binoculars away from his eyes. "If you think it is a crop duster, then, yes, it is."

Rebecca glanced around the roof. "But how are we supposed to…?"

That did seem to be the question of the minute. Talli was doing a decent job of keeping the enemy pinned to the office.

There was some noise at the roof door, but that was going to take them a few minutes to get past. Which should have been plenty of time for Lopez to land on the roof, scoop them up, then head over and pick up Davidson. It should have been with a helicopter, but *no*.

"What are we going to do?" Rebecca asked.

Time to think like Lopez again. Which meant he had to throw any concern for personal safety out the window. He also had to think about five times faster. Not necessarily better, just faster. However, the one thing about Lopez was, he was extremely goal oriented.

If the corporal stole a crop duster, he had a plan to get them off this roof with a crop duster. It was probably not a good plan or a practical plan, but it was a plan.

Brandt turned to Levont. "Do we have any grappling hooks?"

The point man shook his head. "Sorry, Sarge."

"Any repelling gear at all?" Brandt asked but already knew the answer.

"Not a speck."

This is what happened when you got kidnapped from your wedding. You weren't exactly packed for a major mission. The fact they had scraped up as much equipment as they had was pretty impressive. However, none of those weapons were going to help them get onto that crop duster, though. Unless, of course, you counted shooting Lopez out of the sky. Which Brandt wasn't entirely discounting at the moment.

As the crop duster flew closer, he wasn't even coming directly over the roof. What was he playing at? The small plane slowed, enough to sputter the twin engines a bit as it flew right past them.

Lopez had the pilot-side window open. He thrust his thumb to the rear of the plane. "Wire…" he yelled, but whatever else he said was snatched by the wind. "Next!"

Then Lopez was past. Only Vakasa's smiling face in the rear window, waving wildly at them, kept Brandt from going on one hell of a cursing streak.

Rebecca spied the large hook on the back of the plane. "There!" she said, pointing at the metal device.

"There, what?" Brandt said as he squinted.

"I should have realized," she said. "The Egyptians covet organic produce and cotton." Off Brandt's frustrated expression, she hurried on. "Sorry, it means that, about ten years ago, they banned crop dusting, so the pilots had to get creative on ways to use their planes. From the looks of it, this plane had been modified to pull those large advertising banners."

Levont backed her up, handing Brandt the binoculars. "I think he brought the grappling hook to us."

As Lopez banked the plane around for a second pass, Brandt studied the hook. He then scanned the roof. This being a third world country, there were no sleek satellite dishes or encased electronics. Rebecca realized that the roof was a veritable maze of antennas and wires.

Brandt's strong brow furrowed. "He really expects us to catch hold of that thing with one of these wires." Then he smiled. "Lopez *really* is a genius."

That is not exactly how Rebecca would have described it. That hook wasn't all that big. And a lot of those wires didn't seem all that sturdy. But hey, she was the one who'd insisted on coming along. There would be no whining.

"He wants us to do what?" Talli said.

Well, except for Talli.

"Levont?" Brandt asked his point man. "You up for this?"

The big man's smile eclipsed the setting sun. "Really? I get to go first?"

Seriously, there was something wrong with these men.

"That's one of the privileges of being a point man," Brandt confirmed.

Levont didn't waste a single moment. As he slung his rifle, he hacked off a long piece of stiff wire and wrapped it around either wrist, creating a loop to accept Lopez's hook.

As the biplane sputtered again, slowing, saddling up to the roof, Levont rushed over, stepping up onto the side of the thirteen-story building as if he were hopping a curb in New York. He reared back as the plane got close. Once the plane slid by, Levont threw his loop forward and, consequently, his body weight off the roof.

"Off the hook!" Levont yelled as the wire loop caught, jerking Levont out of thin air, pulling the point man forward. Actually, it turned out, *on* the hook.

The back of the plane lurched down from the sudden weight. Somehow Lopez not only righted it, but banked into a steep turn. In a feat of muscles over gravity, Levont curled his legs forward, gripping onto the tail of the plane. He unwound the wire, letting it tumble out of the sky as he climbed forward into the plane.

"See?" Brandt said. "Totally doable."

Rebecca let Talli groan for the both of them.

CHAPTER 15

GIZA, EGYPT

9:27 P.M. (CAT)

Frellan strode into the office building. His men were already breaking through the door to the roof. He would have been there, except he had heard whispers between the men. Ugudo would not confirm them.

The upscale office smelled of iron. Blood. He saw his mother first. Her eyes looked to the heavens, but he doubted she found the absolution she wanted. He cared nothing for her. She had birthed him. That was all. She was weak. She had let her own ambition cloud her judgment. Were they not Moshe's descendants? Did they not have an obligation to fulfill his legacy?

He walked past her without another glance. Then he noted the other body.

His father.

Frellan sank to his knees, cradling his father's head. "No," he moaned. "No."

How could God do this? Punish the righteous and let the likes of Brandt still walk this earth? His father had sacrificed everything for the Disciples. He had left with his wife. Not because he had lost his faith, but because it had been redoubled by her betrayal. His father had kept track of Nori to be sure she did not tread too close to the Messiah.

All of those years living with that witch to die in a foreign office building?

Movement caught his attention. Monnie picked up his mother's burka. The revulsion on her face matched his own. In this, the watcher and he were united. The time for grief would be later. His father would understand.

His death must not be in vain.

His death must lead to the Messiah.

It was the path God had chosen.

"We must be sure they receive a proper burial," Monnie said.

"For him," Frellan nodded. "Not for her."

"What do you want done, then?"

Frellan did not hesitate. "Feed her to the street dogs." Rising, he turned to Ugudo. "I want on that roof."

His second-in-command nodded curtly and rushed from the room.

His mother could be blamed for much, but one man, the man who had the Messiah, the man who had precipitated Frellan's father's death, was wholly to blame.

And Brandt would pay.

This is taking too long, Brandt thought.

Even though Lopez banked as hard and as sharp as he could, the turnaround time was killing them. That roof door just wasn't going to hold much longer. Sure, they had Davidson in position, but the kid wouldn't reveal himself until the absolute last second.

His first priority, though, was Rebecca. He checked the wire around her wrists.

"It is going to hurt like a mother when you catch that hook."

"*If* I catch that hook," Rebecca responded.

"So maybe somebody should stay stateside next time," Brandt chided as he tightened the wire. He didn't want her slender wrists slipping through.

Another explosion at the door made her frown waver despite her retort. "The next time you get snatched from the altar, I will seriously consider it."

No matter her words, Brandt knew she'd do no such thing. Even knowing everything she'd have to go through, he felt pretty damned confident she'd come after him again. Even if she had to hook a plane to do it.

"I've got a safety line around your waist…in case…"

Rebecca nodded. "And that would hurt like a mother, too."

"Yes," he chuckled. "I suggest you catch that hook."

She nodded as he guided her up onto the side of the building.

"It's just like at the carnival," Brandt reassured her. Rebecca's glare told him she really didn't appreciate his analogy right about now.

As she stood above him, he stabilized her with his hands on her outer thighs. He could feel her muscles shaking under his touch. That's what made him love her all the more. Not that she was all that brave. Don't get him wrong, she was freaking brave. But the fact she would do anything to follow him to hell and back, even when she was scared out of her mind.

That was his Rebecca.

Making sure he had a tight hold of the safety line, Brandt murmured to her, "You can do this." As the plane came in low and slow, Brandt patted her leg. "Just visualize your loop sliding over the hook."

"Then the pain in my shoulders when it catches…" she finished. He knew Rebecca wasn't complaining. She was truly visualizing a successful maneuver.

"That's right," Brandt encouraged, then realized Lopez was coming in really, really closely. "Duck!"

Rebecca crouched down as the wings sailed overhead. It seemed Lopez didn't want Rebecca to have to jump too far. The body of the plane slid by.

"Now!" Brandt yelled.

Under his palms, her muscles bunched and propelled her up and out. But it wouldn't be enough. She had too shallow an angle. Brandt wrapped another loop of wire around his wrist, ready to catch her. But Lopez was all over it, tilting the plane's belly and therefore the hook toward Rebecca.

It wasn't pretty, but the loop snagged the hook. The corporal nearly turned ninety degrees to make sure that loop stayed on. Levont scrambled out of the plane and down the fuselage to secure Rebecca.

Only then did Brandt release not only the safety line, but also a breath he'd held way too long. Whistling between his teeth, he refashioned the safety line into his own loop.

Now it was just Talli and him.

Of course, that was right around the time the roof door exploded off its hinges.

Fuck.

Talli laid down gunfire while Brandt's mind whirred.

He raised his hand, circling it overhead, then pointing to the other side of the roof. There was no way Lopez would have time to come all the way around. They were just going to have to catch him on the other side.

Lopez banked immediately, bringing the plane around.

"Go!" Brandt yelled to Talli.

As the man ran, Brandt fired to the door. So far, the Disciples hadn't been quite brave enough to poke their heads out, but it wouldn't be long. Talli didn't even have time to set up properly. He just hauled ass, jumped on the ledge, and flung himself at the plane. Thank goodness he had better aim with his loop than he did with a rifle. He snagged the hook square on.

Brandt couldn't watch any longer. He had about a dozen gunmen deciding right about now they were brave. Quickly, he scanned the horizon. It was pretty much getting to the absolutely last second. Why the hell wasn't Davidson firing?

Um, probably because the sniper had already figured out that there was no way Brandt could hold them off until the plane came back around. It was now or never.

Why was it always *now*?

Gritting his teeth, firing behind him, Brandt sprinted for the ledge. Talli was still trying to get his sorry ass off the hook and onto the plane. Brandt tossed aside the wire. There would be no hook in his future.

Lopez must have realized what Brandt was about to do as he cut the engines. Completely. The plane slowed, dropping altitude. Which was a damned good thing since Brandt ran straight off the roof.

Hitting air, his legs still pumped as if they could get him those last few inches. Then he, too, fell. Chest first...right on top of the wings.

Fuck...That *hurt*. He couldn't even breathe, but his finger latched hold of the forward edge of the wings.

He was safe. Well, that was if Lopez could get the plane's engines started again.

Davidson watched as the biplane's engines finally caught and lifted his team out of their rapid descent. He hadn't been too worried. He knew Lopez would get out and flap if he had to. As the night descended quickly, Talli finally, with Levont's help, hauled himself onto the plane. It appeared that Brandt had decided the wings were just fine by him.

The Disciples were firing at will from the rooftop, but the plane quickly flew out of range. Turned out Davidson's services weren't needed. But that was the role of a perimeter specialist. Ninety-nine percent of the time you cooled your heels. Unless, of course, you were on Brandt's team, then you were green-lit most of the time.

Davidson took one last survey of the area just to make sure that his egress was clear. His scope glided past the building where that couple had been...well...

Wait. He went back to the office. Not to be a perv or anything, but something was wrong. The couple was gone. Like, not there. The way those two had been going at it? There was no way they would have just closed up shop.

They had been a distraction. The watch. The sex. Everything had been meant to keep his attention diverted to the south.

Which meant something that really deserved his attention was happening *not* to the south. He brought his scope around to the north, checking those buildings. Most were dark this late at night. Only a few had lights flickering on.

If the sniper were here, he would *not* set up in the lighted offices.

He would be in the dark. Watching. Waiting for his shot.

And the best shot? Right at Brandt's back.

Quelling panic, Davidson scoured the area for any sign of the sniper. If Davidson waited for the guy to take a shot to find out where he was, Brandt would be dead.

There! The faintest-green reflection from a nightscope. Davidson didn't have time to set up a kill shot. He only had time to prevent one.

Davidson fired, shattering the window. He fired again and again in no particular pattern. He just needed the sniper unable to aim as the plane moved out of range, even for a sniper rifle.

Then a bullet whizzed past his head.

Good, Davidson thought as he rolled over onto his back, lying flat against the roof's ledge. The sniper must have given up on the plane and decided to take out his frustration on another sniper. Fine by Davidson.

Now to get out of here and head to the rally point in Sudan, where they wouldn't exactly need travel papers. Cash, American cash, would get them off the continent without a paper trail.

He was good to go, until he heard the rev of a jet engine. Not one jet engine, but two.

Crap.

Davidson took a chance and brought his scope over the ledge. Sure enough, two F-16 fighters were streaking in their direction. They must have launched from the Abu Suwayr Air Base. Whether the Disciples had tipped the Egyptians off or the government assumed this assault on the German building was the result of political unrest, their plane was in trouble.

Real trouble.

Rebecca ignored Vakasa as the little girl tugged on her *jilbab*. She was too busy worrying about Brandt still up on the wings. Why the hell didn't he just get into the plane like any other sane person?

"Damn, I wish I had access to the Internet," Lopez grumbled next to her. Rebecca really didn't want to know why. However, the corporal told her anyway. "I really, really, really need to know the world's longest flight with a guy on your wings. Come on, somebody figure it out."

"No matter what it is," Talli stated, "we will not be able to challenge it."

"What do you—"

Lopez's protest was drowned out by two jets streaking overhead. Their turbulence rattled the plane down to its bolts.

"That is *not* good," Lopez said with an actual straight face. He wasn't kidding. Lopez was actually worried.

Rebecca's stomach plummeted. They were being hunted by the Eygptian air force *and* Brandt was on the wings. There was not time to worry or throw a tantrum or anything. There was only time to plan.

"What are our options?" Rebecca asked.

None of the men answered.

"Guys?" Rebecca urged. "There are always options. Right? I mean, that's what you always say."

"Oh, we've got an option," Lopez said.

"What?"

Lopez didn't answer, though. Levont did. "We land."

"And?"

Talli was the one who finished the thought. "We surrender ourselves."

"You have got to be kidding me?" Rebecca shook her head. After the shoot-out at the building? And what about Vakasa? After what happened to that reporter during the riots? Rebecca shuddered, she physically shuddered, pulling the girl tight next to her.

"No, sorry, that isn't good enough."

"Chica, give me some ideas here," Lopez said as the jets made another pass, this time lower. They hadn't shot yet, but the radio was squawking with orders. They were in Arabic, but it was pretty clear they were saying, "Land or get shot down." The only reason they hadn't fired already was to wait until they got out over the desert to avoid civilian casualties. However how rather callous to civilian deaths the government had become, Rebecca wasn't sure how long they could count on that to protect them.

This was what Brandt was so damned good at. Seeing an impossible situation, then figuring out a way to thread the needle through it. Unfortunately, Brandt was on the wings.

Next to her, Vakasa clapped, pointing to the east. "*Valo dango*!"

"Light show? Is that what she said?" Levont asked. Rebecca wasn't sure, since she was pretty certain Vakasa was speaking in Welsh and Finnish.

Almost against her will, Rebecca followed the girl's arm. In the distance, the Great Pyramid and Sphinx were illuminated in bright greens and reds. It was the nightly laser light show that played out against two of the greatest historic monuments ever built. However, it really didn't help them.

Then Brandt's face came over the front of the wing. His features upside down, he was shouting something, but who could tell what it was?

"Light show!" Lopez said as Vakasa clapped. "I think he's agreeing with her."

"You're just imagining things," Talli stated, but Rebecca wasn't so sure.

"No," she said, trying to read Brandt's upside-down lips. "He is saying light show."

She tried to follow his logic. Why go there? They would scatter the crowd.

That was it!

"Lopez, head there!"

Without even waiting for an explanation, Lopez course corrected, turning them due east toward the pyramid.

Levont's hearty laugh filled the aircraft. "He wants us to land, get those people on their feet, then blend in with the crowd."

Rebecca sighed, glad that someone else had come to the same conclusion. It was such a long shot that they shouldn't even be trying it, yet the upside-down Brandt nodded vigorously, then disappeared. Apparently satisfied that they were headed in the right direction.

Vakasa clapped again. "*Valo dango*!"

"Yes, baby," Rebecca said, pulling her into a hug, "we are going to the light show."

Although, she seriously doubted if it was in the way Vakasa had hoped.

Brandt clung to the plane as it sped toward the Pyramids. The jets buzzed again, this time so close Brandt was pretty damned sure he wouldn't need a haircut for the next three weeks.

The light show played out starkly against the night sky. It truly was a spectacular sight. Somehow the Pyramids looked even more majestic than they did during the day. The history of Egypt played out across their surface.

And thankfully, it was a tourist haven. There were hundreds of seats filled. Brandt hated endangering them, but he seriously doubted the F-16 would fire into that crowd. The international incident that would cause? Their plane making an emergency landing there was bad enough. The Egyptian government seriously didn't want tourist deaths added on top of that.

He gripped even harder as the plane made its steep descent. Lopez, as always, was thinking ahead. If they had descended any earlier, the jet fighters may have shot them down just to keep them from reaching the event.

Even now, the jets came in low and hard, trying to force them down.

Lopez held steady even though the tiny plane, never built to take the kind of punishment the corporal could deal, shook violently. Brandt had a bird's-eye view of their landing. Not that even a bird would be stupid enough to try what they were trying.

Someone in the crowd must have heard their approach. The man turned and pointed.

Thank God. They were almost on top of the crowd. They needed them to disperse. A hue and cry went up as Lopez brought them just over the desert floor. A blur of people scattered, tipping over their chairs, as the plane touched down, bounced…hard, then went back up again. Brandt's sweaty palms nearly gave out as his lower body slid back and forth across the wings. Those twin-engine prop blades only a few inches from his feet.

Brandt pulled himself as tightly to his belly as he could as they touched down again, bouncing again, landing again, bouncing again, until they crashed into the rows of white folding chairs. The blades chewed up the plastic, sending debris flying in all directions. A lot apparently into his back and arms.

Then they were on the ground, really on the ground this time, rolling forward. Lopez cut the engines and hit the brakes, hard. And there was just no way Brandt could hang on. As the plane came to a stop, Brandt flew forward, over the nose of the plane, and crashed into the front row of chairs.

His shoulder hit the sand, finally bringing him to a stop as well.

Brandt rolled over onto his back as the sound of rattling machine-gun fire filled the air. Guess the Egyptians weren't as worried about bad press as he'd hoped. The others fled the plane as bullet holes tore into the thin metal.

Grunting, brushing plastic off his back, Brandt rose.

No rest for the weary.

Rebecca kept a tight hold of Vakasa's hand as they ran from the plane. The crowd wasn't much farther ahead. They should have been able to blend in before the jets made their next pass. She tossed a glance over her shoulder, expecting Brandt to be hot on their heels. Instead, he was running in the opposite direction.

Why the hell would he go that way?

Then the high-pitched squeal of the other plane explained why.

Another fighter jet, new to the hunt, honed in on Brandt, firing at his heels. Dust kicked up, chewing up the sand.

"Brandt!" she screamed, but he kept running.

"Damn it! Change of plans!" Lopez shouted next to her. "Get the girl to safety!" he said, pushing her toward the crowd. "We'll get him!"

Before the men could head out after Brandt, Vakasa squirmed out of Rebecca's hold and ran across the desert.

"Thor!" she called out.

"No!" Rebecca yelled, but it did no good.

The men fired up at the jets as they all raced across the desert. The pyramid was still blanketed in reds and greens as scenes of the building of the great monuments played on despite all the chaos.

Vakasa was fast. Like, crazy fast. She caught up to Brandt, then passed him, heading straight for the pyramid's entrance. The little girl stopped at the tomb's entrance, waving as if she expected Lopez to take a vacation photo. Rebecca was sure that he would want to. However, he was a little busy trying to keep the jets from mowing them down.

Brandt reached the entrance first, scooping Vakasa up into his arms. He made to head toward them, but Rebecca waved him forward. Using what little lung capacity she had left after the sprint, Rebecca shouted, "No! Go inside."

There was no way they could make it back to the crowd. It had way too much of a head start, and the only cover was that pyramid. Brandt looked like he was going to fight her on it. After all, it would trap them inside. However, Vakasa wiggled out of his arms and fled into the darkness.

Brandt held out his hand, but not to Rebecca. "A gun!"

Levont supplied him with one. As bullets pelleted the stone, the point man led them into the pyramid. He swept his light from side to side.

"Where did she go?"

"Just go down," Rebecca said. This shaft of limestone went down at about a thirty-degree angle until there was a juncture.

Half-sliding, half-running, they made their way to the T. One shaft went up into the king and queen's burial chambers. The other continued downward to a subterranean chamber that was oddly incomplete. Scholars still debated the use of such a chamber.

"Which way?" Brandt asked, puffing air himself.

With the roar of the jets outside dampened by the walls, Rebecca cocked a head, trying to hear the patter of little feet. However, there was nothing. Just the sound of their harsh breathing.

Which way would Vakasa have chosen? Which way would a little girl have run? Or more aptly, which way would a supposed Messiah have chosen?

Either way, up would be the most obvious.

Rebecca pointed down. "I think she went below surface."

"Good enough for me," Brandt announced as Levont made his way down the limestone passage.

"Shouldn't we split up?" Talli asked. "Cover both options?"

Brandt shook his head. "If we go down…"

"We go down together," Lopez agreed.

Rebecca wished just once that *going down* wasn't the most likely option.

"Holy shit!" Stark announced, pointing to one of the many news channels he had on his screen.

Grainy cell phone footage showed a biplane landing near the Pyramids, disrupting the popular light show. Oh, and did she mention that there was a man clinging to the wing? There was no doubt who was flying that plane or who was hanging on.

Bunny crossed her arms. "So does this qualify for the Disciples knowing where Brandt and the others are?"

"I do think this might qualify for an event that allows us to break radio silence," Emily added.

Prenner still frowned. "I know what you two want, but my brass is never going to authorize us stepping in."

"Just call Brandt," Bunny suggested as she watched the group run inside the pyramid. Where the hell did they think they were going? Every passage within the tomb was a dead end. Of course, as jets apparently streaked overhead, looking for a target, a pyramid was as good a place to hide as any.

Finally, the lieutenant gave the nod. Stark keyed in the commands, pushing his earpiece farther into his ear. He tilted his head. "No joy. They aren't responding to my ping."

"Try Davidson," she said, counting off the people who had entered the temple. Only six. And no skinny-assed white boy.

Stark typed rapidly. "Nope."

Bunny chewed on her lip. It made sense the others didn't respond. She could remember the press of those tunnels. The limestone was probably blocking the signal. Davidson, though? If he were true to form, he should be set up somewhere along the periphery of the Giza pyramid complex.

Unless he didn't realize they were going to land near the light show. Come to think of it, that didn't sound exactly like a precalculated rally point. So Davidson was in the wind. Or he was…

Nope, she wasn't going down that road.

If he was alive, why wasn't he answering?

CHAPTER 16

GIZA, EGYPT

9:42 P.M. (CAT)

"*Il suo bene*," Davidson said. "It's okay" in Italian. Yet the three sweaty men still advanced. He'd already tried Arabic, Farsi, and even Armenian, yet the men didn't seem to speak any of the most common languages in Egypt.

His only solace was that he was pretty sure these men were not Disciples. Dressed in near rags and smeared with urban detritus, they seemed to be street thugs. Three street thugs with knives. Sure, Davidson could shoot, but that would advertise his location to not only the Egyptian police who were crawling all over the area, but the Disciples who must have descended upon the area since Lopez's little circus landing.

The men looked like they came prepared to loot. A common occupation these days in Egypt. Some gangs were even accused of fomenting riots just so they could loot afterward.

Now, though, these men had a far more valuable prize in sight. An American. An armed American. How much would the government pay as a bounty? Or how much could they ask as ransom from the US? Either way, it wasn't looking so good for Davidson. He needed to get out of this situation quietly and quickly.

Neither of which looked very likely at the moment.

Davidson secured his rifle onto his back and pulled a knife out of its sheath on his leg. The men brazenly smiled. Davidson pulled a second knife from his belt. Holding both weapons in the blade-back position, Davidson nodded to the men.

Funny, their smiles faded. They were used to ambushing tourists. Mugging them for their valuables, then running. Not a one of the three seemed any too happy about going up against a trained man. Yet the odds were still on their side, so they advanced.

Davidson danced back, waiting for one of them to commit.

The largest of the bunch grunted, shoving the smallest guy forward. The man stumbled, righting himself. He glared over his shoulder yet found no support there. Davidson flipped one of the knives, caught it, aiming it forward.

The guy must have decided to just dive in, as he charged at Davidson. He sidestepped, dragging the knife's edge along the man's arm. Davidson could have gutted him, easily, but the less mess the better. The man grasped at his bleeding arm, wavering to the left, then to the right.

Davidson grabbed him by the collar and shoved him back to his gang. Then he set up in attack position again.

The largest man glared, his jaw muscles working up and down. Finally, he must have decided that this little payday wasn't worth the effort. With a guttural signal, he urged his gang back down the alley.

Not taking any chances, Davidson headed off in the opposite direction. This building would have made a nice perch, but now he would have to go find another one.

He could only hope he didn't miss too much.

"I've got her!" Levont shouted from up ahead.

Rebecca pushed past Talli. "Vakasa, stop!"

Brandt brought up the rear. "Catch our six," he ordered Talli as he moved forward to see what all the fuss was about. Rebecca was struggling to pull the little girl from the end wall. Her fingers were bloody as she dug into the limestone.

"Honey, no," Rebecca coaxed, but the girl just wouldn't leave it.

The little girl's resistance didn't matter as Brandt picked Vakasa up by the waist. "Maybe we can get back—"

That had just been wishful thinking, as footsteps echoed down the tunnel. Getting chased into the pyramid by two jets kind of gave law enforcement a heads-up to their location.

Which meant they were trapped. Brandt set down the girl. She made a beeline to the wall. Her only stop? To grab a knife from Levont's leg.

"Hey!" the point man protested.

She seemed deaf to his concern and used the point of the blade to dig into the thick wall. Brandt ignored her. As long as she wasn't hurting herself or anyone else, Brandt said go for it.

"What is she doing?" Levont asked, although his tone didn't hold out much hope for an answer.

Rebecca put her hand out. "Do you have another knife?"

"Yeah, but—"

Brandt studied Vakasa's work. She was determined. "Give it to her," he instructed the point man.

Levont turned over the knife, and Rebecca sank to her knees alongside the girl, chipping away at the wall.

"Want to share?" he asked his fiancée.

"Want to lend a hand?" Rebecca replied.

Since they were trapped and all, just waiting for the authorities to figure out they only needed a couple of flashbangs or a tear gas grenade, Brandt pulled his knife and dug into the limestone.

"How about now?" he asked.

Rebecca frowned. Sometimes she liked to let a theory run its course before discussing it. This was not the time he could indulge her.

"I either need to know," Brandt stated, "or start prepping for an assault."

"There have been rumors for years that there are tunnels that run beneath the Pyramids," Rebecca said. "That run all over this plateau."

Levont knelt next to them, adding another blade to the mini-excavation. "Why haven't I ever heard of that?"

She nodded next to Brandt. "Because the Egyptian government has not just vehemently denied it, but gone to great lengths to cover it up."

"Which, in our experience, usually means that they do exist." Brandt sighed. Why couldn't ancient history stay fucking ancient?

Rebecca nudged him with her shoulder. "That's what I was thinking. I mean, several well-respected scientists have done ground-penetrating radar studies and found results very consistent with an intricate and elaborate system of passages."

Wiping dust away from his nose, Brandt dug harder. Even if it was only a rumor, that was better than a deadly shoot-out any day. And if anyone could find a secret entrance to a millennia-old hidden tunnel, it was the woman he was engaged to.

"Why hasn't the History Channel picked it up, then?" Levont asked, then coughed. The tight passageway was not ideal for all the dust they were churning up. Brandt could begin to taste why the rock was called limestone.

"Because each of the scientists had their equipment and findings confiscated, then were systematically discredited," Rebecca answered, using the side of her arm to brush back her unruly hair.

Great info. Just not exactly helping right now with the thick limestone wall that blocked their escape.

Then his knife hit something even harder. As a matter of fact, it broke off the tip of the hardened-steel blade. "I think I've got something.

More carefully, he dug around the hold he'd made to expose a slab of black rock. Across the glassy surface were hieroglyphics. Brandt didn't even bother to wait until Rebecca asked. He just got up and out of her way.

This slab of ancient Egyptian writing was possibly the most exquisite find of ancient hieroglyphics in more than a decade. Not that Rebecca voiced her fascination. They weren't on an expedition. They were trying to formulate an escape.

Her fingers ran over the otherwise-smooth surface, reading the carved-out symbols like reverse braille. Well, "reading" might have been a bit generous. Hieroglyphics weren't her thing. Where was Bunny when you needed her? She was much more adept at ancient languages. Why hadn't the woman gotten on that chopper with her?

Oh, yeah, because then she'd be stuck far underground with the entire Egyptian police force after her. That's why.

Vakasa put her tiny finger on the stone as well, smiling, tracing the ancient letters.

"Any clue?" Brandt said. "Any at all?"

Rebecca didn't respond to him. She studied the little girl's face. Was that comprehension? "Can you read this?" Rebecca asked.

The girl's smile widened as she put her cheek against the cool slab.

"Was that a yes?" Brandt asked. "Is this some kind of door? Can we blow it open?"

"I'm not sure," Rebecca answered.

"Rebecca, a little late for modesty."

She shook her head as Vakasa went back to outlining the letters. "Trust me, I'm not. These aren't just hieroglyphs. These are from the Early Dynastic Period."

"What's that?" Levont asked as he helped chip off more limestone to reveal exactly how wide the wall was. All the more letters to *not* understand.

"Exactly my point," Rebecca said. "This is seriously ancient writing."

Brandt rocked back onto his heels and up. "That's it. We're blowing the wall."

"But—"

The look on Brandt's face stopped Rebecca cold. She knew that look. The look that said, *Our lives are on the line, so I am in absolutely no mood to have an academic debate about this.* Unfortunately, Rebecca had seen it too many times before.

"On it, Sarge," Levont said.

Rebecca tried to move Vakasa out of the way, but she refused. As Levont got out the C4, Rebecca took picture after picture of the letters with her phone, trying desperately to record at least some of this ancient find. Snapping the shots, she translated as best she could.

Okay, so hieroglyphs were read left to right. They didn't really use vowels, so there was that. Unfortunately, the ancient Egyptian language was partly phonetic. Like English, you put the sounds together to make the words. Which would be great. However, they only did that about a third of the time.

Sometimes the duck symbol meant "duck." Other times it was the "st" sound. Still other times it meant "son."

Then another really awesome habit of the ancient scribes was to just throw in symbols for aesthetic purposes. Meaning, if they didn't like the look of a sentence, they'd just drop in a seated god or add a scarab beetle to make the passage prettier.

Oh, yeah, and their modifiers could be before the word, in the middle of the word, or after the word. No biggie when trying to speed-read ancient Egyptian.

Damn that Bunny. Rebecca hoped she was happy wherever she was, tucked safely away.

Bunny frowned as she pushed the earphone tighter to her ear. The audio feed was scratchy and mainly filled with police officers shouting in Egyptian. Stark was putting it through a filter and translation program, but even he didn't look too hopeful.

So it was up to her to try and figure out what the hell was going on at Khufu's Great Pyramid. It was chaos over on the other side of the world. And no wonder. It wasn't too frequently a bunch of Americans landed during the complex's light show, then escaped into possibly the world's most treasured landmark.

The police had sent in search teams. However, they were having just as much trouble contacting their own people inside the pyramid as Bunny was trying to raise Rebecca or Brandt.

Then she heard it. "*Elasepha.*"

Down. Brandt and Rebecca had followed the lower passages.

"They headed down," Bunny informed the group. "Bring it on screen," she encouraged Stark, who brought up a map of the passages.

"It's a dead end," Prenner stated.

No duh. Everything in that pyramid was a dead end. Unless...

Was it by accident they went down, or did Rebecca remember the controversy of the 1996 documentary *Sleeping Prophet*, which suggested that there were a series of tunnels under the Pyramids and Sphinx, linking them all?

"Get me"—Bunny snapped her fingers, trying to remember the name of the quasi-scientist—"Dr. Schor. I think that's his name. There should be a diagram in his most recent paper."

Emily stepped forward. "Dr. Schor. Should I know who that is?"

Bunny didn't answer. She wasn't sure yet. The idea had been so crackpot at the time. As a matter of fact, Schor and a few other researchers who had joined their voices to the "There are tunnels under the Pyramids" theory had flip-flopped so many times it was hard to keep track of them with a scorecard.

"Here we go..." Stark said as the elaborate tunnel system came up, overlaid on the map of the Pyramids.

Underground passages that were supposedly "documented" were in green. Others were yellow, orange, and red. The warmer the color, the more it was based on speculation.

"What are we looking at?" Prenner asked.

Bunny pointed to the green tunnels, which were the fewest in number. "These were 'discovered' with ground-penetrating radar…These others were guessed at to complete the circuit."

If these scientists were correct—and Bunny was nowhere close to saying that they were—it did give Brandt and the rest a chance. A slim one, but a chance.

"But how are they going to find it?" Emily asked. "After the hundreds of excavations of that pyramid, how are they going to find it?"

Bunny stared at the very-red tunnel that abutted the western-most wall of the lower passage. Was the tunnel just a figment of the scientists' imagination or a real structure the Egyptians had used to unite the Pyramids? Either way, it was obscure. Superobscure.

"Hell if I know."

You had to give it to Rebecca. She was snapping pictures and trying to read the chicken scratch even as Levont was rigging the C4.

"Update," Brandt asked Talli.

The man craned his head over his shoulder. "Best I can tell they haven't attacked because they think they have us cornered, and the tourist bureau doesn't want any permanent damage to the tunnels."

Yeah, they really wouldn't appreciate what Brandt was about to do. But they couldn't count on the cops to stay their hand just because their government told them to. All it took was one yahoo with a hero complex and *boom*.

It didn't matter what country or what situation. There was always one of them in the bunch that had to make it go *boom*.

"Hold on," his fiancée said. "Think…I think this wall may be booby-trapped."

"Rebecca…"

"No, really," she protested. "This here…*Any trying to pass will meet, or visit, or run into, the wrath of Anubis.*"

They really didn't have time for this, but this was Rebecca. He couldn't just order her to shut up. If only he could in situations like this.

"Any other bright ideas, then?" he asked. If you couldn't beat her straight on, let her beat herself.

"I just need a few more minutes to translate…"

She stopped as Vakasa laughed merrily, then kissed the black stone. The little girl jabbered in at least five different languages. Brandt caught, at the least, German, Russian, Arabic, possibly Norwegian, and Swahili.

"Say it again," Rebecca said. "But slowly. *Lentement.*"

"*Katika*," the little girl said.

Levont nodded. "That's Swahili for 'in the.'"

Vakasa smiled. "*Olhos de.*"

"'Eyes of,'" Lopez filled in. "It was Portuguese."

Brandt encouraged the girl to continue. Rapidly, she spat out another sentence, which took the entire room to translate the translation.

Rebecca finally summarized. "In the eyes of Khepri, find the rise and fall."

Frowning, Brandt gave the nod to Levont. "Put the detonator in."

"Wait," Rebecca begged.

"That makes about as much sense in English as it did in the fourteen other languages she used."

Rebecca ignored him. Of course. Instead, she muttered to herself, "Eye of Khepri. Eye of Khepri."

Brandt was right. The passage made no sense, but the way Vakasa beamed up at her, it had to mean something. And the ancient Egyptians were known for booby traps. Possibly even biological weapons. Just ask anyone on the Tutankhamen expedition. Oh, wait, most of them you couldn't because they had died shortly after the opening of the tomb. Currently, the hypothesis was that the tomb was coated in a deadly strain of E. coli.

But what in the hell did Khepri have to do with anything? Rebecca scoured her ancient religions memories. Khepri was the god of something. But wasn't everybody a god in legend?

"Atum," Vakasa said.

That was so not helpful. "Anybody?" Rebecca asked the group, but they all shook their heads. Between Brandt, Lopez, Levont, Talli, and her, they had every major language group covered.

"I don't understand, Vakasa. Atum?" Rebecca asked.

The little girl's smile only spread. "Ra."

Now Ra, Ra Rebecca got. The Sun God. The head honcho of the Egyptian Heliopolis. Rebecca nearly smacked herself on the forehead. Atum was a sun god as well. Only, Ra had a lot more charisma or something, because Atum was phased out for Ra as the cult spread in ancient Egypt.

Khepri! Now Rebecca got it. He was the god of the sunrise.

"Which way is east?" Rebecca asked. When Brandt looked confused, she grabbed his shoulder. "East!"

Lopez was the one to point to the wall to his right. "Thata way."

Vakasa joined her as Rebecca dug into the wall.

Brandt was none too happy about it. "Rebecca, we've got to get a safe distance up the tunnel before—"

"No," Rebecca protested as the limestone chipped away. "It's here. If there is a tunnel, it is here."

"Guys..." Talli said, backing up toward them. "There's some guy up there rallying the troops to get this over with. He's got a flash bang."

"Damn it," Brandt spat. "Rebecca, we don't have time—"

Her knife hit something hard. "There!"

Rapidly, the crumbling wall revealed another black slab. Only, this didn't have any hieroglyphics. Rebecca figured if you got this far, the ancient Egyptians assumed you knew what you were doing.

Wasn't there a second half to that passage? *Find the rise and the fall*?

What in the heck did that mean? Well, she'd better find out quickly, as Brandt's thumb was over the detonator.

Then she heard it. The tinny sound of something bouncing. Not something. A grenade.

Vakasa put a palm on the slab and pushed up. Desperate, Rebecca helped her. With a groan, the stone gave way. Unfortunately, so did the ground they stood on.

Fuck.

What was the rule? What was always the goddamned rule? Don't fucking touch ancient artifacts.

Guess Rebecca forgot, as she tumbled down a dark passage.

"Do I shoot it?" Talli asked as he aimed at the grenade bounding its way to them.

"No!" Brandt barked. He didn't have time to give any more orders than that. He just grabbed Lopez by the collar and chucked him down the stone slide. Levont seemed to get the general idea and dove headlong right behind the corporal. Good thing, because the trap door was beginning to close.

Talli jumped out of the way of the grenade. Brandt simply shoved him, sending him down the secret passage. He made it, but damn, that doorway was getting narrow, and Brandt was *not* a skinny guy.

Hurling himself, Brandt went in headfirst, but twisted mid-air. He watched the grenade bounce past. Waiting one heartbeat, Brandt hit the detonator. The wall blew at the same time as the grenade. Chips of limestone flew through the closing door, peppering Brandt's side.

But it was worth it. The grenade explosion should cover up their C4 explosives. Hopefully the Egyptians could never prove Special Forces were there.

Then he was slipping and sliding down the slick stone, gaining speed. Brandt only knew the ramp actually ended by the sound of groans as the others hit bottom.

"Incoming!" Brandt warned. He could hear the others scramble to get out of the way. He tried to slow his descent, but there was just nothing to grab hold of. Finally, he gave up as he rounded a curve and slammed into Talli. Bouncing off the sniper, he ran into Levont, who wasn't a lightweight himself. The three of them crashed into the wall.

Shoving the men away, Brandt made it to his feet, a little wobbly but on his feet.

Lopez swept his light at their surroundings, which looked very similar to the tunnel upstairs. Chiseled limestone.

"You okay?" Brandt asked Rebecca, who stood to the side, guarding Vakasa in her arms.

Rebecca held up a hand. "I know, I know. Don't touch the artifacts." Then she smiled. "This one, though," Rebecca said, indicating to Vakasa, "I think this one actually enjoyed it."

The little girl's bright smile took some of the sting out of the multiple bruises he'd just received.

Talli and Levont rose more slowly, brushing off the debris.

They all stood silently for a moment. Craning their ears to see if anyone was going to follow them down the ramp. Sure, there was plenty of noise up there, but their escape seemed undetected.

Brandt swung around to face Rebecca. Her eyes darted to the rest of the men.

"What?" she asked. "Why is everyone looking at me?"

CHAPTER 17

UNDISCLOSED LOCATION

2:44 P.M. (EST)

Bunny watched the live feed from the video screen. No, they didn't have satellite feed, but they did have CNN. Reports were still sketchy. The only thing everyone could concur upon was that there had been an explosion.

For now, they were blaming it on an overzealous officer, but after watching the base of the pyramid shake and the amount of dust that blew out the entrance, it looked as though it might have been something with a little more kick that was set off.

"It's good they haven't reported any remains," Emily stated as she got her phone out.

Bunny had tried to block that sequela out of her mind. Rebecca had to have found that entrance to the underground passages. She just had to.

"Listen to this!" Stark said as he put the audio feed from the police radio on speaker. Everything was so garbled it was hard to make out anything specific.

"Where could they have gone?" an English-speaking voice called out. "Where?"

She hugged Stark, who blushed. Bunny didn't think Davidson would mind, given the circumstances.

Even in an explosion of that magnitude, there would have been body parts, well, all over the place. If they were asking where Brandt and the others had gone, they must not have found any—at all.

Emily answered her phone and spoke quickly, relaying the information to her boss. She put a hand over the phone, indicating to the schematic of the underground tunnels, which it turned out were no longer theoretical. "Which way are they going to go?"

Bunny studied the map, trying to think like Rebecca. She tried to imagine herself suddenly in a millennia-old system of tunnels built by ancient engineers. Surprisingly, it wasn't all that hard. Not after spending any time with Brandt and company.

The question was, how well did Rebecca remember the layout of the tunnels? After about two hundred yards, the tunnel from the Khufu pyramid split into three. One tunnel went out to the Cheops pyramid. The second tunnel emptied out into a near labyrinth of passages that crisscrossed between the other, more minor pyramids. The third main branch angled out to the Sphinx.

Breaking Bunny's concentration was a strange beep. One. Then a pause, then a second one.

"What's that?"

Stark's eyebrows merged into a unibrow. "Not me." Then his face opened up into a grin. "I left the channel open."

It took a moment for Bunny to realize which channel he was talking about. Davidson's channel.

Bunny snatched the headset from Stark. "Sam, is that you?"

Davidson hit the sat phone button once. The faint click was far quieter than if he'd whispered.

"Oh, thank God." Bunny sighed. He liked the sound of it. Living in isolation for most of his life, it was odd for someone to worry about him. And a girl? Davidson had written that concept off even before all the burns.

"Yeah, okay," Bunny continued, clearly nudged on by someone else in the room with her. "Lieutenant Prenner thinks that you have probably set up across from the Great Pyramid. Is that correct?"

Looking through the scope at the sheer and utter chaos at the entrance to the monument, Davidson hit the button once.

"Great—well, not great," Bunny corrected. "I think Rebecca found them a way out of there, and they are heading away from the pyramid."

Davidson let out air through his teeth. Since that explosion, he'd been worried he was protecting a perimeter that no longer needed protecting.

He clicked the button once.

"There is three ways they could go…" Bunny's voice trailed off. She wasn't the most decisive of women. Actually, she kind of hated making decisions, especially big decisions. The ones where your backside was on the line.

He clicked the button once to give her some reassurance.

"I think…Emily needs a direction to go to. She's arranging an extraction team."

Davidson clicked it again. He had so little information he couldn't even begin to help Bunny decide. And it seemed like she had an army guy and a CIA operative. Neither of them was going to know Rebecca and her mind better than Bunny, though.

A rustling sounded when Bunny put her hand over the receiver. He could only make out mumbling until she came back on the line.

"Everyone else disagrees, but I think Rebecca is going to head to the Sphinx. The others think she's going to head toward the smaller pyramids. They are closer to the city, but I think she's going for the Sphinx."

He gave another click.

"I am assuming you are thinking, 'Why?'" Bunny stated quickly. "Besides it being what I would choose, it is the only site that a door has been found. The Egyptian government has never allowed it to be opened, but the Sphinx is the only one we know for sure that has an exit."

That deserved another click.

Davidson could hear the relief in her voice. "Great. Okay, Prenner says that you should set up on the north since Emily's extraction is coming from the south." Off Davidson's click, Bunny hurried on. "Be careful..." Then, much lower, "Come *home*."

That almost got him to break his silence. But he couldn't.

Instead, Davidson broke the connection. He couldn't even give her a click. He couldn't guarantee he could fulfill a "yes" answer.

Besides, he had another nest to set up.

Rebecca stood at the crossroads of three different tunnels. So once again, all eyes were on her. She glanced over to Brandt, who was carrying Vakasa on his hip. The little girl looked so right there that Rebecca almost lost her composure. Despite the heartbreak of him being married to another woman earlier this year, Rebecca knew how disappointing it had been when Maria's baby turned out *not* to be his. She knew how much he wanted to be a dad. To think that the world might never see a child of Brandt's. That by her screwing up which direction they went, they could all die.

"Which way?" Brandt asked. Not demanding. Not cajoling. Not even desperate, although Rebecca knew his heart must be pounding a thousand times per minute. "Don't think about it, babe. Just choose. We'll follow."

Oh great. No pressure there.

But he was right. Her gut told her to go east.

"That one," Rebecca answered, nodding to the third tunnel.

"All right," Brandt said, setting Vakasa down. "Levont, east it is."

As the point man moved out, with Lopez right behind him, Rebecca took Vakasa's hand and fell into position. Still, she queried Brandt. "Are you sure you don't want my reasons?"

In a surprising display of PDA, Brandt kissed her on the forehead. "Nope. I trust that big beautiful brain of yours." Then, of course, the smile fell. "Now move out."

Rebecca did as asked. Although, it was hard to keep up with Levont. He moved at a pretty clipped pace, and Rebecca was busy trying to take pictures of the walls as the men's lights flared against them for a second, then went pitch-black again.

Whoever built these tunnels had taken great care to line them with incredibly detailed hieroglyphics. If she weren't mistaken, the information was mainly about the history of the building of the Pyramids. The inscriptions on these walls could solve about two millennia worth of speculation and academic argument.

And luckily, she had Vakasa with her. Apparently, not only did the little girl speak a dozen languages, she could also read ancient Egyptian.

Bunny's question flared in Rebecca's mind. *Is it her?*

The child was remarkable. There was no question of that. And delightful, too. But was she a messiah? Rebecca looked down at the little hand in hers. It felt so vulnerable in her palm. How could someone so tiny hold all the world's hope?

It just didn't seem possible.

That didn't exactly matter to the Disciples, though.

"Hey, not to be a wet blanket or anything," Talli said, which even Rebecca knew meant that he was about to be a wet blanket, "but let's say best-case scenario we bust our way out of these tunnels, what then? Won't we just be back where we were before we ran into the pyramid?"

Brandt didn't miss a beat. "I guess we're just going to have to count on the fact that Davidson has been very busy."

"Wow, dude," Lopez said, feigning shock, "don't go all mushy on us.

The corporal was right. That was about as inspirational as Brandt got. Usually, he was all "Shut up and hoof it."

And with them all being safe, for at least the moment, which was a high point, really, on this mission, Rebecca delighted in the feeling.

The trek wasn't long. For which Brandt was grateful. That last stunt down the ramp had at the least bruised a rib, his abdominal scar ached, and if he turned quickly to the left, his vision blurred. Par for the course.

"We've got a turn up ahead," Levont informed them, slowing to a stop.

Brandt looked to Rebecca, who frowned. "My best recollection of the tunnel system in this grid…" She sighed. "My best guess is that this leads to only one outlet."

That was good enough for him.

"Take it at half speed," he ordered.

The point man got back to what he did best. Muscles tensed, Levont ducked his head around the corner, then pulled back rapidly. That quick scan must have been negative for any company, as Levont stepped into the possible kill zone. Sweeping his light side to side, up and down, he checked his corners. He checked as far as he could see.

With a curt nod, Levont let them know it was okay to follow.

Rebecca was nearly as well trained as his men when it came to protocol. And little Vakasa? She was a trooper. Not a squeak of complaint. Not a moment of hesitation. Even though he resisted the idea of her divinity, Brandt knew the moment he laid eyes on her that she was special. Back at the village, she'd done what was right when all the adults had shrunk back in fear.

In this part of the world, bravery usually got you killed.

Had Vakasa just not learned that lesson yet, or was she truly that courageous?

"Dead end up ahead," Levont reported.

Well, they were about to put his rather optimistic outlook to the test, weren't they?

Again, the passage ended in a blank wall. Not exactly blank. The limestone was carved in elaborate hieroglyphics. Hundreds of them. No, on second count, probably thousands of them. And that wasn't counting the rest that lined the walls.

So Brandt wasn't surprised when Rebecca asked, "Can I have a few minutes to translate?"

Purposefully, Brandt yanked the Velcro off his watch face. "Five minutes."

Rebecca's lips formed a firm line, but she nodded.

Actually, in their current circumstance, Rebecca could probably have as much time as she needed. God love her, though, the woman performed better under pressure. If you gave her a day, she might never get it done. Second-guessing and cross-referencing took over.

Give her five minutes, though?

The chick could perform miracles.

Rebecca tugged her lip between her teeth. None of this was making sense. She needed her laptop and about seventeen assistants. What in the hell could she accomplish in five minutes?

The line she was currently working on had a hawk, a squiggly water icon, and a farmer. Was the hawk an actual hawk, or was it the "a" sound? Or was it being modified by the little snake under it? Was that snake part of this sentence or the one beneath it?

Given the fact people were still arguing over the Rosetta Stone found by Napoleon's troops in 1799, this task was hopeless. The Rosetta Stone's black granite surface was etched with a decree from King Ptolemy V. It wasn't the decree so much—as a matter of fact, Rebecca couldn't remember what in the heck Ptolemy wanted so badly he had a huge block of granite dug up and put into a temple—but the fact that the words were written in three languages was the big deal for Egyptologists. Ancient Egyptian "priestly" (or higher-form) hieroglyphics, Demotic script (which was considered the "commoner" form of the language), and most important, ancient Greek.

Despite researchers having over two hundred years to translate the stone, you could still find arguments in the journals. Rebecca slid her eyes over the thousands of lines of inscriptions.

The debate about these passages would probably rage until the next millennium.

That was if they ever got out of here.

"Hey, do you mind if I film this?" Lopez asked.

"I'm just going to be sitting here reading," Rebecca answered.

"I know," Lopez acknowledged yet still pulled out his little flip camera. "I want to record something a little boring so that Ricki Junior can appreciate how exciting our escape on the other side is. You know, give him some perspective."

Yes, Rebecca loved being the straight man for Lopez. But who could resist the corporal's devil-may-care grin?

"Sure, why not?"

Having her useless intellectual flailing recorded for all eternity seemed fitting.

"Hey," Levont said. "Brandt, what's the English equivalent of the Russian word *lew*."

Her fiancé turned to answer. "It's not Russian. It is Polish, and it means 'lion.'" Brandt turned back to Talli, then cocked his head. "Why?"

"Yeah, why?" Rebecca added.

Levont pointed to the ground. Rebecca almost couldn't see what he meant, since Lopez was right there with his camera, panning the area in question. Between his sweeps, Rebecca made out words written in the dust on the floor. Apparently, Vakasa had been hard at work on her own.

Only, the little girl had actually produced results. Again, it was a translation that required translation, though.

The point man added, "The African stuff says, 'and here'"—he pointed halfway down another sentence—"'Terrifying One,' and 'fear its wrath.'"

"I can't speak to the ancient Aramaic," Talli said. "However, the Farsi says, 'union' and 'ever.'"

Lopez turned the camera on himself. "And the Latin-based languages—you know, the best ones—say, 'have no,' 'grovel,' and strangely, 'panties.'" After Rebecca smacked him, he corrected himself. "My bad. It says, 'lady coverings,' but come on, if that isn't panties, what is?"

Rebecca didn't answer the corporal. She was too busy adding in her limited French and Swedish knowledge.

She read aloud as much as she could. "*Quake before the Terrifying One.*" Off the men's questioning looks, Rebecca explained, "That was the Egyptian's name for the Great Sphinx."

Could that really be? Could they actually be under the Great Sphinx? It seemed so improbable that the single-largest monolith sat over them. The thing had been carved out of a single limestone block. A feat of incredible engineering nowadays, let alone at the dawn of civilization.

Getting back to the passage Vakasa had translated, Rebecca continued. "*Know this god, made of the union of the lion and man, shall live eternal. No veil shall cover him. No man can destroy, or damage, or harm him. Grovel before him and fear his wrath if you ever*...I can only assume that the last word means 'try.'"

Rebecca rocked back on her heels. It was a brilliant translation of the ancient hieroglyphics. However, it didn't exactly get them out of here.

"That's it?" Brandt asked, obviously figuring out the same thing.

"Um," Levont said, moving out of the way. "No..."

Vakasa had scrawled her writing all over the floor. Translating ten times faster than Rebecca could even do with her laptop. Getting over the sting to her ego, Rebecca stood up.

"Okay, we can't do this piecemeal," she explained. "Everyone just chime in if it is a language you speak."

Brandt listened to the others as he prepared to translate the Russian, Polish, and Turkish. So far, it had just been more ancient Egyptian hyperbole about how incredibly awesome the Sphinx was. Like just looking at the thing didn't tell you that already. Even just flying by it, hanging onto the wings, the Sphinx had impressed him.

Lopez stopped his interpretation. "What about the Riddle of the Sphinx? Shouldn't we be looking for something about old men crawling or something?"

Rebecca shook her head. "No, that is actually a Greek fable. And the answer is the life cycle of man. First we crawl. Then we walk upright. Then we use a cane. Not exactly applicable here."

"Are you sure?" Brandt asked. She seemed a little frazzled and really hated being interrupted.

She sighed before answering. "That riddle was written about a completely different sphinx that guarded Thebes. The sphinx was a *she*, and the legend arose around six hundred BC. This sphinx, the one sitting on top of us, is speculated to have been carved before thirty-four hundred BC."

Little did she know how glad Brandt was that Rebecca was slightly annoyed with him. It usually meant brilliance was on the horizon. So he pushed. "Speculated, but not *known*?"

You could see her hackles rise.

"I'm not sure you noticed the waterlines that striate the statue?"

Brandt just shrugged. This wasn't about what he knew or didn't know. It was about Rebecca pushing herself past her rigid academic thinking.

"Those were created by rains, heavy rains. Rains that *predate* three thousand BC."

Oh, yeah, she was getting up on her high horse.

"So there's a little rain damage?" Brandt pressed.

Her pupils dilated slightly, and her breathing increased. This was like academic foreplay or something. Brandt had no idea why she'd get so worked up, but hey, if it worked for her then, by extension, it worked for the entire team.

"First, it's not a *little*. The water erosion is significant, indicating flooding. Second, this implies that the Sphinx was actually built *before* the heavy-rain period."

As she went to take a breath, Lopez jumped in. "Because why would the Egyptians build such a huge monument on a floodplain? Right? That would just be stupid." Off Rebecca's nod, Lopez turned the camera to him. "Score one for Daddy-O!"

Brandt shook his head, feeling maybe a little worried for Ricki Junior.

Rebecca, however, was undaunted. If anything, she seemed to be gaining steam. "Thirdly, all of the causeways—the ramps used to slide the limestone blocks up to the Pyramids—were built *around* the Sphinx."

Levont was the one to jump in this time. "Which implies the Sphinx was there *before* the pyramids, not after or even at the same time."

"Bingo," Rebecca said, tapping her finger to her nose. Her smile faded quickly, though, as she spun on her heel, looking up at the stone ceiling. "Causeways. Causeways. Causeways."

A casual observer might conclude that Rebecca had lost her mind. Brandt, though? Brandt repositioned his gun, getting ready. Because this phase usually lasted all of ten seconds. Then they'd be on the move.

He'd bet his life on it.

Actually, he was counting on Rebecca. They all were.

Why hadn't she thought of it before?

Rebecca might be a little fuzzy on the "theoretical" tunnels they traveled, but the causeways above surface she knew cold. They were an interconnecting series of ramps and stone-lined paths. Several were at odd angles because they had to avoid the Sphinx. But one in particular seemed to be strangely out of place. Scholars had spent decades trying to decide why the ancient Egyptian engineers had built a causeway so out of the way.

There were more plausible theories, such as the supposition that an ancient temple had stood on the area at the time of building the causeways to the less plausible suggestions that the ancient Egyptians were trying to replicate the stars of Orion's Belt.

But what if the obstruction hadn't been aboveground? What if there was something under the sand that the builders had been avoiding? Any large tomb would make the ground above unable to support the weight of the causeway and the enormous limestone bricks transported over them.

In her mind, she could see the causeways and the strange space left between them and the Sphinx. The tunnel she stood in was just to the south of it. She spun to her right to look at the north wall.

A laugh erupted out of her lips before she could stop it.

"Oh, this is going to be good!" Lopez exclaimed from the side, moving to get a good angle for his video.

It had been there the whole time. Of course, it had been buried in thousands of hieroglyphics. A simple cartouche of a lion stacked on top of a monkey stacked on top of an ibis.

This was some old-school Egyptian religion. Before Ra. Before Osiris. Before Isis. These were the animal gods worshipped *before* the dynasties. The Egyptians worshipped animals above all else. It wasn't until thousands of years later that they morphed mankind into their pantheon.

"This is it," Rebecca said, reaching out to the symbol, but Brandt's forearm stopped her.

"What's the rule?"

Rebecca grinned. She just had gotten so caught up in that moment of discovery. "No touching the artifacts."

Brandt nodded. "At least not until we are secured properly." He turned to the men. "I want everyone tied to each other, with tighter bindings between pairs."

The men complied, except Levont, who looked around them, seeming to take in the fact they were in a newly found ancient passage about to open another secret millennia-old hidden passage.

"Can I just say?" the point man said. "You guys *rock*."

"Tie in, Levont," Brandt ordered, but Rebecca noticed he had the tiniest grin at the edge of his lips.

Rebecca picked up Vakasa as Talli finished cinching them together.

Once they were all tied in, the men raised their guns. Well, not all of them. Lopez had his camera up.

Brandt looked to each man. Once he got a nod from them, Brandt put his palm on the cartouche and pressed. Nothing happened. He pressed again, with the same result. Rebecca only took a little step forward. "Maybe you need to—"

A loud grinding filled the tunnel. Brandt urged her back, his gun raised as the wall moved laterally, revealing a dark passage. Once the rumbling and dust had settled, it became apparent it wasn't a passage, but a set of stone steps.

Brandt flashed his light down the steep tunnel.

"How far does it go?" Rebecca asked as both she and Vakasa craned their necks to see.

"Pretty damn far," Brandt answered, not looking any too happy about it. Then resolve replaced concern. "But it's our only way out, so…"

He indicated for Levont to take point. Without a word, everyone got into position and started down the steps. Lopez swept the camera side to side. Halfway down, the corporal began his narration.

"What will we find, RJ? What mysteries will we uncover? Will Daddy go in the record books? Along with, you know, all these other people?"

Brandt gave Lopez a three-out-of-five death stare.

The corporal just shrugged. "What? Who's going to hear me? Mummies?"

To Rebecca's surprise, Brandt didn't bark for Lopez to shut up. The corporal's soft whisper seemed to dull the edge of anxiety as they descended farther and farther into the ground. Would they find another dead end? After all of this, would they have to throw themselves on the Egyptians' mercy?

The girl in her arms didn't seem to mind, either. She would brace against Rebecca's body to lift her head above the men, constantly trying to see what was up ahead. Ah, children and their boundless curiosity. Someday Vakasa would learn that not everything up ahead was a wonder. Or maybe Rebecca hoped that the little girl wouldn't learn such a harsh lesson. Maybe she could learn it was okay to poke your head above the crowd and expect good things to come of it.

"I've got a door," Levont reported from the front. They all climbed down to join him on the landing.

Rebecca searched the surface for any hieroglyphics or cartouches, but found nothing. Just a hand-chiseled door. She shifted Vakasa's weight to the other hip. Brandt didn't even bother to ask her opinion. How could she have one with no writings?

Brandt gave the nod for the point man to open it. With a heave, the door slid across the uneven ground, grinding and protesting the whole way. Why wouldn't it? It had been shut for how many generations?

Levont took a decisive step into the next room. "What the...?"

Lopez was next and gave a whoop. Talli walked in, his jaw dropping.

Rebecca followed closely behind. "Oh. My. God."

However, it was Lopez who summarized it best.

"In your face, Geraldo!" he announced to the camera. "This is how you open up a chamber!"

CHAPTER 18

UNDISCLOSED LOCATION

3:01 P.M. (EST)

Bunny nearly jumped out of her skin when the click came over the line.

"Yes?" she answered. Silence stretched. Hope faded. Davidson didn't have any new information. He was checking in to see if they did. "Sorry. Nothing more."

Her eyes scanned the dozens of newscasts that Stark pulled up. Sure, theories were rampant. However, not a one had identified Brandt and the others. Which was probably a good thing. However, not having word from them for nearly a half hour was not such a good thing.

The longer they dallied, the greater the chances the Egyptians discovered the hidden tunnel. Okay, so Rebecca and the others probably weren't dallying, but still.

"Let him know the extraction team is nearly to the area," Emily stated. "He should be looking for a large van. Blue. Windowless."

Bunny nodded and repeated the information. She got a click in response.

It was a little hard to gauge Davidson's mental status through a series of clicks, but still. Something felt off. Wrong.

"Are you okay?"

That click came back way too fast.

"Something's wrong," Bunny said, glancing over the news feeds again. Everything seemed quiet on the eastern front. Then it had to be something with Davidson himself.

Prenner frowned. "But he just said he was fine."

The lieutenant didn't know Davidson like she did. Like the sniper would admit anything was wrong.

"Is there anything I can do to help?" Bunny asked.

No response. So her hunch was right.

"Except, of course," Bunny continued, "for us to pray."

A click was her answer.

Davidson turned off the sat phone and shook out his right hand. That Bunny was a little too insightful for her own good.

He willed his fingers to loosen, but they had seized down into a knot. A minor wound like the one he'd taken in the alley never would have affected him, but the damaged nerves in his hand had something else to say about it.

A sniper kind of needed his fingers to work. It was one of those deal-breaker kinds of things.

Lying flat on his belly again, Davidson tried to relax. Maybe if he could convince his body that he was on a nice hot Bahamas beach rather than a grungy Giza rooftop. A grungy tin rooftop.

He'd had to abandon all of the residential rooftops since, well, most of the occupants were out on them. With all the sirens and police activity, it had roused everyone from their apartments.

Not exactly ideal conditions for a stealthy extraction.

Trying to ignore the cramping of his fingers, Davidson did a perimeter sweep, again. Besides the constant influx of police and army vehicles, there was nothing to prove that Bunny had been correct in her assessment. He could be sitting on the wrong side of the pyramids for all he knew.

Or the others were all dead.

Davidson shook his head, sending a spray of sweat off his forehead. He couldn't let the nauseating pain get to him. An equally likely scenario had him placed within only minutes from Brandt's reappearance.

Okay, maybe equally likely wasn't correct, but even if there was the slimmest of chances, Davidson would wait out the week for them.

Not like this, though.

Pulling his hand away from his rifle, he had to admit he couldn't shoot. At least not with his right hand.

Jerking the rifle's butt up, Davidson positioned it against his other shoulder. He was trained to cross-shoot. However, being trained in it and actually doing it were two different things.

Yeah, their best-case scenario now required that Brandt and the rest had survived in a cave under a pyramid, somehow made their way to the Sphinx, broken out, then threaded the needle of hundreds of enemy forces, all with the support of their sniper, shooting *left-handed.*

Nope. Nothing to go wrong there.

Brandt tried hard not to be impressed or overwhelmed or shocked. He failed on all three accounts.

The chamber alcoves lined the walls, filled with urns. Tables overflowed with artifacts.

Thank God there hadn't been any threat in here since Levont had flat-out forgot to clear the room. Brandt had barely remembered to remind him. And Rebecca? Forget about it. The woman dragged her finger along objects circumventing the room. It was like her brain was trying to upload all the objects and categorize them.

Lopez was filming the whole thing, of course. Along with commentating. The only sound in the room was his voice.

"This is like King Tut's tomb on steroids, RJ..."

And the corporal wasn't wrong. There was a statue of an ibis that must have stood seven feet tall. The top of its head brushed up against the ceiling. Vakasa picked up a cobra circlet and put it on over her head scarf.

She then mimicked the "Walk Like An Egyptian" dance, looking very *unlike* a messiah.

The only English Vakasa seemed to know were American idioms. It was pretty damn cute.

After nearly tripping on a jackal vase, Brandt stopped.

"What is this place?" he asked.

Rebecca turned to him, wonder softening her tired features. "Anything that would come out of my mouth would just be a guess." She looked to Vakasa, who was trying to incorporate a moonwalk with her strutting. "Maybe she can help us translate some of the tablets..."

Ah, yes, the tablets. Brandt couldn't even count how many tablets were scattered around the room. He was no Egyptologist, but he would bet this doubled the known amount of knowledge about ancient Egypt.

"Guys," Levont breathed out, his eyes wide with delight. "I think…I think this is just the *antechamber*."

"Get out of here!" Lopez exclaimed. Even Talli looked impressed.

Levont seemed spot-on, though, as they all made their way to the far end of the room.

"I think these panels slide apart."

The point man was right. Those panels covered in hieroglyphics did look like they slid.

"Rebecca?"

She stepped up to the entrance, then put her hand out for Vakasa to come forward. The young girl cocked her head, studying the symbols. Then she reached out and opened them. Everyone scrambled back.

Okay, that was one way to do it.

"Levont, this time let's try and clear the room by the book," Brandt reminded the point man before they all got excited about the next discovery.

"You got it, Sarge."

However, as they entered the new chamber, all thoughts of the enemy vanished.

Rebecca wanted to breathe. Her lungs wanted air. Her brain wanted oxygen. They would all have to wait.

The sight before her was…staggering. The cavern was predominated by a huge pedestal, which served as the base for possibly the largest sarcophagus she'd ever seen. Dark-blue lapis lazuli had been laid into the sides. The stone was considered a precious gem, given its swirled mineral pattern. Each piece completely unique. And there were hundreds, if not thousands, used to adorn the stone coffin.

It was the only adornment, though. This tomb was so ancient it predated Egypt's fascination with gold.

"There's more," Levont shouted from up ahead.

How could there be more?

But there were more. Dozens, as a matter of fact. Dozens upon dozens of "smaller" sarcophagi. And by smaller, Rebecca meant they were only seven feet long and four feet across.

"Whose tomb is this?" Talli asked as they found the back of the cavern, then made their way back to the main sarcophagus.

That was a great question. Rebecca surveyed the hieroglyphics they passed. There was a lot of chatter about the upper and lower kingdoms. About the two becoming one. That event, the unification of Egypt, was perhaps one of the single most important joinings in history. After the two kingdoms merged, a true golden age of humanity began. But maybe all this hype about the unification wasn't just talk. Rebecca put all of this into perspective, given the timeline they had built regarding the Sphinx.

Rebecca clasped her hands over her mouth.

"What?" Brandt asked.

Rebecca backed away from the tomb. It couldn't be.

Yet there it was. She read the cartouche. There was no mistake.

"I think..." Rebecca had a hard time speaking. "I think we've found the first pharaoh's tomb."

Lopez whooped, although Rebecca wasn't quite sure even he understood the magnitude of the find.

"Narmer?" Talli asked in a much more measured tone.

Rebecca shook her head. "No." She pointed to the cartouche. "I think this is the Scorpion King."

"The one The Rock played?" Lopez asked, looking very skeptical.

"No," Rebecca hurried on. "The movie totally twisted history, but there was a rumored Scorpion King—Selk was his given name—but most historians dismissed the story out of hand."

"Guess they didn't see this," Levont commented.

Again, Rebecca couldn't help but laugh. "No, I guess they didn't."

To say this was the find of the century was an understatement of an understatement.

"This is the man that singlehandedly birthed nearly everything we know of Western civilization…"

"Which is great and all…" Brandt stated.

Rebecca tried to shake off her awe and turned to him. "But how does this get us out of here? I have no idea." She pointed to the towering sarcophagus. "Come on, though, it is pretty cool."

Brandt graced her with a rare in-combat smile. "I will give you that."

"The Sphinx wasn't just a random, catchall protector of Egypt," Rebecca rushed on. "It was protecting *this* tomb. The tomb of Egypt's first, unified ruler."

Vakasa ran up to the coffin, putting her arms around a corner. "*Babushka*!"

"Grandmother," Brandt translated, although he wasn't sure if he really needed to.

Rebecca tried to get the girl away from the sarcophagus. "Honey, your body oils are going to stain the surface."

However, Vakasa wouldn't budge. No wonder, given that explanation.

"*Babushka*," she murmured, resting her face against the cool stone.

"Wait..." Rebecca said, backing away from the girl, cocking her head, studying the hieroglyphics.

"What?" Brandt ribbed her. "You going to tell us this really is Vakasa's grandmother. The virgin mother of the virgin mother?"

"No," Rebecca said with a wave of her hand. "But I'm not so sure this is the man I was thinking."

"Levont, Talli, find us a way out of here," Brandt ordered. He didn't bother asking Lopez, as the guy was too busy filming. He turned to Rebecca. They had maybe two minutes to indulge her history geek side.

"Want to share?"

Rebecca chuckled again. "We always assume it's a guy, don't we?"

Brandt frowned. "I don't understand."

"'Pharaoh' is actually a unisex term," Rebecca explained. "As is 'king' in ancient Egyptian." Brandt still didn't have any idea what she was driving at, but hey, she usually landed her point—in time. Rebecca pointed to the cartouche. "This is the Scorpion King, only I think there's a chick buried in there."

"Whoa!" Lopez exclaimed. "Did you hear that, RJ? Girl power, man. We've got some competition."

Rebecca grinned at the corporal, then turned back to Brandt. "I think a woman united the two ancient kingdoms."

Lopez snapped his fingers. "Hey, wasn't there that other broad, Hapsi-put or something?"

"Hatshepsut, the female pharaoh," Talli corrected. Brandt was pretty damn sure he'd tasked the sniper with another duty, but they were playing it pretty loose and fast today.

"Yes," Rebecca confirmed, then went on. "But she wasn't the only female pharaoh. She was the best known and considered not just a female pharaoh, but one of the most successful monarchs of Egypt. She expanded trade and the arts. As a matter of fact, if a museum has an Egyptian artifact, it is probably from Hatshepsut's reign."

Brandt gave her that look. The one that said, *I'm feeling pretty generous, but move it along.*

Rebecca seemed to get the message, as she hurried. "Anyway, there were at least five other recorded female pharaohs. Even one called the 'Warrior Woman.' But this…this means the originator of Western civilization was a woman."

Vakasa kissed the coffin. "*Babushka*."

"Which, again, great footnote to a paper but—"

The ground beneath Brandt's feet shook.

"What was that?"

Dust filtered down from the ceiling as dirt particles danced along the top of the sarcophagus.

Fuck.

"Cave-in!" Lopez shouted.

No, no, no, Davidson prayed.

But the sight in his scope confirmed the worst. The Egyptians' attempt to clear the rubble underground had triggered a cave-in of the tunnel system that led away from the pyramid.

Sink holes—actually, sink *troughs*—were poking the desert floor. Radiating out from the Great Pyramid like a destructive spiderweb. Men ran from the monument, fleeing the catastrophe. The tanks they had brought in aimed to escape, but their treads did nothing but exacerbate the damage. One fell gun first into the sand.

Another tipped backward as the ground gave out from under them. Police cars swerved and dodged, trying to keep themselves on firm ground. The scattered chairs of the pyramid light show disappeared out of sight.

And the far-reaching tendrils were advancing rapidly. The crack of the earth filling the air.

At first, they confined themselves to the pyramid complex, but one leg aimed straight for the Sphinx. Straight for Rebecca and the others.

"Is this as bad on the ground as it looks on TV?" Bunny asked in his ear.

He gave a single click.

Actually, Davidson was certain that it was far worse than it looked. However, he didn't have a code for that.

"If it gets much farther..."

Yeah, Davidson got it, but he wasn't sure what he could do about it.

It sounded like Bunny was holding back tears. "I don't know how we are going to get the van to them."

There was that problem. However, Davidson feared that Bunny wasn't really allowing herself to go the worst-case scenario. That Sphinx had to be heavy. Even if the encroaching cracks didn't collapse the tunnel where Brandt was hiding...any damage to the bedrock around the Sphinx would bring it down, right on their heads.

Rebecca finally got Vakasa away from the sarcophagus as larger boulders began falling. She'd been in a cave-in before. Make that several. They never went well. And this time they didn't have hyper-buoyant water to save them.

"Go back out?" Talli suggested.

Brandt shook his head sharply. "At least *here* we've got some maneuverability."

To accentuate his words, the tunnel past the antechamber shook once, then collapsed.

"Can we get inside these?" Levont suggested.

"So we can get double-buried inside?" Brandt retorted. He was pissed. Not at his point man, but at the situation. Rebecca couldn't find fault with that. She covered Vakasa's head with her hand, trying to protect the girl's fragile skull. Not that a hand would help if one of those boulders fell here.

"Look," Lopez shouted over the increasing rumble. "That corner. There's no cracking."

Everyone followed his finger. The northwest corner did seem intact.

"Great." Talli frowned. "We stand over there and pray?"

That was looking like a viable option, and Brandt seemed to agree, as he urged them over there.

"No, smart-ass," Lopez retorted. "I say we get the lids and prop them up to act as a shelter and a bracing."

"Do it," Brandt ordered before his team could ask any more questions.

Rebecca huddled in the far corner with Vakasa as the men grabbed the nearest lid. They didn't bother with the main sarcophagus. That thing would take a crane to lift. Lopez handed her the camera.

"Film this, will ya?"

Rebecca obliged but feared she would catch Lopez's death on tape. Not the thing that the corporal had in mind for his son.

She watched on the screen as the men broke the seal on the first coffin. The stone fell to the side with a loud thud.

"We can't carry it," Brandt admitted. "So let's walk it over!" He had to shout the last part as rubble tumbled from the ceiling.

Even before that slab of stone was firmly in place, tilting over Rebecca's head, the men were on to the next one. Despite the fact the men were being pelted by debris, they brought the second lid over.

"Get in!" Rebecca urged as the front half of the chamber collapsed, crushing the Scorpion King's tomb. But the men refused. They hauled the third slab over. Talli got knocked in the shoulder by a huge piece of ceiling. He stumbled into their meager shelter.

"Brandt!"

The men were trying to secure the last slab, but it refused to cooperate.

She grabbed Brandt by the sleeve and hauled him inside. Lopez and Levont followed. He wrapped his arms around her and Vakasa as the roof cracked and split. It sounded like the world was ending. As her joints shook, it *felt* like the world was ending.

Lopez took the camera. "Looks like this may be the end of the road..." The corporal gulped as a huge section of ceiling shattered. "Know I loved you, buddy."

He turned off the camera and held it close to his chest as their world collapsed.

CHAPTER 19

UNDISCLOSED LOCATION

3:14 P.M. (EST)

Bunny watched the screen, refusing to believe what she saw. The entire tunnel system had shattered, which was almost to be expected. What wasn't expected and what never should have happened was the Sphinx cracking in half.

Clearly, the ground beneath the giant statue had become unstable. So right at the rib line of the beast, it split and sank a good twenty feet. One rear leg broke off, tumbling to the side. An ear flew off.

The Sphinx's serene face was marred by a network of cracks, making it seem like it was made of parchment rather than limestone.

Then it stopped. The destruction *stopped*.

Bunny held in a breath. Could they really get that lucky?

No. They could not.

With a resounding *bang*, the Sphinx's head tilted to the left as if someone had taken an ax to its neck. The visage teetered there for a moment, then crashed to the ground, rolling between its legs.

Whatever had been holding up the weight of the Sphinx gave out. The body split into a dozen other chunks and tumbled into the sink hole. Only one foreleg, broken and ragged, stuck up from the sand.

As the dust settled, Bunny poked Stark in the arm. "Can we get another angle?"

Stark shook his head. "No one was set up over there."

There was no movement. Nothing. The shattered Sphinx just sat there mocking them.

Where the hell were Rebecca and the others?

Davidson wiped his scope—again. The dust plume was still settling out over Giza. Blue-and-white strobe lights illuminated the grainy cloud with an almost-supernatural glow.

He didn't care about any of that. Davidson blocked out the sirens, the screams, the wailing. He only cared about movement near the Sphinx.

The army was already cordoning off the area, keeping everyone away.

This wasn't supposed to be the way this went. None of it was. He shouldn't be out here. He should be in there, with them. Finding a way out.

Gritting his teeth, Davidson shoved down the doubt and recrimination. They had both been close friends to him after the fire. After his old life had been burned away. Rebecca, though, had found him in that Moroccan hospital, scarred and suicidal, yet she had given him hope. Like a present, gift-wrapped. He wouldn't throw it away, just because…well, just because everything seemed hopeless.

Davidson swept the area again, searching for any sign of life. But there was none. Given the level of destruction, it could take days, if not weeks, to find any remains. If they even could. With a crushing collapse like this…

Wait. Davidson panned back to the paw that jutted up out of the hole. Was that a hand? A dark hand? He punched up the magnification.

It was! It was bloody and dirty as all get out, but it was a hand. Then Levont's face came into view. It was a dusty mess, but Davidson could have kissed it.

Abandoning protocol—because who really was going to hear him over the sirens and yelling?—Davidson brought the sat phone to his ear. "Are you seeing this?"

"Yes," Bunny said through tears.

"You've got to get that van over there."

There was a delay. Why was there a delay?

"Bunny?"

"We're not sure…" She paused. He could hear her lick her lips "With the army over there, guarding the perimeter…"

Davidson gritted his teeth and braced the rifle against his right shoulder. "Get them on the move."

Then Davidson did what he did best.

Shoot.

Brandt held tight to the little girl, protecting her with his body. The mass of broken rock and debris was unstable at best. Levont had tested it with his weight, but everything was still shifting, trying to find its equilibrium.

Rebecca was right in front of him, trying to scale the uneven, rocky precipice. Her foot slipped, nearly kicking him in the jaw.

"One foot at a time," he encouraged.

Then the bang of a gun sounded. Then another.

"Are they shooting at us?" Talli asked, a few feet above them.

Did it really matter at this point? It was only a matter of minutes before the whole Sphinx completely collapsed.

"Move it."

Rebecca scrambled past Talli, still keeping her head low. The handholds were too damn far apart. Brandt was going to have to trust that the girl could hold her own.

"You've got to hang on, honey," he cooed to her. Vakasa nodded her head, burrowing it against his shoulder, her little arms clutching around his neck, her legs wrapped around his chest.

Now able to use both hands, Brandt scaled the pile, arriving at the top with Rebecca and Talli.

"It looks like somebody's shooting at the army perimeter," Levont reported.

Brandt nearly stumbled a step. Davidson had come through. He had been very busy, indeed.

"Look!" Lopez exclaimed. "The van."

From the south, a blue van careened through the dark desert. It punched through the perimeter where Davidson was scattering the men. Good thing, too, because that fucking deep rumbling started under his feet.

"Get clear!"

Everyone climbed over the huge paw. There was no jumping straight off it, though. Levont must have figured that out, as he leapt down onto the Sphinx's head, slid down its nose, and hit the dirt feetfirst. Lopez went next and caught Rebecca at the base.

Then it was just Talli, then him.

"Smile for the camera," Lopez said.

Brandt was about to rip him a new one, but he realized that the corporal was actually talking to Vakasa, who had raised her head and waved to Lopez. Anything to keep the child calm.

But what was going to keep him calm as the last of the Sphinx shook underfoot, the head of the statue rocking backward into the maw? It was no longer a slide, but a scramble, running *up* the nose now, trying desperately to stay one step ahead of gravity. Finally, he reached the tip of the nose and slid down the lips as the head tipped straight back and fell out from under him.

They landed hard next to Rebecca. Brandt pushed forward, making sure there was plenty of solid ground beneath them.

"What's wrong with them?" Talli asked, pointing to the van, which did look like it was driving around in circles.

Levont nodded to the fissures and cracks that scarred the desert. "I think they are avoiding fault lines.

Fuck.

Brandt realized there was no avoiding the fault lines. They were everywhere. And worse? There was a linear gouge in the ground that ran between them and the van. There was no way the van could make it over that earthen moat.

"We've got to meet them halfway," Brandt ordered.

They were going to have to rely on Davidson supplying cover as they dashed across the desert. The point man was the first one over. He cleared the deep fissure easily. Lopez sailed across as well. Talli, however? Talli's boot caught the edge of the other side. If it hadn't been for Levont grabbing his shirt, the sniper would have fallen down the thirty-foot gash in the ground.

As much as he would have liked to think himself a far better athlete than Talli, Brandt realized he could never make it over with the girl in tow. Rebecca, too, had stopped on this side of the fissure.

He hugged Vakasa quickly. "Honey, I am going to have to toss you over."

Brandt had no idea if the girl really understood him or not. She just clapped. However, that was her response to just about everything.

"Levont!"

"I'm ready!" the point man yelled back.

"One," Brandt said, swinging the girl's body back to get some momentum. "Two." Another swing. "Three."

Channeling every bit of high school javelin throwing, Brandt let Vakasa launch. The light girl was so light that he actually overthrew her. Levont had to jump up to catch her before she flew past.

Rebecca looked to him. "I'll never make it."

"I know."

Tears threatened. Seriously, after surviving the Sphinx falling on her, she was going to die because she didn't have thighs of steel?

"And you can't throw me. I weigh..." Well, even at death's door, Rebecca wasn't going to admit that. Maybe Brandt could throw Bunny, but not her.

Still, he took her hand in his. "That's why we are going to run."

"Run?" she asked, but he had already turned away, circling his arm over his head.

"Get in!" he yelled to the others.

The words were barely out of his mouth when he tugged her forward.

"Where are we going?"

"With any hope," he answered, "to a part of this fissure that narrows."

Rebecca ran, having to really press to keep up with Brandt as the men loaded into the unmarked van. Her fiancé was such an optimist. However, the gap only got larger and larger. And it began to send off side cracks. The van easily caught up to them, but had to veer off to avoid a four-foot dip in the desert.

She slowed, tugging his hand. "Just go, Brandt."

"*No.*"

Rebecca pulled to a stop. "You've got to get over before it's too far for even you."

There was no time to argue. The Egyptian army was regrouping. Not even Davidson could keep that many away. And the longer the van lingered trying to pick them up, the more likely the entire team, including Vakasa, would be captured.

"Jump, damn it," Rebecca insisted.

"Sarge!" Levont yelled as the van pulled to a stop as close as it could get to the edge. He waved a coil of rope. "We've got you."

As the point man tossed the end of the rope over, Rebecca turned to Brandt. "What does he mean?"

Brandt caught the rope, wrapping it around his wrist over and over again. "I'm going to anchor this side, and you are going to climb the rope across."

"What? No. Huh?"

As Davidson kept a halo of bullets around them, Brandt urged her to grab the rope with both hands. That disastrous time in Pushchino flashed.

"I don't do well with heights."

Brandt tugged on the rope, tightening it down even further. "It's not a height. It's a *depth*, so get moving."

Yep, that was her inspirational honey, all right.

Taking a deep breath, Rebecca stepped off the edge, her weight suspended only by her grip on the rope. Kids did this kind of thing on the monkey bars, right? Usually without gunfire and an abyss beneath them, but still.

Hand over hand, she made her way across the gap.

Only, the gap was getting bigger. And bigger. The sides crumbling away. She couldn't climb as fast as the edge disintegrated. The rope went slack, dropping Rebecca several feet, as Levont had to back away from the edge before he fell.

"Legs up!" Lopez shouted to her.

She rationally didn't know what he was saying, but her body, keen on survival, did as he said. With her weight more evenly distributed, she climbed faster, hauling it across the rope.

Talli grabbed her as she reached the edge, helping to pull her the rest of the way.

High on success, she turned to find the gap so much larger than she'd remembered it. Way wider than even Brandt could jump.

Her excitement turned to fear as Brandt frowned.

Yeah, he was never going to make that.

Fuck it.

"Get ready!" Brandt yelled as he backed away, then charged the edge. It was a great feeling flying through the air. Until he started falling. As predicted, the other wall came up fast.

Brandt turned his shoulder into it, hitting the limestone rather hard. He clung to the rope, falling another ten feet, until Levont caught up on his end. Then it was just a matter of climbing up the side.

Right.

But he made it. Cresting the edge and getting hustled into the van were a blur.

"Is everyone okay?" Brandt asked, trying to right himself.

A murmuring of affirmatives came back at him.

"Bloody hell," a voice said as the sliding door slammed shut and someone hit the gas, rocking them all back. "Do you destroy everything you touch?"

He looked up to find Vanderwalt smiling that crooked-ass British smile of his.

"What the…?"

They met in a bro hug.

Vanderwalt chuckled. "Let Emily know she owes me."

Bunny hugged Stark, who hugged Emily, who hugged Prenner, who didn't exactly look thrilled about it, but also didn't fight the expression of group affection.

That was the single most awesome extraction in the history of extractions.

"Davidson, get out of there," Bunny exclaimed, so happy to give that directive.

Prenner took the phone. "The rally point is the British consulate. You'll get whisked to Turkey from there."

A single click answered them.

Then reverie was short-lived, however, as a beep came from one of the computers.

"What was that?" Bunny snapped. She didn't like beeps. In her world, beeps were usually bad. And from Stark's frown, she wasn't wrong.

"Someone is trying to hack their way in."

Prenner stepped forward. “I thought you said you were unhackable?”

Stark held up a finger. “Statistically speaking, I am.”

“However?” Emily asked.

The tech didn’t answer. He just started the counter-hack, or whatever you called two geeks going at it. Normally, Bunny would have found it all amusing. The only problem was Brandt and the others’ lives were still in jeopardy.

“Should we move this to Langley?” Emily asked.

Stark just held up a hand, then waved it, whisking away her question.

“This is all going to be a moot point in a few hours, correct?” Prenner asked Emily. “Once they are in Turkey, I am assuming they will be coming straight home.”

The CIA operative looked to Bunny. She didn’t need to voice her question. Bunny had already been asking it in her own mind.

“Right?” Prenner pressed.

“Sure,” Bunny answered, but Prenner wouldn’t let it go.

“Why *wouldn’t* they come straight home?” Emily asked.

Bunny squirmed. She’d sworn she would never breathe a word of what Rebecca and she had found on those stone tablets.

“I don’t think they’ll come home until they feel it is safe.”

“And why exactly wouldn’t it be safe?” Prenner pressed.

When Bunny didn’t answer, Emily squinted. “What do you know about the girl that we don’t?”

Bunny slapped her hands together. “Who else is hungry?”

From the German building’s rooftop, Frellan watched the van fleeing the pyramid plateau. The Egyptian army gave chase, but the desert was riddled with fissures and cracks. The escape vehicle made it into narrow streets lined by tenement buildings. It would soon be lost within the maze of alleys.

To his left, Mikhal stirred. So strange to see the man actually move. The sniper glared as he freed the rifle from his shoulder. Frellan had given strict orders to not engage in this little battle.

"Do not."

Mikhal didn't slow his motion. Instead, he lowered himself to the roof, setting up a shot.

"We cannot risk the girl," Frellan urged.

Still, the sniper set up his shot.

"Do not test me," Frellan warned. That got a cocky grin from the sniper.

Frellan could call over one of the mercenaries. It was within his prerogative to end the sniper's rebellion with a shot to the back of the head. But as Aunush found out, the sniper had friends in the inner circle. The Master's pet.

So he did nothing but watch as the sniper took his shot. The left rear brake light exploded as the van fishtailed, then punched the gas.

Had the sniper missed?

Pleasure dulled to realization. No. The sniper had simply marked the van, making it far easier to track. The sniper rose, swinging his rifle over his back, daring Frellan to criticize him. Also gloating, just a bit.

Mikhal had made two points. One? He could have taken out the van if he had wanted to. Two? He could have taken out the van if he had wanted to. The first was based on his skill as a sniper. The second was based on the fact Frellan hadn't dared intervene.

He tried to allow the fury to bleed from him. Impulsive action was his sister's weakness, yet he feared his fist would fly of its own accord. Then Monnie put her hand in his. Drawing his finger along the veins, Frellan could feel tension bleed from him as he imagined dissecting one of the blood vessels out, putting a metal band around it, then sewing the vein back in. That way, he could squeeze it, close it off, then open it again at will. The body was meant for so much more than one could imagine.

"Where to?" Ugudo asked.

Anger rose again, but there was Monnie's hand in his.

"Think," she said. "The burka was bloodied. Someone was there when she died."

The watcher was correct. It had to have been Dr. Monroe.

"What would your mother have told her?"

Still, Frellan did not know. He had been estranged from her for years.

"I know of her research," Monnie admitted.

Many knew of the watcher who wandered from her path. His mother's defection had never been a secret. He had faced manhood under its shadow. The fact that she had gone out into the world, sampling DNA, trying to scientifically find the Messiah, was closely held knowledge.

Monnie was a watcher herself, though. She swam in the lives of the past watchers.

"Based on her research, here are five locations that are probable," Monnie stated.

"And?" Frellan asked.

"I think one will be of specific interest to Dr. Monroe."

CHAPTER 20

ANKARA, TURKEY

MAY 28, 5:14 A.M.
(EEST, EASTERN EUROPEAN STANDARD TIME)

Rebecca stepped out onto the tarmac, her entire body aching. She really, really missed the billionaire's luxury jet. Sure, they had taken a diplomatic plane from Egypt to Turkey, but it did not have a hot tub. She really missed having a hot tub on a plane.

However, beggars couldn't be choosers. Vanderwalt had worked his butt off to get them out of Egypt, so she didn't express just how much her lower back hurt as they crossed the tarmac and headed toward the private terminal.

In the still-dark mist an *ezan*, a call to prayer, carried over the wind. It must have been the *fajr*, the pre-sunrise service. Had they really been fleeing Egypt all night? Could it really be a new day?

Vakasa squeezed Rebecca's hand, almost as if answering her unasked question.

It indeed was a new day. A new country. A new sense of hope.

Not existential hope, but a more practical hope. The hope of a hot shower and fresh clothes.

However, even that was dashed as Brandt stopped short of entering the terminal. Vanderwalt held open the door, cocking his head.

"I know you won't tell me anything you are up to, mate, but at the least let me buy you all breakfast before you head out."

Brandt held out his hand to shake. The two men had spent most of the travel time reliving past glories. What else could they talk about, though? Vakasa? The Disciples? Not very likely.

When Vanderwalt didn't shake it, Brandt smiled. "Walt, you know how much I appreciate you pulling our asses out like that, but I gotta do what I gotta do."

The thin Englishman finally shook Brandt's hand. "Apparently right *now*."

"I swear, when I can, I *will* tell you all about it." Brandt pumped Vanderwalt's hand. "Even over a warm damned beer."

That got a grin from the affable British agent. "I'm going to hold you to that. Including why you are carting along a little girl rumored to have healed a fatal bullet wound of yours."

What the…? Rebecca turned to Brandt. He'd never said anything about Vakasa healing him. Before she could say anything, Brandt shook his head sharply.

She got it. *Not in front of Vanderwalt.*

The smile that had nearly flickered out on Brandt's face returned. Only Rebecca knew it wasn't a real smile. It was the smile Brandt used when he wanted to get out of a conversation, just like this one.

"You know how it is, Walt," Brandt said. "Villagers aren't quite used to bulletproof vests."

Vanderwalt searched her fiancé's face, then shrugged. "Just another story to add to the mythos of Brandt, then."

"Damn straight," Brandt answered, this time a true grin on his face. He then put his hand on Rebecca's back, guiding her away from the main terminal door. The pressure he was using though felt like he wanted to get out of here ASAP.

She couldn't just leave like that, though. Dropping Vakasa's hand, Rebecca went over and hugged the MI-5 agent.

"Thanks, Walt," Rebecca said, giving their Brit guardian angel a kiss on the cheek before heading back to Brandt. The other men may not have hugged Vanderwalt, but they all gave him a warm handshake on their way out. Especially Talli.

Following Brandt, she glanced over her shoulder as Vanderwalt gave a final wave good-bye. Vakasa nearly broke her elbow returning the gesture.

Brandt seldom felt bad about doing his job. He kept secrets for a living. He'd accepted that a long time ago. Still, walking away from a man who had not only saved his team's life, but Rebecca and Vakasa's as well? He wanted to tell Vanderwalt everything. Hell, the guy might even be able to help them, but Brandt couldn't risk it.

Look at how the story of the gunshot wound in the Congo had spread all the way to Thames House. He couldn't risk any kind of leak. The less Vanderwalt knew, the less he could unintentionally compromise their mission.

Once they were out of earshot, Levont trotted up to Brandt. "Sarge, I know we want to get out of here, but come on"—the point man threw a thumb to the glass window that looked down upon the Esenboga International Airport—"their food service was rated number one in Europe. Number *one*."

Even Brandt had to admit the terminal that was a testament to modern architecture did look tempting. The thing was all steel and glass, with a huge open food court that reflected Turkey's bi-continental culture. A European delicacy café stood next to a traditional Afghan restaurant. His stomach rumbled.

"A quick bite?" Talli asked, seeming far more excited than he did going into the field.

"Thanks, but no thanks," Lopez said before Brandt had to. "This is Turkey, guys."

When Levont and Talli didn't seem to understand, Davidson chuckled. "I think they might still be a little pissed about Istanbul."

That was an understatement.

"If it helps," Rebecca interjected, "in about five hours, we are going to be in Basque country, a foodie's heaven."

Levont rubbed his belly. "Why, yes, that does."

Brandt turned away from the elegant airport. "Lopez, you need to secure us a craft." The guy was nearly halfway down the long hallway when Brandt shouted, "Something *nondescript*."

The corporal gave a head bob before he disappeared around a turn. Lopez would bring back what he brought back.

Brandt sighed, draping an arm over Rebecca's shoulder. She leaned her head into the crook of his arm. It almost hurt to have to talk shop.

"You sure about Spain?"

Rebecca lifted her head, giving a shrug. "More sure than I was about the tunnels under the Pyramids, and less sure than I was that St. Basil's held a clue to the Ten Commandments."

"So," Brandt responded, "not sure at all."

She cuddled against him again. "Pretty much."

"I am telling you, man," Levont barked a laugh, "you've got to start *charging*—I mean, charging *serious* money—to be on your team."

The air was fragrant with the smell of oranges, leather, olives, and sweat. The atmosphere was heavy with it, so much so that it almost became another personality to add to the eclectic mix of nationalities in this press of human flesh. Gypsy women bustled forward, trying to force flowers into his hand, or to read that same hand, the easier to then extract a "favor" of some spare change.

"Master Frellan," a voice called out amongst the bustle of the Madrid marketplace.

Frellan turned on his heel, making sure to keep his hoodie all the way forward. Who would call his name so freely? His mercenaries were out arranging transportation to the Basque region of the country. Monnie and Mikhal were the only ones by his side.

A black-robed priest hurried amongst the early-morning crowd at the Plaza Mayor, Spain's largest open-air marketplace, weaving his way amongst the stalls and shoppers. He had the pasty-fleshed and squint-eyed look of a man who spent far too long reading books inside. While out here in the bright Spanish sun, it gave him an appearance of constant unpleasant surprise.

The chubby man finally caught up. An overexuberant smile upon his face.

"Do I know you?" Frellan asked. Seldom did he spend much time in the company of Roman Catholic priests.

"Yes, yes," the man said, trying to catch his breath. "Well, no, not really. I am Father Benedicto."

Frellan more sensed than saw Mikhal pull a knife from its sheath. Little did the priest before them know he was moments from death.

"We have a mutual friend," the priest finally clarified. "Aunush."

"In here," Frellan hissed, urging the priest away from the linen-lined stalls and into a small *sustantivo* that operated at the edge of the marketplace. The scent of bitter coffee mixed with sweet milk pressed upon them. "How do you know that name?"

Benedicto's pleasant smile was replaced by a sharp glare toward Mikhal. "You can put the knife away. Lest you wish to openly kill a priest in possibly the most devout Roman Catholic city short of Rome."

Frellan glanced around to the patrons. Nearly three-quarters of the women—even the younger business woman getting ready for their day at the capital, or at an international conglomerate such as Telephonica, or even the Olympic planning committee—wore a cross around their necks.

The home-court advantage did indeed go to the priest.

"We are no longer at cross-purposes," he explained.

An eyebrow shot up. The Disciples and Roman Catholic Church not at odds? That was like saying Mossad and Hamas were suddenly allies.

Frellan switched to Latin. Even in this internationally diverse city, these espresso drinkers should not have been fluent in the ancient language. Although, he was certain the priest was. If he knew Frellan's sister's name, then he must.

"We wish to bring the *true* Messiah to the world," Frellan said slowly and carefully.

The priest got into the long line leading up to the barista. Several people moved out of the way, allowing Benedicto to jump ahead of them. If only the masses respected the Disciples in such a way. *Soon, though. Soon*, Frellan reassured himself.

"I did not say we would always be aligned," he explained in ancient Greek. "But today, today we both seek the same thing."

Monnie interjected. "And that would be?" she asked in Aramaic.

"Come with me," the priest said with a knowing smile, "and I shall show you."

Frellan glanced about. "And your escort?"

Benedicto shrugged. "There is only I."

Alone? Who was this priest? To walk freely amongst the Disciples? Once outside of the city, they could easily gut him and leave his carcass on the side of the road with no one the wiser.

However, the priest seemed decidedly unconcerned with his fate. "Latte anyone?"

Apparently, things weren't going well. Stark's fingers flew over not just one keyboard, but three. For hours. For hours, he had fought off the attack, deflecting the hack, but it looked like the defenses just wouldn't be enough. Prenner had wanted to pull out hours ago, and Emily was telling Langley they would be there in fifteen minutes all night long.

The only reason they had stayed was that Stark was learning as much has he could about the hacker. His style. His moves. And hopefully, his identity.

However, Stark finally threw his hands up in the air. "That's it."

He reached over and pulled the plugs on the CPUs. Drives winded down as Stark turned off the screens.

"All right," Emily said, getting her phone out again. "The car is waiting around the block. I can have it here in just a minute."

"What do you mean?" Stark asked.

Emily looked to Prenner, then to Bunny. "We need to establish a new HQ."

"Duh," Stark said, standing up and stretching, probably the first time he had in six hours. Without another word, he led them out of the basement and into the kitchen, where they found his mother, who shook her head.

"Burning the candle at both ends. Not good for the skin."

Stark went over and gave her a kiss on the cheek. "Mom, how about some breakfast?"

"Animal pancakes or biscuits and gravy?"

Stark looked to the group. "Well?" When no one answered, he turned back to his mother. "How about both? Plus some hash browns. My brain needs a carb kick-starter."

"Only because we have guests."

Stark gave her another kiss on the cheek and led them upstairs.

"I am not going to remind you of the incredibly tight timetable we are on," Prenner said as they climbed up to the second floor.

"Yeah, thanks for trusting me so much. You didn't have to remind me of that."

Stark grabbed a chair, stood on it, and pulled down the staircase to the attic. Obviously intrigued, no one asked where they were going. Once in the attic, Stark turned on a light to reveal a techno-geek's wet dream. If the basement had been a command center, this was the mother of all command centers.

Computer after computer booted up.

"I don't understand," Bunny said, trying to count the number of screens lining the walls.

"It's my doomsday room. I set this system up, routed it through Thailand, and have never used it since. This baby is virgin. No IP addresses. No browsing history. No cookies."

You know what? If Davidson weren't just so damned sweet, Bunny might have learned to love the geeks.

Even Davidson could hear the squawk of the air traffic controller through Lopez's earphones. Although, to be perfectly honest, Davidson was pretty dang sure the corporal was enjoying the berating. How often did Lopez get to use his colorful Spanish language on someone who actually understood him?

"What's happening?" Rebecca asked from the seat behind. Brandt still hadn't popped an eye open, although Davidson knew the sergeant was wide-awake.

"It sounds like air traffic control is trying to wave us off because our plane is too big," Lopez reported.

Rebecca looked back over her shoulder from the first-class section to the hundred-plus empty seats behind them. At the time, ditching their small prop plane and stealing a Boeing 747 that was scheduled for maintenance in Athens, Greece, seemed like a great idea. It hadn't occurred to anyone that the closest airport to the northern region of Spain would be a small regional airport.

Although, the more he thought on it, the more Davidson began to wonder if Lopez in fact *did* know this information. Because, come on, they weren't being shot at. There was no bizarre weather disturbance, and Brandt had forced the corporal to fly at "regular" speed. Lopez had bellyached the whole way about the embarrassingly long flight time.

So the only way Lopez could make this one-on-a-scale-of-ten routine flight into an eight was to increase the difficulty of the landing.

And trying to set down a jumbo jet on a tiny airstrip might just do it.

With the cockpit door propped open, Davidson could hear Talli complain, "They're saying if we try to land, we're going to crack the pavement and go nose first into the ground."

"Sure," Lopez agreed, "if *they* were flying the plane."

Lopez hit the mic and threw out a string of what Davidson could only imagine were choice Spanish curse words. For once, he was glad he wasn't fluent in the language.

Vakasa pointed out the window as the Pyrenees Mountains came into view. She clapped loudly, pointing and speaking in her catch-as-catch-you-can manner.

He didn't think he needed to translate. She liked mountains, that was pretty clear.

"Aren't we coming in a bit fast?" Rebecca asked. "And steep?"

"I think that's part of the deal," Levont said, grinning ear to ear.

Rebecca was right, though. Davidson rose and made his way to the cockpit.

"Lopez," he tried to reason, "there's having fun, and there is unnecessary risk."

The corporal shrugged him off, too. "Says the guy who was *outside* the Sphinx when it came down."

There was no more time to argue, as wind screeched as the flaps went up, finally slowing them—some.

"Come to Papa!"

Davidson braced himself as the plane leveled out for a split second, the ground rushing up at them. Then Lopez brought the plane's nose up. He tugged hard on the yoke. Was he trying to land them on their tail?

Hysterics with rolled *r*'s and lispy *s*'s spewed from the radio. They were tilted so far up Davidson couldn't even see the ground anymore. Then their back tires made contact with the ground, but Lopez kept enough thrust that they were literary wheeling down the road rather than landing. Slowly, the corporal lowered the front tire.

And that was it. They were out of the air and on the ground. They had barely felt it. Davdison looked back out of a window. Not even a scratch on the runway.

"Um, Lopez," Talli said in his "I'm panicking but trying not to seem like I'm panicking" voice, "this isn't a very long runway."

Talli was right. Sure, they were on the ground. However, they were rolling down the runway at breakneck speeds. Literally *break their necks* if they hit the retaining wall at the end of the runway.

"No," Lopez admitted as he put the flaps up farther and tapped the brakes. "No, it's not."

If the corporal tried any harder to stall their speed, he could end up putting them nose first into the runway, which, of course, was not ideal. Behind him, Davidson could hear Rebecca getting Vakasa into crash position.

Which was what Davidson should have been doing, only he had a fascination with watching Lopez work his magic. As the plane shimmied around them, Lopez worked the flaps, the brakes, and the radio all at once.

"Here's for nothing!" Lopez said as he turned the plane. The craft careened for a moment, then fell into sharp left turn, which evolved into a full-on spin. They doughnuted down the short runway. The smell of burning rubber filled the air. Then they were out of rubber, as the metal axles screamed against the runway.

That wall was still coming up fast. Then Lopez put the flaps up full. Their last wide arc brought them around to the wall. With an almost gentle tap, the wing hit the wall, then they stopped.

For a moment, no one moved. Then Lopez whooped.

“That is how it is done!” The corporal turned to Levont. “Well? Did you get it?”

“Duh, man,” Levont answered as he lifted the camera for all to see.

Davidson sat back in his seat. That was quite the introduction to the Basque region.

CHAPTER 21

BASQUE REGION

1:36 P.M. (CEST, CENTRAL EUROPEAN STANDARD TIME)

As the SUV revved up the mountain, Rebecca settled in for the long drive. Even though they had landed in San Sebastian, they were still a good three and a half hours out from the Basque village of Lennore. Vakasa seemed to understand this was going to be a haul and snuggled up against her leg, folding her hands on Rebecca's thigh to act as a pillow.

The scenery was magnificent, rich and lush and rocky and mountainous all at once. It was the variation that Rebecca had come to identify with Spain in general. So many different types of terrain, all existing in a space that you could fit inside of Texas and rattle around. It was astonishing, really. Those extremes could often be found right next to, or even right on top of, one another.

Rebecca put her hand on the little girl's shoulder. As Vakasa drifted off to sleep, her lips formed a lazy smile. Rebecca glanced up to find Brandt equally ready to nap.

"Are you sure that you don't want me to explain why Basque? Why this village?"

Her fiancé didn't even crack his eyes open. "Nope."

Still, Rebecca tried again. "Not any historical context of the region or how it impacts Vakasa?"

"Still nope," Brandt stated, then turned his head to the side, resting it against the SUV's doorjamb.

She should have seen it as a sign of trust and respect. Unfortunately, Rebecca wasn't all that sure she had it right. Without a sounding board, talking it out, she was getting more and more anxious that she had missed something. And when you were talking about millennia-old mysteries, missing something pretty much meant you were screwed.

Hell, she'd even take Bunny right about now, but they were still under radio silence. After contacting Bunny and giving them the cursory details, all electronics had been abandoned and new ones bought at the airport.

"You guys are kidding me, right?" Levont asked from the backseat.

The rest of the men shook their heads. Talli even snorted. "Get some sleep while you can."

"Sleep?" Levont questioned. "I don't want to blink around you guys." He glanced to Rebecca. "Ma'am, if you are game, I would love to know what's going on."

Rebecca smiled. It had been a long time since she'd been called ma'am. It felt kind of good. "All right, then. What do you know of the Basque region?"

"Wait," Levont said, his easy grin fading, "is this going to be a quiz?"

"I am a professor first and foremost," Rebecca confirmed. How she loved a fresh new mind to explore.

"Um, well..." Levont fumbled a bit, then found his intellectual footing. The guy looked like a brute linebacker, but she knew he could speak five different languages and had proven himself incredibly bright and flexible in the field. And how she wished she'd only known that from Brandt's stories. Rebecca had experienced it firsthand.

"All right," Levont said, starting slowly, then gaining speed. "The Basque region is known for its hyper-patriotism. It is now an autonomous state within Spain after a pretty brutal road to independence. A lot of which would put the IRA to shame. But since the accord in the seventies, the violence has died down. The state department lifted a visitors' advisory a decade ago. Now the danger in Spain is the economic crisis and the bands of bandits that have formed to steal from the tourists."

Rebecca shook her head, laughing lightly. "That would be an awesome briefing for the team. However, what I am looking for is why the Basque people are so nationalistic? Why they wanted their own government? Why we are here?"

"Oh crap..."

"Ha!" Lopez announced from the driver's seat. "Even I know that one."

Rebecca knew she looked skeptical, but come on, this was Lopez. He probably knew the driving time between each and every city, town, and village, but their history? That would be a first.

"Enlighten us, then," Rebecca encouraged.

Lopez glanced to her in the rearview mirror. "I shall, little missy." The corporal took in a deep breath before starting. "Okay, the Basque people have been settled in the region for like... ever. At least ten thousand years, which makes them the longest continuous European population. So they are kind of proud of that. Like, super proud of that. They have their own language that predates any others in the region and is more like Arabic than Spanish. So they pretty much figured they should have their own government as well."

"A-plus," Rebecca commended. "And how did the Basques avoid being assimilated into all of the conquering nations that swept through Europe over the ages?"

Lopez nodded out the window at the steep cliffs rising up around them. "These mountains, darlin'. Geographical isolation. It was just too hard or expensive to mount a campaign up here."

"Like I said, A-plus." Rebecca smiled as Lopez beamed. "Now the bonus round. What does that have to do with Vakasa?"

At that, Lopez frowned. "No clue."

Before Rebecca could answer, Talli stirred in his seat. "All right, let me give a stab at it."

She was as surprised as the rest of the car that Talli was contributing. He'd been fairly withdrawn this mission, more than usual.

"Christianity," he stated. Off her nod, he continued. "Strangely, this region was the first to be evangelized as early as the five hundreds yet resisted the new faith more than any other population."

"Whoa there, *chico*." Lopez chuckled. "This area is hardcore Catholic."

"If you'd let me finish," Talli retorted, "I was going to say, once they adopted Catholicism, however, they took to it like fish to water."

"All right, then," Lopez answered, seeming satisfied.

"And what does that have to do with Vakasa?" Rebecca asked Talli. The man squirmed a bit. Because he didn't know the answer or didn't want to speak it?

Davidson spared Talli Rebecca's expectant glare.

"The Black Madonna," Davidson stated.

Rebecca grinned. "Exactly."

Levont looked from Rebecca to the little girl curled up on her lap. "I don't get it. I mean, I get it. She's supposed to be the Messiah, and she's black—and *representing*, I might add—but..."

Davidson's eyes flicked over to Rebecca. She didn't seem nearly as confident about this aspect as she had the rest. He stepped into the silence. "The Black Madonnas are revered by some and dismissed by others."

Lopez shook his head. "They are just paintings for statues that have been stained black over time."

"Case in point," Davidson retorted.

"*Prove* it," Lopez challenged.

Davidson sighed. While fallen, Lopez still held on to his Catholic roots. His *Hispanic* Catholic roots. They were some of the staunchest anti–Black Madonnas around.

"If the white skin of the statues were stained by age and soot, why are the golds in their gowns still gold? Or the blues, blue? Or the reds, red? Why is only the skin affected?" Davidson overrode the corporal. "And why are other paintings of white saints still *white*."

Lopez sputtered, "But, but...Even though the skin is dark, the features of those Madonnas are European."

"Only some," Rebecca corrected. "The *later* ones. Many consider them knockoffs. Artists indulging in the fad. The first ones, though? Those created in the early AD years? Those show definitive negroid features."

The corporal huffed and went back to driving. Which is just as well. He didn't stand a chance against Rebecca.

"Okay, great," Levont commented. "But what's that got to do with a remote Basque village?"

Davidson looked to Rebecca, who gave him the nod to explain. "It is where the first Black Madonna was ever created."

With half an ear, Brandt listened to the rise and fall of conversation. Rebecca was going into detail about the history of the Black Madonna. Its acceptance, then rejection, then acceptance by the Catholic Church. She was really getting her history geek on.

Brandt didn't need to pay particular attention to her, since he pretty much already knew the story. There was a Black Madonna in the church across town. His friend had taken him to see it as a kid. He'd thought it would be dumb, as all kids thought religious artifacts were when they were kids, but even at ten years old, Brandt had been stirred by the beauty of the statue.

He'd learned that the church had even tried to cover the color, but the congregation had complained so vehemently that they had to paint it back. When his priest couldn't explain the phenomena, dismissing it out of hand, Brandt even talked his mother into letting him bicycle to the library to research it.

So when Rebecca mentioned the Basque region, he'd pretty much known where she was going with it. This area was ground zero for Black Madonnas.

"Turn left up ahead," Rebecca broke off from the history lesson.

"You sure?" Lopez asked with a frown. "The GPS says left is going to take us off a cliff."

Rebecca leveled her gaze. "Ricky. Left."

"You've been here before?" Talli asked.

Brandt shifted to get a better listen. The conversation still wasn't eyelid-raising worthy, at least not yet.

"Yeah…" Rebecca said, sounding far less excited. "Yes, I have."

Levont's smile was so bold that Brandt *heard* it. "Ah, come on. You can't drop a hint like that and not follow it up with the story. 'Cause we know there's a story there."

Brandt was pretty sure Levont got a smile out of Rebecca. She was a little bit of a sucker for flattery. Why she hung out with *him*, he wasn't quite sure.

"I did some DNA research based on the Basques' assertion that they had DNA unique to the European continent…"

"And?" Levont pressed.

"Well, unfortunately, beyond the fact they have a very high Rh-negative blood factor, they are pretty much a Pyrenees Mountain mutt mix."

Davidson turned in the seat next to Brandt to rejoin the conversation. "That wasn't all, though, was it?"

Huh. The kid knew something about Rebecca that he didn't. That wasn't being a very good fiancé. However, after hearing about three dozen different research grants, his eyes kind of glazed over.

"Well," Rebecca answered, not sounding all that thrilled that Davidson had brought up the subject, "I also proved that they didn't have the 'smart gene' that I'm looking for."

"Ouch," Levont exclaimed.

"Yes, I'm a little bit of *persona non grata* around here."

Brandt peeked open an eye, to find Rebecca blushing and suddenly becoming interested in the hem of her shirt.

She even looked pretty as an outcast.

Frellan peered at Benedicto, who sat across from him. They'd found a small table in the shade of an alley to talk. They were sheltered from view of the main street by a row of almond trees, their trunks short and squat, their branches and leaves wide and spread. The trees were in bloom, their perfume scenting the air with a sweetness that contained just a touch of raw almond to it.

His men stood guard at either end of the street, making sure no tourists decided to crash their awkward party. Monnie sipped a *café con leche* and munched on *magdalenas* that she occasionally dipped in her cup as Benedicto licked the thick, dark chocolate where it dripped down from his *churros y chocolate.*

This black-frocked man seemed little the holy man.

"My *monsignor* is arranging for transportation to the village of Lennore."

"We know where we need to head," Frellan stated coolly, still trying to puzzle the man out. "We do not need your help."

"Ah, but your master seems to feel differently."

Frellan looked to Ugudo. The priest only seemed amused. "Please. After the Congo and then Egypt?" He chuckled. "For such an ancient society, you aren't exactly batting a thousand out in the field."

Frellan's fingers dug into his own skin. He had suffered much, sacrificed much, to lead the search for the Messiah. To have this *priest* speak to him in such a way?

"But I am not here to babysit," Benedicto announced. "I am here to kill the girl."

Monnie coughed out creamy coffee, patting her chest, trying to stop the near convulsion. Frellan was equally horrified yet kept his visceral reaction inside. Really, in retrospect, he shouldn't have been even surprised. At least not the kill part. But admitting that the priest had planned to kill the girl, that was surprising.

"And you told the Master?"

"Of course," the priest said with a shrug. "We could have spun a tale of wanting to study her ourselves, but why? We both know she is a danger to my church."

"The pope knows of this?" Frellan asked.

Again, the priest shrugged. "As your master knows everything that you have done or plan to do in the field?"

So true.

Frellan picked up his black coffee and drank half the scalding-hot liquid. "If you know where we are going, then might I ask why you need *us*?"

Benedicto nodded to Monnie. "We do not have what is in her head."

"Why?"

"She holds the key to proving the girl's divinity." The priest seemed delighted by Frellan's ignorance. "You did not know, truly? Well, I guess your master also knows more than she is sharing."

Frellan turned to the watcher. "What is he taking about?"

The petite woman looked down at her cup.

"What?"

Before he could press further, a set of SUVs drove up to the alleyway, squealing to a stop. There was no way the large vehicles—much more suited to the US than to Spain—could ever navigate the narrow stretch where they sat. Benedicto rose from his seat.

"Please, does it not make more sense to kill me *after* I've helped you? It will feel far more satisfying, I assure you."

Oh, the priest had no idea what Frellan had planned for him. Perhaps genital jewelry was too tame. Frellan had been itching for a subject to try dermal weaving. He'd seen the technique at a small, discreet body boutique in Singapore. The subject's skin was flayed off the muscle, cut into strips, then woven as one might a basket. Of course, the man having the procedure had topical anesthetic and painkillers on board. How would Benedicto feel when Frellan put the knife to his cheek without the benefit of such numbing agents?

Satisfying only began to describe the feeling.

Rebecca exited the car with a bit of trepidation. Her last departure from the village had not gone well. There hadn't been tar and feathers, but she was pretty sure that was only because the villagers didn't have them handy.

Brandt put a hand on her back, ushering her toward the tiny church set off from the rest of the village. "You've got this."

But looking toward the stone building, with a belfry topped by a cross poking out over the rest of the squat, whitewashed town, she wasn't so sure. It was a small church, especially by Spanish standards, but it still demonstrated its dominance, the dominance of the *Católico Apostólico Romano* church. The afternoon sun beat on her back, practically pushing her into the shade of the church. Brandt opened the door. However, it wasn't for her. It was for Levont. Their point man.

Even though it was a church in the middle of one of the most isolated regions in the world, they still observed protocol. And for that, Rebecca was thankful. There was a certain comfort in it. The men moved with military precision. Except for Lopez, of course. He stayed with the car, and Davidson had vanished as usual.

Although, the village offered very few spots for a nest. Her guess? The sniper was heading for the tree line. Well, their unofficial sniper was heading there. Talli was second into the church. Rebecca took Vakasa's hand as Brandt brought up the rear.

The interior of the small church, unlike many of the great, sprawling houses of worship they had visited, was nearly spartan. Instead of gold chalices and thick red velvet, above the altar there was only a single wooden figure of Christ on the cross.

Brandt quickly dropped to one knee, crossing himself. Then he was up again, on the job.

A woman—who, from the look of her formless dress and cleaning rag, seemed to be the church's caretaker—approached from the back of the church. Then her eyes narrowed as she spotted Rebecca. The woman turned on her heel and rushed back the way she had come.

Slowly, they made their way down the central aisle as the heat followed them in. Even the heavy stone walls could not keep the summer heat out.

A scrape of wood as the antique door opened announced the priest as he hurried to meet them. Clearly, he had hurried to don his formal robes. His biretta, a four-cornered hat, sat askew on his head. The black pom at the tip listed to the right side. He met them at the altar.

"Father Hernández," Rebecca said as she held out her hand.

The man spit into her palm.

Okay, so that's how this was going to go.

Brandt put his forearm between the priest and Rebecca. The guy was a man of the cloth, but no one—and Brandt meant *no one*—spit on his fiancée.

"I'd back that up, Padre."

Hernández, however, did not seem to understand or care. While he kept his spit in his mouth, he went on a verbal tirade.

Brant heard something along the lines of "*Me cago en tus muertos*," whatever that meant.

"Um," Levont said as the priest went on and on, "my European Spanish isn't all that great, but I think he's—"

"Yeah, I think we get it," Brandt said, not wanting Rebecca to have to hear the curses in stereo.

He glanced over, but instead of finding Rebecca looking hurt, there was that steel glint in her eye. Brandt had seen it before. Many times when he suggested they go to the sports bar for dinner. But this time it was even more pronounced.

"Borgoña," she said quietly. Brandt vaguely remembered the name from the plane ride lecture as the sculptor who had first created the Black Madonna.

At first, Hernández didn't seem to notice that Rebecca had spoken. Then he suddenly sputtered, his face glowing an unseemly ruddy red.

She repeated the name, "Borgoña." Only, this time she put her hands on Vakasa's shoulders. The priest followed her gesture, appearing surprised the little girl was even in the church. Then his eyes dilated to the point they seemed pitch-black. He stumbled back a step.

"Shiva."

Rebecca frowned. "Shiva is the Hindu god of—"

"Creation and destruction," Brandt finished. Seriously, didn't Rebecca know by now his interest in world religion?

By the look on her face, Rebecca's mind was not focused on Brandt whatsoever. She had that "I wish I had my laptop" frown.

"It is also means the 'Auspicious One,'" she explained.

The priest stepped forward, placing a hand on Vakasa's cheek. "Mari."

The girl covered his hand with hers.

Rebecca raised an eyebrow to Brandt. "Well, Mr. Ancient Religions?"

He didn't bother to answer. Basque pre-Christian beliefs were not part of his repertoire, and they both knew it. She flashed a grin at him before continuing. "Mari Urraca was the Basque goddess. The head of their pantheon. Their messiah."

The priest's hand dropped away from Vakasa's cheek as he sighed. He looked none too happy about it, but he bowed his head to their group. In thickly accented English, he urged them out of the church and toward his cottage. "Will you join us for *el almuerzo*?"

Lunch.

While Brandt was hungry, he wanted to get the hell out of here ASAP.

"We can talk here just fine."

Rebecca nudged him. "We would love to, Father."

Hernández, his hand on Vakasa's shoulder, led them out the side door of the church.

Brandt hung back, gently catching Rebecca by the elbow. "What was that about?"

Rebecca kept her tone quiet. "These people are extremely traditional. If we don't allow them to feed us…if we don't break bread with them, they are not going to give us the information we need."

Brandt did enough work in foreign countries to understand the need to observe and interact in local customs. It didn't mean he had to like it, though. However, with the rumbling above his belt, his stomach was pretty keen on the idea.

Rebecca sat on the hard wood bench, watching as the villagers piled plates and more plates on the table. Competing for their attention were *bacalao al pil pil, tortilla con chorizo, jamon ibérico de bellota*, and pretty much every imaginable kind of tapas you might encounter on a traditional Spanish Basque bar crawl, or *txikiteo*.

They had included both *manchego* and the more traditional Basque *idiazabal* cheeses, as well as black and green olives. The green ones were *aceitunas rellenas de anchoa*, or stuffed with anchovies.

Included in the beverage department were the Basque cider *sagardo*, the *Cava* sparkling wine from Cataluña, and sherry from Jerez. The meal was fit for a king—or in this case, fit for a little girl whom they were all clearly fascinated by.

And Vakasa returned the affection, taking nibbles of everything offered. Rebecca noted, though, that she was also hiding about half the food under her plate. Even supposed messiahs didn't like *seso frito*—fried pork brains.

Though Brandt had objected to the lunch, he was plowing through his second plateful of *paella*. Levont might have been on his third, yet took heaping servings of any new dish put in front of him. Talli was the only one who appeared to have a discerning palate. It seemed he wasn't all that fond of olives, which was a slight problem since just about everything had olives in it.

"Lopez and Davidson are going to be so pissed," Levont said, shoving another forkful of food into his mouth. Brandt just grunted his acknowledgment. "This food rocks."

Rebecca couldn't argue. The *bacalao al pil pil* was her favorite from the last time she had visited the village. It was a soup made of salted cod, olive oil, garlic, and a pinch of chili. Didn't sound like it would be much to write home about, but when made with skill, it was mouthwatering. And not nearly as salty as one might think.

And was she just that hungry, or was the *tortilla* twice as delicious this time? She remembered the first time she had been served *tortilla* in Spain at a tapas bar. She had expected a round, flat cake made of corn or flour and had ended up with a savory omelet of egg, potato, onion, and heavenly *chorizo*—red sausage. What she had meant to be a side dish ended up being most of her meal after she had taken that first bite.

She noticed though that Hernández hadn't touched his food. Instead, he stared at the little girl as if visual inspection would be enough to tell if she were divine or not.

"Has she performed any miracles?" he asked, obviously sensing her inspection.

Rebecca looked to Brandt, who blew a breath out through his nose as he lowered his fork. "The kid had a reputation as being an *ajuogo*, a female witch doctor."

"But a miracle?" Hernández asked.

"Your gunshot wound?" Rebecca prompted Brandt.

Brandt leaned back on the bench. "I got shot. It hurt. It looked like it was bleeding a lot. She put pressure on it, and it stopped. No big deal."

"That's when the first earthquake hit," Levont added, taking a huge bite of *lentejas*, a Spanish lentil stew. Brandt glared at his point man. Levont shrugged. "It was, Sarge."

"A three-point one," Brandt countered. "We barely felt it."

Rebecca looked to her fiancé. This was her first time hearing about an earthquake. "Anything else you are holding back?"

"No," Brandt stated, then leaned forward to take another bite. "Nothing at all."

"Well…" Levont said, flinching as Brandt glared at him again. Still, he went on. "The witch doctor dude we left her with called her a *mo-mo*. That means 'messiah' in Swahili."

CHAPTER 22

LENNORE, SPAIN

5:48 P.M. (CEST)

Brandt was seriously going to have to give Levont a refresher course on which glares to stand up to and which to back down from. Like don't tell everyone the witch doctor had called the kid sitting next to him a messiah. Although, in this discussion, Brandt had the upper hand. All he had to do was point toward Vakasa, who currently had olives on each of her fingertips after sucking out the anchovies. She was now eating each one off at a time.

"Look at her," Brandt said, shaking his head. "She's just a kid."

"That she might be," Hernández said, nodding to one of the women serving them. The villagers began clearing off the table.

"Wait," Levont said, scooping huge spoonfuls of *guiso* from one of the pots onto his plate. "Why are they taking away the food?"

Brandt wasn't sure, but took a few scoops himself. Apparently, he'd pissed off the priest. Even though they had come here to prove beyond a shadow of a doubt that Vakasa was not in fact the Messiah so they could get the Disciples off their ass, Rebecca had warned them to keep the "This isn't the Messiah" rhetoric to a minimum.

Quickly, though, it became apparent why they had removed the food. They needed the table for something else. On a large wooden platter, one of the women presented a burnt statue. Not any statue, but that of the Black Madonna. Even though half of her face was blasted away by flame, it was clear this was a treasured relic. And there was not doubt that the artist had meant for this Madonna to be dark skinned. From the striations, it was clear he'd used several different types of wood to complete the statue. Her features were also clearly African.

"Borgoña," the priest explained, "dying, covered her with his body, sparing the Madonna for generations to come."

The villager set the platter down in front of Vakasa. The girl stroked the wood, then laid her face against the figure. "Momma."

"That doesn't prove anything," Brandt said.

Hernández actually agreed with him. "No, it does not."

Rebecca put her hand on Vakasa's arm. "We need your help to prove whether she is or is not the child of the Black Madonna."

"Are we not all children of her blessed womb?" the priest asked, his accent thinning. The guy clearly spoke more English than he liked to let on.

"The Disciples commissioned this statue, didn't they?" Rebecca asked.

Brandt watched the priest's face as he clearly struggled with how much to share with them. In the end, he stood, smoothing his robes.

“There are some preparations to be made, but as much as we can answer, we shall.” His face softened as he looked to Vakasa and then the statue. “We owe her that much.”

Brandt wasn’t sure which “she” the priest was referring to, but he’d take it. The sooner they got out of Europe and back to the States, the better. The villagers left the room, taking the Black Madonna with them.

“So,” Talli asked, “are they really getting ready to help us or…?”

“Firebomb us?” Levont finished.

Brandt wasn’t sure which way that one was going to go, either. “Check the doors.”

The men set up on either side of the room, protecting the only two exits out of the room. Rebecca rose, keeping Vakasa close.

“If we do prove she *isn’t* the Messiah,” Rebecca asked quietly, “what happens to her once we get home?”

It was getting a little old not having any firm answers. “I don’t know.”

Rebecca crossed her arms over Vakasa. Like a mother would her child. “I was thinking…”

She didn’t need to finish the sentence. Brandt knew exactly what she was thinking.

Rebecca waited as Brandt studied her face. She knew what she asked was a lot. A whole lot. More than she thought she’d ever be ready for, but with Vakasa’s hands in hers, it felt right.

“I was thinking the same thing,” Brandt answered.

“Are you sure?” Rebecca asked, wanting to make sure he’d understood her unspoken question. “What about your family?”

To her surprise, Brandt chuckled. “Are you kidding me? Vakasa wouldn’t be stateside a week before Mom had her entered into a beauty pageant, and trust me, the family Christmas letter would announce, ‘Three generations of beauty queens.’”

Rebecca smiled back. Could something so good come out of such a horrible set of events?

Before she could ponder the notion any further, Hernández returned. “Follow me.”

Vakasa didn’t hesitate, skipping after the man. Rebecca had to grab her hand and keep her in proper formation as they made their way out of the cottage and toward an older, overgrown monastery. The wooden structure had fallen into disrepair. Tiles hung down from the roof, and it looked like squirrels had set up housekeeping in the eaves.

Ahead of her, Levont had to lower his head to make it into the broken doorway. Once inside the monastery, it seemed like they had stepped back several centuries. With no electricity and branches covering most of the windows, Levont and Talli turned on their flashlights, the beams cutting across stucco walls and leaf-covered floors.

Was it just Rebecca, or did the wind rustling through the vines sound like a monk’s devotional chant? Nothing, however, adorned the hallway. Not a single cross or painting. Had the monks taken everything with them, or had the place been looted?

Hernández led them through an ivy-choked chapel and back into the living quarters. Here there was more filtered light through the broken windows. The priest pushed aside a large swath of moss from the floor and moved a board to reveal a stash of artifacts.

Silently, he brought them out one by one, laying them on the lone moldy bed.

The first item was a *hilarri*—actually, it was a small pendant shaped in the image of a *hilarri*, or Basque gravestone. The top was a disc shape that connoted the rising or setting of the sun. This disc sat upon a triangular base. Several ancient Basque symbols filled both the disc and its base.

Vakasa smiled as her finger traced the six-leafed rosette. The most ancient of iconry. Yes, primitive man drew bulls and horses, but those were meant to be literal. They were drawing animals. Many scholars tried to argue that these stylized flower petals were only meant to represent the plant and nothing more. Others argued that the sun-like disc and rosette were representational of the gods' gifts to man. Sun and foliage. The two things man needed to survive. Included inside the base were several lines of ancient letters and a crude symbol for running water.

Rebecca had never really had an opinion one way or the other. In some ways, she felt it was splitting hairs, but seeing the ancient totem, it did feel like whoever had carved it was trying to send a message.

Who knew what it was, though? Rebecca couldn't translate the lettering. She turned to Hernández. "What does it say?"

"That is what I hoped the child would tell us."

Vakasa, though, simply picked up the *hilarri* pendant and tied the leather cord around her neck. She patted it as if to make sure it was going to stay there. Vakasa then moved on to the second item. An unusual cross lay on the tattered blanket. With a circle encompassing the top of the cross, used to represent Christ's death and resurrection, Rebecca was certain it was a Coptic cross. Silver and apparently heavy, Vakasa picked it up.

"*Hermano*," she whispered, touching her lips to the center of the cross.

Brother.

"Don't start," Brandt said from the corner of the room. "Are we learning anything of value here?"

Vakasa took the cross and whacked it against the wooden frame of the bed.

"No!" Rebecca cried out, trying to get the artifact from the child before the priest had an aneurysm. "Honey, no."

But the girl wiggled out of her grasp and hit the cross again. It cracked at the base of the circle, revealing a small compartment down the shaft of the cross. Vakasa pulled out a small piece of parchment. With a smile, she walked over to Brandt and handed it to him.

Rebecca looked over Brandt's shoulder as he carefully unrolled the parchment. The drawings on it seemed to be a map. Only, a map of what?

Bunny paced behind Stark. "Well, is it going to work?"

"Everyone does realize I am hacking into the NSA's central database, right?"

Prenner frowned. He'd voted against them, of course. Luckily, he was outvoted.

"I still think we should move to Langley," Emily added for like the thousandth time.

Stark nodded toward the leftovers. Only the trunk of a pancake elephant and tiny shreds of crispy hash browns survived. "And exactly what are they going to serve us there?" Before Emily could retort, Stark overrode her. "And these computers are more secure than any CPU in *any* government building."

To underscore his point, the computer dinged, indicating he had in fact just hacked his way into the NSA's hub. Stark rubbed his hands together. "Let's see what they've been up to since Vanderwalt dropped them off in Turkey."

Bunny really hated this whole radio silence thing. But with the Disciples hot on Rebecca's trail and half the US military wanting to pull in Lopez and the rest, it was the only way to keep them safe. Stark flipped through reams of data, apparently sorting it in his head.

"Here we go," Stark stated, bringing up a photo of a jumbo jet parked on a pretty small runway. "That's gotta be Lopez."

Yes, Bunny had to agree. Which meant they had headed to the Basque region. Which meant they were going back to Rebecca's old stomping grounds. "Can you get us some satellite coverage of the northwest area of the Basque region?"

Emily shook her head. "There's not a lot over that area. Not since the separatists agreed to the cease-fire."

Bunny frowned.

"Sorry, darlin', she's right," Stark said. "I can't pull up footage that isn't there."

"What about the Disciples?" Prenner asked. "Can you pick up their trail from the Congo?"

"Well, I already knew that they followed Brandt to Egypt after chartering a plane out of Cameroon…" Stark stalled out as he brought up and rejected several maps. "Out of Egypt, though? That is a problem. After the Sphinx disaster, only three planes made it out before a complete lockdown of Egyptian airspace. One was the Turkish plane. The other two were headed nowhere near Spain. One went to India, and the other headed to South Africa. It doesn't look like they followed Brandt at all."

Stark was good. Extremely good at his job. However, the tech had never gone up against the Disciples. They didn't give up. They didn't know what giving up looked like. But how else could they have gotten out of Egypt?

"How long until they locked down the ports?" Prenner asked Stark. "Those are usually far more porous than airports or even train lines."

"Good question," Stark commented as his mouse flew across the multiple screens. "For major ships? They were pretty quick, but look at what we've got over here..."

He brought up a map of the long coastline of Egypt. A satellite feed showed numerous small crafts launching from non-port locations. Actually, it looked a little like rats fleeing a sinking ship. If anything, there were too many boats to track.

"This is going to take a while."

Prenner shook his head, though. "There's no way they were going to stay on the water. Too high a probability they could get stopped and searched."

"And it would just be too slow," Emily added. "The Disciples must have known Brandt was going to take to the skies."

"All right. Let's see if anybody's flight path crossed a—" Before he even got the sentence out, he found a seaplane that had landed near a boat. Sure enough, from Brandt's description, that was Frellan and his team.

Bunny watched in horror as he shot the crew and pitched their bodies over the side. Yes, that was the Disciples for sure.

"Looks like they headed to Italy, then took a charter to Madrid."

"Madrid?" Emily clarified.

"Yep."

Prenner frowned. "But look at the timeline. Lopez hasn't even stolen that jumbo jet yet. How could they know Brandt was going to Spain?"

"Don't know," Stark admitted. "But let's look at Flickr to find out what the Disciples did once they got to Madrid."

"Flickr?" Bunny asked. "You're joking."

"Nope," Stark said as he brought up the photo-sharing site and started grabbing photos from Madrid. The vast majority were from cell phone shots. Candid pictures taken by locals and tourists alike. It was weird looking at the Spanish city through the eyes of hundreds of lenses. "Got 'em."

Rapidly, the tech brought up a series of photos that, cobbled together, formed a crude and jumpy video. They watched as Frellan was met by a…

"Is that a priest?" Prenner asked.

It certainly looked like it. Stark's fingers flew again. "Let me backtrack and see where he came from."

If watching the cobbled-together video was odd going forward, it was mind-bending going backward. Yet somehow Stark followed the priest all the way back to *Iglesia de San Andres*. A prominent Catholic cathedral.

"Unless the guy thought he was being followed," Stark announced, "it looks like he is a bona fide priest."

"Where did they go from there?" Emily asked.

"Working on it," Stark said, fast-forwarding through thousands of photos. Then the video came to a stop as Frellan and the others climbed into three SUVs. "Gonna have to switch to real-time cams and hope we've got an angle on them."

Stark flipped through every traffic cam in Madrid, coming up empty.

"Check the official Spanish website," Emily suggested.

Even though Stark looked about as confused as Bunny was, he did as ordered. "Now what?"

"Check out the scenic cams. They stream live video of rural Spain."

Bunny nodded. "Look at highways heading toward the Basque region."

No one spoke as a clear shot appeared of the three SUVs heading up into the mountains. Heading straight for Rebecca and Brandt.

Brandt studied the parchment. It looked like an old Crusader's map, judging by the Jerusalem cross in red along with the standard waving of an antique English flag.

"Does it show a location?" Rebecca asked.

"I'm pretty sure it is of the Holy Land, but this arrow is pointing off the map."

"Is that a Star of David?" Levont asked, indicating to the last item on the bed.

Drawn to the artifact, Rebecca left Brandt's side. Just as well. Half a map didn't get them very far. Vakasa picked up the steel star and spun it on her hand. After playing with it for a few moments, she laid it back down.

Not exactly the actions of a prophesized messiah.

"I don't get it," Rebecca said, looking to each of the artifacts.

Which was not good news. If Rebecca didn't get it, none of them could. Brandt was beginning to feel like it was time to pull the plug. Head home, face the consequences of their actions. Actually, Brandt would have done that several injuries ago. His instinct was to get stateside ASAP, hopefully ditching the Disciples. But there was that little girl and her radiant smile. If they went home now, without clear answers, Vakasa would be whisked away, taken to some DARPA research facility.

Rebecca leaned over to study the Hebrew symbol. "A *hilarri*, a Coptic cross, and a Star of David—what made you collect them?" she asked the priest.

"It was not I, but the monks that originally settled here," the friar stated. That didn't seem to help Rebecca any, though, so he continued. "Look to the back of the star."

Turning over the star, Rebecca read an inscription on the back. "*Shechinah.*"

Brandt frowned. He'd heard the word but couldn't place its origin. Rebecca turned over the broken cross. The same inscription. Vakasa twirled her *hilarri* around her neck to reveal the same word.

He was about to ask Rebecca what it meant but realized she was "processing." Not emotionally. Hell, Rebecca was worse than his men at dealing with her feelings. No, her mind spun, trying to tie everything together. Vakasa. The items. The inscription. Asking Rebecca anything at this point would only slow her coming to a conclusion.

Unfortunately, the friar didn't seem to understand this concept. "The girl was born in Solomon's mines, was she not?"

"What?" from all four of them echoed off the mossy walls.

"We don't..." Rebecca stammered. "We're not sure...What?"

The priest seemed nonplussed by their surprise. "In the Congo region. The child came from deep within East Africa."

Normally, Brandt would find such a statement almost insulting and racially charged, yet the friar did not seem to be making any kind of political statement. He really wanted to know where Vakasa was born.

Rebecca cleared her throat. "We don't know for certain where she was born, but we did find her in the Congo."

The friar bowed his head, taking in a deep breath. "The monks that lived here were devoted to the Black Madonna, but when the Holy See discovered their endeavors to bring all the relics to this place, the monks were taken from this place, and the monastery closed." The priest pointed to the items. "They begged my ancestors to protect these artifacts. We were to watch for an earthquake in the Congo. Two sunsets later, we were to embrace any dark child that entered our church."

The man put a hand on Vakasa's shoulder, seeming to want to test that she was in fact tangible. Real.

"For centuries, we have waited for—"

A window shattered behind them. Brandt pulled Rebecca and Vakasa to the floor. Although, to be honest, Rebecca was already on her way down. Talli shoved the friar down as he made his way over to the window. Levont checked the exits. They still seemed clear.

As Brandt prepared to give the order to retreat to the car, another window blew out. There was no way in hell that was the Disciples' sniper. He didn't miss. And neither did Davidson. Which meant that the kid was trying to send them a message.

They weren't alone.

Rebecca risked reaching out a hand and grabbing the cross and Star of David. Whatever was happening, their trip was being cut short.

Another window shattered. Even though the shots didn't seem aimed to kill, Rebecca still flinched. Vakasa plugged her ears with her fingers.

"Father, thank you," Brandt stated, "but we've got to bug out."

Hernández shook his head. "You must follow the map. It is the only way to know if she is the child of God."

"Yeah," Brandt countered. "We'll catch that one on the flip side."

"No," the priest said, reaching over and grabbing Brandt's arm. "The other half of the map is in a brother to that cross."

“That’s great and all, but we need to leave.” Brandt looked to his point man. “Levont.”

Hernández seemed pretty desperate, though, physically blocking Levont. Not that he would last long if the muscle-bound point man decided to do something about it. “The cross is hidden at the El Salvador Church.” Off Brandt shaking his head, the friar hurried on. “It is just over the ridge.” Levont went to brush past the priest, but the man held his ground. “There is but one paved road out of the village.”

Brandt looked to Levont, who nodded his head. “Go on.”

“If you leave your vehicle here, making it seem you are still in the area, it will delay your pursuers, no?”

Rebecca watched Brandt’s frown deepen. “It could.”

“Then you hike out on foot through the forest. The church is along your path to town. You will know the place.”

Rebecca gulped. It was a risk. Actually, anything they did at this point was a risk. Which one would Brandt take?

He looked to her. “Well? I’m sure you’ve got an opinion.”

“It *is* on the way…”

Brandt grunted, then let off a single shot out the window. It must have been a signal to Davidson. He swooped up Vakasa as he rose, settling her on his hip.

“You better be right, Padre,” Brandt said through clenched teeth. “And you better have our backs.”

The priest pressed his palms together as if in prayer. “We shall.”

With that, they were out of the monastery. Lopez was there with the SUV, doors open and everything.

“Change of plans,” Brandt announced. It was Lopez’s turn to frown. “We are hiking our way out of here.”

“Hiking?” Lopez said. “This thing is a V-ten with four-wheel drive. I can get us anywhere.”

"Park the car as if we are still at the church."

The corporal was clearly confused but also seemed to know that now was not the time to ask any more questions. He knew Brandt as well as Rebecca, if not better. Quickly closing the doors, Lopez climbed in and followed orders, moving the car.

Brandt didn't even wait for him or Davidson, who approached from the south. Instead, Brandt just started climbing the ridge. He turned to Rebecca. "Well?"

Rebecca hesitated for a moment. Over the southern ridge, she could see dust being stirred up by the Disciples' advance. And they were hiking? Rebecca could now see Lopez's point more clearly. She felt exposed. Vulnerable.

"Thor," Vakasa said with a sigh, laying her head on his shoulder.

The little girl was right. Brandt would get them through this.

They were rapidly approaching a dense forest made up of maple, beech, birch, and ash trees, many of them pollarded. Pollarding was a pruning technique, used since the Middle Ages. It created what almost looked like a tabletop bunching in the trunk about four feet up, from which the rest of the branches would then climb. The trees ended up looking twisted and tortured, the effect more than a little bit creepy.

Climbing up beside him, they followed Levont up the hill, rapidly hidden by the forest. Each step taking them closer to Vakasa's destiny.

CHAPTER 23

UNDISCLOSED LOCATION

10:33 A.M. (EST)

Bunny picked at the last of the hash brown shreds and popped them into her mouth. She had to do something to keep distracted. Never mind those potatoes were soaked in saturated fat. Once the team was home safe, she'd have to do like a hundred crunches to burn off the calories.

With no more food around, Bunny was about to resort to biting her nails.

"Shouldn't they have intersected by now?" Prenner asked.

Stark checked a dozen different calculations. "I am hooked into every Spanish police scanner, CB radio bandwidth, and cell phone tower. When the Disciples and Brandt meet on the road up to the village, we are going to know about it."

Only, they *didn't* know about it. The first window had been over two minutes ago. That was with the Disciples going seventy miles per hour and Lopez going a hundred, which was a pretty accurate speed. Bunny watched the numbers flicker. Even if the Disciples had been going fifty miles per hour and Lopez eighty, they should have met on the sole road out of the village.

"Maybe they are planning an ambush," Emily suggested. "Stayed at the village and are lying in wait."

Bunny couldn't help it—her thumbnail found its way between her teeth.

Prenner shook his head. "With Lopez's speed and control? I think Brandt would have taken to the road. Setting up an ambush could backfire, leaving them trapped."

They both looked at Bunny like she was some kind of Brandt expert. Okay, maybe she was as close as they could come.

"His priority is going to be protecting Vakasa and Rebecca."

"Not exactly helpful," Prenner commented—unnecessarily, in Bunny's opinion.

Stark threw up his hands. "They would have to be crawling to have missed each other by now."

"So Brandt *did* plan an ambush," Emily stated, seeming a bit more pleased with herself than usual.

"Without satellite feed, we're blind..." Stark said even though his fingers still tapped away. "But maybe I can pick up some audio—"

Static burst from the speakers, nearly rupturing Bunny's eardrums. Stark couldn't dial the volume down fast enough, but then the sound abruptly stopped on its own.

"What was that?" Bunny asked, rubbing her ears.

Stark didn't answer her, though. He just kept typing, scanning the screens until the static returned, albeit at a quarter of the volume. Then he pushed back away from the keyboard like it had zapped him.

"No," he said, cocking his head at the screen.

"What?" Prenner asked, studying the same screen. However, he clearly had no idea what information it held.

"That was a high-frequency homing beacon."

Emily frowned. "It couldn't be."

"Care to fill us in?" Bunny suggested.

"The frequency?" Prenner asked, somehow in the know.

"Twelve hundred ninety-eight."

Prenner and Emily shared a look.

"Guys," Bunny insisted, "tell me what is going on."

Emily stepped back, clearly turning over the task of educating Bunny to Prenner. The lieutenant cleared his throat before explaining, "Someone from Brandt's team is broadcasting their location intermittently."

No, no, no. "It's gotta be Talli or Levont." Talli was lazy, and Levont was new.

"Twelve hundred ninety-eight HZ was Davidson's signal when he was with the Knot."

Bunny felt her knees shake. If Prenner hadn't put a chair under her butt, she probably would have fallen to the floor. "It can't be."

Stark gave a sympathetic smile. "It is, though."

She looked down to the phone still in her hand. The same phone she'd called Davidson with. The same phone she'd informed Davidson of the exact location and speed of the Disciples.

And now someone was using his beacon to draw the Disciples to them.

"So it's not so much going to be an ambush as a massacre," Bunny stated, putting the phone on Stark's desk.

Surprisingly, Prenner was the one to put a hand on her back. "We're just going to have to wait and see."

Somehow that didn't really comfort her.

Frellan got out of the SUV as his men swept the area around the church. One of the men put a hand on the only car parked in front of the chapel.

"Still warm."

So Brandt was still here. An ambush on his mind? Funny, that was what Frellan had planned. Monnie joined him as Benedicto smoothed his robes. "Ah, how quaint," he said as he studied the small church. Such an odd little man.

"It looks like all of the villagers are inside the church," Ugudo reported. "No sign of Brandt and the others."

Good. So much easier than rounding them up for questioning. It was looking more and more like Brandt had simply gone to ground, hoping to hide his way out of a confrontation. Clearly, the sergeant did not understand exactly how efficient Frellan was at teasing information out of people.

His man held open the door to the church. Frellan stepped inside. It took a few moments for his eyes to adjust from the stark sunshine outside to the murky light of the chapel. The men fanned out down the side aisles as Frellan walked up the main passage. He would have time to enjoy the villagers and their resistance.

For how many centuries had the residents of Lennore been lying to the Disciples? They had sworn they knew nothing of Borgoña's work. Nothing of the Black Madonnas lost to history. Nothing of the blessed child to come.

Liars.

They would be his finest works of art.

One of his men's faces twisted into a scowl. Frellan picked up his pace, arriving to the first set of pews. He grabbed the woman by the shoulder and turned her to him.

Blood splattered across his shoes as it gushed from her neck. The woman's body knocked into the man next to her, sending him reeling into the next and then the next.

"They're all..." Monnie stated, her hand to her mouth.

Benedicto had a bit more fortitude and checked the next row. "Yes, I believe they all committed suicide."

"Rather than give up Brandt's location." Frellan had underestimated those of Lennore. They would rather die than see the Messiah in his hands. Frellan turned to Ugudo. "Search every millimeter of this village. *Find them*."

"Don't bother," Benedicto stated, waving the men toward the car.

"You have no—"

The priest waved him off. "I know. I am not in charge. I have no authority. I am not the boss of you." Frellan could feel his cheeks flush as Benedicto continued. "However, I think I might know where they headed."

Frellan's eyes narrowed. The man was insufferable. However, Frellan did not have time to be choosy regarding his source of information. They were so close on Brandt's heels. They could not fall farther behind.

"And how would you know such a thing?" Monnie asked.

"Oh, I have a little birdie." Benedicto shrugged. "We're hitting the road, then?"

After only a moment of introspection, Frellan turned to Ugudo. "Do a quick sweep of the area. If nothing turns up, we will follow the priest's direction."

Benedicto took in a deep breath, patting his expanded girth. "I really should get out of the abbey more often."

Brandt crested the ridge, joining Levont. The guy had set a hell of a pace, but they'd made it. Well, most of them.

"That was a workout," the point man said, stretching out his calves. No shit.

Brandt shifted Vakasa on his back and gave Rebecca a hand. Davidson had to help Talli up the last section. Through the break in the trees, they could look down upon the outskirts of the town, Cuellar.

"Well, at least the priest wasn't exaggerating," Rebecca said as she pointed to a small church at the foot of the hill.

When the man had said, "You'll know the place," Brandt had had his doubts. Spain was riddled with old churches and chapels. You couldn't throw a baseball without hitting one. However, it turned out this one truly was unique. And not necessarily in a good way.

This church had flying buttresses, except they were attached to the first-floor walls and the ground. Brandt wasn't quite sure what a mildly rounded, ground-level wall needed huge flying buttresses for, but hey, it made the El Salvador Church easy to find.

"Notice anything weird?" Davidson asked as he pulled the rifle scope from his eye.

"Besides one well-secured church wall?"

"The people—or lack thereof."

Levont lowered his binoculars. "He's right. There's no one around."

Brandt took the binoculars and surveyed the streets. There weren't people, cars, children, trucks. Not even a dog. He passed the binoculars to Rebecca.

"Any idea what's going on?"

She shook her head. "Maybe it's a Spain-specific holiday?"

Whatever it was, Brandt didn't like it. He liked normal. He liked routine. This was anything but. However, they couldn't stand here with their knees knocking together. They needed to get on with it.

"Just keep an eye out," Brandt warned Levont as he moved them down the hill. This side was decidedly easier on the calves as they made their way to the town. He set Vakasa down but grabbed her by the back of the shirt as she went to run ahead to Levont.

Despite the down-turned lips when Rebecca held out her palm, Vakasa took it, swinging their locked hands up and down.

As they approached the tree line, Levont stopped and checked out the area again. "Still clear. *Way* clear."

Great. Somehow they had stumbled into a ghost town.

"Lopez, find us a car."

Unlike his usual bravado, Lopez hesitated, glancing up and down the empty street. "Yeah, um...this could take a while."

"Just do it," Brandt ordered. "Davidson, find a perch."

"Will do," Davidson said as he headed up a tree. Guess he was going native, finding an actual perch.

"Levont, take us in," Brandt ordered, gripping his gun tight.

"There it is again!" Stark announced, pointing on the map to where the last high-frequency burst had originated.

"Cuellar," Prenner read aloud. "What are they doing in Cuellar?"

"Hell if I know," Bunny breathed out. Even with Stark hacking into the Stanford University database, they really didn't have much more information regarding Rebecca's stay in the Basque region. She was all about the blood samples and the genealogies.

Not so big on giving details of where she had stayed or sites she had visited.

And now Cuellar? That didn't even show up on her spreadsheet.

Worse, the Disciples were being tipped off by...Bunny couldn't bring herself to say it. They were being tipped off by someone *inside* their team. Did Brandt suspect? Did they know that a traitor walked amongst them? Or was perched above them?

"We've got to mobilize the local police or something," Bunny suggested. It might get them all arrested, but at this point, it was probably better than the alternative. They could sort out the mess later.

"That's weird," Emily said, hanging up a call, then redialing. Bunny could hear the phone ring through without being answered. "No one at the Cuellar police station is picking up."

Bunny looked to the Google map that showed only static streets and points of interest. What in the hell was going on in Cuellar?

Rebecca kept tight hold of Vakasa's hand as they crossed the street. It really was eerie. There wasn't a soul to be found.

"Ouch," the little girl complained. Perhaps Rebecca had been holding on a bit too tight. She loosened her grip, only slightly, as they approached the church. The flying buttresses were unusual enough in such a small church. At ground level? They were rare. Abutting a *Mudejar* aspe? Downright unique. Instead of just a semicircular stone wall, this church's nave was covered in brick in such a way that it appeared the wall had many windows. It was only an illusion, though. The wall was solid brick.

Such an odd fusion of Islamic and Christian architecture. But that was Spain for you. So many cultures had come through the region, even as far as the Basque region, and each had left its mark on the culture and the architecture.

Levont disappeared around the curved wall, only to return within seconds. "The church looks clear."

Swiftly, they entered the shelter of the church. Even though it didn't seem like there were any prying eyes on the street, with the Disciples, you just never knew. Inside, they found the church empty. It clearly no longer served worshippers and was maintained as a museum. Which was fine by Rebecca. Less furniture to move.

"Where do you think the cross is hidden?" Brandt asked after Levont swept the area.

"I am guessing it will be in the rectory, similar to the monastery and—"

Before Rebecca could finish her sentence, the little girl slipped her grasp and was off, running through the doorway, ducking under Levont's attempt to grab her.

"No!" Rebecca yelled after her, but the kid didn't even swivel her head as she streaked down the long hallway. They were all on her heels as she entered the rectory. Vakasa stopped abruptly, kneeling down onto the wooden floor. She patted a plank.

Brandt looked to Rebecca. "As good a place as any to start."

Talli knelt down beside Vakasa and began tugging on the boards. Brandt leaned over to Rebecca. "We are going to have to get that kid a leash."

She nudged him with her elbow but regretted the motion as he flinched. It was so easy to try to put the trauma of the last few days behind them. Unfortunately, their flesh wasn't quite as over it.

Still nursing a rib, Brandt watched as Talli struggled with the floorboard. Seriously? When they got home, the guy was going on protein powder for his muscles and vitamin A for his aim.

"Talli," he finally said, "you keep Vakasa back." As the supposed sniper urged the little girl away from the board, Brandt knelt to the floor. He would have landed on his good knee, except he really didn't have a good knee at this point.

Brandt flipped open his service knife and used it to pry away at the seam between the boards. It took a little bit of leverage, but the wood plank popped up, revealing a dirt-lined space. And there glistened a silver cross.

Just as Brandt's fingers closed around the crucifix, the sound of clapping filled the room.

"Jolly good show, mate."

Brandt tossed the cross to Rebecca as he drew his sidearm, leveling it at the intruder. He knew who it was before the sandy-haired man entered the room.

"Vanderwalt, you do not want any part of this."

The MI-5 agent walked in as casually as if he were joining Brandt at a pub. "Ah, but you see, I've been waiting for this for quite some while. I just need the girl and the artifacts, including the latest cross."

Brandt didn't even have time to figure out how Vanderwalt had found them or what his angle was here. He just needed to get into a better shooting position.

"Chap, don't bother," Walt said, indicating to the three thugs that lined up behind him in the hallway. "I brought company. Now, hand over the girl and the items, and we will be on our way."

"Her name is Vakasa," Rebecca stated beside Brandt, hands shaking as tears glistened in her eyes.

"Ah, the always lovely Dr. Monroe. Do not worry. I plan to take good care of her."

"Once she suits your purpose?" Brandt asked, pretty much knowing the answer.

Walt shrugged. "Promotions are hard to come by these days."

"You fucking..." Brandt didn't waste his breath. The guy had been as close to a friend as a covert operative could have outside his unit. To think that eating grubs together wouldn't bond you for life. At least not when career trajectories got in the way. He should have known something was up when Vanderwalt showed up personally in Egypt. A little too-white-gloved service, even for MI-5.

A ping sounded from behind him.

Vanderwalt drew his weapon. "What are you playing at?"

Was that Davidson? Then another ping and a piece of brick flew across the room. A bullet chased after it, nearly catching Talli in the ear. The man danced away, lowering himself and the girl to the floor.

Not Davidson, then.

"That is not us," Brandt answered, ducking down.

No, it was the Disciples. More accurately, the Disciples' sniper.

Walt smiled that crooked—actually *crooked*—smile of his. "As a kicker, I have a way out of here that avoids the sniper." As another bullet whizzed into the room, shattering against the far wall. "I will allow you to follow us, but only if you give us the girl and the artifacts. Your call."

Brandt was so busy calculating the odds of him being able to get to all three of Vanderwalt's thugs before he got taken down, that he had nearly missed the part where Rebecca tossed the two crosses to Walt, along with the Star of David. Walt frowned. "And the pieces of map."

Rebecca complied. The die was cast. Brandt couldn't do anything to stop her. What was her plan? She had one, right? She had to have one. One that was better than a shoot-out in an enclosed stone church.

"The girl," Walt said, his hand out.

Talli, though, wouldn't let go of the girl. "Talli…" Brandt warned. "Give her over."

"No," the man said, shaking his head vigorously.

Great. Perfect time for Talli to get all brave.

"I'm done," the sniper said, still ducked down under the window.

"Just give me the girl," Walt warned.

But Talli just kept shaking his head. "I want out."

What the hell was he talking about? "Out of what?" Brandt asked.

Surprisingly, Talli turned to Walt. "I want out." Talli pointed to Brandt and Rebecca. "They are insane. You said you would pull me whenever I asked."

"Pull you?" Brandt growled, a bitter realization growing. One he didn't want to admit, but one that made a whole lot of sense. "Talli, you fucking traitor."

Walt sighed. "If it is any consolation, that is not *Talli*."

Brandt nearly got clipped by a bullet as he just stood there. Rebecca tugged Brandt back, jarring him out of his shock.

"Then who the fuck is he?" Brandt demanded.

"It is a long story, chap, told over a warm beer."

"Try me, *now*," Brandt said, clutching his gun as the Disciples' bullets began chipping away at another window. Damn, how he wanted to take Talli down right about now. Consequences be damned. You would think after being betrayed so often it would take the sting out of it. Think again.

Walt sighed. "Ibel here was SRR on a joint mission with Talli's unit in Dakuh."

"SRR?" Brandt repeated. "You've got to be fucking kidding me. They are surveillance personnel. You sent me out into the field with a *fake* sniper?"

"Honestly, chap, I didn't mean to. Ibel was just there. Talli and the rest were killed. Talli had no family." The Brit sounded almost remorseful. *Almost.* "We had the perfect opportunity to insert one of ours into the American Special Forces. You would have done the same."

Brandt snorted. "Send you out without perimeter support? Have you fucking lost your mind?" And here he thought he knew Vanderwalt.

"Now, wait," Walt retorted. "We were going to have him fake an injury to get him off sniper duty, but *you* requested him."

"Because he was graded an A-one sniper, you jackass."

"Yes, well…" Walt conceded. "That was unfortunate."

All of the various scenarios played out in Brandt's mind. How fucking frequently Talli's lack of skills had endangered their lives. Rebecca's life. Vakasa's life. Walt had played Russian roulette with them all.

"But now we must be off," Vanderwalt announced, waving Talli and Vakasa over to him. "My men will have shoot-on-sight orders, so give us a two-minute head start. Then you can blend in with the crowd."

What crowd?

Before Brandt could ask, Levont chimed in. "But wait. I don't get it." The beefy point man turned to Talli. "Why do you want to leave the team?"

"Levont…"

"What? I mean, really, *why*?"

Walt waved the question away and ushered Talli and Vakasa down the hallway. Rebecca took a step forward. Brandt grabbed her by the wrist, but it turned out he didn't need to.

"Vakasa," she said, "we are right behind you."

The girl smiled, holding Talli's hand. "Ta-ta."

She then skipped on after Vanderwalt, heedless of the danger she was in.

This was going to be the longest 120 seconds of his fucking life.

Rebecca ducked her head as the sniper punched through another window. He peppered the wall with shots. Although, none seemed necessarily aimed at them. Weird.

"One hundred fifteen," Levont counted down.

You could tell each second was eating at the point man. He itched to move out. But not more than Brandt. He wouldn't look at her. Wouldn't hold her hand. Wouldn't talk about it. He'd gone full-on caveman mode. There was his job, and then there was "making things right." She didn't care about any of that. She only cared about that little girl she'd made a promise to.

"One hundred twenty," Levont announced as he burst through the door and headed down the hallway Vanderwalt had taken. Three of the team, now down from five. It didn't feel right, yet they rapidly found what must have been a storage room. A trapdoor was propped open. At the least, Vanderwalt hadn't been lying about that.

Levont shone his light down the rickety staircase. "Looks a little sketchy."

Rebecca shook her head, urging him down. "It was built during World War Two," she explained, but Brandt still frowned.

"While Spain was essentially neutral, it became a massive underground for Jews escaping from Eastern Europe." When neither man seemed to get it, she continued. "And while the Vatican was also supposedly neutral, Catholic churches were a major sanctuary and transfer stations. Now, can we go?"

Brandt gave the nod, and Levont headed down. "Clear, at least as far as I can see."

Rebecca hurried down the rickety stairs, with Brandt on her heels. The tunnel stretched out into the distance. Levont started at a quick walk, then picked it up to a trot. Rebecca breathed in the stale air through her nose and out through her mouth. It seemed like they were running into oblivion, as the tunnel just kept stretching out farther and farther away from the church. Exactly how far was the exit? Then as light could be seen farther down, Levont kicked them up into an all-out run, only slowing as they reached a door, cracked open an inch.

Even though the men barely seemed taxed, Rebecca was winded, trying to catch her breath as Levont tested the door. A strange roar came from the other side. The point man jerked open the door, revealing…well, the crowd that Vanderwalt had promised them.

All of the missing people were *here*, at the center of the town. They were shouting and waving Spanish flags in the air. Like she had guessed. It must have been some Spanish holiday. Which clearly everyone and his brother were attending.

"Time to get lost in the crowd," Brandt stated, urging her toward the revelers. He then whispered in her ear. "Tell me you know where they are taking her."

Rebecca just nodded. There was no time to explain. Just to escape.

CHAPTER 24

CUELLAR, SPAIN

6:41 P.M. (CEST)

Davidson watched through his scope as the sniper took shot after shot at the rounded church. Sure, the guy was good, but he certainly wasn't the only thing keeping Brandt and the others inside. Davidson would have bet money, even if they couldn't find the matching cross with the map, that Brandt wouldn't have stayed inside the church for more than a few minutes.

Something was wrong. Unfortunately, Davidson had no idea what it was or how to help. Instead, he had concentrated on the conundrum in front of him. The Disciples' sniper hadn't bothered with Davidson at all. Of course, Davidson hadn't fired at him, either. Mainly because it seemed that the other sniper wanted him to, almost baiting him to take a shot.

And there it was. Davidson found the tiniest glint of metal in a tree across the way. That wasn't a sniper up there. A sniper's scope had antireflective gel and the rifle itself a black matte coating. Nope, that was just a plain old mercenary out in those woods. Probably more than one. Probably more like four or five.

If Davidson had taken a shot, they would have honed in on him, leaving him no room for escape, until the sniper himself took the kill shot.

Davidson brought his rifle up and prepared for the move. There was no point in staying here. He could give no tactical support, at least not for long. Besides, the chances that Brandt would come out into the hot zone were nil.

Straddling a branch, Davidson pulled out his sat phone. Perhaps Bunny and the others had an idea of what in the hell was going on in the church. He popped the battery back in and dialed the number Bunny had provided him.

It rang and rang. No one picked up.

Davidson checked the battery level, the number he'd dialed, and the connectivity. All showed ready to rock and roll. He dialed again. Still, no answer.

Fantastic. They were in a ghost town. Brandt and the others were AWOL, and now Bunny wasn't answering.

No wonder Levont loved working with this team.

Bunny stared at the phone as the light blinked out.

"You couldn't answer it," Emily comforted. "Not until we know more."

Still, it killed Bunny to ignore Davidson. The man she knew and the man who would betray everyone just didn't jibe. She knew he'd done it before, to tragic consequences, but that was *before*. Not now. Now he took responsibility for his actions and was making amends.

"Yeah, um…new problem," Stark said as another alarm went off.

"Do we really need auditory prompts?" Prenner asked, wincing at the sound.

Stark ignored him. "Whether it is Davidson or not, someone has given our hacker some serious intel. They must have been watching Madrid and back-traced my patch into the cameras."

"What *exactly* does that mean?" Bunny asked, knowing without the word "exactly" in her question, the tech would meander off into computer speak for five minutes before returning to his point.

"My first firewall has been breached," Stark hurried on, "but I've got nine others. We've got to figure out the leak, though, or I give us half a day max before they worm their way in."

No one spoke. If the enemy could compromise this pristine computer system so quickly, what chance did they have anywhere else?

A loud buzz filled the attic.

"Another breach?" Prenner asked, tilting his head to the side while plugging his ears.

"No, duh," Stark answered. "That's facial recognition."

Quickly, he scanned the screens, pulling up a series of photos showing Brandt, Rebecca, and Levont pushing their way through a large crowd.

"Where is everyone else?" Emily asked to no one in particular.

Bunny's heart fluttered thinking what could have happened in that stone church. What could still be happening?

"Wait," Stark announced, "I've got Lopez."

He showed the corporal nearly flying down the road in a stolen car, speeding back toward the church, only to slam on his brakes and do a U-turn in the middle of the intersection.

"That was two and a half minutes ago."

None of this made any sense. How had Brandt and the others gotten all the way to the heart of Cuellar from the church? Where was Talli? Where was Davidson?

They watched the flickering, disjointed footage of Brandt play across the screen. Suddenly, he stopped and it looked like asked to borrow someone's phone. Almost immediately, another buzz emanated from the speakers.

"He's using the text drop box," Stark stated. "They must really be in trouble."

Bunny looked to Emily, whose frown echoed Stark's statement. "It is a dummy text account we have set up for emergency contact. It is only supposed to be used in the most exigent of circumstances, since it leaves both them and us open to exposure."

Well, given everything that had happened, it was no wonder Brandt was willing to risk it.

Stark read aloud as the text showed up on the screen. "*Vanderwalt has Vakasa and not in the good way. Disciples on tail. Talli traitor.*"

Not Davidson. Davidson hadn't betrayed them or anyone. Bunny's pulse pounded against her ears. "Yes!" she shouted. "In your face!" she said, pointing to Prenner, who seemed almost disappointed it wasn't the sniper. "I *told* you it wasn't Davidson."

"Vanderwalt?" Emily said, her voice sounding distracted and tinged in pain.

Bunny calmed herself. Davidson might be free and clear, but some serious stuff had gone down.

"Talli must be the one feeding the Disciples information."

"Guys," Stark announced, "we've got a bigger problem than that."

Really? Because Talli and Vanderwalt teaming up together to kidnap Vakasa seemed like a pretty big problem.

Then Bunny looked up at the mosaic of snapshots tracking Brandt.

"Is that Frellan?" she asked.

"Yep," Stark confirmed, then scanned to the left. "And there's Monnie and Benedicto."

The trio was making their way through the crowd in the direction of Brandt. Stark split the screen, showing Vanderwalt, Talli, and Vakasa moving toward the east side of town, away from Brandt. The Disciples, though, they were heading straight for the remnants of Brandt's team.

"Except, that isn't the problem I was talking about," Stark corrected, bringing up a completely new screen.

Bunny took a step back. No. No, that couldn't be.

But as Stark opened up the search criteria, giving them a panorama of Cuellar's town center, not only could it be. It *was*, and it was happening right now.

"Text him back," Bunny urged. They had to warn Brandt.

"He's moved on," Stark said, bringing up the latest images.

Everyone sucked in a breath as Brandt helped Rebecca over the boards that lined the street.

"They're never going to make it," Prenner said.

The crowd booed as Brandt hopped the barricade. The Spanish took their celebrations a bit too seriously. Even Lopez, though, in the car across the alley, was waving his hands in the air, yelling something.

Then Levont swiveled sharply. "Bull, he's saying *bull*."

Fuck. Brandt didn't wait for clarification. If Lopez said bull, he meant *bull*. Then a cheer went up from around the corner, and the sound of stampeding hoofbeats followed. They couldn't get over the other side or back over their side in time. Not as a bull, with three-foot long horns, came charging at them.

Levont must have figured out the same thing, as he sprinted down the street, away from the enraged bull. Rebecca and Brandt followed, but there was no way they could outrun a pissed-off bull. Then Levont, moving way too agilely for such a big man, parkoured his way against the barricade, got enough momentum to hit the side of a store's facade, and then launched himself onto a fabric awning.

He lay flat against the material, shoving his hand down. "To me!"

Running at full speed, Brandt urged Rebecca to the side. "Jump!"

And Rebecca did, hitting the barricade with her feet, giving her enough height for Levont to catch her by one hand. Out of the corner of his eye, he watched the point man use Rebecca's momentum to swing her up onto the awning. The fabric ripped from their weight, but she was safely out of the bull's path.

Unfortunately, Brandt could not say the same thing for himself.

He could feel the damn bull's hot breath on his back. The beast was way too close for Brandt to try Levont's stunt. And he hated to admit but he was too *old* to try it. And too injured. Instead, he just hauled ass down the street, trying to keep at least a few inches between himself and the bull.

Brandt had seen too many news clips of people trying to escape by running to the side. That was how you got gored. Of course, trying to outrun a bull was the way you got trampled.

But wait. What if he…?

Without giving it any more thought, Brandt veered to the side. The bull took the bait and lunged toward the wall. Only, Brandt wasn't there. Brandt had tossed himself to the center of the road. The tip of the bull's horns narrowly missed Brandt's shoulder, and he got one good hoof to the hip, but then the bull was off, running his two tons of weight down the road, scraping the barricade with his horns.

Brandt rolled up, intending to get the hell out of the road, when a cry from the crowd warned him. Three bulls, side-by-fucking-side, charged toward him.

Without even bothering to curse, Brandt just ran for it.

Davidson crept along the game trail, scanning for trip wires. The sniper's perch was nearby, and he would never leave it unprotected. There. The slightest bend to a leaf and Davidson found the wire. The sniper was good, but Davidson wasn't new to the game.

Lifting one foot over the wire, Davidson felt the sat phone vibrate against his hip. He forgot to take the damned backup battery out. Fumbling for the phone, he nearly stepped on a secondary trip wire. No, not just a secondary, but a third and even a fourth. The entire trail was crisscrossed with them.

Shifting his weight, Davidson startled a bird, who squawked, fluttering up, barely skimming past his head. If the sniper hadn't heard the sat phone, he definitely heard that. So it was no great shock as Davidson felt a bullet tear through his sleeve. His only recourse was to throw himself backward, past the trip wires, then scramble for cover.

Swinging his gun up, Davidson let off a few shots. High up in the tree, he got a fleeting glimpse of the sniper jumping from one tree to the next. Davidson would have loved to track him on the ground, except for the honeycomb of trip wires.

Finally, he lowered his gun and answered the phone. "Not exactly the best timing, Bunny."

He didn't even have time to process her words. He just secured his gun and set off at a run, in the opposite direction of the sniper. In the direction of the town center.

"Brandt!" Rebecca screamed as he disappeared around a corner, but Levont pulled her toward the alleyway. "No," she protested.

"We've got to get to the car," Levont said. "It's his only chance."

Yes, the car. Lopez. He could outrun a bull. And the car was right there in the alley. Perfect. Levont helped her slide down the wall until her toes touched the roof of the car. She landed there, slid down the windshield, onto the hood of the engine, onto the pavement, and then into the backseat. Levont was right on her tail, loading into the passenger's seat.

Lopez didn't even wait for the point man to close the door as he hit the gas, speeding them backward down the alley.

"Leave you guys alone for five minutes and look what happens," Lopez joked as he slammed on the emergency brake, spinning them into a tight ninety-degree turn. He then released the brake and hit the gas, nearly slingshotting them down the street.

"So is Talli taking care of Vakasa?" Lopez asked.

Levont went to answer, but Rebecca overrode him. "Something like that."

They needed Lopez's attention focused on one thing and one thing only.

Catching up to Brandt.

Frellan gave a rare smile as the sergeant hurled himself down the street, desperately trying to stay ahead of the bulls. Perhaps it was time to put the man out of his misery. Prove this soldier was no god.

He gave the nod, and Ugudo raised his gun, setting his sight on Brandt's chest, when a loud honking interrupted him. The crowd on the other side of the street dove to get out of the way as a car careened toward them. It broke through the wooden barricade just ahead of Brandt. The sergeant flung himself up onto the hood of the car as it accelerated in front of the bulls.

No, this could not be happening. God could not be so cruel. Ugudo fired, his shot ricocheted off the hood, slicing Brandt's temple. The car swerved as it pulled around the next corner.

"The car," Frellan barked to the men standing next to him. They turned and ran down the side street. The doors were already opened by Monnie. Once loaded, Frellan ordered, "Go!"

Everyone gripped their seat as the car leapt forward. Well, everyone but Benedicto, who smiled congenially. "Spain. Such a rich cultural history."

The hardware on Frellan's face jingled as his facial muscles twitched. "You could have warned us."

"And miss the look on your face?" Benedicto responded. "I think not."

Brandt clung to the front of the hood as his legs swung back and forth behind him. It wasn't helping his grip to have Lopez squirting down the windshield, trying to wash his blood off of it.

But they were good. They had pulled away from the bulls, dodged the Disciples. All they needed to do was get far enough ahead, and he could get into the car, and they would be on Vanderwalt's six.

Then, through the windshield, he saw Lopez's eyes dilate. Anything that caused the corporal's eyes to dilate was something *serious*. Brandt risked a glance over his shoulder, to find the lone bull standing in the middle of the street, facing them. Apparently, he wasn't done with Brandt.

With a pawing motion, the bull prepared to charge.

Lopez, of course, didn't slow. Instead, he started honking, angling toward the next barricade. Townspeople leapt for safety as the corporal gunned the car through the wood. Splinters flew up, adding to the debris already lodged in Brandt's hair.

They had nearly made the sharp turn when the bull hit their rear end. Brandt was nearly thrown clear as the car swerved to the left. Then Lopez course corrected, pushing Brandt's body back onto the car.

That had been too fucking close.

Lopez accelerated again, putting some serious distance between them and the bulls that charged behind them.

Brandt looked up to find Rebecca smiling at him. He grinned in response. They were home free.

That's about when the other car hit them.

Rebecca's head hit the windshield as the other car slammed into their side. The two cars were locked as they raced down the alleyway. Metal screeched as Lopez tried to get them untangled.

"Gun!" Levont shouted as he raised his own, aiming at the other car. Lopez leaned back as Levont fired past him.

Rebecca ignored the gunfire and looked to Brandt, whose left hand was slipping off the hood. He was falling. And that wasn't the worst of it. A huge Dumpster, heaping full, blocked their side of the alley.

"Roll down your window!" Lopez yelled.

Rebecca didn't even question the order. Not as Lopez slammed onto the brakes. She hand-cranked the window, even as everyone was tossed forward. The brakes screaming in protest. Brandt flew up the windshield, then onto the roof and down the back window. His hand lashed out, catching the rear doorjamb.

The two cars separated as Rebecca reached out and grabbed Brandt's hand. Levont leaned over the front seat, helping her haul Brandt inside the car. Lopez cornered around the Dumpster, hitting the gas.

"Now let's see how you like it," Lopez growled as he steered toward the car ahead of them. Only, they didn't move forward. In fact, they started *tilting* forward.

"That bull really wants a piece of me," Brandt groaned. Then Rebecca saw what he meant. The bull had used its horns to pick up the back of the car. Their wheels spun useless in the air.

"Four-wheel drive!" Levont shouted.

Lopez ground the gears as bulls surged around them. The smell of burning rubber filled the air. Finally, the front wheels found traction, grinding into the cobblestone. Brandt used the butt of his gun to break open the back window. He fired, but the bull didn't seem to mind in the least.

"Let it go!" Brandt yelled at the beast.

Whether it was his appeal, the multiple gunshots, or the fact that the front wheels finally got some purchase, the bull dropped the car, and the rear wheels hit the ground spinning. The car popped up, racing forward amongst the other bulls. One slammed the side of its horn into their side, denting the car.

"I know this is tense and all," Levont said, "but oh my gawd, this is awesome. Talli does *not* know what he is missing."

Unfortunately, he did not.

"Take the next right," Brandt urged.

"I've got a side of beef in the way," Lopez informed him.

"Exactly," Brandt answered.

Lopez's hand went to the emergency brake, preparing for a hairpin turn. Slamming on the brakes, they turned to the right. The closest bull continued ahead, getting knocked in the hindquarters by a car nearly its own weight. The bull spun out, falling to the ground in a tangle of limbs.

The car streaked to the right, ducking into a side alley. The rest of the bulls tried to follow, but the cobblestone was too slick, and they ended up in a nice big steak pile.

"Get us—"

Brandt didn't finish his sentence, as the Disciples' car had tagged them in the rear, sending them spinning.

Gunfire filled the air.

This was *not* how his honeymoon was supposed to go.

Davidson shot. He didn't have time to actually set it up, but by God, he shot. The bullet went wide, disappearing into the alley. Correcting, Davidson shot again, this time shattering the back window of the Disciples' SUV.

That gave the driver pause. Enough to allow Lopez to control the spin of their car and head down the alley, in the *opposite* direction. That didn't mean Davidson had lain off. If anything, it gave him more motivation to keep the Disciples right where they were.

With each shot, Davidson increased his precision. Taking out the rearview mirror. Hitting the steering wheel.

It was only a bonus when the bulls caught up with the Disciples' SUV. They seemed pretty dang determined to vent their frustration on something. Davidson was glad that it was the Disciples.

Figuring the bulls could pin down the SUV as well as he could, Davidson slung his rifle and took off over the rooftop. Leaping, he made the jump and landed on the next tile roof.

Time to head to the rally point.

Rebecca cried, laughed, and sighed, all at the same time. They had done it. And she supposed that Lopez had footage of their narrow escape. They were halfway across town and not a single bull. That had to be some kind of record.

Brandt looked in front of them, behind them, to each side. Finally satisfied they were safe, he reached over and hugged her.

Then Levont screamed, a chunk of his shoulder flying off and out of the car. Brandt pulled her down as Levont's hand clutched at the wound, blood pouring between his fingers.

No one asked what had happened. Everyone knew. The Disciples' sniper.

Lopez made a hard left turn, getting them out of the sniper's line of sight as he reached over and put pressure on Levont's wound.

"Dude, it's a flesh wound, buck up."

Levont gave a weak smile as he dug his finger into his skin, trying to staunch the flow. Rebecca, a little too familiar with gunshot care, ripped a sleeve off and, keeping her head low, packed the wound.

Then a bullet caught her forearm, taking a piece of seat upholstery on the ricochet. Lopez took the next right.

"How's he hitting us?" she asked, clutching the wound.

Brandt searched the skies above them. "The steeple."

The spire of the San Francisco Cloister stood high above the small town. The sniper had direct aim of wherever he wanted.

"In there!" Brandt yelled, pointing to a vacant shop. Lopez didn't hesitate as he crashed them through the glass window of the store.

He braked hard, stopping them short of the back wall.

Everyone listened as the motor rumbled, waiting on their next orders.

Levont gulped, finally getting the bleeding under control. "Now what?"

"Now?" Brandt responded, helping Rebecca tighten the packing. "We wait for Davidson to do his job."

How the hell did the sniper get positioned so quickly? Did it matter, though? He had, and now Davidson had to get him out of the steeple.

With Brandt and the others safely stowed, at least until the town police found them, Davidson took in a deep breath and let the tension course out of his muscles. His hands were tired. His fingers were nearly numb. And he was up against one of the best snipers he'd ever seen. Worsening his slim odds, he was on the wrong side of the cloister to take a kill shot.

Again, none of that mattered. Only the shot mattered. He may have just one. At maximum, two shots. There was no time to find adequate cover. Once Davidson shot, he would be a target. He had to make it good.

Not just good, but perfect.

Davidson blocked out the shouts from the streets. He ignored the revelers fleeing the town center. He ignored everything but the light breeze playing in his hair and that steeple.

Of course, he couldn't see the sniper. The man was too well hidden beneath the retaining wall. And Davidson noted that the sniper had secured his rifle's muzzle so there wouldn't be any shooting the barrel out of the way.

Once again, he was going to have to get inventive. Davidson let the world slip away as he aimed. His heartbeat became his guide. His breath a rhythm to mark time. Then he let loose the shot.

It hit the rope of the bell precisely midway. The cord frayed but did not give. Davidson ejected the shell casing, jerking the bolt to load the chamber, as the Disciples' sniper turned the muzzle of his rifle toward Davidson. Too bad the sniper had secured it so tightly to the ledge.

Davidson fired again, hitting the rope in exactly the same spot, snapping it in half. The huge bell fell from its assembly, clanging loudly. So loudly Davidson cringed. Imagine how the sniper felt.

Disoriented, the man nearly fell off the ledge. Davidson fired, but the shot went wide as the wind kicked up. Before he could recover, the sniper jerked his rifle from its mooring, sliding down the roof and out of sight.

It wasn't a kill, but it did get the sniper out of play. Davidson swung his scope around to see Lopez peel the car out from the shop and toward their third rally point.

Time to get out of Cuellar.

CHAPTER 25

CUELLAR, SPAIN

8:29 P.M. (CEST)

Frellan sat on the balcony of their hotel room as he watched the townsmen repair the damage along the bulls' path. His team waited until sundown so they might slip into the dark and meld together with the forest. Their heads held in shame. There was no need to rush their exit. The girl was gone, with no way to track her.

Centuries of contacts now useless. Yet somewhere in his heart, Frellan still held hope. Their enemies could not keep the Messiah's location a secret for long. God's will would force her from hiding. It was Her time. It was *his* time to find her. He felt it in each scar. Each tattoo. Each branding. Even in defeat, he cut a symbol into his flesh. That of a bull to remind him always of his mission in God's name and grace.

It was hard to concentrate on the sweep of the bull's back, however, as Benedicto chatted casually with Monnie. The two acted as if the Messiah had not been snatched from their grasp, headed into the unknown.

Instead, the two spoke of ancient religion. Monnie shared such secrets with the priest. Words that had only been spoken within the walls of the sanctuary for millennia. He might have protested if Benedicto's execution was not hours, if not minutes, off.

Mikhal stood in the shadows of the hotel room. He looked his same stoic self, except for a rather large bruise across his forehead. For all of Frellan's failings, Mikhal's were twice that. Yet the Master still seemed to favor him. He had let the Ten Commandments slip through his fingers and now the Messiah. How long could the man hope to stay within the Master's good graces?

A rattling brought Frellan back to the table where the priest's cell phone bounced on vibrate. Benedicto picked it up and read the text, then laid it back down.

"Now, where were we? Rehoboam?" he asked Monnie.

"The text?" Frellan prompted, tiring of having to bend to this small man's whims.

Benedicto shrugged. "My contacts believe they will head to Morocco."

Frellan squinted against the late-afternoon sun. "Why not to Rota? It is the closest military installation with American jurisdiction." Morocco was many hours farther.

"Nonextradiction," the priest explained. "We don't believe they will head back to the States. Brandt—God bless his Catholic soul—wishes to protect the girl."

Protect her? To stay within the cobra's reach? The sergeant was either full of hubris or truly deluded if he thought he could stay ahead of the Disciples in their own backyard.

After his phone danced a bit more, Benedicto reported, "We will have a helicopter at Bilbao. Once we have firm word of Brandt's destination, we will give pursuit."

The priest then smiled at Monnie. "Seriously. I must know more of Bathsheba's son."

Frellan went back to his carving, letting the blood flow freely. He wished God to know his unwavering faith.

Rebecca let the soft clattering of the rail train lull her into relaxation. Out the window, Lourdes streaked by. Vakasa was curled up next to her, playing quietly with a string of bull's tail. Wonder where she got that.

"Just a few more hours," Brandt said, hugging her.

To what, though? Rebecca almost asked but stopped short. It was bad enough Brandt was running from his own government. That they were taking refuge in a nonextradition country until they could figure out how to protect Vakasa long-term.

For now, she enjoyed their almost leisurely trip as they crossed from Spain into France. Davidson and Levont also took the opportunity to stretch their legs across the seats, getting some well-deserved rest. The only one not relishing his downtime was Lopez. He was still sulking. Over Talli's defection or the fact Brandt wouldn't let him steal a plane, Rebecca wasn't sure.

Talli's defection. Actually, it wasn't a defection at all. They'd never known Talli or Ibel or whatever his name was. She could remember him stepping next to Vanderwalt—with Vakasa at his side, a wide smile on her face.

Vakasa.

Rebecca started awake, disoriented and near panic. She reached for the girl in her arms, but it was just a backpack. She'd been clutching a backpack. Trying to get her bearings, Rebecca glanced around the private compartment. They were on a train, but the men weren't relaxing. Instead, they were assessing, checking, and loading their weapons.

"You okay, babe?" Brandt asked as he stuffed another gun into his bag.

"Yeah," she answered automatically, even though she was pretty sure he knew it was a lie. Instead, she felt like her right arm had been ripped off. She'd only known Vakasa for a few hours, yet Rebecca could swear she'd given birth to the girl. It ached to not have her by her side.

"We'll get her," Brandt reassured, slapping a clip into his sidearm.

Rebecca gave a wan smile as the train slowed. She looked out the window. Instead of Lourdes, they were pulling into Barcelona. A major metropolitan city. A city that would have the goods they needed to mount a mission to follow Vanderwalt and Vakasa.

They had given their tickets to Morocco to a young Portuguese couple in exchange for this private compartment headed to the coast. Once again, they were totally off the grid.

"Everyone's got their orders straight?" Brandt asked.

The men nodded in unison.

"Lopez, get us something fast, and by fast, I mean *fast*."

The corporal's eyes dilated. "Commercial fast or *experimental* fast?"

"I mean fast *fast*."

This was one of the reasons Brandt had chosen Barcelona. He'd explained that the city had one of the few aviation research facilities in Europe.

Lopez raised his hand to Levont. "It is *on*."

The point man slapped Lopez's palm. "You know it."

Brandt turned to her. "You are sure about Jerusalem?"

"I only got a brief glance at the second half of the map," Rebecca explained "but yeah, it did look like Jerusalem."

As the train pulled to a full stop, the men stowed the rest of the gear. When finished, Brandt took Rebecca's hand. "Remember, until we rendezvous at the airport, we're just a vacationing couple. Keep your head down, though, to avoid the cameras."

Yeah, Rebecca wasn't going to have any trouble with that. Not with worry for Vakasa so heavy on her heart, but stepping out into the train's aisleway with Brandt, Rebecca smiled brightly. Whatever it took to get to Jerusalem as quickly as possible.

Another alarm went off. If Bunny hadn't lost count, that was number five. Stark's ten firewalls weren't looking all that many nowadays.

"Why aren't they on the train in Lourdes?" Prenner demanded. He then turned to Emily. "And where the hell did Vanderwalt take the girl?" When neither of them had adequate answers, the lieutenant turned on Bunny. "Well?"

Bunny threw her hands up in exasperation. "You tell me." First the Brit's betrayal. Then Brandt going radio silent again. Why could nothing ever go linear with those men?

"If someone would shut up for a second," Stark said, then had to break off as he worked on the latest breach, "I think I know where the girl is."

"What?" the three said in unison, leaning over the tech.

"Back it up," Stark complained. "Except, of course, for you, Bunny."

The kid did like the occasional side boob action. And if he'd found Vakasa, Bunny would give it to him. "The girl?"

"Yeah," Stark said, bringing up a map of Europe and Africa. There were a bunch of dots. Like, a *bunch* of dots. None of which seemed to make any sense.

"Not seeing it, Stark," Prenner complained.

The tech then highlighted the area of the Congo. "Let's look back seven years…" Most of the dots vanished, leaving a large square marker over the Congo. "That is the Kalemie earthquake. A six-point-eight."

"So?" Emily pressed. Vanderwalt's actions had hit her the hardest. Whatever casual elegance the woman had retained over the past days had vanished. The CIA operative was cranky and not afraid to show it.

"So?" Stark said. "I think that is the moment of Vakasa's birth."

Bunny sank into the seat next to Stark. Prenner and Emily still seemed confused.

"You might as well tell them," Stark prompted Bunny.

She looked to him with a new appreciation. "How did you know?"

"Please, Cuellar?" the tech chided. "A Congolese girl going to the heart of Black Madonna country? Come on. I'm a Googling god."

Bunny turned to Emily and Prenner. It was time to come clean. She would need their help, and to help they needed to know the full truth. "Stark is right. We—Rebecca and I, and apparently the Disciples—believe Vakasa is the female Messiah prophesized by the tablets of the Ten Commandments."

Emily, then Prenner, sat down.

"Whether you believe it or not, Frellan and now apparently Vanderwalt do."

"What's this got to do with earthquakes?" Emily asked, seeming slightly less shaken than the lieutenant.

Stark picked up the strand of logic. "Philosophically, who cares? Geologically? That girl tends to make the ground shake—a lot." Bunny watched as Stark brought back up the hundreds of dots. "These are all of the three-point-zero earthquakes in the Congo region over the last seven years. Anybody see a pattern?"

Bunny shook her head. She hadn't realized Africa experienced so many earthquakes. It was like LA out there.

Stark pealed away dot after dot to reveal a set of quakes that seemed to unfold in a linear pattern. "If, for theoretical purposes, we mark the six-point-eight as Vakasa's birth, we have got this set of quakes that occur well off the major fault lines and continental rifts."

"You can't be saying that earthquakes follow the girl?" Prenner asked.

The tech looked to Bunny, who answered for him. "No. He is saying that Vakasa *creates* them."

"Whoa," Emily said, "I'm a little used to how you guys roll, but this—"

"This is only the tip of the iceberg," Stark said. "Let's fast-forward to last week." He pointed out a 3.3 quake. "That one is within minutes of Brandt getting shot." Without waiting for anyone's response, Stark went to another point. "That one is approximately the time Rebecca and Vakasa were captured by Frellan's men." He whisked the screen to the next point. "And that one is when the crocs attacked."

"The Congo is a very geologically active area," Prenner tried to explain. "Those could all just be aftershocks."

Stark shrugged. "Okay, then how about Egypt? You are seriously going to tell me that an aftershock reached several thousand miles away?"

"This is all speculation and—"

"Then speculate about this…"

The tech brought up a new screen. It showed small quakes across the Mediterranean. In a *line* across the Mediterranean. "These microquakes are exactly in line with his plane's flight path. Stark then overlaid this map with that of a plane's trajectory. They were a direct match.

"I think Vakasa is leaving us bread crumbs," Stark finished.

Bunny was glad she was already sitting down.

Davidson trotted up to the private hangar, his new gear in tow. It looked like the rest were already loaded onto the plane, with the exception of Levont, who was packing their gear into the hold. Davidson tossed him a bag.

"Got a couple more for you."

"Don't know how much more it can hold," Levont said. "This plane is lean."

Lopez came out of nowhere and took the bag from Levont. "No, this 'plane,' this Marchetti SF Five Hundred, is not just the fastest, most sophisticated plane to ever grace the world, it is the Porsche of planes, it is a true work of art, and I won't have you scratching her."

Levont put his hands up in defeat. "Sorry, man. I'll take care of your girl."

"That's better," Lopez said, then headed to the steps that led up to the plane.

Davidson helped Levont load the rest of the gear, then joined Brandt and Rebecca in the tight cockpit. The thing was built for four, but they were going to have to make do for six. Make that five. Talli wasn't with them. Not that Davidson was grieving all that much over the loss of their "sniper." The other men seemed to have barely blinked at the loss, either. Was this how they had felt after his betrayal? Had they just moved on like this?

Brandt rose and went to get into a jury-rigged jump seat. Apparently, the sergeant thought he was going to cram his large frame into that tiny chair.

"Sarge, I got it," he said, shaking off his concern. They had a mission to complete.

Brandt looked to argue, but Davidson held up the video camera. "Lopez has already asked me to tape his beating the airspeed record for a four-seater."

"No way we can beat that," Levont said, settling into his co-pilot seat. "We've got five people, plus all the gear."

"You doubt me?" Lopez asked.

The point man laughed. "Hell no."

"All right. Let's go make history."

Brandt shook his head but rose, taking the seat next to Rebecca.

As they rolled out of the hangar and onto the tarmac, Davidson pointed the camera toward the front window. "*Guinness Book*, here we come."

Frellan walked down the gangway. The spices of Morocco filled his nostrils. Despite the late hour, the airport was still filled with gamblers trying their hand at slot machines, desperate to win back some of what Morocco had taken.

Benedicto stopped mid-stride, though, looking to his phone. "The child is not with Brandt." Frellan waited as the priest read the rest of the text. "She was taken by a British agent."

Another turn of luck. Brandt was the bane of the Disciples. This British agent did not know what hurt he had invited upon himself. "Then they head north?"

Shaking his head, Benedicto reread the text. "They head *east*. Their flight path appears to be directed straight at Jerusalem."

The Holy Land? Could God truly smile down upon them?

Then a man trotted up to Frellan and handed him a slip of paper. His joy dashed by the note. "Brandt is not on the train to Lourdes."

Monnie's smooth skin creased at the brows. "They must have found something in Cuellar that indicated where the British would take her."

"We must hurry," Benedicto stated, heading back to the plane.

Frellan, though, simply sat down in one of the chairs, opening his phone.

"What are you doing?" the priest asked. "We are hours behind."

"You are not the only one with contacts," Frellan reported, dialing his Russian brethren.

Bunny had given up trying to keep track of the alarms. A cacophony rang around them. Some were breaches, others were earthquake alerts, while still others were based off facial-recognition programs at every major airport, train station, or port in Europe. Hence the variety of buzzes.

"Can we turn some of these down?" Prenner asked.

Stark just waved him away. "This high-speed plane must be Brandt's team," the tech said, showing a flight path nearly identical to Vanderwalt's British jet. Better yet, they were catching up with Vakasa.

"Where are the Disciples?" Emily asked.

"I picked them up in Morocco, but they fell off the map after that."

Another alarm rang.

Bunny tensed. "Is that another breach?"

"Nah," Stark answered. "The eighth wall is holding strong." He flicked through several different screens until he finally found the one sounding the alarm. "It is the earthquakes…"

"What's wrong?" Prenner asked.

Stark shook his head. "They've diverted from a straight path to Jerusalem, heading ten degrees north."

"Why?" Bunny asked.

The tech shrugged, sorting through a variety of screens, finally settling on an air traffic control feed. "Yep, the plane is heading north. They informed Atarot Airport that they are not landing there but haven't registered a new flight plan."

Bunny picked up the sat phone. "We've got to warn Brandt." Even as she dialed, she knew it was futile. Davidson must have removed the small crystalline battery from the sat phone. It rang and rang with no answer.

"We've got to figure out another way," Bunny said, slamming down the phone.

Before Stark could answer, the room filled with the sound of Klaxons as the lights blinked out and red flashing strobes replaced them.

"That," Stark stated, "was the eighth firewall coming down…" He fussed for a few more moments, then threw up his hands. "All right. That's it." He turned to Bunny. "Go get Mom."

"I'm sorry?" Bunny said.

"Oatmeal-and-raisin cookies," Prenner stated, "no matter how good, are not going to get you out of this mess. We need to move on."

Emily nodded. "Agreed."

Stark ignored the other two and addressed Bunny directly. "Get. My. Mom."

Not knowing exactly what else to do, Bunny obeyed.

Rebecca held on to the armrest as her seat shook from the airspeed that Lopez was attempting to achieve.

"Sorry, dude," Levont reported. "Only two hundred and fifteen knots."

Only 215 knots? That meant they were traveling around four hundred miles per hour. No wonder the seat was shaking. Rebecca would put up with the annoyance. They were less than an hour out of Israel. They would start descending as they passed the coast and head inland. At that point, Lopez would have to cut speed, but clearly he was not willing to give up the record just yet.

"The wind is against you," Davidson stated beside her. "With our weight and that headwind, you just aren't going to be able to overcome the air resistance."

While Lopez didn't argue, he certainly did frown.

Rebecca let the men's discussion flow over her. She knew that they really didn't care about their airspeed—well, Lopez might. No, the others, even Brandt, had taken part in this race to keep their minds off of Vakasa. Rebecca wished she were as adept at blocking out the fear and pain.

She'd replayed the scene in the Cuellar cloister over and over again. Should she have let Vanderwalt take the girl? Should she have let Brandt try to shoot it out? Or would they have had a high body count and still no Vakasa?

"Whoa!" Levont yelled, pointing ahead.

Lopez squinted. "What the…?"

Rebecca looked out the window, to find the Mediterranean water roiling, bubbling, churning. It was pretty far down there, but something massive was happening to the usually calm Mediterranean waters. Then a plume shot up from the sea, creating a wall of water in front of them. An undersea volcano.

"Crap!" Lopez yelled, diving them nose down.

They streaked away from the plume, the plane shaking violently. Rebecca looked over her shoulder. The water turned to steam as ash sailed high above them. Volcanoes could shoot debris twenty-five kilometers into the air. They weren't safe until they were outside of the plume radius.

"Another one!" Levont shouted, pointing ahead.

Only, this one wasn't just shooting water and ash. Lava burst from the cone, nearly taking out their wing.

"Turn south!" Rebecca yelled. "Due south."

Lopez banked the plane hard as wind screamed around them.

"We aren't going to make it," Rebecca moaned. Lopez was good, but he wasn't that good.

"Make a—" Brandt started to say, then stopped as a third volcano erupted in front of them. It was twice the size of the others. The blast slammed into the wings, sending them reeling to the right as if they were nothing more than a paper plane.

They were flying straight over the Aegean Arc. A set of four ancient volcanoes. The increased seismic activity must have destabilized the mantle cap. As the fourth exploded directly under them, lava splattered against their underside as the rest of the molten-hot spray coursed around them.

"Hang on!" Lopez shouted as he laid them over ninety degrees, cutting through the eruption.

They cleared the lava, then the smoke, then the steam, exiting out into the clear evening sky.

"Just like dodgeball!" Lopez announced. "Only, with lava."

Rebecca looked over to Brandt, who wore the deepest frown she'd seen yet. She reached her hand out. He didn't take it.

"The end of days."

For a moment, Rebecca didn't know what he meant, but then realized he was putting together the earthquakes and now the volcanic eruptions. If Vakasa truly was the Messiah, would she fulfill other prophecies? Prophecies like the apocalypse?

Apparently, Brandt's faith that Vakasa was *not* the Messiah seemed to be wearing a little thin.

"We're looking pretty good," Lopez said, easing them down in altitude, getting ready to make the approach toward Israel.

"Um, except we are kind of on fire," Davidson noted.

"Well, yeah, there's that."

"And we've got incoming!" Levont yelled over the sound of the inferno behind them.

"Incoming?" Lopez asked. "Who in the hell—"

Brandt felt the sonic boom all the way down to his marrow, and it didn't let up. They must have been in the jet's sonic carpet, feeling every last molecule displaced by the other plane. Then the tail boom, which nearly jarred him out of his seat, restraints and all.

Lopez banked them to the left. "How did the Disciples get a supersonic jet?" When no one answered him, since they were too busy holding on for their lives, Lopez continued. "Seriously? How? I want one."

Finally, they came out of the sharp bank, but the supersonic jet wasn't idle. They were making a tight turn to come back around for another pass. If the jet got close enough, the force could shake the bolts holding their little plane together.

His concern nearly made Brandt miss the minor detail that Lopez was heading back *toward* the volcanoes. "Lopez..."

"What?" the corporal asked, never wavering from his course. "Nobody is stupid enough to follow me in."

"That is kind of what I am worried about."

Lopez rolled his eyes. "Please."

And then they were back into the smoke plume. The world contracted down around them as ash and airborne lava shot past them.

"Levont, find me one ready to blow."

"Lopez..." Brandt growled. There was courageous, and there was suicidal.

The corporal leaned forward as he took them low enough to get out of the plume. The four fiery volcanoes each looked prepared to erupt again. Their molten core bubbled and spewed.

"Last time I wasn't ready. This time—"

"There!" Levont didn't get the word out before Lopez slid them over to the second volcano, just in time for a huge steam plume to shoot out of the cone.

The plane shimmied but rode the column of superheated air. The metal around them became hot to the touch, but still, they climbed in the sky. Finally, the eruption ended, and they flew out of the blast zone, far above where they had entered.

The jet had slowed considerably to circle the volcanoes. And now their plane was above the Disciples. Lopez angled them downward.

"Now let's see how you like it!"

Brandt wasn't quite sure what Lopez had in mind, but it wasn't going to be pretty. They approached fast and hard on the jet. Someone on board must have spotted them as they tried to accelerate, but not even with a supersonic jet could they outrun Lopez, at least not in time.

The corporal aimed them straight at the jet. It wasn't until the last moment that he realized Lopez had no intention at all of waving off.

"No!"

Brandt's order was too late. Rebecca braced for impact, but she couldn't be prepared for the actual impact. Lopez slammed their landing gear on top of the jet's back. Both planes lurched. Their vehicle bouncing up. Lopez wasn't done, though, as he hammered the plane back down. Then again.

"Lopez!" Brandt barked. "They've got way thicker steel."

"But a way higher stall speed!" the corporal countered, pounding down again.

It took one more time, with each of the planes falling out of the sky. Then it suddenly got a whole lot quieter as the Disciples' engines cut out. Lopez still wasn't satisfied, though. He brought their landing gear down again, shoving the jet's nose downward to the Mediterranean Sea. Only then, as the supersonic jet hurled toward a crash landing, did Lopez pull them up. But not quite as far as she had hoped. Then she saw why. Their left wing was engulfed in flame. Make that both wings. Make that the tail, too.

"Lopez!" Brandt shouted.

"Jeez," Lopez said, working the controls. "Calm down."

Calm down? They were on fire. *Fire.* Oh, yeah, and about to crash land.

Then the plane jerked, and it sounded like a rip cord was running out directly above her. They were suddenly pulled up. The draft was so quick it brushed the lava flames off the wings.

Rebecca craned her neck to see out the window. Above them, a huge plane-sized parachute had opened. Lopez cut the engines and let the plane drift down toward the water.

"There," the corporal said. "Happy now?"

As the plane gently landed on the water, Davidson popped off his restraint and made for the hatch. There were still smoldering fires all over the hull of the airplane. The lava had tagged them nearly everywhere.

Davidson opened a storage compartment, grabbed a fire extinguisher, then undid the hatch. They were lucky the winds had shifted. The parachute, still filled with air, tugged them along toward Israel. Even without his scope, Davidson could make out the coastline.

All in all? *Not too shabby*, he thought as he climbed out of the cabin and onto the back of the plane. He hit a few flames with the extinguisher, dousing them, as Brandt and the rest joined him. Then the wind shifted and the parachute collapsed. Brandt and Levont rushed over, grabbing the sagging material before it hit any of the flames. The last thing they needed was the thick material catching fire.

Lopez detached the chute from its anchor, and they threw the material over the side.

Dousing another bit of lava that was about to cut into a fuel line, Davidson scanned the horizon. The Disciples' jet seemed to have sunk completely. Just as well.

"Um," Rebecca said, scooting her way toward the nose of the plane, "are *we* sinking?"

Levont nodded. "It's all the gear in the hatch. It is dragging the tail down."

"Shark!" Lopez announced. Davidson looked over as a dorsal fin cut the surface.

"Of course there's a fucking shark," Brandt rumbled. "But somebody's got to dump the gear out of the hold." The sergeant began stripping, but Davidson stepped forward.

"I'll do it."

Levont also stepped forward. "I'm an excellent diver."

Lopez, though, shooed them all back. "Maybe, but each of you is like a bloody 'Come Eat Me' sign to the sharks."

No one could argue with that as Lopez pulled his shirt up over his head. Davidson's neck bandage was oozing as they spoke. Levont's shirt was saturated in bright red and Brandt…Well, he had a litany of cuts and scrapes.

"Be careful," Brandt ordered as Lopez took a knife from his leg holster. "I mean *my* kind of careful, not *your* kind."

"Come on," Lopez scoffed. "I've pearl-dived off of Sri Lanka." He waved his hand over the water as a shark came in close, then darted away. Not just any shark, but a bull shark. "This is nothing."

"Just film it!" Then Lopez gripped the knife in his teeth and dove off the side.

Brandt rushed to the side, but the plane tipped with his weight. Rebecca screamed behind him as one of the sharks got a little impatient waiting for them to sink and all. It threw itself halfway up the side of the plane, snapping and thrashing. Brandt only had time to grab Rebecca by the waist and swing her around, out of danger.

Levont leveled his weapon, but no one fired. With Lopez down there, they couldn't risk a feeding frenzy. Actually, once the bags were out of the hold, Brandt wasn't sure they could stay afloat. No need to get the natives too agitated.

The bull shark clamped his jaw one last time, then thrashed its tail, sliding back down into the water. His eyes, though, his eyes said, *We'll meet again.*

Fucking bull sharks. Great whites usually *accidently* bit you. They wanted seals. Once they took a bite and figured out you tasted bad, they were more than likely to spit you back out, giving you a chance to survive.

The bull shark? No such luck. They bit and held on—tight. If they did happen to let you go, it was only for a moment. They latched right back on. They were ferocious and committed to eating whatever they had caught.

Not a good combination.

"It's working!" Levont announced, and sure enough, the back of the plane wasn't quite as underwater as a moment before.

But then the water churned as several dorsal fins cut the water. Rebecca clung to Brandt as Lopez's head popped above the waves. Just as a shark lunged for him, Lopez hit the shark square in the nose with a pack. The beast reeled away as Lopez tossed the bag onto the plane.

Brandt rushed over to help Levont haul the corporal out of the water, while Davidson filmed it all, of course.

Lopez pulled a string of life vests after him as well. "I've got four vests that—" Another shark jumped out of the water, snagging the last vest, cutting the line, taking his prize with him. "Make that three vests."

"Ricky!" Rebecca chided him, helping him climb farther up the plane.

Lopez shook off all the help. Instead, he dropped to his knees and opened the gear that he'd salvaged. It was a pack of two rather large lifeboats. He pulled the cord and they began to fill with air.

"What the…?" Levont said, dancing back from the inflating rafts.

Lopez shook his head, spraying water on all of them. "Please, these experimental planes crash as often as they land. They've got the most sophisticated emergency rescue equipment on the planet."

"You are expecting us to take those out…in those waters?"

It wouldn't be long before sharks realized that rubber was not tooth-proof.

"Nah," Lopez stated. "Levont, let's put those muscles to work."

Actually, it took Levont, Rebecca, and himself to maneuver the first life raft under the wing and secure it. The second was easier to position. Suddenly, their sinking plane was now floating peacefully on the sea.

Lopez grabbed two paddles and held them up. "Who wants to row?"

Frellan breathed in the stale oxygen of his face mask. The pilot and copilot were both dead, along with two of their men. The rest braced themselves against the back of the chairs, keeping their heads above water.

The water was surprisingly warm, almost soothing. God's small gift to them.

"We've got to find a way out," Monnie complained, as was her want.

He indicated out the window where a shark tail glided past. "Feel free." Because beyond the sharks were bright flashes of red and orange. As a matter of fact, their jet had gone down nose first into a lava flow. Slowly, they drifted down the molten slope.

So perhaps he should not have characterized the pilot and copilot as dead. They were more dissolved down to their elemental components than simply deceased.

"I do have to say," Benedicto said, pulling his mask away for a moment, "the Disciples know how to treat a guest."

"How long will the oxygen last?" Monnie asked.

Frellan did not bother to answer her. Their SOS had gone out. They were only a few miles off the coast of Israel. If there was anywhere to crash-land into a volcano surrounded by sharks, it was here.

He looked over to Mikhal, who stood stoically as always. Without even a mask on. Frellan would never speak it aloud, but standing here, waiting while sharks circled, he began to understand the sniper perhaps a bit more.

"We can't have more than a half an hour of oxygen," Monnie informed the group.

Ah, dear, sweet, innocent Monnie. Now she had stirred fear. Fear he would now need to extinguish. He gave the slightest nod to Mikhal. Three muted *pops* sounded, and half of their mercenaries slumped forward, abandoning their now useless oxygen masks.

Monnie sucked hard on her mask, those pretty green eyes of hers dilating. She did, however, quiet.

Sometimes stillness did win the game.

CHAPTER 26

UNDISCLOSED LOCATION

3:27 P.M. (EST)

Bunny burst in to find the attic in just as much disarray as she had left it. Stark's mom was right behind her.

"Oh, honey," she chided, "how many times have I told you to bring your dishes downstairs?"

"Mom!" Stark exclaimed, pointing to all the red flashing lights.

The woman gave out a heavy sigh as she sat down at a workstation. "All's I am saying is a messy desk leads to a messy mind."

"I'm sorry," Prenner said, shaking his head as the woman logged in. "But we can't have someone without the proper—"

Stark stood up. "Look. My mom might or might not have been on the FBI's most wanted cyber crimes list during the nineties. She may or may not be in the Witness Protection Program.

She may or may not be foreign royalty." He put his hands on his mom's shoulders. "What I can say for sure is that she is the best damn hacker I know. If we want to save Brandt and the rest, we've got to let her help."

Finally, Prenner nodded.

Stark's mom patted her son's hand. "That was so sweet, dear. However, it isn't going to get you out of trouble for laying down such sloppy code. Your reliance on spaghetti code is really not doing you any good."

"*Mom*," Stark complained as he sat down at the desk again.

Bunny looked up as footage of a volcano played out. "What's that?"

"Oh," Emily chimed in, "there are now four volcanoes in the Mediterranean, Rebecca's plane crashed, and Vakasa's micro-tremors have stopped."

"Oh, is that all?" Bunny groaned. She just went downstairs and maybe grabbed a Tab cola, but that was it.

Stark's mom nodded to the screen. "Hon, you worry about where that little girl got off to. I'll handle this hacker punk."

Immediately, the red flashing lights faded out as the normal lights came back on, and then there was silence. No alarms. No buzzers. No Klaxons.

For the first time in two days, Bunny felt like they might actually be in control.

Brandt sloshed through the shoreline waters of Palmachim, a small Israeli beachside resort. He carried Rebecca in his arms. Not that she was injured, they just needed her to look injured.

The other men followed along, abandoning their floating plane. They'd hit the shore just in time, as the hold had taken on too much water for even the lifeboats to hold up. A crowd met them at the water's edge.

Davidson explained in Hebrew that their plane had been downed by the volcano and that Rebecca needed immediate medical help. For once, it was a good thing there wasn't a doctor in the house.

One of the older men pointed to his old beat-up Hyundai pickup truck. He handed the keys off to Davidson. That was the kid for you. Even scarred up, he could charm the coat off an Eskimo.

Brandt loaded his fiancée into the back as the other men piled into the cab. He hugged Rebecca close as Lopez pulled them out of the seaside parking lot and onto the road. Not until they turned the corner, heading east toward Jerusalem, did Brandt let her up.

"Great job."

"I didn't have to dig all that deep to play injured."

They both watched the new volcanoes sputter and spew. They were throwing up more ash than lava now. The sky becoming a dark-gray smudge. The sun barely peeked out from the horizon, flaring its last rays. If these explosions were anything like the Icelandic Eyjafjöll eruption, they wouldn't be seeing the sun for a few days, if not weeks. More than likely, air travel all over Europe and the Middle East would grind to a halt. Perhaps as far as western Asia and northern Africa.

Even if Command wanted to send them support, they were shit out of luck now.

As the sun set on the glowing volcanoes, Rebecca looked toward the east. "Do you think Vanderwalt would really hurt her?"

Frowning, Brandt sighed. "A few hours ago, I would have said no way, no how. Of course, at that point, I thought Talli was a sniper, too."

Rebecca lightly punched his leg. "No, you didn't."

He couldn't help but smile. "I guess that one didn't come as a complete shocker."

She snuggled up against him as they finished their most unusual pilgrimage.

"Where are they going?" Emily asked, pointing to the map of Israel. The last-known trajectory of Vanderwalt's plane showed them heading northeast of Jerusalem.

No matter how long Bunny stared at the screen, it made no sense. Unless, of course, they were shooting for Syria. Which made even less sense.

Jerusalem, now Jerusalem had made sense. Where else do you go if you've got the next Messiah? The city was rich in religious history. That is what made it such a political hot potato. The Jews, Christians, and Muslims all claimed the ancient city for their own.

In addition, the area under the Temple Mount had never been excavated due to political tension between the three religious groups. Who knew what was under there? So Vanderwalt *should* be heading to Jerusalem. He could visit the site of Christ's crucifixion. He could visit the Wailing Wall. He could visit half a dozen historic sites, yet he had flown past them all.

Why?

Unfortunately, she was the one tasked with the question. Bunny laid aside the "shoulds" and "wouldn't it make more senses." She went back to her roots. Ancient civilization for a thousand.

Jerusalem had been the capital of Israel for millennia.

Wait.

It wasn't the *first* capital.

"Bring up an ancient map," Bunny asked Stark. The tech complied, even though he looked confused. "Now overlay the flight path."

"I'm not sure what—"

"Do it."

There it was—Shiloh. Israel's first capital. Now it was just a small village out in the middle of nowhere.

"That's it," Bunny stated. "That is where they are headed."

"Why?" Prenner asked.

"I don't know *why*," Bunny admitted. "I just know that Shiloh is the only place they *could* be going."

"Damn, she's right," Stark added. "Vanderwalt is making their descent."

Bunny looked to Prenner. "So how about we figure out how to tell Rebecca and the others before they get all the way to Jerusalem?"

They all looked to the sat phone that perched on the desk. Bunny snatched it up and dialed, but got the same response she'd gotten all evening. Nothing.

Stark's mother sighed. "Think outside the box, son. Think big. Think *wide*."

The tech smiled and gave his mother a high five. "You know it."

"Going to share?" Prenner asked.

"Nope."

Yet again, Lopez hit a pothole in the road a tad too fast and nearly popped Rebecca and Brandt out of the back of the truck. Seriously, this truck ride was more traumatic than the last few rides, and that included volcanic eruptions, a sideways bump of the airport wall, and a crash landing into the Congo. Her kidneys were never going to forgive her.

They were passing through the town of Ramia, heading due east for Jerusalem. Less than an hour out, Rebecca tried to rest but couldn't. Too much was at stake. And Jerusalem was a large city. She could only assume Vanderwalt would head for the old city, but she couldn't take any chances. She had to turn the history of the biblical city over and over again.

Finally, Lopez slowed as they reached the heart of Ramla. For so late in the evening, there were a lot of people out. Mainly gawking at the sky and the fiery display off in the Mediterranean. Stores were still open, accommodating the crowd, she supposed.

She had gone back to her contemplations when Davidson banged the side of his fist against the truck's back window. He was saying something, gesticulating to the people on the sidewalk, but Rebecca had no idea what he meant.

"They are all checking their phones," Brandt said next to her.

He was right. Every single person was looking to his or her cell phone. But why?

Then they passed an electronics store. Each and every television, computer screen, and tablet flashed one word. "Shiloh."

Shiloh?

Lopez picked up speed as they headed out of the town center. He was about to get onto the 1-Freeway headed east to Jerusalem. Rebecca pounded on the window.

"No! Go north!" she shouted. "Take the Six-Interchange."

Apparently, they were having as much trouble hearing her as she had hearing them.

Brandt rose up, leaned through the driver's side window into the cab of the truck, and pulled the wheel to the left.

Well, that did the trick, as they cut across two lanes of traffic and hit the on-ramp at an angle.

Lopez corrected their skid and off to Shiloh they were.

The shark thrashed away from the plane as Frellan's diver sent an electric shock through its snout. Bull sharks were determined, but not *that* determined. The diver waved the survivors away from the side emergency door, then used a handheld hydraulic expander to pop open the hatch.

Taking a deep breath from the waning oxygen mask, Frellan pushed off the seat and was helped out by the diver. As sharks circled, swishing their strong tails in frustration, his small group made their way to the surface.

Breaking water, Frellan could not help but gasp. The world was redone. Molten lava shown brightly in the night as four new volcanoes rose proudly from the sea. The sky was completely obscured by the ashen clouds roiling overhead.

Hooked up to a harness, Frellan and the others were brought aboard a marine helicopter, which was having a bit of trouble staying in the air as winds ripped across the open sea. Once aboard, he reached out a hand to Monnie.

"Ye of little faith."

She did not retort. She simply bowed her head as she made her way to her seat.

Benedicto, though, clapped Frellan on the shoulder. "It does all seem a bit biblical, does it not?" When Frellan didn't answer, the priest chuckled. "Quite the time to be a religious zealot!"

Frellan did not grace the man with a response. He only looked across to Mikhal. They seemed to have reached an understanding on the plane. With a single flicker of his eyes, Frellan marked the priest for death.

Once the girl was found, Frellan would be rid of them all.

"Got 'em!" Stark cried out, bringing into focus a satellite image of the truck. He then brought up another five shots of Brandt's team heading north.

"Where did you get those?" Emily asked.

"Um? In this part of the world? We've got enough satellites tasked to the region to have a sat-link smorgasbord."

To prove his point, Stark brought up another half dozen images of Brandt and the others taking the turn away from Jerusalem to Shiloh. So Stark taking over the airwaves had worked.

"So what is Vanderwalt's end game?" Prenner asked.

"No idea," Stark said. "But they landed in a small regional airport just ten miles outside of Shiloh."

"Again," Emily stated, "why Shiloh?"

Bunny had been sorting through that as well. "Well, Shiloh was the first capital of ancient Israel."

"I thought Jerusalem was?" Prenner asked.

She shook her head. "Nope, it was Shiloh for three hundred years before King Solomon built the First Temple in Jerusalem."

"Even so, I don't get it," Emily stated. "Why take Vakasa to the old capital? Why not Jerusalem? There is just so much more history there."

As Bunny geared up, Stark flipped through several stills of Vanderwalt. The group got into several cars and headed out. "You want history? Did you know that there were over one hundred and forty-seven legends about King Solomon?"

Clearly, this group did not.

"Lost 'em," Stark said, working the multiple satellite feeds.

While he tried to pick up Vanderwalt again, Bunny continued. "I think the single most incredible thing about King Solomon is in how high a regard we hold him," Bunny hurried on. "Sure, he seemed wise—the whole 'cut the baby in half' thing, and he built the temple—but he had over seven hundred wives and three hundred concubines, and let's face it, some of the exploits are pretty weird."

"Bunny," Emily said, unconsciously touching the cross around her neck. Amazing how open-minded people could be until you brought your point too close to home.

"Besides being able to fly and control demons," Bunny explained, "the part that affects us is the fact that, later in life, he seemed to have a crisis of faith. He began building temples for his many, many, many wives. Foreign gods. Pagan gods."

"Got them!" Stark announced bringing up a live feed of Vanderwalt's groups pulling up to the one and only site of interest of the present-day Shiloh.

"Should we try to contact Brandt?" Stark asked. Alarms blared as red lights flashed again. Firewall number nine had just gone down. "Mom?"

The woman furiously typed. "This isn't a hacker. This is a team of hackers. We've got a full-on daisy-chained siege going on."

Bunny wasn't quite sure what that meant, only that it was bad. Super bad. She patted Stark on the back. "Don't worry about Rebecca. She'll figure out where she needs to go. Help shore up our last firewall."

Bunny glanced up to the screen showing Brandt and the others entering Shiloh. They'd made great time—Lopez was driving, after all. But Vanderwalt had over an hour lead time.

Could they catch up to Vakasa in time?

Brandt helped lift Rebecca from the back of the truck and to the ground outside of what looked like a tabernacle, a Jewish holy place once used to worship in the open desert. Only, it wasn't created as a tent, but fashioned out of wood. While it seemed to be a fairly accurate replica of the biblical Tabernacle of Moses, it didn't exactly look like the site to unveil a messiah.

"You sure about this?" Brandt asked.

"You're the one that didn't want to hear about my reasoning," Rebecca chided.

Okay, at the time, getting bounced around in the back of a truck, all he wanted to do was meditate on materializing a thick steak and a cold beer. And not Bud Light, either. No, he wanted a dark lager. A beer you had to chew. He wanted to imagine their life after this mess. When the only thing they had to worry about was who was going to take out the garbage and how he was going to keep his sisters from giving Vakasa a makeover.

Now, though? His eyes flickered over to the other cars parked in the dirt lot next to the synagogue. Vanderwalt certainly seemed to think this was the right spot as well. For what, Brandt had no idea. He gave the nod for the men to do a sweep around the building. It seemed dark and deserted, but they knew better.

What the hell was Vanderwalt up to? He doubted, even with Rebecca's extensive knowledge, that she would know. Otherwise, she would have volunteered that information. Normally, he would have let the situation play itself out. Only, there was nothing normal about this situation. And there was a little girl who thought he was Thor. He couldn't disappoint her.

As the men assembled in front of the tabernacle, Brandt realized they didn't have time for show-and-tell. They were going in blind, then.

"Boss?" Davidson asked, the question clear. There was no cover. None. The synagogue was perched on a hillside. It was the highest point for miles. And given this was eastern Israel, there were no trees. Not even a tall shrub.

And they were a man down. Granted, it was Talli, but still a man down.

"We all go in," Brandt decided.

Lopez pocketed the truck keys and raised his rifle.

Brandt gave the nod.

Time to find a little girl and kick Vanderwalt's pasty-white ass.

Rebecca fell into line with the men. At the head was Levont. The men's flashlights crisscrossed the synagogue. While it looked like a tabernacle from the outside, the inside was just a small house of worship not unlike any other synagogue. The pews, the alcoves, the bema where the Torah was read during ceremonies.

Then the ark, which held the sacred scrolls.

The synagogue was one large open room. With no one in it.

It took the men a few more seconds to clear the space, but empty it was.

Brandt looked to her. "Well?"

She didn't have a clear answer for him. This was the place, Rebecca was sure of it. This synagogue had been built in exactly the site of the first Jewish tabernacle. It had served as the sacred gathering place for Jews for centuries. Excavations around the area had confirmed religious activity in the region for millennia.

This had been the first *Shechinah*. The term that Nori had spoken as her last word on earth, and the word etched into the back of the monk's artifacts. *Shechinah* translated as the place or the dwelling of God. It could be used in just about any synagogue or temple. However, it was normally used to refer to the First Temple.

The one that Solomon had built, moving his people's capital from Shiloh to Jerusalem. Exploring under the Temple Mount would bring all the threads of this mystery together. Unfortunately, all she was left with was a handful of frayed ends.

One of them being that *Shechinah* was the *feminine* version of the word. Many scholars argued that the ancient Hebrews chose the word to reflect the duality of God. To bring the feminine element into their religion. That the temple was the womb, so to speak, for their faith.

What if it was for an entirely different reason? What if it had always been meant to bring forth a woman savior?

"Rebecca?" Brandt urged.

She brought her mind to the present puzzle to solve.

Where had Vanderwalt and the others vanished?

Davidson checked out the door as Rebecca answered.

"Solomon had an affair with the queen of Sheba," she announced.

Not even Davidson knew where she was going with that one.

"And that's important because?" Brandt asked.

Rebecca walked up to the bema, checking up and down the length of the wooden pedestal. "They had a son," she said as she moved onto the ark. "And legend has it, Solomon gave him the Ark of the Covenant."

"What?" Brandt said.

She nodded vigorously. "I know, right? Solomon supposedly gave away the Jews' most precious artifact. Just that fact alone helped keep the Ethiopian royalty in power until the nineteen seventies." Opening the side of the ark, Rebecca sorted through the scrolls. "Anyway, right about that time is when he turned his back on the priests and started building a whole swath of temples. Many in Shiloh."

"Great history lesson, babe, but I need—"

"I think…" Rebecca blurted out, then stalled. Davidson had seen it before. It was when her analytical brain worked faster than her interpretive brain. She was on to something. To prove his theory, Rebecca stroked the side of a papyrus roll, a smile slowly spreading. "I think those other temples were just to keep his wives happy. But I think he built in Shiloh to cover his true ambition."

They all waited as she sat cross-legged on the floor, reading through the scroll she had picked. But she just kept reading. Her eyes sliding across the ancient Hebrew words. Davidson didn't think she was actually comprehending the information. He guessed that she was just letting the language roll over her, allowing her to sink into the mind of Solomon. She could probably feel the dust in her throat. The feel of coarse cotton upon her skin.

Davidson had been raised amongst antiquity. So much so that he felt that he'd almost walked alongside Mary and Peter. But never had he felt as close as Rebecca seemed to be to Solomon right now. He did not envy her. Davidson's scars were a constant reminder of the price one paid for getting too close to the past.

"Babe?" Brandt prompted.

Rebecca's eyes were still unfocused as she set the scroll down beside her. Rising, she laid a hand upon the top of the ark. On top of the winged angels.

"I think Sheba convinced Solomon to open the covenant," she said, sounding miles off. "I think he read what I read." She paused, letting her finger run down the course of the gilded wing. "I think he decided to build a new temple. A temple to the new Messiah."

"Great," Brandt announced. "Where?"

Rebecca seemed startled by the question as she shook off the trance she'd been under.

"Oh, I have no idea."

CHAPTER 27

UNDISCLOSED LOCATION

2:26 A.M. (EST)

"What is taking them so long?" Bunny asked as she stared at the screen that showed the tabernacle. The boring, nothing-happening tabernacle. Just a few lights shown through the windows and that was it. For over half an hour.

She didn't expect Stark or his mom to answer. They were hella hard at work trying to keep the hackers out. Bunny turned to Prenner. "Well?"

The man's chiseled jaw worked up and down as he studied the screens. "Vanderwalt clearly went in but didn't come out. Brandt is betting on Rebecca following in his footsteps."

Bunny had already figured that out, but how long would Brandt stay? When would you finally give up? When would Rebecca's skill and Lopez's luck run out? And they couldn't give any aid. With the violent eruptions and aftershocks from the Mediterranean, even if Vakasa produced microtremors again, they wouldn't be able to see them amongst the jittering needle of the seismograph.

She knew what it felt like to be out in the field. To have no idea what you were doing, yet having the fate of the world on your shoulders. Rebecca must have been going out of her mind right about now.

A screen off to the far left flashed briefly. Out of the dozen or so alarms blaring, this one barely seemed worth mentioning. Only, it was perhaps the most important one, as Frellan's face filled the screen.

The Disciples had not only survived the crash, but were en route to Shiloh.

"What can we do?" Bunny asked Emily, knowing she wouldn't have any better answer.

The CIA operative shook her head. "The area is a disaster. An internationally declared natural disaster. Even if I could raise Israeli forces, and even if they could mobilize anything, I doubt after Jordan they would be any kinder than the Disciples."

Bunny turned to Prenner.

"The United States military has no knowledge or hand in the events occurring in Shiloh, Israel."

She could have punched him, but the lieutenant was right.

Rebecca and the rest were on their own.

Brandt lifted a Star of David from the wall. Nothing happened. Just like nothing happened the last five times he had lifted this particular item. The synagogue was not all that big and not all that elaborately decorated. They had tested each and every piece of iconry in the place and come up with squat.

Rebecca had wandered back to the ark. He joined her. "Any inspiration?"

She shook her head. "I must be losing my mojo." Then she cocked her head. "The ark is never supposed to touch the ground."

"Okay..." Brandt said, backing up as Rebecca searched around the replica. "It also isn't supposed to have doors on the side, either..."

"And this is way too big," she said, hurrying on. "It should only be two and a half cubits in length."

"Again," Brandt stated, "also not supposed to have doors in the front."

Rebecca's hand ran over the back wall.

"We've already moved everything on—"

"And where are the gold rings to hold the shittim wood rods?" She was really getting amped up, shoving on the ark. Apparently single-handedly trying to tip the thing over. "I mean, this is one of the ancient resting places of the ark. You'd think they would get it right."

Yes, you would, but he didn't quite see what bullying the ark was going to get them. "Rebecca, let's take this slow and—"

"The *parachot*," she said, spinning on her heel. "Where is the veil?"

Rebecca began tugging at the other wall hangings.

"Honey, you've got to tell me what you are—"

"God ordered Moses to always have the ark covered by a veil." Rebecca climbed up on the ark, searching up high for something. She found a curtain rod. A bare curtain rod. "Vanderwalt took it."

"And that means?" Lopez asked.

Rebecca smiled fiercely. "Vanderwalt doesn't know ancient religions as well as he thinks he does."

"We're talking about Solomon, aren't we?" Davidson asked.

Brandt looked from his sniper to Rebecca.

"Why, yes, we are," she said, walking back and forth atop the ark. "And one of his most famous legends? The conundrum of two women who claimed the same babe. What was Solomon's advice? Split the child in two." Rebecca looked down at the ark. "And what does this ark represent?" she asked.

He hoped she was asking Davidson, because Brandt had no idea.

"The moment that Moses stood before God," Davidson filled in the gaps, "he stood between two cherubims."

Before he could stop her, Rebecca raised her foot and slammed it down on the ark. Wood split as grinding filled the room. And then she tipped over backward, disappearing into a dark passage.

Brandt charged the ark, leaping up onto it as the wall behind her closed. He punched the wall to no avail. It was as solid as it could get. The top of the ark, though? Not so much. He kicked the remaining wood, hitting some sort of metal rod. Then he, too, felt the world tip as the other men rushed forward.

Slipping and sliding down the long, slick shaft, Brandt didn't bother trying to find purchase, as there never was any. Instead, he spun around, feetfirst, prepping his weapon. Light shone up ahead—the ramp was about to dump into a chamber. He'd done this dance enough to know that Vanderwalt would have a guard posted at the bottom. If he didn't, the Brit was a way bigger idiot than Brandt had thought.

Ready for the end of the line, Brandt hit the floor at a run, using the momentum of the slide to carry him into the chamber.

Unfortunately, Vanderwalt was just a douche, not a stupid one. He had posted not just one, but four guards. The rightmost of whom had Rebecca by the neck with a gun pointed at her temple.

"Drop your weapons," the second guard said in crisp British, "or she dies."

Brandt didn't even bother to argue as Rebecca mouthed, *Sorry.*

He ditched his rifle, kicking it over to the nearest guard. Then he pulled his sidearm out of its holster and slid it across the stone floor. Next came his knives, two grenades, and a pack of C4. What could he say? He was prepared this time.

"Follow us," the guard stated, shoving Rebecca toward him.

"Super sorry," Rebecca apologized.

"New rule," Brandt said. "No kicking artifacts until you are secured on a line."

A smile flickered on her lips. "You got it."

Then they walked out of the simple rock-hewn chamber and into…well, into King Solomon's temple.

Rebecca sucked in a breath. The vestibule wasn't very wide, but it was stunning. Every surface—the walls, ceiling, floor—was gilded. So much gold that it glowed a ruddy yellow under the light of the burning torches. Many scholars argued that King Solomon could not possibly have been as rich as the Bible implied. That there was no way for an ancient king to have collected 666 talents of gold per year.

By the sheer square footage of the gold lining the walls, Rebecca guessed the number was way, way, way higher than that.

They passed through the vestibule into the Greater House—and *greater* it was. Columns soared to the ceiling a good twenty feet above their heads. Again, everything was covered in gold. Well, not just gold. This gold was etched with drawings, passages, and pagan gods. Each of which were adorned with gems. Diamonds, rubies, emeralds. Especially the ancient goddess Astarte.

Many had guessed that Solomon had begun worshipping this deity after his affair with Sheba. None, however, knew the extent. But it all made a type of logic, though. If Solomon had read of the female Messiah, why wouldn't he look to the strongest female god to grace his world?

Later, Astarte had been adapted by the Greeks as Aphrodite, relegating her to the goddess of love. But in ancient times, Astarte was so much more. She was the goddess of the evening star, the goddess of virility, and the goddess of war. To hear the Phoenicians tell it, she had birthed mankind.

However, Solomon did not build this temple to Astarte exclusively. As a matter of fact, if you looked hard enough, you could find every major god upon these walls. And the inscriptions? They might as well have been made by Vakasa. They were written in every conceivable language. Was it a jumble of foreign words meant for one specific little girl to understand?

"Thor!" a familiar voice yelled.

Rebecca had been so fascinated by the columns she didn't even see Vakasa at the front of the temple. The little girl ran hard across the marble floor and leapt into Brandt's arms.

The rest of Vanderwalt's party stood on the steps, which climbed up to the Holy of Holies's door. The innermost temple. The chamber where the ark was normally kept. Although, looking around her at the plethora of pagan gods, Rebecca was pretty damned sure they would find something altogether different inside.

"Brandt," Talli—or whatever his name was—said, nodding to his old sergeant.

"Liar," Brandt retorted as menacingly as he could, with Vakasa showering him with kisses.

"She won't tell us how to get inside," Vanderwalt stated.

"And what makes you think she'll tell us?" Rebecca asked, but then again, Vakasa was still planting kisses on Brandt's cheek.

"Ask her," Vanderwalt demanded, his disheveled hair no longer cute. Even his crooked teeth took on a menace. The ground trembled beneath their feet. Not even the glittering surroundings could take away Rebecca's sense of dread.

Davidson kicked at the ark again, to no avail.

"Hang on," Levont suggested, shining his light into the broken wood. "There was a rod, but it's bent." He tugged on the cherabim's wing. "I think we just had to crank one of these bad boys down, but now..."

Yes, but now Brandt and Rebecca were under the tabernacle, and they were stuck up here.

"Um, new problem," Lopez announced, cracking open the door. "Looks like the Disciples want to join the party."

Davidson jumped down from the ark and made his way to the door. Sure enough, two SUVs snaked their way up the road to the hilltop.

"Blow it?" Levont suggested, indicating to the ark.

"No," Davidson stated. He turned to Lopez. "I've got an idea, but it is a little risky."

Lopez cocked his head. "You had me at idea, but now that I know it's risky?"

Davidson could only hope all of Lopez's enthusiasm was justified.

Brandt tried to extract Vakasa from his embrace, but she wouldn't let her clutch hold of his neck go until he gave her raspberries against her neck. She giggled so loudly that the laughter echoed off the walls.

"The ark," Vanderwalt said, pointing to the door.

Finally, Vakasa let Brandt lower her to the ground. "And if I get her to open it? What do we get in exchange?"

Vanderwalt grimaced. Not a good look on him. The affable boy-man worked a lot better. "First, you aren't Davidson, so don't try and charm me. Secondly, I've got your woman and the kid." The ground shook, hard. Golden dust rained down upon them. "Thirdly, I think the world might be coming to an end, so how about you just open the bloody door?"

The last part was more of a maniacal shout.

Brandt glanced to Rebecca. Vanderwalt might be losing it, especially keeping Talli back for close protection—had the Brit not read any of Brandt's after-action reports?—but he wasn't all that far off from the world ending part.

He gave the nod to Rebecca. His fiancée kneeled next to the girl.

"Vakasa, do you know how to get into the Holy of Holies?"

The girl reached out and touched the thick carpet that hung behind her. The central image was that of a huge lotus blossom.

Vakasa went to open her mouth, but a loud *boom* filled the chamber. Followed shortly thereafter by gunfire. Someone had breached the temple. Vanderwalt snatched Vakasa away from Rebecca.

"Tell your men to stand down!"

Before Brandt could answer, one of the British soldiers hauled ass out of the vestibule. "He can't! It's the Disciples." The guy fired back into the antechamber. "And they are *seriously* packing."

Brandt turned to Vanderwalt, his hand out. "Give me a weapon."

The MI-5's eyes flickered to Brandt, then Talli.

"Phhh, I say give him a gun." Well, at least he could count on Talli for something.

Vanderwalt lowered his weapon and turned the grip to Brandt. "We are not done."

Hell no. But right now, they needed to survive the next few minutes. Checking the chamber, he urged Rebecca and Vakasa behind the nearest column. Setting his sights on the arch that led to the vestibule, Brandt had only one question.

Where the fuck were *his* men?

Sitting tight was tough, Davidson thought. Especially when you could hear gunfire and corresponding screams. He could only pray they weren't Brandt's or Rebecca's. But they had to stay hidden until it was clear.

Which hopefully would come soon, as the three of them were crammed down within a space under the floorboards. This was Israel, after all. This region had been occupied or exchanged hands a dozen times over. They knew the use of a good hiding place. Unfortunately, this one clearly was meant for small children, not three grown men.

"Get down here!" a shout seeped in through the boards overhead.

It was what they had been waiting for. Davidson had gambled that the Disciples would find the damaged ark and decide to just blast their way through the wall. Which they did, promptly heading down the same shaft as Brandt and Rebecca. They had left two guards up top, which made attacking from the rear a little complicated.

Levont lifted the board with the tip of his rifle. "There they go."

Cautiously, in case the Disciples had left any traps, the three of them made it across the room. And there they caught their first break. The Disciples had secured ropes to the ark that led down the shaft. They could make a controlled descent.

Levont went to go down first, but Davidson stopped him.

"I have another idea."

The point man nodded. "Risky, I hope."

Oh yeah.

Rebecca tucked down, trying to keep the girl shielded, but Vakasa squirmed against the protection. Bursting from Rebecca's grip, Vakasa ran the short distance across the temple and, on all fours, climbed up the steps to the veil.

"Vakasa!" Brandt shouted, but the little girl paid no heed. Instead, she ducked under the tapestry and disappeared behind the thick material. Brandt tried to lash out to catch Rebecca, too, but she bolted.

His curses filled the air as Rebecca ran. He probably would have been right behind her if gunfire hadn't split the air between them. As Brandt returned fire, Rebecca scrambled up the steps and dove under the tapestry.

The woven material cut down the sound of rattling gunfire to the point it seemed not any louder than a pachinko machine. Vakasa pressed her palm against the gilded door. Which was oddly Jewish. Not that the door to the Holy of Holies shouldn't be Jewish, it was just, in this place, with its foreign gods, the strict Hebrew seemed, well, odd.

"How do we open it?" Rebecca asked.

Vakasa answered by picking up Rebecca's hand and placing it against the cool gold. The ground beneath them quaked, giving a sharp jerk, then settling down again.

"Say the words," Vakasa said in plain English.

"Which words?"

Then the earth shook and didn't stop.

So much for a controlled descent, Davidson thought as he braced his legs against the side of the tunnel. He waited, taking deep breaths, preparing to be discovered. Luckily, the swaying of his rope must have been chalked up to the earthquakes, or they hadn't even noticed, given all the trembling.

Heading down the rope facefirst, Davidson let up a little on the rope and slid down enough to get an angle on the rock chamber. Sure enough, the Disciples had left two men to guard the entrance. And their backs were turned to Davidson.

Even so, taking them both out before either could fire?

He would only get one chance.

Gripping the rifle to his shoulder, Davidson set his sight on the first man. He swiveled without firing to aim at the second. He imagined the pop of the gun. He imagined the kick of the recoil. He imagined the other man turning to the sight of his fallen comrade.

Taking a deep breath, Davidson was ready.

He saved the easier shot for the second shot and prepped for the farther man. He tugged the rope once. Once the shots were off, the other men would repel down. First, he *had* to get the shots off.

His fingers ached. He promised them a nice hot paraffin wax bath when all this was over. Exhaling, he bottomed out his diaphragm and took the first shot. He didn't have time to see if he had hit him square. By the time he got his rifle around, the other man had turned his upper body, making the second shot almost easier.

Letting go of the rope, Davidson slid down the rest of the tunnel, landing palms first. He launched up, pushing to his feet. He got his rifle up just as two guards came to investigate.

There was nothing tight or sophisticated about this shooting. Davidson just needed a spray of bullets to force the men back. Lopez hit the ground next to him, firing as he came out of the hole. Levont was only a step behind. They broke formation and headed to the cover of the wall as the guards shot into their little chamber.

"Perfect," Lopez congratulated Davidson. "Now what?"

That was a very good question.

Finally, Brandt thought. His men must have joined the party, since the Disciples' force was now split. The forward half were still firing toward Brandt and Vanderwalt's men. However, the back guards were now occupied with their rear.

What do you do when you are grossly outmanned? Force them to fight on two fronts. Hitler hadn't understood that, and look how World War II had gone for him. The Disciples might have invested as much time studying their military history as they did their religious history.

Using the brief respite, Brandt glanced over his shoulder. The tapestry didn't move. The only bright spot was no blood running out from under the veil, so there was that. He didn't like being out of the line of sight, though. He didn't like it at all.

Testing the waters, he flashed his sleeve out from behind the column. A bullet hole ripped through it. Okay, so the Disciples weren't that distracted.

Brandt could not believe he was saying this. "Talli, cover me."

"Oh no," Vanderwalt said from the other side of the column. "Cover *us*."

"Then exactly who is going to cover me?" Talli asked.

At least the fake sniper was an equal opportunity coward.

Great. Brandt was stuck with Vanderwalt, who had minimal field experience, and the ex-sniper, whom he had absolutely no faith in.

"Fine," Brandt said, firing in the direction of the Disciples.

Rebecca had better come up with something quickly, as the enemy had regrouped, firing with gusto.

Vakasa sat next to Rebecca, beaming that smile of hers. Clearly, the girl expected the "words" to come tumbling out of Rebecca's mouth at any moment. Sure, lots of words had come out of her mouth.

She'd tried the *Shemoneh Esreh*, the standing prayer, the first prayer listed in the *siddur*. She'd tried it in Hebrew, Yiddish, ancient Greek, and English, to no avail. Then she tried Psalm 146 and even Exodus, but the door didn't budge. Hell, she'd even recited the Christian Lord's Prayer, with equal luck.

The floor nearly dancing didn't help her concentration any.

Vakasa cocked her head and spoke. At first, Rebecca didn't understand even what language she was using. Then it hit her. Coptic. Rebecca translated quickly. "What shall I give you?"

Rebecca's eyes narrowed. Was the girl quoting I Kings 3:5? The question that God asked Solomon?

Vakasa took Rebecca's hand and put it to the door as the tapestry ripped from the ceiling. The sound of gunfire came in a rush as Rebecca spoke the words.

"*Therefore give to Your servant an understanding heart to judge Your people, that I may discern between good and evil.*"

A rumbling, deep beneath their feet, shook the marble underfoot. The shock wave came up and through the floor, cracking the great gilded door down the exact middle. Parting the opening, sending out a great sigh as if woken from a long sleep.

Suddenly, the gunfire waned.

Rebecca knew that was never a good sign. Not when it was the enemy who had stopped shooting. From down the long temple, she watched a grenade fly through the air.

"Brandt! In here!"

CHAPTER 28

SOLOMON'S TEMPLE, SHILOH, ISRAEL

10:32 P.M. (IST, ISRAELI STANDARD TIME)

Rebecca did not need to tell him twice. Not with two—no, make that five—grenades heading their way. Brandt turned on his heel, firing behind him, making for the door. The grenades bounced on the floor, skipping happily toward the altar.

Brandt heard footsteps behind him as he leapt up the stairs. Someone knocked him to the side, sprinting through the open doors in front of him. Vanderwalt. Son of a bitch. But the Brit was only a few steps ahead of him. Brandt made it through the door into another gilded room. He didn't have time to assess it much more than that as he turned to close the damned doors.

Talli raced toward him, with the grenades dancing behind him. "I tried the best I could!" he yelled as he streaked toward Brandt.

Despite the plea, Brandt kept right on closing those doors. Only at the last second did he slow enough to let Talli slip through.

"Get the bar!" Brandt shouted as he pushed the two sides of the door closed. Together, Talli and Rebecca shoved the bracing bar down. The damned thing had barely sealed the doors when explosion after explosion rocked the Holy of Holies.

Brandt grabbed his girls and got them into the corner to ride out the worst of it.

Finally, the *booms* died, and the world stopped shaking. Thank God for thick stone walls. The ancients really knew how to build them.

"Bloody hell," Vanderwalt cursed behind them. Brandt turned to get a look at the Holy of Holies. To be honest, beyond the gilded walls and jewel-encrusted etchings, it wasn't much to look at. There were two smaller doors on the other side of the room.

"Where is the ark?" The MI-5 agent asked.

Rebecca helped Vakasa get up. "Most likely? Ethiopia."

"Then what are we doing here?" Vanderwalt demanded.

Brandt sighed. "Welcome to my world."

The Brit didn't seem to appreciate the joke, however, as he raised his gun. Brandt did him one better. He raised two. One pointed at Vanderwalt, the other at Talli.

"Yes, Walt, I know you could kill Rebecca or Vakasa before I could kill the both of you. However, let's face it, neither of you have the stomach for playing chicken."

Proof positive of his statement, Talli handed his gun over to Rebecca. "I just want out. I didn't even want to get on the plane in Madrid."

Vanderwalt's eyes flicked between Brandt and Talli and the gun in Rebecca's hand.

"Just go, Walt," Brandt said, indicating to the doors. "We take one door. You take the other." Still, the Brit wavered, so Brandt pressed. Vanderwalt was a douche spy, but he had proved he wasn't an idiot. "It isn't going to take the Disciples long to get through that door. I would prefer to be as far away as humanly possible when that happens."

"Which door are you taking?" Vanderwalt asked, his voice cracking.

Rebecca nodded to the left door. "That one should represent 'good,'" she said, then indicated to the right door. "That one 'evil.'"

"Funny," Vanderwalt spat out. "I will take the left, then." Keeping his gun pointed at Vakasa, he backed his way to the door. With a light push, it swung open. That old grin appeared as if the last twenty-four hours hadn't just happened. "I'm still looking forward to that warm beer, mate."

"Just go," Brandt urged, then turned to Talli. "What are you doing?"

"I'm going with you," Talli said.

"Oh, no, you aren't," Brandt countered, cocking the gun pointed at his old sniper. "You picked your bed."

Talli reluctantly followed Vanderwalt through the left door. Brandt waited a few heartbeats, then went to the door, cracked it open, and made sure the men followed the path rather than doubling back again.

He turned to Rebecca. "You did tell them the wrong door?"

"Duh."

Rebecca pointed to the rightmost door. "This one faces east. The direction of Jerusalem."

Brandt nodded. She knew that he was fluent enough in Jewish religion to know that Jerusalem was considered sacred, even by Solomon, at least before he took a gander at the Ten Commandments tablets and all the secrets they held.

“Good enough for me,” Brandt said, checking the other door quickly before doing a sweep of the eastern door. Rebecca took Vakasa’s hand and followed Brandt down the new hallway. It was adorned in the same manner as the main temple.

She wished she had time to translate the myriad of inscriptions that lined the walls. The insight into ancient times they held…Well, it was priceless. At the least, she would have loved to take photos, but Brandt set such a pace that, even if Rebecca had had a camera, it would be nothing more than a blur.

They reached another set of doors, side-by-side.

“Do we go east?” Brandt asked, going to open the rightmost door.

“I think it’s more complicated than that.”

“Great.” Brandt sighed. “Another maze or labyrinth or whatever the ancients called a screwed-up mess?”

Rebecca studied the figures on each door. “No. I think these doors represent a series of choices we must make.”

“And the difference?” Brandt asked, clearly not in spirit of debate.

“I think we have to prove that we are the Messiah, or at least with the Messiah.”

“So?”

To the left was a beautifully rendered etching of Moses. He looked younger, though, than most of the descriptions. Certainly long before the tablets were found. Perhaps at the beginning of their long trek across the desert. To the right was another stunning depiction of the goddess Astarte. She seemed so human yet divine.

“Still looking like we take the right door.”

Rebecca wasn't so sure about that. Astarte was simply an imaging of what the Messiah might be in the future. Moses, however, was real. And just beginning his journey, just like Vakasa.

"I say we go left."

Brandt studied her features for a moment, then shrugged. "My motto?" he said, entering the left tunnel. "Never argue with a woman in the middle of a global religious crisis."

Frellan strode across the gilded temple's marble floors. The click of his boot heel ringing out in this place of God. Not a place of God, but truly God's place. This temple had been built by David's son, Solomon, for Frellan's messiah. In a world that he simply slipped from shadow to shadow, this felt like home.

His men came down the steps. "It is locked, sir."

Brandt yet again was ahead, but only for the moment. "Rig it," Frellan ordered.

"No," Monnie protested. Frellan turned to the watcher. How he dreamt of putting a bar through one of those pretty green eyes. She cringed at his stare but continued. "You cannot defile this place any more than you already have."

"Oh, I can," he promised her. "And I shall."

She took a step closer. "No. You won't."

"And who is going to stop me, little one?"

Frellan felt a sharp sting in his gut. He reached down to find a blade buried up to its hilt. A delicate, pale hand held the knife. He searched Monnie's eyes, finding the timid watcher gone as her lips curled into a fierce smile.

"Finally," Benedicto said, nodding to Monnie.

Her glare shut up even the verbose priest.

Monnie turned her attention back to Frellan, turning the knife sideways, twisting his bowel. "You and your sister. I should have known twins born to a treacherous mother would come of no good."

Frellan looked to his men, his mercenaries, yet not a one raised a gun against her.

"Fool," Monnie mocked. "*I* pay them."

As blood rushed from his brain into his belly and then out onto the white floor, Frellan still did not understand, or refused to understand.

Monnie, however, made it abundantly clear.

"I am your *master*."

"Whoa, whoa, whoa," Lopez hissed next to Davidson. "When did the religious hottie go all psycho ninja?"

"Shh!" Davidson responded. "I can't hear."

The Disciples' master was so young. However, that wasn't unprecedented in bloodline-based societies. It didn't matter their age, but the blood that ran through their veins. More than likely, the young woman currently shoving Frellan to the ground was a direct descendant of Moses. That heritage trumped any age issue.

Davidson watched as Monnie turned to the priest. "Do we have a problem?"

"If you hadn't done it," the priest answered, "I was about to."

The two moved farther away, toward the Holy of Holies's door. Davidson strained but couldn't make out what they were saying. Then Monnie turned and pointed an arm straight at them.

"Guys…"

"Yeah," Lopez agreed. "Time to boogie."

Levont fired into the vestibule as Davidson and Lopez hit the ropes.

"Come on!" Davidson yelled, but the point man wouldn't leave the archway.

"You're going to need cover," Levont protested.

Lopez was already halfway up the tunnel.

"Next they are coming with—"

A grenade rolled into the room. But didn't go off. They weren't going to get another chance like that. Levont hustled over to the ropes, climbing hand over hand, nearly overtaking Davidson.

The bounce of another grenade echoed up the tunnel. This one was not a dud.

The concussive force pushed them up and out of the shaft. Davidson and Levont flew over the ark as a fireball whooshed over their heads. The flames licked at the curtains and wood, setting the entire synagogue on fire.

Davidson and Levont were hot on Lopez's heels as he burst through the door into the already-smoky night.

"How the hell are we getting back through that?" Lopez asked as the building's roof caught on fire, the blaze now raging.

"Wait until it goes out?" Levont suggested.

Davidson looked to the ground, though. "This hill isn't cylindrical."

Lopez shot him a glance. "Um, no."

Ignoring the corporal, Davidson walked off the distance he thought the temple below occupied. There was still a lot of hill left—to the east.

"You think there's more down there?" Levont asked.

"Yeah," Davidson answered. "That temple down there isn't a replica of the First Temple. It is an homage to the Jewish place of worship. I think King Solomon built a whole new shrine to his messiah."

"That's great and all," Lopez agreed. "But what is our next move?"

Davidson looked to the surrounding area. "There are a number of fables involving King Solomon, any of which—"

Lopez held up a hand. "Hold on. We barely tolerate it when Rebecca does it, and she is way crazy better looking than you."

"Fine," Davidson replied. "Then how about I have a plan?"

"Like the rest have gone so well," Lopez said. Then when Davidson didn't continue, he finished. "No, I was serious. Love your plans. Let's do it."

Davidson pulled out his sat phone and replaced the battery. Bunny and her crew might come in handy. He dialed the number, but it went to voice mail. Really? An emergency field line going to voice mail? He couldn't worry much about it, though. He had an insanely flawed plan to execute.

Bunny dove for the sat phone, but the line was dead by the time she answered it. She tried to dial back as the entire room went dark. No lights. No sounds. No sat phone uplink.

"The last wall. It's been breached," Prenner whispered into the dark.

No, this couldn't be happening. Not with three of the men outside the temple and Rebecca and the rest missing.

Then the lights came back on.

"Oh, please," Stark said as he rebooted the system.

"I stopped them at the sixth wall," his mother continued, "while I was making your toast."

"Then why?" Emily said, indicating to all the equipment.

Stark shrugged. "Because we had to make someone believe we were knocked back on our heels so they would get bold and go for the kill shot."

"Your spaghetti code really was a delight, dear," his mother offered. "A true Gordian's knot."

"Wait," Bunny announced, her brain catching up with the current events. It turned out she was way better at keeping track of ancient ones. "All these alarms and outages were faked?"

Stark's fingers flew across the keyboard. "Those hackers weren't nearly as smarty-pants as they thought they were." He brought up a line of code, which made no sense to Bunny. "Off of this little gem, Mom backtracked them to the Pentagon."

Emily pulled a gun out of Bunny didn't want to know where and trained it on Prenner.

"What?" Prenner said, backing away, going for his own sidearm.

"Don't," Emily warned. "Not until we know more. Stark?"

"Once we identified the hack was coming from the E-ring, we did a little digging into Prenner's files…"

A page came up on the big screen. Bunny skimmed it, then found a passage that begged to be read aloud. "*In my opinion, Brandt's command has been riddled with unjustified off-the-book missions, questionable judgment, and near-negligent homicide risks.*"

"That is a sealed document," Prenner growled.

"Yeah, right. From me?" Stark said. Then his mother cleared her throat. "And my mom?" The tech held up a hand. "Plus, it turns out that Prenner didn't just happen to stumble upon this mission."

"Please," Prenner said, his tone losing its dangerous edge, "don't."

"Sorry, dude, the time for don't ask, don't tell is way over." Stark brought up a picture of Brandt's deceased point man, Svengurd. Bunny barely recognized him. She'd known him for about twelve and a half minutes. His height and stark-blond hair were kind of memorable, though. The photo morphed into a candid photo of Svengurd and Prenner in an embrace. "Prenner here was Svengurd's boyfriend."

Bunny turned on the lieutenant. "I knew it." When everyone looked to her, she clarified. "About him batting for the other team—I knew that part."

"Yes, Svengurd and I were engaged," Prenner admitted. "And yes, I did and still do blame Brandt for his death, but I would never betray my country or put Brandt's men at risk—certainly not a little girl."

Prenner searched the eyes of everyone in the room but came up with no takers. Not Bunny, either.

"Get his gun," Emily ordered.

Bunny approached Prenner as he put his arms out to the side. "I'd say I'm sorry," she said, "but you know, I'm not."

Prenner leaned in. "You think I'm a tight ass." She didn't answer that clearly rhetorical question. "So think about it. Would I break the rules like this?"

She grabbed his gun and backed away. "I've given up wondering why sick creeps like you do anything."

Handing the gun to Emily, Bunny accepted a ball of wire.

"Tie him up," the CIA operative instructed.

As Bunny obeyed, Stark clapped his hands together. "All right, now that we don't have to worry about any interruptions…"

He called up the tabernacle, now on fire. The three men had been busy, though. Strangely, not putting out the fire, but carving letters into the hillside.

GPR.

Bunny racked her brain for some ancient meaning to those letters. “It isn’t ancient Greek or Mesopotamian.”

Stark’s mother chuckled. “No. It is ground-penetrating radar.”

“Yes,” Stark answered. “I think we’ve got a satellite nearby equipped to identify underground bunkers.”

“So they must think Rebecca and the others are alive.”

Emily nodded. “Alive, but trapped underground.”

As Stark retasked the satellite, Bunny was going to concentrate on the *alive* part.

Brandt kept an eye on their tail as they approached yet another set of doors. How many had they passed through by now? He simply deferred to Rebecca each time. They had tried to consult Vakasa, but she was too busy either rebraiding her hair or playing with her necklace. For a supposed messiah, she wasn’t exactly the type to take the lead.

“Um…” Rebecca said, indicating to the doors. Brandt wasn’t sure why until he realized that neither of them had any symbols. They were simple stone doors. This couldn’t be good.

“What do you think it means?”

Rebecca wouldn’t meet his eye. Instead, she looked down to Vakasa who was playing a phantom game of hopscotch. The kid never stopped surprising him.

Well, they had to pick one of the passages. Brandt went over and pushed open the door on the left. Its floor sloped upward.

“That could lead to the surface,” he said, trying to pack as much hopeful optimism as he could into the statement.

“Or to a dead end,” Rebecca countered.

The other door showed a passage that went down. Steeply.

Brandt didn’t even bother to argue.

They were going down.

As they passed through the door, the ground jolted to the right, then the left, then undulated underfoot. His and Rebecca's eyes met. At least they seemed to have chosen correctly.

The passage was steep and had become uneven. What had once been gilded surfaces now descended into hand-chiseled stone walls. Rocks cluttered underfoot, making the going slow.

Vakasa tripped, so Rebecca picked her up as they ventured deeper and deeper under the temple. A stone tumbled down from above. Brandt swung around, flashing his light, trying to see if they were being followed. Did an errant footstep dislodge the rock or was it simply the nearly nonstop trembling of the earth?

He waited, holding his breath. No one emerged. No shots were fired. No grenades tossed.

Brandt did pick up the pace, though. If the Disciples didn't get to them, these tunnels were apt to collapse if shaken much more. Finally, they arrived at a door. A single door with only a lotus blossom etched into its surface.

Rebecca moved out of the way so he could enter first. Even if they were entering the Holy of Holies, they still needed protocol. This door was heavier than the rest. He had to put his arm into it. Then it budged, opening into a large chamber.

Shining his light, they were nearly blinded by the reflection.

Brandt thought he'd been impressed back at the temple. He had been wrong.

CHAPTER 29

TEMPLE OF HOLINESS

10:45 P.M. (IST)

Rebecca spun in a slow circle, trying to take it all in. Resplendent didn't even come close to this most Holy of Holies. Forget gold. Solomon had brought out the big guns here. The walls were lined with every precious gem you could think of. Gold filigree wove around the dazzling jewels.

And the statues? The entire chamber was filled with rows upon rows of them. Every ancient god was represented. Anubus, their old friend Moloch, Diana, and so many more. Each faced east. Each knelt down on one knee. Each faced a carving that seemed fashioned out of one enormous piece of onyx. They all bowed before the Black Madonna.

Only, she didn't seem a Madonna at all. The statue before them appeared to be just a beautiful African woman with a babe in her arms. Not just any babe, though, but one with rows of braids just like Vakasa.

"Don't let her—" Brandt yelled.

However, it was too late, as Vakasa had rushed forward and hugged one leg of the statue. It was the only thing her tiny arms could encircle.

"Momma."

Rebecca braced for whatever happened next. The roof to split open. The floor to cave in. Anything. Seconds ticked by, nothing happened. If anything, the earth beneath their feet seemed to quiet. The constant quaking died down to silence.

"Maybe it's because she is home," Rebecca suggested.

"Or she isn't the Messiah, after all," Brandt countered, although his features didn't seem as hardened as they usually did. If anything, he seemed simply relieved. As did Rebecca. If Vakasa really wasn't the Messiah, then her chances of having a normal life exponentially increased.

"Of more practical concern," Brandt stated, "I don't see another exit."

Unfortunately, neither did Rebecca.

As the tabernacle burned to the ground, Levont held up the C4 block. "Well?"

Davidson paced it off again. But without blueprints for the temple, how could he know for sure? He turned around and counted his steps again, trying to get a more thorough understanding of the underground temple.

"Things have quieted down," Lopez remarked. "We could just wait."

Davidson glanced over his shoulder with a look that, even with his damaged lips, should have said, *Really?*

"If we place it wrong..." Levont didn't seem to want to finish the statement. Who did? They could only begin to imagine how unstable the ground beneath them was. An inaccurately placed charge could bring the whole hillside down on Brandt's head.

They had to gamble, though. They had to think proactively. Maybe if the Disciples weren't down there with them, they could wait. But with that she-cat down there, along with the priest? They had to make a move.

Davidson indicated to the easternmost slope. "At the least, let's set the charges so we are ready."

"For what?" Lopez asked.

"Who the hell knows?"

"They are on the wrong side," Stark said, pointing to the screen. "They are going to blow the wrong spot."

Bunny tried the sat phone again. Nothing. She checked the ground-penetrating radar readout. The largest, most elaborate chamber was due west of them. Worse, if they took out that corner of the temple...Bunny was no architect, but a house of cards was more stable.

"Think," she said aloud as if everyone in the room, with the exception of Prenner, wasn't already. "We've got to get them a signal."

"Out in the middle of nowhere," Stark complained, cracking his knuckles. The nearly forty-eight hours of straight hacking was beginning to take its toll on the young man.

"Hold on," Bunny said, her mind racing. "What if we dumped the satellite? I mean, dropped that puppy out of the sky."

Stark's brow creased with confusion. "I mean, sure we could, but why…?"

His mother, though, smiled. "I like the way this girl thinks. You need to find a girl like her."

As Stark blushed a thousand shades of crimson, Bunny asked, "The satellite is in ultra-low orbit, right?" Stark nodded. "So it is right over their heads, and if we force it into the atmosphere…"

Clearly, Stark began to get it. "It would light up even that ash-filled sky."

"They will have to know something was up."

Stark nodded. "I'm on it."

"No," a voice said from behind them. "I don't think you are."

The CIA operative still pointed one gun at Prenner but the other at Stark. "God will decide what happens."

"Emily?"

"I am not thinking of just our lives," the woman said. "I am thinking of the global clu-taster-fuck that will happen if that child emerges from the temple." Emily nodded to Bunny. "You of all should understand. You know of her potential, yet you said nothing, why?"

Bunny shook her head. "All's I did was keep my mouth shut. I didn't actively endanger my friends. A little girl, Emily. Doesn't that cross around your neck mean anything to you?"

"It means everything," she said, fingering the crucifix. "Which is why we are going to simply watch and see what happens."

How Bunny wanted to just strike out and pimp-slap the CIA operative, but Prenner gave the slightest shake to his head.

Didn't the lieutenant know? Patience was *not* Bunny's virtue.

Brandt cocked his head. "Did you hear that?" he asked Rebecca as she and Vakasa made their way around the statue.

"Did you *feel* that?" Rebecca countered as she rejoined him.

She was right. A distant rumbling vibrated through his boots. It felt like thunder that began on the horizon, then powered toward you. That was not the immediate concern, though. The immediate concern was the door to the chamber opening and a grenade sailing through the air.

That was the concern.

"Get down!" Brandt shouted, knowing that it probably wouldn't make a difference. When the thing landed, it just spewed smoke, though. The Disciples must have been trying to keep the structural damage to a minimum. Good for them.

"Get Vakasa behind the statue," Brandt whispered, urging Rebecca away from the center of the room. Pulling up his shirt to protect his lungs, Brandt slunk forward, keeping a statue of Anubis between him and the door.

Through the chamber's haze, Brandt saw the flash of a muzzle as a gunman braved the smoke. He held his fire, though. The Disciples had too many men with them. Brandt had to wait to make his stand count. More than one must have made their way through the series of doors. Sure enough, another stepped into the chamber.

Behind him was the girl, Monnie, Brandt thought her name was. She appeared unarmed. Before the group got much farther, Brandt braced his bad shoulder against Anubis and fired, hitting the first gunman in the gut. He winged the second gunman. Monnie darted deeper into the temple as another figure entered. Brandt had the bead on him but pulled up short.

A priest. Why did it have to be a priest?

The chamber shook as smoke churned. Gunfire pinged off a statue. Rebecca held Vakasa tight to her. The air cleared as a form approached. It was too short to be Brandt. Should she call out for him, or would that only draw the danger closer?

Instead of the monstrous Frellan, a lithe, young woman emerged. With her smooth skin and emerald eyes, she should have seemed nonthreatening. That was not the case.

"You know who I am?" the woman asked.

Rebecca had no clue, except for the fact that religious megalomaniacs usually gave themselves away. They wanted you to know who they were. Rebecca could piece together the rest. A female Disciple. The only one to find the Holy of Holies. Rebecca could venture a pretty damned good guess.

"The Master?"

The woman's lips spread into a smile. "So you know that you must give the child over to me."

Rebecca knew no such thing. However, she did note that the Master had a knife, and Rebecca was weaponless. Underfoot, the floor gave out as steam rose from the earth. Scrambling back, Rebecca avoided falling into a huge crack in the ground. Would it be enough to keep the Master back?

Unfortunately, the Master had that wild look in her eye. The one that religious zealots got just before they did something really crazy.

"God shall guide me," the woman said, rushing toward the gap, easily clearing it.

Perfect time for him to take sides, Rebecca thought.

The woman slashed with a knife, narrowly missing her arm. Rebecca pushed Vakasa out of the way. The Master cut upward. Rebecca barely danced out of the way in time. She'd gotten lucky.

But how many more of those could she evade?

Brandt finally took down the guy he'd winged, but the priest was in the wind. Or more accurately, in the smoke. A scream rang through the chamber. Turning, Brandt was too worried about Rebecca and ran smack into the rod that the priest wielded. Reeling backward, blood coursing down his forehead, Brandt brought up his gun.

Again, that damned black robe and white collar made him hesitate just a split second too long as the staff arced up again, coming down on Brandt's shoulder. That was completely unnecessary.

Brandt brought his gun around to bear, but the damned priest used the butt of the stick to hammer his obliques.

As he doubled over, the priest smiled. "I didn't think that wound had completely healed."

Oh, game on.

Brandt didn't bother rising from his position, he just ran at the guy like a linebacker. The priest apparently didn't play many sports in seminary school. He tried to dart to the left, but Brandt was all over that. Tackling the priest around the waist, Brandt slammed the man into a statue of Moloch.

He might not be able to shoot a man of the cloth. But knock the wind out of him? That Brandt could do.

Rebecca dodged to the side. God love Brandt. He'd tried to teach her hand-to-hand combat. Every time they practiced, though, they usually ended up in bed. It was not a very productive teaching environment. As the knife swept sideways, nearly slicing her open, Rebecca really, really, really wished she'd paid more attention.

Watch the attacker's shoulder, she could hear Brandt demand.

It was a little hard when that shoulder moved all over the place, smoke blocked her vision, and steam from the earth's interior made it hard to breathe. There it was, though. Before the woman even made the swipe, Rebecca jumped to the side, avoiding the sharp end of the blade. She was sure Brandt could have maneuvered a way to disarm the Master, but hey, Rebecca would take not being gutted as a win.

Distract your opponent, her memory of Brandt reminded her.

She had never quite gotten that one down. How could you distract your opponent without distracting yourself. But she had to try, as another blow had nearly landed.

"Is this what your God wants?" Rebecca asked.

"*My God has wiped out many nations. Devastating their fortress walls and towers.*"

"Zephaniah Three:Six," Rebecca said, identifying the passage.

A flicker passed over the Master's face. Surprise? Doubt that another could know the Bible as well as she? Whatever it was, it transformed into anger pretty damned quickly.

The woman charged, a war cry on her lips. But it was a ruse. Her shoulder wasn't committed. Rebecca held her ground, ready to leap in the opposite direction once that shoulder told her which way to go.

Rebecca should have gotten away cleanly, except for the condensation on the floor. Her foot gave out, and she fell into the attack. The stabbing didn't hurt as much as Rebecca would have imagined.

Still, she couldn't help but scream.

A pained cry filled the air. Brandt pushed the priest back, but the guy just would not give up. And Brandt really needed him to get over it. Rebecca needed him.

"You will have to kill me." The priest sneered.

Could he? Could he kill a priest, even if he was one evil son of a bitch? Brandt raised his gun, a prayer on his lips, when a plume of lava jetted through one of the fissures on the floor, dousing the priest in molten flame.

The man flailed, spraying himself further with liquid heat.

Brandt backed away as the priest lunged for him. Blinded, the father must not have seen the growing gap. He fell headfirst into the churning orange lava, boiling the priest as he hit the surface.

Crossing himself, Brandt backed away as the floor split in two.

Throwing caution to the wind—since how much had it really helped him in the past?—he charged forward, to find Rebecca crumpled beneath the Black Madonna. Even injured, she tried to keep Monnie away from Vakasa. The little girl tried to cling to Rebecca, but Monnie jerked her to her feet, put a knife to the child's neck.

"Drop the weapon," she demanded.

"You won't kill her…" Brandt said, advancing slowly, trying to find a window.

Monnie's eyebrow went up. "Clearly, you don't know exactly how nice it is to be the Master." The woman brought the knife even closer to Vakasa's jugular. "It would have been far better to bring her to the sanctuary to prove my devotion than have the girl die a tragic accident, but I am sure I can wing something."

Brandt wanted to believe Monnie was bluffing, but the cold look in her eyes didn't melt as the room steamed up. He was going to have to take a shot, any shot. Then the entire chamber shook, cracking like it was a snow globe. Only, it wasn't snow that welled up from the floor, but lava.

Monnie lost her balance, Vakasa rushed away from the woman. Unbalanced, as the marble underfoot had tilted forty-five degrees, Brandt tried to shoot, but Monnie launched at him. His shot would have tagged her if the slab hadn't shifted another twenty degrees. Now he couldn't worry about firing, Brandt had to worry about not falling in the bubbling, gurgling lava.

Everything the liquid magma touched. And given that everything in the shrine was gilded, the gold melted off, dripping into the lava, giving it a golden sheen.

The chick threw a kick, knocking Brandt's gun from his hands. It slid into the maw, sinking beneath the molten surface.

"Will you fight a woman?"

"I just killed a priest, bitch."

She spun, bringing the knife around. Brandt blocked it with his left hand as his right hand jabbed her in the solar plexus. He had to give the chick credit. She didn't double over or even stop. The only concession to the injury was her arm tucked against her side. She kicked again. Brandt blocked again.

The blade sliced through the air. Too bad Monnie had a tell as obvious as Rebecca's. Brandt caught her wrist, bending it backward. She tried a knee to the groin. Monnie found out that was what knees were for. To block a move like that.

Brandt was two moves away from not only disarming her but subduing her.

Too bad the floor lurched up three feet.

"That was not me!" Levont yelled.

Davidson believed him, but then what was that...?

Wait. It wasn't over. The ground beneath their feet split, sending chunks of hillside tumbling down the ravine. They all scrambled to get to higher ground as the outline of the temple broke through the surface. *Hold on.*

"What the—" Lopez said, focusing his camera on the next hill over. It was getting lower. Or were they getting higher?

Lava burst through the dirt, flowing in a swift river. Yet still they climbed.

"Is this…?" Levont didn't seem able to finish the sentence.

"The birth of a volcano?" Davidson obliged. "Yes."

"With us on top of it?" Lopez added.

"And them inside of it," Davidson concluded.

Rebecca clutched her belly. Blood still oozed through her fingers, but adrenaline must have kicked in, as she rose to her elbow, trying to find Brandt amongst the chaos. Huge slabs of wall and roof fell all around, smashing through the floor, bringing more lava to the surface.

The heat was unbearable. It was like standing in the Sahara in the noonday sun. Her face felt baked through and through. How did Brandt feel standing out on a precipice only inches from falling into the abyss?

Monnie parried and stabbed, knowing that he had no way to maneuver. Brandt was so skilled, but none of that mattered when you couldn't back up a step.

Another violent jerk of the ground and the onyx statue cracked at its base as the ceiling shattered. Debris reigned down, making Brandt's position even more dangerous.

"Help me," Rebecca urged Vakasa as she dragged herself over to the Black Madonna. "Push, baby, push," she urged.

The statue teetered on its broken legs. Rebecca forced herself to her feet, putting all of her weight into the onyx. For once, being a size eight was actually beneficial. The Black Madonna leaned, then fell to the side.

"Left!" Rebecca screamed.

Brandt didn't have time to have his brain register, process, and decide what the hell Rebecca meant. Instead, he just flung himself to the left. Monnie backed away from the precipice.

"You can't run forever."

No. No, he certainly couldn't. Luckily, he didn't need forever, as the huge black statue fell. At the last moment, Monnie must have sensed the rush of air above her. She turned, but too late.

The statue creamed her. Smashing her body against the marble. Her knife falling useless beside her.

He did not have time to gloat, however, as the entire section of floor quavered, then broke, chunk by chunk, into the lava. Just like he used to play "hot lava" when he was a kid, jumping from chair to couch to chair again pretending the floor was on fire until his mother scolded him, Brandt leapt from foothold to foothold—only, in this scenario, it really was lava.

Landing on the only stable piece of floor, Brandt rushed over to Rebecca. Her midriff was a bloody mess. She tried to smile but only managed to grimace. Vakasa smoothed Rebecca's forehead as Brandt pulled up her shirt.

"Let's see how bad it is."

"Pretty bad," Rebecca groaned.

But what he found was a minor gash. Sure, it was bleeding, but it was a gash, after all. "You're good. Let's get you up."

"No," Rebecca said, looking down, fingering the wound. "That went in my abdomen." Brandt helped her up. "I felt the knife bounce off my spine, Brandt."

He draped her arm over his shoulder. "You know that little fat pooch on your belly you hate so much?" Off her nod, he continued. "It saved your life, so can we take this as a win and get the fuck out of here?"

Feeling stronger, Rebecca was more than happy to, only how? And where? They were standing in the middle of a boiling cauldron of lava.

Bunny gripped Prenner's sleeve. She didn't know why she did, but she had to have something to hold on to as the hill shattered. Davidson and the other men desperately sought stable ground, only there wasn't any.

From five different satellites, they watched the dome of the hillside bulge. Then, from deep belowground, lava burst forth, pushing up with it an island of marble. Standing atop of it were Rebecca, Brandt, and Vakasa! Her joy was short-lived, as the lava churned and overturned their stone raft. The three seemed prepared for that, though, as they jumped in unison—onto a huge onyx slab.

No, not a slab, a statue turned on its side. A statue of the Black Madonna.

As the volcano erupted around them, they rode the statue down the lava flow.

What about Davidson and the others?

Rebecca clung to a fold in the statue's dress, practically covering little Vakasa with her body. Brandt's arm was over both of them, trying to keep them on their extremely slick raft.

Then, from above, a slab of marble angled toward them, carrying Davidson. He tossed a rope to Brandt. "It should stabilize us!"

She wasn't so sure about that, but was so glad to see the sniper. Before she could ask about the others, another slab jettisoned from above them. Lopez rode the marble like a board.

"Lava surfing!" he cried out as he worked that molten wave.

A last slab tried to make it past the crest, but just couldn't. It carried Levont. As the stone raft angled back, their point man waved.

"Tell my parents. Off. The—"

Then he was gone.

"Levont!"

But no one answered as they coursed down the magma. Rebecca could feel the stone's heat beneath her feet. Would they make it to the bottom before their own raft burned them alive?

Then their speed slowed. They were reaching the bottom of the hill, where the ground sloped more gently. Brandt got them to their knees.

"As soon as we get close enough to some real ground, we've got to jump."

Rebecca nodded, more than happy to oblige. She gripped Vakasa's hand, making sure the girl understood the plan. "We're going home," she reassured her.

Vakasa smiled that bright smile of hers, leaning her head into Rebecca's shoulder.

Then a shot split the night. Vakasa jumped up, leaning in front of Rebecca. She felt the bullet's impact through the little girl's palm. Hot blood splattered on Rebecca as Vakasa fell into her, blood coursing down her dress.

The little girl patted Rebecca's cheek. "Momma," then her hand fell away.

"No!" Rebecca screamed, gathering Vakasa in her arms.

Davidson tore his eyes away from Vakasa and found a helicopter rising from behind the volcano. The Disciples' sniper hanging out the side, training for another shot.

Go to hell.

He brought up his rifle. He barely aimed. He let his instinct carry him. Let this one prayer be answered in full.

Davidson let loose the shot. It coursed upward, hitting the sniper's scope, shattering the tempered glass, then sliced through the sniper's eye. The bastard fell from the helicopter, dangling from his safety line. The chopper dragged him along the lava, then cut the line before it, too, was pulled into the magma.

The Disciples' sniper was finally dead.

That did not bring back Vakasa, though.

Brandt grabbed hold of the nearest shrub and pulled the statue they were riding on toward solid ground. Rebecca was putting pressure on the wound. It was bad. He had no doubt it was bad. But it had to be fixable.

He scooped them both up in his arms, lifting them from the onyx, taking them to higher ground. As soon as he set Rebecca down, she put her ear to Vakasa's chest.

"Start compressions," she said, breathing into the little girl's mouth.

Brandt did as he was told, giving five quick compressions, then pausing for Rebecca to give a breath. But in the next five compressions, he noticed that Vakasa wasn't breathing anymore. The blood was simply pooling by her. He felt for a pulse. None. He moved the fabric aside to find a mortal, a way-mortal, wound in her belly.

"Compress!" Rebecca demanded.

What would he say? No amount of CPR was going to bring Vakasa back. That had been a "shatter" round. The bullet had exploded inside of the girl.

"Babe, she's…"

His fiancée ignored him. Instead, she started doing the compressions herself, then breathing again for Vakasa. He tried to gently urge her away, but she shoved his hands aside. Davidson rushed over, but Brandt shook his head. The private sank to his knees, his head in his hands.

"Rebecca…"

"No!" Rebecca answered, shoving Brandt away. Why couldn't he see it? "She can heal herself."

Rebecca started more compressions. They just needed to keep her heart beating until they could get her to medical care. Then Vakasa would take over from there.

"Babe, no, she can't," Brandt whispered, holding his hands over hers.

Screw that. She kept up the compressions.

"She healed me," Rebecca stated, only stopping to give a breath. "She healed you."

Vakasa couldn't be dead. She just couldn't. But when Rebecca put her lips to Vakasa's, she could feel how slack they were. How the girl's body moved like a ragdoll's when Rebecca did compressions.

Tears burned hot down her skin. She couldn't give up. She couldn't lose Vakasa.

"You've got to let it go," Brandt urged, trying to pull her hands back from the girl. "You've got to let *her* go."

"*No*."

No. Rebecca couldn't and she wouldn't.

They all watched the monitors in stunned silence as Rebecca continued chest compressions and Brandt continued to coax her away from the girl. Thermal imaging showed Vakasa's bright-red heat signature cool to orange, then to yellow.

Bunny turned abruptly, trying to get a gun from Prenner's hand.

"I can't let you."

Fine. Bunny abandoned the quest for a gun and lunged at Emily. She grabbed the CIA operative around the throat. "How could you?"

The woman, though, only smiled sadly. "It was God's wish."

"*God's wish*?" Bunny repeated, clamping her fingers around Emily's windpipe. "If you hadn't—"

Prenner tugged on Bunny, trying to get her away from the traitor. "Can't let you do that, either."

Bunny stopped struggling against the lieutenant and allowed him to pull her back. "Guantanamo won't be good enough for you."

"Trust me," Prenner said, "she'll pay."

What exactly could Emily pay that would bring back Vakasa? Bunny spun around and faced the monitor.

"Stark, make arrangements to fly me there ASAP."

"With the eruptions and ash, it could be weeks before—"

"*Get me there.*"

"Ya," Stark said, typing rapidly. "On it.

Bunny reached out and touched the screen. How could she care so much for a little girl she'd never even met?

God, how he wished circumstances were different, but they weren't. Brandt had been in the field way too long. He'd seen this type of injury way too often. He put a hand on Rebecca's back as she sobbed even as she continued CPR.

Lopez trotted up to them, a broad grin on his face, pointing over his shoulder. "Did you see that?"

Brandt gave a sharp shake to his head. The corporal's smile fell. "Oh shit."

"You two go find Levont."

"Levont?" Lopez said, his head swiveling. "Where's Levont?"

"Find out," Brandt growled. Davidson pulled Lopez up the hill. Although, Brandt didn't have much hope that the men's search would end any better than Rebecca's attempt at resuscitation.

"Hon," he said, putting his hand over hers again.

"She can do this," Rebecca choked out. "She's got it in her."

Brandt squeezed his fingers around his fiancée's. "She was just a little girl."

"Don't you *dare* use the past tense," Rebecca hissed.

"A brave, remarkable little girl, but just a *little girl*."

Rebecca shook her head, but when she went to compress her arms, she gave out and crumpled against Vakasa. He pulled them both into his embrace. Rebecca's sobbing racked the both of them.

He leaned his forehead against Rebecca's and gave up the fight against his own tears, letting them flow down his cheek. They joined Rebecca's and, together, splashed down upon the girl they'd come to love.

CHAPTER 30

UNDISCLOSED LOCATION, ISRAEL

THREE DAYS HENCE

Davidson held Bunny's hand as their turn came to view Vakasa's coffin. It was a simple ceremony. A simple grave deep in the desert. Only they would ever know where the unmarked grave lay. Bunny had made sure that Stark blanked out all satellite feed of the area.

Lying in the wooden coffin, the little girl looked like she was just sleeping. That if he reached out, he could rouse her. That he could wipe the guilt away for not saving her. For not seeing the sniper. For not being fast enough.

Bunny must have read his scowl and squeezed Davidson's hand as she put a lily inside the coffin. Davidson put his own hibiscus next to Vakasa. It was the only thing he could remember about his own mother. How she smelled of the pink flower. It seemed a fitting tribute to the little girl who had saved them all.

Lopez followed. There really should have been two ceremonies today. One for Vakasa and one for Levont, but Lopez refused to declare the point man dead. "We need our drummer" was the only thing Lopez would say on the subject of Levont. So, for now, the point man was only MIA.

The corporal placed a carnation in the coffin. He leaned over and whispered, "Don't worry, RJ will know all about you."

It shouldn't have been like this. It shouldn't have been just them here. There should have been heads of states and a sea of people to grieve Vakasa. But that was kind of the point, wasn't it? Her secret needed to be buried with her. The world would never know the spark of her smile.

Then a bright light flashed in the sky. Davidson shielded his eyes against the glare. Was that a satellite falling from space? As the fiery object streaked overhead, commemorating Vakasa, Bunny nudged him.

"I think you're really going to like Stark."

Brandt wrapped his arm around Rebecca's waist as they approached the coffin. She seemed strong and all, but his fiancée had sat shivah for the past seventy-two hours. Rebecca hadn't left Vakasa's side for three days. Although, Brandt wasn't so sure she was actually mourning rather than she was hoping. Hoping against hope that a miracle really could happen and Vakasa would awaken.

This morning, though, Rebecca seemed clear-eyed, not arguing or fussing when he reminded her that if they wanted to honor

Jewish tradition, they would need to bury their little girl today. She'd just nodded and headed off for a well-deserved shower.

Now, though? To see Vakasa in that coffin? Brandt wasn't sure how Rebecca was going to hold up. He guided her forward, but she sidestepped him.

"Let me go last," she requested.

He didn't argue as he stepped up to the pine box. He wished he had something more to give the child than a yellow jessamine, the official flower of South Carolina. He wished he could have shown her his hometown. Brought her into his family. He'd had so many wishes for her, but this flower would have to do.

Brandt was about to move on, but the rabbi stepped forward and handed him a red rose along with a note. Without another word, the rabbi turned and walked back toward the waiting cars.

Opening the note, Brandt almost dropped the card. It was signed by Vanderwalt. The bastard hadn't even bothered to show his face after the girl's death. Probably just as well since Brandt would have shot him on sight. He was about to crumple the damned thing and kick it across the desert, until he read the man's words.

I would do everything differently.

Why the hell did tears spring to Brandt's eyes? Vanderwalt didn't deserve his forgiveness, but Vakasa would have wanted it that way. She'd already forgiven the MI-5 agent with her "aloha." So alongside his jessamine, Brandt put the rose and the note.

He moved aside as Rebecca approached. She seemed to want a moment alone, so he turned to look at the others as they grouped to the side. Bunny seemed five years older than the last time he'd seen her. Lopez was telling a story about Vakasa, making both Bunny and Davidson smile. Leave it to Lopez to lighten the mood.

A rustling behind him drew Brandt's attention. What was Rebecca putting in the coffin?

"I thought you said the flowers would be enough?"

Rebecca shrugged. "Just a few tokens," she said as she reached down and gave Vakasa a kiss on the forehead, then laid a lotus blossom on her bright-orange dress.

Brandt guided her away. There was no need for her to see the coffin lid nailed down. It was time to move on.

Rebecca leaned her head against the SUV's window as they bounced their way out of the desert. Rebecca kept her eyes glued on the fresh burial mound until she could not longer make it out in the distance.

Her eyes were dry for the first time in days. Maybe her tear ducts had just given out? Or maybe she was ready to say good-bye.

"Lopez, where are you taking us?"

"I know we are bummed and all, but you've got to see this." He drove them up a low hill, then parked the car. "Come on," he said, getting out.

They followed him the rest of the way to the plateau. Rebecca's feet stalled. The volcano that had erupted in Shiloh stood starkly against the dawn. Over the past few days, a weather front had moved in, bringing with it rain and cold air. The volcano's sides had cooled rapidly, transforming the orange magma into slick black volcanic glass. Not just that, but gold etched its surface. The veins running throughout the slope, glistening in the early morning light. Most remarkable of all, the Black Madonna statue, half-buried in volcanic glass, stood almost as a sentinel.

"They're calling it a miracle," Lopez said, nodding to the growing crowd at the volcano's base.

Brandt pulled Rebecca close, kissing her on the top of her head.

"That it is," Davidson remarked.

The others moved to get a closer look, but Rebecca stayed in Brandt's embrace. He turned her toward him, tilting her chin to him.

"Marry me."

Rebecca sniffled, grinning. "Of course."

"No," he said. "Right now." He tossed his head toward the volcano. "I don't want to wait. I don't want to go another minute without us…"

His throat squeezed off, betraying him. How many ways could they have died in the past week? What would next week bring? Brandt went to explain, but Rebecca seemed to get it.

"What about your family?" she asked. "A big church wedding?"

Brandt stroked her hair back. "We'll put on a dog and pony show from them, but I want us…I want to be your husband. *Today*."

She searched his eyes a moment as if testing to see how serious he was. She must have liked what she found, as her lips curled up into a grin. "All right, then," Rebecca said, turning to the rest of the group. "Looks like we need to find ourselves a rabbi or priest or—"

"Look for?" Lopez scoffed. "You've got *me*."

Brandt frowned at his corporal. "Lopez…"

"What?" he said. "I'm ordained in eight countries, Israel being one of them."

"I don't think—"

Lopez overrode him. "We can do this right here. Right now. 'Not another minute' and all that, right?"

Good to know Lopez was also as proficient at eavesdropping as he was at driving.

"You've got your maid of honor and best man…" Bunny added.

"I appreciate the thought, but—"

Rebecca took his hand, though. "I think we should."

He looked to her. She looked tired, drained, yet strangely happy. "This is your wedding day, Rebecca. We should at least go into town. Get a dress and—"

"Brandt," she said softly, "we aren't shiny, happy people." She indicated to the rough countryside around them. "For better or worse, this is who you and I are." She gestured to the others. "Who *we* are."

"If you are good to go," Brandt said, raising his hands in mock defeat, "I'm good."

And he was. Despite everything that had happened, with Rebecca in his arms, he was good.

Rebecca held Brandt's hand as Lopez continued on with the wedding ceremony. The moment was surreal with the volcano simmering in the background. Still, her hand shook. This was certainly not the wedding of her dreams. The pictures were going to be a bit…odd, but unique.

She wouldn't have it any other way.

"All right," Lopez said. "Let's get to the good part." He looked to Brandt. "Sergeant Vincent Paul Brandt, do you take this incredibly hot paleo-DNA-archaeologist for your wife?"

Even Brandt cracked a smile at that. "I do."

Lopez turned to her. "Chica, I am not sure what he's got that I don't."

"Ricky," Rebecca warned.

"What? I'm just saying you've got options."

She just glared at him.

He smiled broadly. "All right, all right. Rebecca Elaine Monroe, do you take Mr. Pecs over here for your husband?"

"I most certainly do."

"Cool," Lopez said. "You many now kiss the bride."

Their lips met tenderly at first. So much had happened that they both seemed hesitant. Could one grieve and still love? Apparently, they could, as the kiss warmed. Brandt put his arm around her back, pulling them close. Her hands found his chest, gripping at his shirt, narrowing the space between them ever further.

"Yeah," Lopez announced, "it's like thirty-five miles to find a room for you two, so why don't you dial it back a notch?"

They broke off the kiss, chuckling. They should have known what they were getting when they agreed for the corporal to officiate.

Bunny embraced her. "Congratulations."

Davidson went to shake Brandt's hand, but he pulled the younger man into a bear hug, clapping him on the back. Behind them, the volcano bellowed and lava danced in the air, then slowly streaked down the side, cooling as it went, turning into black glass before their eyes.

She hugged Brandt. No, she hugged her *husband*.

As the rest watched the sight, Rebecca's eyes slid to the east. To Vakasa. She hoped that the little girl was looking down upon them. Rebecca knew that she'd sworn off religious controversy before, but this time she was serious.

Now she had too much to lose. Too much to live for.

EPILOGUE

UNDISCLOSED LOCATION

UNDISCLOSED TIME

Vakasa awoke slowly. She did not force her eyes open. Did the stars rush to shine at night? Did the sun hurry to rise? She let her senses drift, assessing her new abode. The smell of dirt was strong. Vakasa didn't mind. She liked the scent. It reminded her of home. Her tongue, though, was thick in her mouth, dry and tasteless. She cracked her eyes open, to find complete darkness.

It did not scare her. She was born in darkness so was not surprised to awaken in darkness.

Her fingertips felt rough wood beneath her. They moved to her dress, a tightly woven cotton fabric. She hoped it was orange. Wouldn't that be something? She smiled at the thought of an orange dress.

Taking another deep breath, Vakasa relished several other scents. Flowers, she thought.

She was reminded of God's grace. She had always felt His touch. Even as she was birthed, she'd felt it. Even as her mother gave up her life to bring Vakasa into the world, she had felt it. God's love was in each leaf of a tree. Each breath of air.

The love of mankind, though, had not been so clear. The cruelty she had witnessed? The needless pain that man dealt to himself? She had always tried to see past it, to see through to their hearts. She had not been successful.

Until the man with the strong arms and the woman with the kind smile.

She did not have to search hard to see their compassion.

Their love, though? Ah, their caring was tangible as her fingers moved to her side. The presents the woman had given proved that mankind's love could be as precious as God's.

Vakasa clicked on the first gift from Rebecca. A flashlight.

The second?

A shovel.

ABOUT THE AUTHOR

Photo by Ben Hopkin, 2011

Born in San Francisco, Carolyn McCray grew up in Napa Valley, California. A natural-born storyteller, she used to "direct" the other kids from her neighborhood in recorded readings of Nancy Drew mysteries. A lifelong animal lover whose first word was "rhinoceros," she managed to fulfill her twin passions by growing up to become a veterinarian *and* a writer. She is the author of *Heartsblood*, *Fated*, *30 Pieces of Silver*, and *Encrypted*.

15821912R00258

Made in the USA
Charleston, SC
22 November 2012